The Ghosts of Lille

KIMBERLY KOCKEN

One Printers Way
Altona, MB R0G 0B0
Canada

www.friesenpress.com

First Edition — 2023

Edited by Tom Kocken & Danika Peters

ISBN
978-1-03-919412-0 (Hardcover)
978-1-03-919411-3 (Paperback)
978-1-03-919413-7 (eBook)

1. FICTION, GHOST

Distributed to the trade by The Ingram Book Company

For Tom, my partner in fishing and in life.

For Mason, for always listening to and questioning my ideas.

INSPIRATION

"No, the menace of the supernatural is that it attacks where modern minds are weakest, where we have abandoned our protective armour of superstition and have no substitute defence."

– Shirley Jackson, *The Haunting of Hill House*

"...for the poor wren, the most diminutive of birds, will fight, her young ones in her nest, against the owl."

– William Shakespeare, *Macbeth*

THE GHOSTS OF LILLE

CHAPTER ONE

Mother Earth dictates that mountains should never move. Sentinels of time, they stand and observe the passing of the ages, marking the years only by the slow degradation of old age, like an elder, slowly shrinking and too stubborn to be moved. People, on the other hand, do not hold still for long. From the time they are born until they die, they continue to move forward, some slower than others; but measured against the lifespan of the mountain, their time is brief, regardless of how long and fruitful a life they have lived.

Mountains have known time without the presence of man. How quiet it must have been for them, how peaceful, as no other creature has ever disregarded the grandiosity of a granite monolith like man has. None other than man would think to go through the heart of a mountain, rather than over or around it. No other creature would think to pillage the depths to steal what treasures lie there, instead relying on the mountain to parse out those treasures at will, leeching rich life-giving minerals into the frigid streams. Since the time of man, a mountain's lifespan is no longer as sure as it once was, but still, as a rule, mountains do not move of their own volition, *until they do.*

There are places in this world where the natural laws do not always apply, or rather, a different set of natural laws are present for reckoning. Who is to say what is natural and what is not? There are places where the mountains move and people stay still, stuck in time for what might seem like forever. But who is to say? Forever is a very long time, and unlike the mountains, people haven't really been around all that long, so maybe all that is natural for people is not fully understood. Perhaps some people are like mountains: they cannot move on; they cannot go away; they are stuck.

There is such a place which breaks the natural laws, or which recognizes a different set of laws altogether perhaps. It is a collection of tiny communities cut into the mountains, still in view of the foothills, which stretch out to the oceans of golden yellow prairie land to the east. Reaching to the border which divides Alberta from British Columbia, it is a gateway to the Rockies and a pavilion for the wicked winds of the west. Not for the faint of heart, as the westerly winds are strong enough to hurl chunks of rock and gravel into fragile window panes, the Crowsnest Pass is comprised of former coal mining communities which have more in common than they do which separates them, though one would be wise to keep that opinion to oneself when in the company of a resident, as *they* tend to see it quite differently. *The Pass*, as it is commonly referred to by locals and nearby Albertans who flock there for summertime outdoor excursions, is home to the worst mine disaster in Canadian history, the *Hillcrest Mine Disaster*, in which 189 miners lost their lives, leaving ninety grieving wives widowed, and 250 traumatised children fatherless. This came just over a decade after the Frank Slide, Canada's deadliest landslide, which nearly destroyed the town of Frank, killed up to ninety of its residents, and toppled half of Turtle Mountain. The mountain had *moved* after all.

With such a rich and devastating mining history, it is no surprise that the community of the Crowsnest Pass is littered with homes with a rich and devastating history of their own. From the far-west town of Coleman to the eastern hills of Bellevue, there are a scattering of old houses which had their start in a place called Lille, a relatively short-lived mountain mining community, which is now a ghost town. Though the term *ghost town* means nothing more than a town which has shut down and essentially 'died', there are those who claim that upon hiking to the abandoned town high up in the mountains behind the Frank Slide Interpretive Center, they have had the sense that they are being watched, and that their presence is not really welcome.

There are also those who live in these once-nomadic abodes who claim to have had other-worldly, sometimes even frightening, encounters with past residents. Though it may be easy for most to deny the possibility of people who haven't yet moved on, it's not so easy for anyone to deny the eerie and ominous atmosphere felt when passing through the towns, especially when driving past the slide, where the highway is flanked on both sides by millions of tons of limestone rubble, a century-old graveyard for so many who are still buried in the exact spot where they died.

In the shadow of Turtle Mountain, it's easier to fathom that mountains do indeed move. It is still monitored daily, in light of the fact that another slide is likely to occur at some point in the future, though according to the experts, not any time soon. If mountains can move, perhaps there are also people who cannot. Perhaps there are people who stay in one place far longer than they were ever meant to, far longer than they ever should.

CHAPTER TWO

Startled to awaken in a strange bed, in an unfamiliar room, in a house she did not know, yet which seemed vaguely familiar, Emma threw off the heavy blanket weighing her down and making her skin itch. The floor was cool and rough beneath her feet and she rubbed at her eyes, trying to make sense of where she was. For reasons she could not understand, she was eager to find her mother, though something told her that this did not make sense, as she knew her mother was back at her own house, but in her mind, which was foggy and bewildered, that did not matter in the least.

As she tiptoed across the room she was careful not to make a sound, so as to avoid waking anyone who might be sleeping. The velvety depth of the darkness made it difficult to find her way to the door, but she steadied her breathing to calm herself until she was able to grip the doorknob. It was heavy and seemed massive in her hand, making it difficult to turn, but her patience paid off and the solid wooden door swung open on creaky iron hinges. With an absence of windows, the long hallway lined with doors was darker than the room she had escaped. Using her hands to guide her way, she made her way out of the hallway, into an open foyer and out the front door of the unfamiliar house.

The night air was crisp and cool on her warm face as she stepped onto the front porch and made her way down a short flight of white wooden stairs. She made her way down a short path leading to a dirt road, which was just as foreign to her as the house had been. The sky was bruised black and blue, the stars an impossible riot of sparkling diamonds, as though she were camping in the middle of the forest, far from civilization and its unquenchable thirst for light. Beyond a short row of tiny and unfamiliar wooden shack houses, a path turned off into the forest, and though it was brutally dark, as the sliver of a new moon was the only light to go by, she followed it into the forest. It felt as though she had no say in the matter, as though someone else were guiding her. Somehow it felt like she was reliving a memory, but she had no recollection of ever being in this place.

The terror of what might happen in the forest was overwhelmed by her instinctive need to find her mother. Trees so close that the branches caught in her hair and scratched at her face like claws confronted her at every turn. Strangely, they seemed to be grumbling and groaning, getting louder with every step she took into the forest. The path she was on opened up to a bank beside a wide river. The stream roared over stones worn smooth by time and the rage of the current.

Even in the darkness she could see the shimmer of the water in the starlight. The night fell eerily and unnaturally silent. The ground began to rumble and shake beneath her and she was knocked to her knees, digging pebbles into the palms of her hands. Her hands were not her hands at all. They were too small to be hers. Before she had time to make sense of such a strange detail, a deafening roar pulled her attention skyward. She realised that she was facing a massive mountain, its peak visible like a jagged shark tooth digging into the sky, its face a dark mass of forest.

In seconds that lasted an eternity, yet happened so quickly that she had no time to react, she watched as the shark's tooth dislodged itself from its majestic seat and came hurtling through the air as the face of the mountain began to slip and pour toward her like a lava flow, the dust spraying into the air like water vapour rising from a waterfall. In the final moment, as the limestone behemoth came hurtling toward her, a terror arose in her mind like none she had ever felt before. Though her mouth opened wide, the scream caught in her throat before the world turned black.

Emma was startled awake to the darkness of her bedroom. Her hair was plastered to her forehead in a sheen of sweat, and she had to stifle a scream that had started just at the moment that she had awoken. She cupped her hand over her mouth to be sure, her nostrils engorging as she fought for more air. Fortunately, John was still sleeping soundly beside her, oblivious to the drama that had just played out while they slept. It was pretty obvious that she had been dreaming about the Frank Slide. Clearly her anxiety was on full alert, now that the decision had been made to move into a house directly in the path of one of the most infamous disasters in the world.

They had not even seen the house yet, that was the plan for the morning, but she knew that the view from the back of the house was the face of the slide. Emma had been telling herself that any concerns she had were unfounded and that she would get used to the idea in time. Passing up the chance to live out their dreams based on her anxieties would be a choice she would always regret, especially since she was sure that deep down John would always resent her for it. They were to meet the estate lawyer in the Crowsnest Pass at two. They planned to leave in the morning, allowing themselves time for a scenic drive through the foothills on the Cowboy Trail and a leisurely lunch in the Pass. Emma was both excited and nervous to see the house her husband's great aunt had left him when she passed away.

When the lawyer had informed them of the inheritance, she had assumed they would use it as a vacation property, a getaway from the mayhem of city life. They would go there to hike, camp and fish. The other possibility she had considered was selling it outright, as they had never even spent time in the Crowsnest Pass together, despite being only hours away. So she was stunned silent when he told her that he wanted to uproot their lives and start over somewhere they had never even been together.

Despite her recent attempts to avoid looking at the clock upon waking late at night, her latest strategy to combat her chronic insomnia, she instinctively rolled over and glanced at the angry red numbers glowing brightly to her left. The time was *4:10.* This was becoming a habit. For the past week she had been waking at the exact same time, which had inspired the attempt to quit peeking at the clock, but her curiosity won out every time and she just had to know. Perhaps this was a part of growing older. She knew she was not that old. Being only thirty-five her mother still called her a *spring chicken* and lectured her on how much she still had to learn about the perils of a: growing old, and b: specifically, growing old as a woman, which apparently was fraught with far more irritation and physical degradation than the process endured by men. Her mother often told her that she, like her own mother, woke like clockwork throughout the night, at increasing intervals with each passing decade.

Assuming her insomnia was hereditary, she also assumed that this recent development was a normal evolution. It was also a tremendously frustrating one, as each time she was literally startled awake. Each time she had the sensation of panic and disorientation when she opened her eyes, then she'd instinctively look at the clock. Though she felt a little disturbed by the repetition, it served as an effective anchor to the real world. After all, *4:10* was not *the witching hour,* which was three a.m., she was pretty sure. Immediately she knew where she was and knew that she was safe. Though she tried, she could not grasp the fleeting ghostly tendrils of the final moments of the dreams that had frightened her so. Emma realised that she was okay with not being able to recollect. They were only dreams after all, and bad ones at that.

Begrudgingly, she realised she had to go to the bathroom (another annoying part of the ageing process), and though her mother would claim a sexist monopoly, she was pretty sure that trips to the bathroom at all hours of the night were part and parcel for both men and women as they aged, though she could not deny she was getting a head start on John for that particular development. Careful not to disturb him, she slipped out of bed in her *Queens of the Stone Age* nightshirt, which was actually an old concert shirt she had confiscated from her husband's closet. With the size difference between them, it served her purpose perfectly, though it was not exactly her sexiest bedtime apparel. It seemed the days of sexy lingerie were virtually obsolete, though she questioned the wisdom of that at such a young stage of her marriage.

As Emma left the room she glanced back at John to be sure he was still sleeping and paused to take him in. She loved to watch him sleep. It was one of the only benefits of her insomnia; he was sweet and sexy all at once. His dark skin and hair were in stark contrast to the bright white of their bedspread, which seemed to glow in the pool of moonlight pouring in through the window. Ironically, he was the dark one of the two of them. Though she was one-quarter Blackfoot on her mother Charlotte's side, no one was ever aware that she was even Indigenous until she shared the fact. In their defence, her complexion was fair and her dark red hair only hinted at her mother's mahogany tresses. But when they were side by side, there was no denying the family bloodline, and it was easy to see her ancestry, though not necessarily easy to place it.

The shadows cast by the window panes crisscrossed John's muscular back. Emma could see from the shadow of his jawline that he needed a shave, though she hoped he would not, as she loved it when he forgot, which was rare. It made him look rugged, which she had expected from an outdoorsman, but John was almost always impeccable. As she admired his masculine physique, she fleetingly decided to dig out his favourite nightgown for the next evening, though she knew it was doubtful she would remember and actually follow through with her late night commitment.

As she made her way to the bathroom, she stopped to look in on Charlie, who was sleeping as peacefully as her father. Luckily, at four-years-old, she was more like *him* in this way, and had slept like a rock from the time she was a baby. Her long curly hair was shockingly dark like John's, but like Emma, her complexion was fair. She did not have any of her mother's freckles, but she did share her curls, her small, slight stature, and her curious personality. Emma attributed her daughter's beauty to John, though he insisted Charlie had inherited it from her.

Emma frowned at the sight of Charlie's puppy sprawled across her daughter's left leg; her right leg was perched up around her waist in a position that made her look like she was about to jolt off of the bed, were it not for a six-month-old Cocker Spaniel keeping her pinned in place. It did not really bother her to see Max sleeping with her daughter; she knew from her nightly rounds that this was a common feat of his lately: jumping up onto Charlie's bed. Emma suspected her daughter might have more to do with it than the dog's budding agility. She *knew* however, that John did not approve of the dog getting up on the furniture, let alone sleeping in his daughter's bed.

In fact, he had barely approved of the dog whatsoever, but Emma had seized on the opportunity to bargain with him when he had presented her with the idea of expanding their increasingly successful cafe bookstore, *The Library*, from the city, into the Crowsnest Pass. She had baulked at the idea. Being the financial and administrative brains behind the business, she felt that the tiny mountain community did not have the local population to support another coffee shop. John, however, insisted it was the perfect opportunity for someone with the right imagination and work ethic. They could fill the same need in the community that they had in their urban neighbourhood, offering book club nights, board game tournaments, paint and sip events and local bands. All events of course would include cover charges, as well as drink and food specials to boost their bottom line. He intended to mimic what they had done in the city, with a small-town approach. They would be living mortgage-free in their newly-inherited home and could slow down their lives and spend more time together as a family. Not to mention, she would finally get the time to start her novel. She had dreamed of being a writer since childhood, when she had written a twenty-six page horror story with illustrations and the kind old white-haired school librarian, Mrs. Moore, had catalogued it and placed it on the library shelf amongst the other fictional stories.

"Small towns almost never offer enough recreational opportunity," John had theorised over a beer one night, shortly after first proposing the idea to her, "especially if there isn't much of an economy. So people are hungry for the chance to do the things they'd normally have to travel hours to do. Imagine the inspiration of being in the mountains when you start writing your novel. Imagine if we could go fishing anytime we wanted."

It was a struggle to argue against his logic, though her business side knew that the reality of the situation was that businesses had a hard time getting established in any small town. She also knew that prior success in one market did not guarantee the same in another, but for some reason, she kept these concerns to herself. In some ways, she was less opposed to the idea than she liked to let on. Dangling the carrot for the opportunity to write certainly did not hurt his chances.

They already had plenty of opportunity to fish in Calgary, with the Bow River running through the sprawling city, but she could not deny the appeal of the breathtaking mountain streams she had heard so much about, yet had never taken the time to visit. It was difficult enough as business owners and parents of a young child to make the time to fish where they lived. This only bolstered his argument that they needed to slow down the pace of their lives. They had already paid the price in more ways than one for not being on guard for the dangers of an overly-stressed life. Emma hoped that the change of scenery would be the inspiration she needed to kickstart her commitment to achieving her lifelong goal of becoming a writer. Despite her feelings on the situation, she was no fool; she knew her husband could be a master manipulator when he put his mind to it.

"If you think about it," John thought out loud, "most of our regular customers are from the neighbourhood we live in, and we do well. The population in the Crowsnest Pass and surrounding areas is definitely greater than our neighbourhood, and there's always the summer crowd to consider as well."

"You know you make a good point, but you bring up another." Emma was sad when considering the fact that they would lose the life they had built in their city neighbourhood with their trendy little business. "We will be leaving behind our family and friends. A lot of those regulars are some of our *closest* friends. My mother lives here. You do not…" she had stopped herself abruptly before finishing her careless thought, as she was about to mention the fact that John did not have any family to consider, though she knew that was not only heartless, but untrue, as he was just as close to her mother as she was. At times she even suspected they might be closer, perhaps because they both worked with food, as her mother had become a baker when Emma was in her teens. John had actually been the first to suggest naming their daughter after her mother, though she had not taken much convincing. Her only sticking point had been that they refer to her with a different, perhaps more modern version of the name. After toying with ideas like Charlize or Charla, and flat-out refusing suggestions like Lotty, they'd settled on Charlie, and when they'd told her together at the moment she got to meet her granddaughter for the first time, she had cried and told them it was perfect.

"I know some parts will be hard." He had taken on a serious tone and pulled her close to him, refusing to let her break his gaze while he convinced her of his plan, "It will be for both of us. But it will be *worth* it. We'll make new friends, and it's not like we're going to lose the ones we have now. We're really only moving a few hours away and we'll have a great place for people to visit. Just think about how much more time we'll have together as a family."

Though she knew the last detail he had offered up was bullshit, as she had barely seen him in the first year of setting up the first business, Emma had agreed anyway. She knew this was what he truly wanted, and she could not deny that a generally slower-paced lifestyle for her daughter's upbringing was appealing. Refusing to be a doormat, however, she was sure to get him to agree to some terms in return for getting his way. First off she had insisted that they finish any work that needed to be done on the house before they ever moved in; she wanted to have the same standard of living she was used to in their city condo, though she knew house living would be much more work and commitment than condo living was.

More importantly, she wanted to continue to work from home, so that she could stay with Charlie until the time she was in school full-time, and perhaps even for a while after that. Her own mother had brought her up on her own and had always had to work long hours, leaving Emma with an aunt, or a neighbour, or eventually on her own, and she had always wanted to be the kind of mother who was waiting at home when her child arrived home from school. She knew that financially it was wise for her to continue working, but she was smart enough to know how to use her abilities to her advantage so that she could have the best of both worlds. Unfortunately, it was often her marriage which took a back seat on the priority list, as she would leave her work for when Charlie was in bed, taking her away from time alone with John. He was always supportive, and when she felt insecure, he reminded her that they had both planned for and agreed on this approach for their daughter's early years.

Emma's final request had been the dog. John had always used the excuse that it was not fair to own a dog in the city, but she knew he was just avoiding the extra responsibility. And so, of all her demands, this was the only one he had hesitated on, and in fact, had fought her on. "A dog's only going to tie us down," he grumbled when she first proposed the idea, though it was not the first time she'd brought it up in the history of their relationship. She had grown up with a dog, *Sherlock Holmes*, though Emma always called him *Shirley*, much to her mother's dismay. Both the dog *and* the name had been her mother's idea. Considering the time Emma spent on her own, her mother felt it would be wise to have a guard dog on duty, and although Emma often doubted the attack-dog abilities of the terrier-cross mutt, she had appreciated the company dearly and worked with him incessantly to make him a good dog, even though he was a terribly yappy one.

"We have a three-year-old," she had sniped, "just how much more tied down can you get? I do not think a dog's going to hamper our social life any further. Besides," she dropped the snarky attitude and opted for sweet manipulation, wrapping her arms around his neck and gazing intently into his water-blue eyes, "if we're going to live in the mountains, we would be wise to have a dog around to let us know if there's a bear in the vicinity."

"More likely, it would lure one right to us," he complained, then tried to distract her by kissing her neck, a well-known point of weakness, but she would not be swayed.

"I think it would be great for teaching our daughter some responsibility. She and I can go on mountain hikes with the dog while you're at work." She dropped her arms from around his neck and made it clear in her tone that she was serious and would not change her mind on this particular caveat. In the end he had no choice but to bend to her will, but made his own demands as he gave her what she wanted.

"Okay," he began, and she squealed with delight, but he ignored her and continued on, "but I have a few requests of my own."

"I'm listening."

"I think that we should get a breed that does not shed."

Emma snickered and he sneered playfully at her and continued with his demands, "We should buy one from a reputable breeder. I do *not* want a shelter dog…"

Emma dropped her jaw and crossed her arms in mock judgement of his demands, but he would not be swayed. " I want to know where it came from if it's going to be growing up with our daughter. And, if you insist on having a dog, I insist it has to be trained to be a good dog."

"Yes sir!" Emma did her best baritone and gave a shifty military salute. She was happy to get any dog.

Afterward she had been committed to researching breeds and had chosen a spaniel. Max was sweet and playful. He was almost completely black with the cutest fawn-coloured eyebrows she had ever seen. Charlie had adored him instantly of course. Even John warmed up to the pup, despite his reservations. Regardless, he would not approve of the dog sleeping on Charlie's bed. Emma however, did not care, and so she left him there, snoring slightly, guarding her daughter in his puppy way. She quietly pulled the bedroom door shut and made her way down the hall to the bathroom.

Emma closed the door but did not bother with the light, as there was already a ghostly-green glowing nightlight plugged in beside the bathroom mirror so that Charlie could find her way in the night if she needed. She peed absentmindedly, propping her chin on her hand, which was resting on her thigh. Her head bobbed and slipped off of her hand, snapping her back to semi-consciousness, though she was still slightly dozing when she flushed and washed her hands.

Even as an adult, Emma always avoided mirrors during the night, after being traumatised by visions of the ghost in the mirror at the *Overlook Hotel* when she would sneak around watching horror films on television at far too young an age while her mother was sleeping. Half asleep, she glanced into the mirror without thinking, something she would do without hesitation in the light of day, but which she always subconsciously, or maybe *not* so subconsciously, avoided in the darkness. Her reflection looked foreign to her, as all faces do at such a late hour. Her face was pale and her eyes appeared sunken and dark. Her pale lips were non-existent in the light, giving her an alien appearance. Emma scolded herself for being so childish as she quickly averted her eyes, but in her haste, she thought she caught a movement in the mirror, something separate from herself. She was too anxious to look again and had already convinced herself that this was the product of an over-tired imagination.

Tomorrow I'll start a fresh regimen of melatonin and get some sleep, she reassured herself, yet without a second thought she backed out of the room in a defensive stance. Prepared for what? She did not know.

What she was not prepared for were the arms that wrapped around her from behind. The weight of a body suddenly pressed against her back, trapping her, heavy breath in her ear. She always thought she would scream in a moment such as this, but she did not. Instead, she let out a pathetic squeal, as though she had seen a spider. But her terror was still evident, and she fought at her assailant, pushing the heavy arms away with all her strength.

"Hey, hey, what's wrong?" John's voice both soothed and confused her. She whipped around to face him, instantly embarrassed at her reaction, but also defensive.

"What the hell? You scared the shit out of me!" Emma punched him half-heartedly in the arm and the spell was instantly broken. It was forgotten that she had even been thinking she had seen something in the mirror. She kissed John on the cheek, plodded back to bed, and was already fast asleep before he returned to their room.

As he drifted off to sleep, he gently stroked her arm with the back of his hand, a habit he'd had ever since the first time they'd shared the same bed for the night. It was one of her favourite things about him, even if it did keep her awake sometimes, though she would never tell him that. When she started to toss and turn as she mumbled in her sleep, he was already deeply sleeping, but instinctively, he pulled her closer to him anyway. She did not awaken, but a salty tear rolled down over the rosy apple of her cheek into her quivering mouth, and she whispered two words nobody heard and which she did not recall in the morning: *Stay away.*

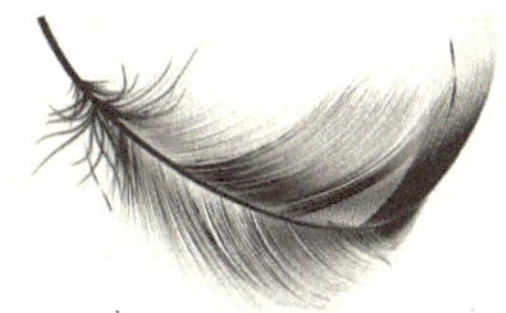

CHAPTER THREE

The next morning, John was already making breakfast and entertaining Charlie, or rather, she was entertaining him, when Emma dragged herself into the kitchen, showered and dressed, but feeling like she had not slept at all. John could see her suffering and handed her a hot cup of coffee.

"Guess what I learned to do Mommy!" Charlie squealed in her high-pitched four-year-old voice.

Emma winced; she had not realised that she was sporting a budding headache and immediately went to the *random* cupboard, which for some reason housed a selection of miscellaneous household items, including: coffee cups, both current and nostalgic; the coffee grinder; a can of sugar for coffee or tea; a variety of plastic storage containers; and a random selection of medication, which for some reason did not ever remain in the bathroom medicine cabinet. She grabbed the Advil as she put on her best smile and asked, "What did you learn sweetie?"

"I learned how to snap my fingers! Watch!" She proudly showed off her new talent and Emma hugged her tightly with genuine pride.

"Wow, Charlie! How'd you learn to do that?"

"Daddy taught me how. It was a secret until I knew how for sure!"

"Well, that's great," Emma announced as she furrowed her brow and lowered herself to Charlie's eye level, "but you do not have any other secrets, do you?" Charlie lowered her eyes and shook her head; Emma could see that she thought she'd done something wrong. "You're not a princess in disguise or anything are you?" With that Charlie's sweet cherub face burst into a smile that stole her mother's heart. She shook her head again, but this time she was beaming.

"Are you excited to go to your Nana's house for the night?" John asked as he brought breakfast to the table.

"Yes! We're going to take Max to the park to learn him to swim!" Charlie exclaimed as she was guiding a large piece of waffle to her already open mouth with intense focus.

"*Teach,*"John corrected her.

"'Scuse me?"

"You're going to *teach* him to swim."

"I know, silly. I already said that."

John bit his tongue and left it at that. Emma put her head down and smirked sideways at her husband as she pretended to eat her breakfast. Charlie continued on, unphased by her parents. "And Nana said we're going to make *bisketti*!"

"You mean *spaghetti*," John corrected her again.

Now she was frustrated with him. "That's what I *said*," she retorted in her most serious tone.

Emma was in the middle of a swig of coffee and spit it all over the table when she started laughing, listening to the exchange between the two people she loved the most in the world. She wiped up the mess with her napkin. The rest of their breakfast was uneventful, yet boisterous, with Charlie's excited conversation, sprinkled with the occasional knock knock joke, which her father had taught her last month. And of course, the newly acquired talent of finger snapping. Emma was hopeful that she would not drive her grandmother crazy during their sleepover, but she was sure her mother could take it and knew she would love the time spent with her only grandchild.

They dropped Charlie and Max off at her mother's place and headed off the main highway, taking Highway 22 to the mountains to see their new home. The drive was scenic and quiet. In fact, they barely spoke to one another on the trip. They were both in a thoughtful, reflective mood and had been together long enough, and had been *through* enough together to be able to comfortably enjoy one another's company in silence. They stopped in Longview, the last town they would pass through before getting to the Crowsnest Pass, but only long enough to top up the fuel tank in the truck John lovingly referred to as *Fred*, because it was a Ford and it was red. This was a silly quip he often shared, thinking it was far more clever than Emma ever did.

When they reached the Pass, John drove right to the house, as though he had been there before. He assured Emma he had never been. He had been surprised when his great aunt Helen had left him the house, but understood once the estate lawyer had explained that she'd had no children of her own after losing a young child long ago. When she passed away after a massive heart attack at a very old age, her estate had gone to her only living family.

John had no siblings and had lost both of his parents in a car accident while he was away in France at culinary school. Emma and Charlie were the only family he had now. It was difficult for Emma, as she felt a loss for her husband because he had not had a chance to know his great aunt, nor had she had a chance to know John. Considering they were both alone in the world, as far as extended family went, it seemed a tragic missed opportunity that they had not spent time together before her death.

They turned off of the highway to the left, just before the notorious Frank Slide. Emma had learned when researching the area that the slide had happened at the turn of the twentieth century, and had been the deadliest rock slide in Canada for generations. She had also learned that although most people know the famous disaster site only as *Frank Slide*, the mountain which crumbled, crushing much of the small town of Frank, is actually called *Turtle Mountain*. It was a surprise to her that on the standing side of the mountain the town of Hillcrest is nestled into a picturesque hillside which foreshadows nothing of the disaster which befell the other side, now a barren and desolate gravesite. The Crowsnest River, which Emma had discovered snakes its serpentine course along the tiny towns which make up the Crowsnest Pass, marked a line between their neighbourhood and the famous landmark.

Emma stared up in awe at the mountain, which had broken in half and fallen on top of the fledgling coal mining town, killing almost a hundred people. Through her research of the slide after they had learned of the inheritance, she had learned some interesting details, aside from the stories John had shared from his childhood, which he was reluctant to discuss after the loss of his parents. She knew that while their own house could be mortgaged and insured, not all houses at the base of the slide could be, so those who chose to live there had to pay up front and take their chances. Emma had also learned that the mountain was equipped with a multi-million dollar monitoring system which closely monitored the movement of the mountain, literally to the millimetre. And it *was* moving, if only by millimetres.

Apparently, another slide, which would complete the destruction of the face of the slide when the eastern side fell, would happen at some time in the future, though the experts determined it would likely not be in the *near* future, which was not very comforting. Apparently the insurance companies and banks agreed with her, or they would have no concerns with issuing mortgages or insurance to those willing to live under the infamous disaster site. Although their new home was on the other side of the bridge which crossed the river from Bellevue and was considered a safe zone, it was clear that the bridge was not enough to to ensure anyone's safety when she saw the enormity of the boulders which still laid at the base of the mountain, reaching across the Old Frank Road, which ran along the river, and the new highway, up the other side of the hill reaching into Bellevue and Frank. Just one of those behemoth rocks could take out an entire house if it bounced in the right direction. She tried not to obsess over the possibilities, though it was not easy. What she avoided in the day had been manifesting in her dreams at night.

When their friends had asked about whether they had any concerns living in such a famous disaster zone, John had responded flippantly. "Well, let's hope that if it takes me out, I'm fishing when it happens, so at least I can die happy." Everyone laughed at his casual take on the situation.

"What about you Emma?" Emma's friend Joni had asked with concern in her voice. Emma knew what Joni was thinking, knowing that her somewhat anxious friend would have reservations about living in such a place with her young daughter. "Do you feel the same? Aren't you a little scared?"

Emma had smirked. "Hell no," she teased. "I've got an escape plan!"

Again, everyone laughed, but Emma could tell that Joni knew just as well as *she* did that any fears she had were being put to the side for John. Wanting to make him happy, she was willing to sacrifice her own needs to do so. What Joni did not understand, as far as Emma was concerned, was that despite her fears, which were not really rational considering all she'd learned about her new home, she really was excited to be moving there herself. She felt privileged to be living in such a famous historic place and thought it would be a great opportunity for Charlie to grow up in such an interesting community, and a home with character, like Emma had always wanted for herself.

An even more important consideration in their choice to move was their shared love of nature. John had introduced her to fly fishing when they had first started dating; they would go on weekend excursions into the backcountry. Emma had teased him coyly when she'd first watched him fishing, with his bulky waders and a tiny fly tied onto the end of his line. But he was incredibly intense as a fisherman, authentically concerned with his surroundings and the wellbeing of the fish he caught and released, as he believed in releasing them all.

His intensity was mesmerising and incredibly sexy, and she found herself watching him fish for hours. When she was not lusting after him as he cast his line with grace and precision across the sparkling stream, she found herself wishing that she could join him. Trying to figure out how to bring it up with him, concerned that perhaps he wanted to keep this one thing, this skill, this *art*, for himself, she had been delighted when he had made it easy on her and brought it up himself.

They were sitting by a bright and crackling fire which cast an eerie flickering glow onto the surrounding pines and onto their faces as they sat and shared their life stories, getting to know one another. John had been reliving a moment from his morning of fishing when he had caught a *Walter*, as he called the big ones, which she knew was a reference to some fishing film he loved, but could never remember which one. At the end of his riveting retelling, which she was sure included many details which he had enhanced for dramatic effect, he had simply blurted it out: "Do you ever want to try it? Fishing, I mean. I could teach you if you like." He had been awkward, but determined and sweet. "No pressure if you do not want to, but it's got to be pretty boring just watching me all the time."

Emma had not even tried to play it cool, as she often did with him at that stage in their relationship, and had responded emphatically, "Yes! I'd love to. I would not cramp your style? I would not have the slightest clue what to do. I might just be an annoyance."

"Well you're an annoyance now, but what does that have to do with fishing?" He'd said this with a straight face, so it had taken a moment to register and then she was punching him in the bicep, as she often did when he purposely went out of his way to annoy or prod her into reacting. He was like a child sometimes, trying to get a rise out of her, but it only added to his charm, as she knew he'd always be lighthearted and young at heart.

Changing his tone, taking her hand and kissing it softly, he kissed her wrist and said with a reverence she was sure she would never forget, "I figure we're going to be spending more and more time together really, so it would be great if you learned and we could do this together. I would not ask just anyone you know." He had been deadly serious saying this; it was clearly important to him. "I've never taken…" He became somewhat awkward and averted eye contact. "I've never taken a *woman* fishing before. Not being sexist or anything, but I'm just saying, I would not take just anybody. I think we have something special. don't you?"

Emma had responded with a passionate kiss, which had led them to fumbling and stumbling their way to his camper as they stripped one another along the way, and enjoyed the most passionate lovemaking they had ever shared. As she laid in his arms, their legs tangled in the sweaty sheets and in one another's, she had known he was *the* one. She had not known if he had felt the same, but she had hoped for it, and in time her hopes had proven true. She married her dream guy after all and had become a fly fisher in her own right. They were an excellent fly fishing team.

Of course, this had proven more difficult since they'd had Charlie, as even in her pregnancy she had fished, sometimes to John's chagrin. But she had done it anyway, though she had tamed down any exploration of overly-rugged terrain. Since having Charlie, her priorities had obviously changed, as had John's, but they still made it a point to get some time to themselves to fish the streams together while her mother watched over their daughter. Aside from that, it had become more difficult to fish together, or at all, and they were hoping that a house in the mountains, right next to a world-class river, would provide them more opportunity and ease to do just that. They were hopeful the lifestyle would rub off on their daughter and she could join them in time. She was already big enough to join them at a big lazy pool for the day, as she had just turned four, but a typical day of trekking the mountain streams was years beyond what was safe for her yet.

They turned left before the bridge to cross the river down a short gravel road. The trees and shrubs lining the road on their left were just starting to show the first buds of spring. Emma found herself excited at the prospect that they might be in their new home by summer, though she braced herself for the possibility that this was an unrealistic expectation, as the old house might need a ton of work. The estate lawyer was waiting on the front step of the small yellow house trimmed in white, which Emma was happy to see had an upper level, as she had always wanted a bedroom away from the main living area, in the hopes that it might help her to sleep better.

Although the house itself was charming, it was surrounded by a rickety white picket fence which was leaning heavily to the east and gave the house a crooked look; it would have to be removed. Inside the fence was an overgrown garden. Clearly John's great aunt had been an avid gardener, but Emma considered that in her old age the upkeep may have become too much. Feeling a pang of guilt that they had not been there for this elderly lady, she dismissed it quickly, as they had not even known of the relation, and would have made the time if they had. She decided that she would do this particular job herself, as a tribute to John's great-aunt. She loved to garden, or at least loved the *idea* of gardening, as she had not really ever had the opportunity while growing up and living in the city.

The lawyer was an older man. Emma guessed he was pushing seventy, yet he still seemed to be full of energy, and he introduced himself as Gary Parsons. As he mopped his profusely sweaty forehead with an old hound-stooth handkerchief, he told them that Helen, John's great- aunt, would be happy that the house would be lived in full time, as she had been a little crotchety in her later years and had hoped it would never end up in the hands of some city slicker *weekenders*, who bought their properties for a steal and only came to the Pass on the weekends and holidays. Helen had believed these types weren't really a part of the community. Neither of them responded to this bit of local politics, but listened quietly and respectfully as he imparted Helen's feelings.

"If I'm honest," he added, "it seems to me there was nobody good enough to take the house. But of course, it needs to go to someone, whether she likes it or not. I'm sure she would be happy to know that it's staying in the family, even though she did not leave us a will to know *what* she really wanted. " The paperwork was ready to be signed and the agent seemed eager to hand over the keys and leave them to their new home.

"Be sure to walk to your right when you leave the house. Where the houses end, the river begins. Do you fish?" He asked them as he was opening his loudly creaking car door. Before they could respond he finished his thought. "Because if you do, this is the house for you, but make sure you look up your regulations; it's all catch and release on the Crow. I would not want to see you get yourselves into any trouble." With this last comment he hurriedly and awkwardly piled into his car.

Emma had the distinct impression that he was in a rush to get out of there, a feeling reinforced by the troubled glance he gave them in the rearview mirror of his rusting purple Roadrunner. She put it to the back of her mind when John took her hand and led her on an upbeat tour of their new home. Aside from some updated paint colours and a desperate need for decluttering and new furniture, the house did not need much work, so it would not take long before they could move in and start their new life. The kitchen was bright and spacious for a small house, made up for by a smaller family room.

The main living area had an open floor plan, which was unusual for such an old house, so they assumed there had been some renovations over the years. There was a mudroom which doubled as a laundry room at the back of the house.

Off of the family room a white painted wooden staircase led to the upper level, where there was only one bathroom. This was an issue that could be dealt with in time, definitely long before Charlie was a teenager. The bathroom was beautiful, with the clawfoot tub Emma had always dreamed of and a stained glass window featuring a gnarled tree which she thought resembled the Burmis Tree, another bit of local information she had gleaned through her research. The tree is a famous skeleton on the edge of the Crowsnest Pass which marks the official entrance to the community. Emma was amused to learn that the tree is so beloved that people stop to have their photos taken with it and the locals lovingly prop it up with crutches over time to keep it standing, which miraculously, it does, despite the monstrous raging winds of the mountain pass. Sitting on the branches of the tree in the window, which was a mosaic of blue, purple and charcoal glass, were three mesmerising black crows. The sky behind them was a muted grey and the effect was beautiful, yet gloomy. A wonderfully gaudy mirror hung over an old cabinet vanity, lit by a stained glass fixture hanging from the whitewashed ceiling.

Though none of the bedrooms were very big, they each made up for it with character, with elaborate crown moulding and beautifully trimmed old windows, which hinted at the age of the house. The floors were wooden and Emma noticed the echo of their footsteps as they moved from room to room. What would be Charlie's room was directly across the hall from the bathroom and down the hall from the master bedroom, which was considerably smaller than the one they were used to in the condo, but it was charming and cosy and Emma felt at home, despite the questionable paint colours in each room.

Though the bathroom was stunning in its neutrality and charm, the bedrooms and hallway were equally stunning in their clashing stabs to the eye. Charlie's room was a shockingly bright yellow, enough so that Emma would worry about the child being able to actually fall asleep in such a bright setting. Any hint of light would suggest full-on sunshine in the room. The spare room was a horrible fuschia pink; not that the colour itself was horrible, but on the walls of the old house, it just seemed so ridiculously out of place. The master was the worst, as it was a bright pumpkin orange; again, a colour Emma actually favoured in the scheme of things, but not in her bedroom. However, if paint was the worst of it, she considered them to be lucky, though she knew this would speed up the timeline of when they would be moving from the city to the mountains. Emma was happy to realise that she was okay with that possibility.

At the back of the house, just off of the mudroom, was a door which was in desperate need of some restoration, as the paint on it was peeling to reveal a kaleidoscope of coloured layers under the most recent glossy white, which did not look very recent. The old white porcelain door knob had a keyhole beneath it which was clearly the old-fashioned style, made of a solid metal. Emma wondered where the key was, or if they even needed one. She tried it, but it would not budge.

"It's locked." She stated the obvious. "What do you think this leads to?"

"Let's see if we can find a key and find out," he suggested. They searched the cupboards above the washer and dryer and found an old pottery bowl with a single old black metal key. "I'm guessing this is it," he announced as he tried the lock, which turned smoothly with an audible *click*. The old door led to a basement beneath the house, which turned out instead to be a traditional cellar, as there were no windows, so the temperature remained constant. Though the room was dark, low and strewn with cobwebs, Emma found it to be quaint and started planning the options for how they could use it.

"We could start canning," she suggested excitedly, "and have our own garden so we can preserve our own food!"

"Or," he interjected, "we could stay true to the history of the Pass and make our own booze down here. Maybe some moonshine! But probably just too much wine and some shitty beer."

"Sounds like a plan," she agreed and kissed him softly on the cheek.

"Do you like this place?"

"I think I love this place."

"Really?"

"Really." And with that, they stood in the cellar and embraced, locked in a long and loving kiss. John kissed Emma on the forehead and continued to explore the dark room. He wandered off to a dark corner behind the old furnace.

"Come see this," he said in a serious tone. She could not see him, but she could hear him clearly, as the cellar was one big room, though the furnace in the middle of the room blocked the sightlines from one side of the room to the next. She followed his voice behind the furnace and found him looking at a decrepit old door, one even more ancient than the one which had led to the cellar. It was clearly heavy, as it was made of thick pieces of lumber attached by a crosspiece across the top and bottom.

"Where do you think it goes?" she asked with some trepidation, but also some curiosity.

"Only one way to find out," he shrugged and undid the latch, then pulled the creaky door open. It led directly to a crooked concrete staircase, leading up to a hatch. John looked back at Emma and smiled. "It's a way to the outside."

She pushed him aside so she could see for herself. "Cool!"

"Totally cool," he agreed. They made their way back to the main level and out to the back yard, which needed some upkeep, but was more than big enough for Charlie and Max to grow up in.

The view was astounding and terrifying all at once. They had already driven past the rockslide on their way into the house, but standing in the backyard, they had a full view of the awe-inspiring sight. Emma could not help but remember the first time her mother had told her the story of Turtle Mountain which had been passed down through oral tradition by the Blackfoot people in the area. Because her mother's grandmother had been Blackfoot, Charlotte made it a priority to know as many of the stories of her people as she could learn. She told Emma that she had learned the story of the mountain when she had stayed with her grandmother on the Piikani reserve when she was little, and had then retold it to Emma when she first brought up John's inheritance and where it was located, as she did with anything that might relate to their culture, even in the most obscure ways.

The story told of a battle at the foot of the mountain between the Blackfoot people who lived in the surrounding area, and the invaders who came from the south, from what's now known as Montana. When the Blackfoot discovered the intentions of the trespassers, they prepared themselves for what was sure to be a bloody battle to defend their lands, believing that the potential loss of life would be worth fighting for what was theirs.

The violent encounter started with an ambush which came thundering down from the mountain as the brave Blackfoot warriors advanced on the unexpecting enemy. But the warriors and the invaders were no match for the rock which had somehow come loose and fell to the earth, crushing men like tiny ants underfoot.

Believing that the unlikely tragedy had been a warning about the evils of battle and killing from the spirit *Napi*, the Blackfoot declared permanent peace in the valley. They named the place *The Mountain That Walks* and avoided staying anywhere near it, understanding the dangers there. Many believed that the slide which devastated the town of Frank happened because the people were unaware of the dangers they faced while making their lives and livelihoods next to such a predictably unpredictable mountain. Emma felt a shiver trace its way down her spine at the thought of the warning from Napi, but mostly, she felt lucky to have such a beautiful view in her very own backyard.

They spent the rest of their day making a list of the necessary fixes which would have to be done before they could move into the house. Before leaving for the day, they took the lawyer's advice and walked to see the river. The house next door was a little smaller than theirs, but was equally charming in a different way, as it had a log cabin feel, whereas their own house seemed more like a cottage than a cabin to Emma. The next house was the biggest one of the three standing side by side. It was white with black trim and was surrounded by budding lilac bushes. On the side of the street opposite the three houses and the other half dozen they'd passed on their way to their place, was a forested area and a marsh, which acted as a buffer zone between the neighbourhood, which consisted of about a dozen small old homes, and the train tracks and highway which ran parallel to the spot, just up the hill from the river. They had been informed that although this neighbourhood was considered a part of the town of Bellevue, it was actually across the highway and closer in proximity to the town of Hillcrest, which was just across the bridge which crossed the river.

Emma noticed that Bellevue overlooked their home, as it was built into the hillside on the other side of the highway, but she could only see a few of the homes. In the distance toward the east she could see the Bellevue Mine, which was now just a tourist attraction, and no longer a functioning mine. Emma had learned in her research on the area that both the Hillcrest and Bellevue Mines had endured their own disasters, both leading to lost lives, and both occurring in the same era as the Frank Slide. She could not imagine why anyone would have stayed living in such a seemingly cursed place at the time of these events, knowing she herself would have left after the first incident. But she knew that the reality of the matter was that sometimes it was not as simple or easy as that. Once people put down roots and invested in a life, it was not easy to just move on and start over. The irony in this thought was clear, as that was exactly what she and John were doing, not to mention what they were imposing on Charlie, who also had a lot to leave behind in the short life she had lived.

Missing her grandmother was enough in itself to upset the balance of the life she was used to, but they knew that she was young enough to adapt quickly. Besides, there was little that could keep the two apart, certainly not a picturesque two-hour drive. Of all her worries, Emma was most concerned about leaving her mother behind. They would all miss having her so close at hand; they relied on her for so much. She would miss the family time they had carved out on Thursday nights when they would take turns visiting each other at home and making surprising new dishes or reliable old favourites. Not to mention the free babysitting for their Friday night date nights. It wracked her with guilt to know that Charlie would miss her grandmother with a vengeance. They were so close it made Emma jealous at times, but mostly she felt grateful that her daughter and her mother could have this unbreakable bond and she did all she could to foster it.

Luckily, kids were resilient if allowed to be, so though she would miss her playdate friends from her mommy group, and Joni's son Eric, whom they'd always surmised would be Charlie's future husband, since they were less than a year apart and nearly inseparable whenever their families would get together. Emma knew however, that Charlie would make new friends in the Crowsnest Pass. She also had no intention of losing touch with Joni, who had been her best friend since university, so Charlie would still see Eric, though probably not as often as she would like.

At the end of the street, only a few houses away from John and Emma's new home, hidden conspicuously behind a low mound and high bushes, was the beautiful Crowsnest River. When they rounded the turn into the lane which turned onto their back alley, they encountered a deep pool with a tiny grassy beach on their side of the stream and a tall, overhanging rock on the other side. It looked like the perfect pool for diving from the big rock into the deep water below or a leisurely swim on a hot summer day, and also for fishing of course. Nothing was rising, as it was too early in the season, but there was no doubt the fish were there. Emma was captivated by the sight and knew that she was where she should be. She was *home*. John squeezed her hand and she looked into his eyes, recognizing the same joy in him that she felt herself. They had no need for words. They just smiled, turned, and walked back to their new home, taking the back lane, which was a direct path to their favourite new pool, *the home pool.*

After making sure everything was locked and secure, they drove around the community, or more accurately, *communities*, looking for potential spots for their new cafe, and actually found a few they thought might be promising. By the time they headed back to the scenic highway to drive back to the city, they were exhausted with all of the activity of the day, yet buzzing with excitement for their new home.

Although they were exhausted when they got back to their quiet condo, and made their way to bed for an early sleep, they both seemed to have too much adrenaline to actually drift off. Instead, they invested their shared energy in a long and sensual night of lovemaking, drifting off and waking again to one another throughout the night. They were happier than they had been in a long time. Change can be refreshing in a marriage, an opportunity for renewal. Good or bad, the unexplored experience will always be unpredictable. For John and Emma it would be no different.

CHAPTER FOUR

Calgary, Northwest Territory, Canada, 1896

"Fisher has asked for my hand in marriage."

The expensive imported china teapot Margaret was holding in her delicate, ladylike manner fell from her hand as her jaw fell from her face with an excessively dramatic flair which was customary for her. Olivia held her smirk as she quickly mopped up the tea, which was everywhere, including on her new baby pink dress (her mother would kill her). She also did her best to scoop up as many of the millions of tiny shards of china which she was pretty sure were also now embedded in her new dress, as she was suddenly feeling a little itchy and uncomfortable, though that may have been in response to her sister's reaction to the news. Margaret ignored the mess she had made, expecting that one of the maids would take care of such a mundane and possibly dangerous chore.

"Oh, quit fussing now and focus for heaven's sake!" She scolded her younger sister in her old schoolmarm voice, the one she had used to bully Olivia into doing her bidding when they were young girls. She had quit bullying her when they were both in their adolescence, but still employed use of the voice whenever it suited her needs, though now that they were full-grown women, it no longer had any effect on her rebellious sibling.

"Calm yourself sister. Harry will think you're hysterical again and ship you off for some respite with our loving parents," Olivia teased her sister lovingly.

"You know he hates it when you call him that." Already Margaret was calmer. Olivia often had that effect on her, when she was not doing her best to frustrate the life out of her. "His name is Harold, and it would do you well to respect a man of his position." She realised her sister's tactic to distract her from the important matter at hand was working and she quickly turned the conversation back to where it began. "So tell me what happened," she pleaded. "do not leave anything out. If I do not soon have an ounce of excitement in my life, I think I'll wither up like a dried up old seed husk and blow away in the wind. Harold probably won't even notice. He'll be too busy chasing the nanny around to realise I'm even gone."

"Do not say things like that Margaret! Harry's a good man and you know it." Olivia defended her only brother-in-law as she always did against her only sister. It was never necessary with their parents; they loved Harold, as he was a man of power, prestige and most importantly, money. She thought it was ironic that her sister always chided her for disrespecting Harold by calling him Harry, which they both knew he did not mind in the least, yet she herself would disrespect her own husband, quipping offhandedly that she had married a bore, and that sometimes the money almost was not worth it. *Almost.* But Olivia knew her sister loved Harold in her own sometimes cruel way, a cruelty which stemmed from the truth of the matter. The truth was that Margaret *had* married for money, as her parents had wished, and although she did love her husband and would always be a loyal wife to him, she had sacrificed what she had once confessed to Olivia was her one true love: a boy who'd worked for her father.

A blacksmith by trade, he had been hired to work on the family estate, including in the stables, which is where he and Margaret had met. Their chemistry had been undeniable and their love affair had been intense, but brief. Olivia remembered questioning her sister about him when she had happened upon them talking innocently outside the stables as Margaret was visiting with her prized thoroughbred. All seemed fine and well on the surface, but the air between them had been electric. Margaret had confessed all, although Olivia doubted she truly knew all of the details of their forbidden tryst. Margaret had seemed relieved to be able to talk to her sister about it and the situation drew them closer not only as sisters, but as friends and true confidantes. Their bond could not be broken, nor could their trust in one another.

When their father discovered the relationship which had been taking place under his very own roof, a relationship he felt he had financed and provided an opportunity for, he was thoroughly disgusted. His reactions were swift and brutal, and Olivia saw a side of him even she could not have imagined him capable of. He immediately fired the boy and kicked him off of the property, leaving him essentially penniless and homeless. He degraded his reputation in town, calling him a liar and a thief, but not of his daughter, as that detail was conveniently kept quiet. There was no need to destroy his daughter's reputation based on a moment of childish impudence, as long as she did what she was told from there on.

As a child, Olivia had always looked up to her older sister and her progressive attitude toward her place in life. In trying to be like her, she had become like her, but the Margaret she had known disappeared when there was no word from the boy whom she had loved so deeply. Her marriage to Harold happened less than a year later and was a grand, yet somewhat sad event, if only in Olivia's eyes. The marriage had not been arranged, but it might as well have been, as their father had also set about finding an acceptable husband for his eldest daughter. Despite his claim that she had been too childish to choose the right husband, apparently she was not too young for marriage, as long as she was willing to pick someone he'd already determined suitable. Margaret was so desperate to get away from his wrath at that point, and because she had never forgiven him for running off her first love, she married the best of the candidates he put before her, and Harold truly was a wonderful man. They never spoke of the boy again, not directly anyway, though Margaret often made reference to her sacrifice or her loss and Olivia understood in the knowing way they shared between them now.

But today was different, because today, *Olivia* was faced with a choice. She carefully chose every word she spoke, knowing the pain it might inflict on her beloved sister. "I think I want to say yes," she said timidly, not sure where this would go.

Margaret's response shocked her.

"If you do not marry him, I might have to become a black widow and marry him myself!" She teased her sister, then her eyes were so sad that Olivia wanted to turn away from her, but she did not and Margaret continued on more seriously. "I know I can be mean sometimes. You know, about Harold. But I really do love him. I know you know that." She looked into Olivia's eyes, clearly wanting a confirmation, and Olivia responded with a quiet nod so Margaret pressed on. "I won't lie to you though and tell you that I do not have regrets. But who does not?"

"But Margaret," Olivia interrupted, ready once again to defend Harold, but Margaret waved her off and continued with what she clearly needed to say.

"I know what you're going to say, and you are right. Harold is a good husband and a good father to our children. Ulrich, *Uli*, was a boy. He did not really love me. I'm woman enough to know that now. After all, if he had loved me the way I loved him, our bastard father never could have run him off the way he did. He would have come to me like the highwayman in the poem: '*though hell should bar the way*.'" She gazed into the distance for dramatic effect. "But he did not, and I have moved on to a better life, I'm sure."

"I'm lost then," Olivia responded with frustration. "I thought you did want me to marry Fisher, but now it sounds like, well, I'm not sure what you mean honestly."

"I mean that I regret that I did not marry for love. Just because Uli was a cowardly urchin, does not mean I could not have waited until I was ready and found someone who was meant for me. I have come to love Harold, but I do not know if I'll ever truly be in love with him, because I did not marry him for love, and I know now, like I knew back then, that marrying for any other reason can never be what it could be or should be."

"So you regret that you married for money, so I should not concern myself with it? Fisher's only a carpenter after all, so my lifestyle will definitely never be the same. But I do love him deeply, and I've never really cared about money."

"Let's be completely honest, Olivia."

"Honest about what? Are you saying I do care about the money? Because I would think that you know me better than…"

"Oh calm yourself girl. I know you do not give a damn about the money. When I said complete honesty I meant two things. First of all, I did not marry for *money*." Olivia eyed her quizzically, "I married for *spite*. And second of all, do not be so naive. At least know what you're getting yourself into, because it's easy to say you do not care about money when you've never known a life without it." Olivia tried to interrupt but Margaret was on a roll and would not be swayed from her purpose. "And do not think that Father will be helping to pay for any wedding. You might as well count yourself disowned. If you ask me, it isn't much of a loss."

Olivia's eyes fell to the floor, realising that she had already made her decision, long before she had even spoken with her sister, and that she had known all along it would be a difficult one. She lifted her eyes, ready to tell Margaret face to face that she would endure all and that she would do anything to be with the love of her life, no matter how difficult it might prove to be. But Margaret's smile said that she already knew all of that. She took Olivia's hand and reassured her. "That's why Harry and I will pay for the wedding. do not you worry about a thing."

Olivia's hand covered her pretty, heart-shaped lips, which always seemed to have their own natural rouge, in a genuine gesture of surprise. She was instantly in tears over her sister's unexpected and heartfelt offer of support.

"I assume after all that I am the matron of honour," Margaret demanded and smiled sweetly at her little sister.

Olivia gathered herself and wiped her tears. She kissed the back of her sister's hand and smirked. "I'll think about it."

They laughed so hard they rolled on their regal teatime chairs, then Margaret bridged the space between them and embraced Olivia as they laughed and cried for joy. They spent the night celebrating with good food and great wine, but they kept the secret to themselves, if only for a little while, so that they could revel in the joy of sharing it together.

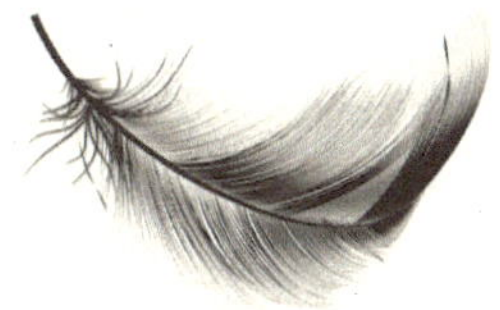

CHAPTER FIVE

Emma had been unendingly busy since they had moved to the Crowsnest Pass and started settling in. As she had hoped, the house only took a few months to complete, as aside from replacing the hot water tank and adding a new central air conditioning unit, most of the work that needed to be done was cosmetic and straightforward. The house had been renovated in recent years to upgrade the plumbing and electrical, so they had not needed to worry about much. They had sold and donated most of Helen's furniture and belongings, though they did take the time to go through it all carefully, choosing their favourite items to remember her by, despite the fact that they had never known her at all.

Having found only a few pictures of Helen herself, mostly in her youth, Emma kept these. She found one tucked away in a shoebox which was taken of a younger Helen in her mid to late twenties Emma assumed. She was holding a little girl on her lap who appeared to be around Charlie's age. They had matching smiles with the slightest space between their front teeth, as well as matching haircuts, with dark, bouncy curls; the family resemblance was obvious. The back simply read *Helen and Lorraine, Summer 1982*. Emma had put this one aside to be framed and had hung it on the wall in the family room with the other family photos she had arranged in a cluster over the mantle.

Now that everything had a place, she could take the time to relax and visit with her neighbour Marin, who had immediately become a new friend, despite the fact that there was a significant age difference between them. They had simply clicked from the moment they had met, though they did not get much time together, even though they lived next door to one another. They were both busy, but enjoyed making time to get together for a cup of coffee or a glass of wine to have a laugh, usually between bouts of local gossip, provided readily by Marin. She had grown up in the Pass and knew just about all of the long-standing locals.

Marin and her husband Stu were both teachers at the local high school, both just a few years off from retirement, though they did not seem in any rush. Marin was an English teacher and Stu taught social studies. They never seemed to run out of interesting subjects to talk about, or hilarious stories about their experiences with kids over the years, though they did not have any children of their own. Emma had not had the nerve to ask whether this had been a matter of choice or circumstance, and Marin had not offered up the information. Emma knew it was not really any of her business anyway, nor did it matter. In her youth, Emma had always harboured a secret suspicion of childless couples, though as a grown woman she had come to understand this to be rude and even cruel in some cases, so she consciously worked to be critical of her own bias.

Since John had taken Charlie to the outdoor pool in Blairmore for the morning, Emma decided to use the opportunity to make the short trip next door for some coffee and banter. Before she even had the opportunity to actually knock, the painted dark green door swung open and she was greeted enthusiastically.

"You do not need to worry about knocking," Marin proclaimed as she pulled her inside. "Just come on in. It's just the two of us today. Stu's at the pub for the afternoon."

She followed Marin, who had short blond hair with a patch of black streaking through long bangs, giving the impression that she was years younger than her age. Just slightly taller than Emma, Marin led her briskly through the front room which was only big enough for a small and plump, velour, forest green sofa; a worn square wooden coffee table with a glass insert top;

and a small television stand with a new flatscreen which was far too big for the proportions of the room. They made their way into the small kitchen at the back of the house and Emma sat in her usual chair, which rested against the wall, so that she could chat with Marin as she busied herself around the outdated yet comfortable kitchen.

"Did you know John's aunt Helen well?" Emma asked while Marin poured the steaming hot coffee.

"As well as anyone I guess. She was not overly social. We've lived in this house for ten years now. My uncle Felix probably actually knew her better than I ever did. We bought the house from him when he moved into the seniors' home in Pincher Creek. He still comes out here every day for a beer and a bullshit at the Hillcrest Miners' Club, but he's too old to be living on his own anymore. Not that he's not spry, mind you. He thinks he's a teenager still sometimes and he's got the attitude to show it, but really he's just a *doll*. Anyway, he might be able to tell you more than I could."

Emma nodded and followed along as she sipped her coffee, which was aromatic and dark. As she measured from a shiny black bag sporting the insignia of a crow flying beside the logo: *Crowsnest Coffee Company*. Marin shared that it had been roasted locally. Emma made a mental note to mention it to John as a supplier for the business. Any time they had a chance to buy locally they did. Besides, the coffee was excellent.

"Do you know what happened to her daughter? I'm surprised Helen did not leave the house to her."

"She had a daughter?" Marin seemed genuinely surprised. "I honestly had no idea. I never saw anyone come and visit really. Like I said, she kept to herself a lot and was not overly friendly. I guess now I understand why. Maybe I should have tried a little harder to get to know her, but she never seemed interested. She was never rude or anything like that, she was just *very* private, and between you and me," she dropped her voice to a whisper, even though it was just the two of them there, "she was a little intense... in a weird way. Kind of spooky sometimes, you know?" Marin caught herself and backtracked with embarrassment. "Not to be offensive. I know she was your family."

"No offence taken; I didn't even know her. Maybe your uncle might know what happened to her daughter?" Emma was intrigued now. This seemed a mystery to be solved, though she reminded herself that Helen was a real person, John's *family*, and she deserved her privacy and dignity, even in death. *Especially* in death.

"I could ask him," Marin offered. She seemed genuinely interested in her own right.

"Maybe we should just leave it be," Emma thought out loud.

"We could," Marin agreed and sipped her coffee. "Or we could ask him. I do not see what it would hurt. He loves telling a good story. You think about it and let me know. I'm nosy, but I can keep my mouth shut. So I won't ask him unless you ask me to."

"Sounds good," Emma agreed, but the subject was never far from her mind, even though they moved on to discuss other more light-hearted subjects, including the most recent local rumours, which were amusing but vague. Still being an outsider, Emma did not know most of the people Marin spoke of.

By the time she was ready to head home to start preparing lunch, she had changed her mind again about her investigation. "Next time you talk to your uncle, maybe you could ask him about Helen's daughter?" Emma asked sheepishly. "I know her name is Lorraine. I assume it's her daughter anyway. The estate agent said she had lost a young child but did not say how. It's the only picture I found of her with the two of them together."

"I'll ask him next time I see him and let you know what he says. I'm sure he'd just *love* to sit with a pretty young woman talking about old times." Marin winked at her, gave her a quick hug and led Emma to the front door. She waved out the window and watched as Emma made her way out the front gate, across her own yard and into the house next door. She smiled a warm and friendly smile until Emma was safely inside her own front door. Then her smile faded to a frown and she pulled the curtains closed.

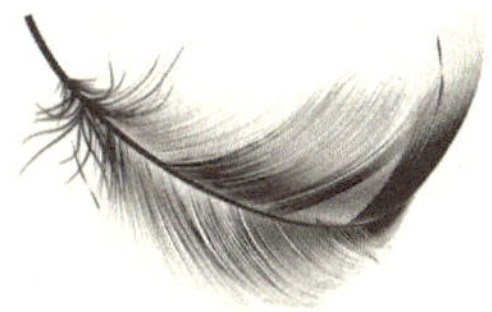

CHAPTER SIX

A few days later, Emma and Charlie went for their daily walk along the river. They had fallen into the habit of walking Max each morning on the path which led from their house to the end of the lane, up a steep gravelly hill overlooking the rolling Crowsnest River. It was early in the summer and the water was still running too high for dry fly fishing. It was too dirty for any kind of fishing anyway, the river was like cold chocolate milk as it raced away from the mountains, heading east into the rolling whaleback foothills and windswept prairies.

Emma kept a close watch over Charlie and Max as they both bounded along the worn path which stretched along above the river toward the forest. The trees marked the divide between the railway tracks and the rushing stream. At first she had believed them to be alone, but then she suddenly had a sense that she was being watched and took a moment to survey her surroundings. There were posted signs warning of bears in the forest, a normal part of living in the mountains, and a species she was used to as a fisherman. But there was no bear.

There was a man standing at the edge of the forest. He was tall, with dark hair and an equally dark beard. His features were vague at a distance, but he was looking in her direction, and she had the sense that he was watching her. Momentarily chilled, though it was warm outside already, she had an intuition that she should turn back. She was just about to call to Charlie and Max to let them know they would be heading back early, when she saw a large black and white dog that looked like it might be a cross between a shepherd and a collie, come sauntering at a leisurely pace toward the man. Emma realised that this was likely why he had been watching her, as she was coming nearer with a small unleashed dog. The dog lowered its head as it made its way to the man's side and sat obediently, without being tied, beside the man who patted the dog's head and led him off the path toward the river.

Emma involuntarily took a deep breath and turned a light shade of pink, embarrassed at herself for overreacting, just because another person was out for the same purpose that she was. She chalked it up to the necessity for vigilance in the city and forgave herself for her foolishness in the moment. They continued on. As they neared the boundary of the forest path, Emma realised that she could no longer see the man and his dog.

Quickening her pace, not wanting to lose sight of Charlie and Max as they ventured deeper into the forest on a well-worn, yet overgrown path which twisted away from the water's edge, she carried on behind as they skipped and hopped their way through the woods, up a small hill which led to a path nearer the tracks. They were headed to the old abandoned colliery which Charlie was convinced was an abandoned haunted mansion. Really, it was an old and crumbling structure which seemed to be sliding down the hill on the other side of the tracks, which the local kids had vandalised with graffiti, ruining the historical presence of the structure, yet adding to its creepy atmosphere. This marked their turnback point, as any further went deep into the forest, where the grasses grew impossibly thick, the tall coniferous trees drew close and a surprise encounter with a bear was a much greater risk than the well-worn and well-travelled path they travelled each day.

It occurred to her that they had not crossed paths with the man and his dog, which seemed strange, as most did not venture past this point for dog-walking, unless they were fishing. She tried to pretend that it did not bother her, but she found herself peering through the trees, trying to see if they were nearby. Nothing. Something about it did not sit right and gave her a creeping sensation. Emma suddenly had the sense that they were being watched again and the feeling instilled a sense of panic.

"Let's get home Charlie," she encouraged absently. She was still searching the woods for the source of the feeling which was a sinking pit of fear in her stomach now. Still nothing.

"Let's race Mommy!" Charlie challenged her and sprinted off for a head start.

Emma gladly followed at a much quicker pace than she normally would have in one of her many races with Charlie through the forest. She kept close at her heels, the dog bounding in front of them both, his ears flopping wildly. Emma slowed only to look back over her shoulder. Once they were free of the forest and on the open path between the river and the railroad tracks, she felt a little less panicked. Free from the woods now, she felt foolish for reacting the way she had. *It must have been a panic attack* she told herself. *It's been awhile. What the hell?* She tried to convince herself that perhaps she'd sensed a bear in the woods and had reacted instinctively, but she knew that was a lie.

The truth she would not admit was that she had been drawn to the man for reasons she could not understand. It did not make any sense. She could not place why or even *how* she was drawn to him, but it made her feel awful and ashamed to know that while she should have been thinking of her daughter, she had been searching the forest for another glimpse of some strange man, though she really was not sure why.

With everything they had endured, John deserved so much more from her. Already once he had forgiven her a betrayal of their love. The truth frightened her. She put her mind back on her daughter and the day ahead, but the sight of the man and his dog tickled at the back of her mind for the rest of her day and followed her into the night.

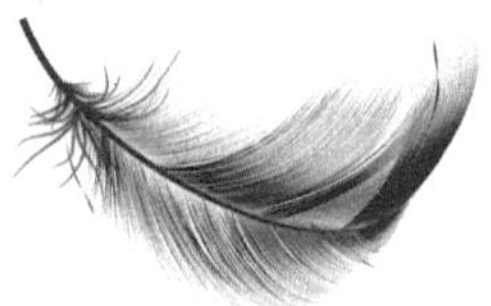

CHAPTER SEVEN

That night Emma dreamed that she was at the river, fishing at a spot the locals called *The Wall.* The water was clear, in contrast to the turbid muddy mess she had observed on her morning walk. The sun threw sparkling ribbons of diamonds across the stream and there was just enough breeze to move her hair lightly around her face.

The rhythm of her cast seemed to move in slow motion. Emma watched as her fly slowly drifted to the water's surface, like the cotton seeds of a dandelion dancing on the river. She mended her line with a flick of the wrist, a motion without thought, an instinct. As the imposter fly twisted slightly to the left, then to the right, she braced herself for the power of the hit that was sure to come. Still, she had not been prepared to see the massive head rise up out of the water, its mouth wide open for its prey, and then the *take*, which snapped the moment back into vivid colour and speed.

Emma fought the silvery torpedo as it launched itself into the air, at least two feet above the water. Its lithe and powerful body was twisting and shimmering its rainbow glimmer as the sun glistened off of the water which sprayed in all directions, forming a halo of mist around the beautiful creature. Emma squealed with delight and swore to herself at the magnitude of her catch. The line burned her fingers as the fish ripped through the powerful current, determined to outrun and overpower its captor. She gave it the lead it demanded and waited for it to calm for just a moment before furiously winding it in, the tell-tale click of the reel matching the rabbit-race rhythm of her heart.

After a long drawn-out battle, she was finally gaining ground and could feel the brute Rainbow trout giving up the fight so that she was able to reel him in. Following a few false starts when she had thought the fight was up and that he was virtually landed, he would circle her feet as the water pushed and pulled at her tired legs. Then he would bolt away again, prolonging the inevitable moment when she was finally victorious. As Emma cradled the massive fish in the net John had bought her for her birthday the year before, she was careful to keep it submerged, as it had already spent itself in the fight. She easily removed the tiny black and white fly from his steely lip, and felt the power of his tail as he flicked it, turning away from her, back into the depths of the stream, thoroughly unharmed and thoroughly insulted.

Smiling smugly to herself, Emma wiped her hands on her waders and her brow, which was glistening with a light sheen of sweat. She shaded her eyes as she looked up at the suddenly sweltering sun and decided she would finish her trip on the catch of the day. When she looked around, she had an overwhelming feeling of vertigo, as she was no longer in the place she had been standing just a moment before when she had landed and released the fish. Instead, she found that she was somehow about a mile downstream from The Wall at her favourite spot, *The Beach*. This spot was named by her and John as a way of communicating where she intended to start for the day, as this was the point just before the trail plunged deep into the forest. John preferred she not go further without him, on account of bears or whatever other wild animals might be lurking in the shadows. She never begrudged his overprotective nature, as it reminded her of just how much he loved her, despite everything they had been through in their past and all she had put him through.

When she finally regained her composure, no longer concerned with how she had gotten to where she was standing at the moment, she noticed a massive crow sitting in a gnarled old evergreen overhanging the river. It seemed to be watching her with its intelligent coal-black eyes. Forgetting about her disorientation, as one does in dreams, Emma focused instead on the huge black bird, which was cawing softly, seeming to speak to her in its own pearly tongue.

She smiled and spoke softly to it, as she always did when she was alone with crows, having loved them the most of all birds from a young age. "Pretty bird, how are you? Why are you all alone today?"

The crow cawed again, though the soft cadence was gone and it seemed almost to shout into the sky. One by one, a whole family of crows gathered on the dying tree; all of them seemed to be watching Emma intently. *A murder*, she thought absentmindedly, and she no longer felt that she was safe where she was. As she stooped to pick up her fly rod from the rocky beach, it was nowhere to be seen and she realised that she was no longer in her waders and fishing boots. Somehow she found herself clad in a pair of tight khaki shorts and a billowy white shirt over a black tank top and sandals. She could not remember what she was doing here on the beach alone or why the crows were watching her.

The crows burst from the tree suddenly, swooping down so close above her head that she ducked down low, almost falling to the uneven ground amongst the diminutive forest of wild chamomile growing everywhere in the sand, amongst the Saskatoon berry and Chokecherry bushes. They screamed at her as she broke into a run, leaving the open air of the beach to take cover in the forest and run for the safety of home. As she stumbled through the winding path, the branches of trees and shrubs hanging in her way swiped at her face like brittle, skeletal hands, reaching out to keep her in the forest. When she broke into the sunshine back in the open next to the river, she found that she was running wildly toward the spot where she had seen the man earlier in the day. She knew he would be there again and he was.

He turned to look at her, still from a distance, seemingly oblivious of her terrified state. Standing at the edge of the river, he turned away from her. The crows were in the forest now, their deafening screeching demanding attention. The man seemed to pay no mind.

Were they trying to tell her something? Telling her to *stop*? Emma turned to look back where she had come from, searching for the crows, which were invisible to her now, calling their death cries from the blanket of the forest.

Turning back toward the river to find the man was gone, she was confused, as there really was nowhere to go where one would not be seen, except into the river.

Emma ran toward home, her dark red hair flying out behind her like a flame in the wind. But instead of staying on the path which would take her home, she found herself at the deep pool flanked by the massive old Cottonwood trees; and again, the man was there. He smiled a dashingly handsome smile at her as though he knew her, and she felt that she knew him too somehow, though that could not be, as they had never even spoken. He waved to her to join him at the pool and she was pulled in his direction, her feet seeming to float over the uneven ground.

When Emma found herself standing face to face with the man, she could not help but stare into his unusual eyes. They were an overcast grey, a stormy evening sky. Though his face and his smile were kind, there was something wicked in those clouded eyes. Without a word he held her face in his hands, a soft smile playing at his lips. He smelled overpoweringly of strong soap; the smell reminded her of her grandmother's house somehow.

He held her gaze as he leaned in to kiss her, his fingers running through her hair, then gently but firmly tugging it back to tilt her face toward his. In a moment she wondered why this was happening and then wondered why she was *letting* it happen. It was like she was someone else, not in control of the moment, not in control of her actions. But she knew enough to know that when his lips caressed her own, she would kiss him back, like she had no choice. She already knew his *taste*. He was so close now that she could feel their breath mingling, just before feeling the touch of his skin on hers.

Emma shot up straight in her bed, sweat plastering her hair to her forehead. Feeling sick to her stomach, she had to stifle a sob, desperate not to wake John. It had only been a dream, a nightmare for sure, but nothing more. Still, she found herself trembling and had to fight to regain some semblance of control. She put the back of her clammy hand over her mouth, the other gripping the bedsheet as she made herself take the deep meditative breaths she had learned from her therapist years before when she had suffered from panic attacks, having been convinced that John would leave her for the things he'd had to endure. Things had been bad for a time, but they had found their way through, though it was always in the back of her mind. She knew she could have lost him, all things considered, but he had decided to forgive her. Emma did not know if she would have been able to do the same had the tables been turned, but luckily, that had not been the case. John would always be the rock in their marriage. She could not imagine her life without him.

With focus, her breathing finally slowed and her heart rate subsided a little. Still sitting up in her bed, she closed her eyes; she was exhausted, as though she'd hiked a mountain, *or fished a river*. There was no moonlight tonight. Emma thought she could hear running water coming from the bathroom. It was not the hypnotic cadence of the old clawfoot tub's faucet, which sometimes dripped in the night if the tap was not shut off tightly. It seemed to be the pouring of a bath. Or perhaps more accurately, the overflowing of the bath, as she could hear the running water spilling over onto the porcelain tiles on the floor. She could almost *see* it, though her eyes were closed and she was in her bed.

John stirred next to her, his fingers lightly brushing her arm in his familiar way. She was momentarily both surprised and dismayed; if John was in the bed with her, then it must be Charlie in the bathroom. Before she even had time to react, the bedroom door slowly creaked open, squealing on its hinges.

Emma opened her eyes, expecting to see Charlie having woken from a nightmare of her own perhaps, wanting to crawl in with her parents for the night. But instead, her eyes, well-adjusted to the darkness of the night, made out the tall form of her husband, as he did his best to creep quietly into the room, likely having gone to the bathroom in the middle of the night while she had been lost in her dream.

Emma's body reacted to the realisation before her mind even registered the meaning. Jolting up out of the bed, stifling a scream, she was not about to stay in bed when someone had just stroked her arm in the middle of the night while her husband was out of the room. But there was nobody there. The bed was empty, aside from the pillows and the duvet, which she had almost pulled off of the bed in her haste to get away from it. John could see her bewilderment and shock and went to her immediately, putting his arms around her tightly but gently.

"Are you okay honey? Were you dreaming? Come on back to bed." John spoke gently as he guided her toward their bed. She followed him hesitantly and let him lay her back and put the covers over her, just as she did whenever she put Charlie to bed. He laid beside her, facing her in the dark of their room, and stroked her damp hair. As he kissed her on the forehead, a tear rolled down her cheek, spreading out in a warm pool on her pillow. Unsure if she was crying out of confusion or fear she realised it was likely both.

As she laid in John's arms, she told herself that she had just imagined the touch on her arm, and that she had been drifting back to sleep when it had happened. She might have been mixing it up with earlier in the night when they had first gone to bed and she had been so exhausted, but struggled to get to sleep. Maybe she had been asleep all along. She told herself all of these things, but deep down, she did not believe any of them. Suddenly, she was reminded of the sound of running water coming from the bathroom. John had been in there after all.

"Were you running the water while you were in the bathroom?" Emma asked quietly, trying to sound nonchalant after her emotional reaction.

John responded sleepily; he was already drifting off. "I washed my hands if that's what you're asking, *germ cop*."

"No; I meant in the tub."

"I washed my hands in the sink, weirdo. Why would I wash them in the tub? Let's go to sleep." He kissed her goodnight and was snoring lightly before she could ask him anything else.

Emma did her best to sleep that night, but her thoughts shifted in a dizzying haze as she remembered the details of her dream, the touch of the hand she had thought to be so familiar, and the clear sound of water spilling onto the floor. She could not remember when it had happened, but she had a suspicion that it coincided with her realisation that someone, or something, not John, had been lying beside her in their bed. As she shivered through the night, Emma fought a rising wave of nausea, the taste of shame and fear at the back of her throat.

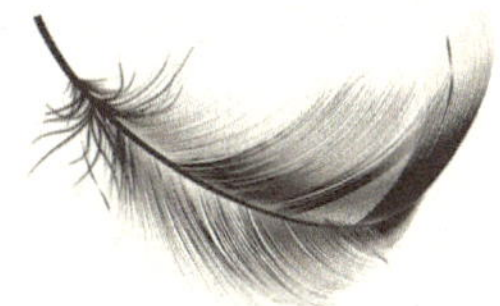

CHAPTER EIGHT

Frank, Northwest Territory, Canada, 1898

Olivia woke with a start as the train announced its arrival in the fledgling town of Frank with a banshee scream even *she* could not have slept through, despite her current state. Her hand went instinctively to her tummy, gently stroking the baby bump which was becoming much more than a bump. She was grateful to have the time to settle in before she was due, though it had not been easy travelling while she already felt ill. The incessant jostling and rocking of the train had not helped any. When Fisher had insisted on paying the extra expense for a private car, she had objected wholeheartedly, knowing they would need every penny they had to get started in their new life, away from the only home she had ever known. But Fisher, having known the trip would be difficult on her, had held firm. She was happy now that she had acquiesced.

Frank was nestled directly under Turtle Mountain, and was a town in its infancy, born of the recent discovery of deep veins of coal running through the heart of the mountain. The Crowsnest River ran between the mountain and the tiny coaltown, which was made up of a boarding house for the single miners who would descend on the town in search of work, and cottages for twenty five families. The cottages were part of an effort to draw more *stable* men to the area and the mine, men who might be more apt to put down roots and become a part of the legacy that the town was sure to become. That was if Mr. Frank, the founder of the town, had his way. There was a bank and a school, as well as a number of taverns and hotels, one of which now belonged to Margaret and Harold, who had recently convinced Fisher and Olivia to follow them to the area. The entire mountain pass was alive with new enterprise and opportunity.

Though they would live closer to Margaret and Harold now, they would not in fact be staying in Frank. Instead, there was a new cottage, as well as a new job for Fisher, working as the carpentry foreman building and maintaining the train bridges which would run between Frank and Lille. Lille was a town six miles away which had just recently been established with its own coal mining operation. It too had a company boarding house and family cottages, one of which would now be theirs, a place to call home as they started their new life and their new family.

After the difficult journey along the foothills, Olivia was glad to be spending the night with her sister. After all, it had been months since they had been together. Margaret was dying to see her in person to witness just how enormous her little sister had become. As they pulled up to the station, which was directly in front of the buildings which were being erected for the mine's operations, Margaret stood with her son, Michael, a fidgety four-year-old, the spitting image of his father; and Angela, an energetic two-year-old, who looked little like neither one of her parents, though she was still young and cherubic, which suited her chosen name. Olivia marvelled at her sister's motherly demeanour, corralling her young children as she hunched down in her ruffled navy blue dress to help them wave to their aunt and uncle through the windows of the train, which was now pulling to a stop, its brakes squealing in protest in the final moments before they were still. She found herself overwhelmed with emotion at the thought of becoming a mother herself, but she could also see herself in her sister's mannerisms and was put at ease.

Fisher sat smiling at her from the seat across from hers, his green eyes twinkling in their conspiratorial way. He always seemed to be plotting something, though he really was not the type. He was as dependable as the mountains were solid. Olivia forced a smile in return, though her stomach had lurched with the jolt of the brakes.

"How are you feeling?" Fisher asked with compassion as he took her hand, rubbing at her wedding ring, which was growing tighter with each passing day now.

"Fine," she assured him, as she waved with her free hand at her sister, niece and nephew.

"Liar," he replied as he took both of her hands in his and kissed them before standing and helping her up. He let her leave the car as he gathered their bags.

Once they were on the new wooden platform, Margaret pulled the children forward to meet them. "Look at you," she teased. "You're the size of a house!" Olivia shook her head and laughed as her sister embraced her gingerly, as though she might break.

"Harold's going to positively flip when he sees you like this. It looks so good on you. How are you feeling?"

This time Olivia opted for the truth. "Absolutely awful," she moaned. "Can we please head straight to your place so I can gather my wits before we head to the hotel for a visit? I was sleeping on the train and could use a little wake up."

"Of course. Let's go get you a warm cup of tea with a shot of brandy. It'll fix whatever ails you *and* the child." Margaret put one hand around Olivia's waist and held onto Angela with the other. Michael had already abandoned the womenfolk to make an alliance with his uncle Fisher.

Fisher took the reins for his sister-in-law and they made the short trip by carriage to Margaret and Harold's new home. Though it was nowhere near as grand as the home they'd had in Calgary, it was at the far eastern end of the town, and was clearly larger than the homes they had seen at the hub of the tiny town. The house was spacious enough for all of them, with an extra bedroom for Fisher and Olivia to stay. Though the house was still brand new, Margaret had already put her special touch on the place, making it feel warm and welcoming. Olivia could see that her sister was truly happy in her new home. Margaret was beaming with pride as she gave them the lay of the land so that they could make themselves at home during their short stay, as they were expected in Lille the following day. There would be a company carriage to take them up the rough new mountain road to their new home.

Once they'd had some tea and a bite to eat, Olivia was feeling more like herself and was up for a walk into the heart of Frank to see the new hotel. Margaret left the children with the nanny while she guided Olivia and Fisher on a walking tour of Frank. Crossing over the diminutive Gold Creek, they could see the Cutthroat trout wavering in the waters. Past the cottages, some of which were still mid-construction, they headed directly to the business district, which was also in the process of being completed.

The Frank Hotel, belonging to Margaret and Harold, had just recently been completed. It stood on the corner of Dominion Avenue and Fifth Street, which sounded so much more grand than the scene itself. In front of the hotel was a dirt road, closed in on either side by wooden sidewalks. It resembled the other buildings, with a hitching rack for horses beneath a wooden porch and a false front, which was the current style, making the building seem taller than it really was on the inside. When they entered through the wood and glass front doors, they were immediately greeted by Harold, who was standing behind the receiving desk with a young man who appeared ready for any task, sporting a sharp red Jacket and a tiny round hat which was cocked to the side and fastened by a black strap under his pointed chin.

Harold kissed his wife on the cheek and immediately set to gushing over his sister-in-law's new appearance. He clapped Fisher on the back as he heartily shook his hand, then toured them around the hotel, showing them one of the simple, yet tasteful rooms, the kitchen, and the tavern. There were already two customers, perched at the bar, though it was still early in the day. Harold invited them to stay for a drink and something to eat, but Olivia had grown tired and promised to see him when he returned home from his day of work.

They made their way back to the house the same way they had come, and Olivia slept the rest of the afternoon away, waking finally just in time for dinner. Harold had left work early to spend time with the family, knowing they would not be staying for long. They spent the night reminiscing and discussing the trials of starting a new business in the *wild west.* Olivia found herself smiling often, happy to be near her family again and to have the opportunity to raise her family with them. After a long evening of banter and laughter, they made their way to their beds after exchanging good night hugs and blessings.

When they were finally tucked into their bed for the night, Fisher draped his arm over Olivia's waist, cradling her tight belly in his strong hand. He kissed her shoulder and smelled her hair, as he always did. "I love you," he whispered as he fell off to sleep. She was already snoring lightly as the moon poured its white light into the darkness of the room.

In the morning they enjoyed breakfast as a family, though Harold had already left for work. "He has terrible hours sometimes, but we'll be up to see your new place really soon anyway," Margaret assured them.

The company carriage picked them up shortly after breakfast and they made the climb up into the mountain, taking the road, instead of the Frank and Grassy Mountain railway, which was on a steeper grade than the road. Fisher, thinking again of his pregnant wife, had requested a carriage, rather than the train. The company had agreed, on the basis that he would come immediately, as the beginning operations were booming, and they needed men who could be relied upon to get things moving in the right direction. Fisher had the reputation of being the kind of man who could be relied upon.

Though the trip was a little rough up the well-worn mountain road, the scenery had been beautiful, a precursor to the town itself. Lille sat on a plateau and was surrounded on all sides by mountain tops. Olivia had the sensation that she was in a bowl, surrounded by trees and towering stone. Like Frank, the company cottages were lined up in identical rows of five. They pulled up in front of one of them, which was no different from the others. This would be their new home. It was tiny and straightforward, much less elaborate than her sister's house, but big enough for their new family. It was new and it was clean. In her mind, Olivia was already envisioning the linens for the curtains and a rug for the wooden floor.

"What do you think?" Fisher asked, hesitation in his voice. She could tell he was worried about what she might think. Though he never brought it up, Olivia knew that he wished he could give her the kind of life she had grown accustomed to when she had lived with her parents, but that did not interest her in any way. There was no doubt about the quality of the man she had chosen to tie herself to. Their love was worth any sacrifice.

She turned to him with a tear in her eye, then sniffed and wiped it away. "I love it! We're going to be a family here."

Fisher smiled widely and swept her up in his arms, kissing her passionately on her lips, then her neck. "Me too. Want to go for a walk and check out our new town?"

As she took his hand and kissed the back of it, Olivia looked into her husband's smiling eyes. "Lead the way, handsome."

He offered her his arm and she took it, as they made their way out into the bright sunlight to explore the place they would begin building their life together.

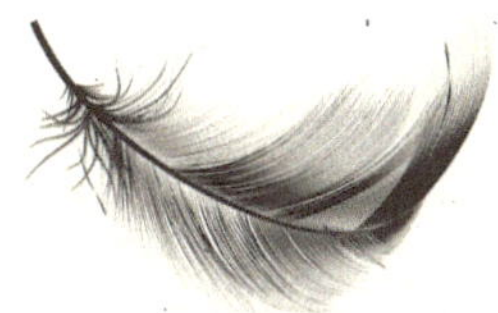

CHAPTER NINE

Though she was still feeling a little shaky from last night's *dream*, as John had referred to it in the morning, Emma accepted the invitation to meet with Marin's uncle Felix with genuine enthusiasm. She would have liked to pretend that she had just dreamed that familiar touch, now so strange, but she could not shake the feeling that she had been wide awake, and that it had truly happened. She could still *feel* it. Now that she'd had time to reflect on it, the only familiarity in it was the action itself: the fingers caressing her arm. But it stopped there, because John's touch was always warm, *always*. Emma liked to tease him about how hot he ran, like a coal-powered furnace. It was why he never gained a pound, despite his weakness for her baking. Last night's touch had been icy cold, but she had been too tired to even notice at the time, with her focus having been on the sound of running, *spilling* water coming from the bathroom.

Although aware of her own preoccupation, and her vacant stare, she was still taken by surprise when John asked her what she was thinking about. "You're a million miles away this morning, sugar. What's up? Are you worried about something?"

"No," she lied. "Just tired is all. I did not sleep well. I'm hoping to get Charlie out for a drive and a swim in Sparwood. She likes the giant dump truck they have there." She turned the focus back to John. "Busy day today?"

"Always."

"Anything special happening?"

"Nah, just the usual."

"Well, let's have something special for dinner then. Any requests?"

Without hesitation he grinned and announced, "Your butter chicken!"

"Wow, you are so unpredictable." Emma returned his grin and came around to his side of the table. She wrapped her arms around his broad chest and kissed his cheek.

"Mommy, ewww!" Charlie whined as she attempted to coordinate eating her Cheerios and milk without spilling the majority on the table on the journey to her widely waiting mouth.

Emma grinned and winked at John then sat across from Charlie, who was engrossed in the challenge of finishing her breakfast. "I have a new friend," she announced matter-of-factly between mouthfuls.

"Oh really?" Emma played along. "What's their name, this friend of yours?"

"It's a secret because it's an extra special *magical* friend who can disappear!"

"Hmmm, am *I* allowed to know their name though, since I'm your mommy? Will you at least tell me if it's a boy or a girl?"

Charlie's face narrowed and she squinted her eyes; she was clearly thinking it through, though Emma took it as a part of the make-believe. Finally she decided, "No, it's not time for you to know yet." Then she returned to navigating her cereal, which Max had discovered and was quickly doing his part to clean up.

There was something in the tone of her words that made Emma pause a moment, as though there were some underlying message, a warning perhaps, but it just barely registered in her consciousness before she was distracted by the ukulele singsong jingle of her cellphone. She frowned briefly then distractedly picked up her phone, saw Marin's name and picture looking back at her, and picked up the call.

"Hi Marin. How are you?"

"I'm just fine sweetie. I wanted to get in touch early, I hope you do not mind, so that you could have time to change your plans around today if you are able to and if you want to." Marin rambled on in her laid back manner.

"Why, what's up?" Emma tried to hurry the conversation along, as it was almost time for John to head off for a long day at work.

"Well my uncle Felix is willing to see you about your aunt Helen if you'd like to meet with him for a coffee and some treats. I told him you're a great baker. I hope you do not mind. He's got a sweet tooth like nobody's business! Get some sugar in him and you'll soften him up like the Pillsbury doughboy! He'll tell you anything you want to know!" She laughed heartily at herself and Emma could not help but laugh along.

"I would love to, but I'm not sure what I'd do about Charlie. John's going to be at work all day today." She looked toward John who was watching her with some curiosity.

"I'd be happy to take her on a tour at the Crowsnest Museum in Coleman if you'd like. There's lots for her to learn about where she lives." Marin paused briefly in thought and added, "Just like you're trying to do by chatting up old uncle Felix, who's a doll by the way. I'm not sure if I already told you that or not. He might flirt with you, I won't lie! Like I said before, you are a pretty young thing after all. But he's harmless, a great guy actually. By far my favourite uncle. I was probably closer to him than I was to my own parents growing up. They had so many kids and uncle Felix was always a bachelor for some reason. I never really understood. He was such a catch. But maybe sometimes your time just passes and then it's too late. I do not know. Anyway, listen to me rambling on about a bunch of stuff you do not care to hear about I'm sure. So what do you say? Does ten o'clock this morning work for you? He says he'll come to your house."

Without hesitation, Emma agreed. Not only was she enthusiastic to hear what Felix had to say, but she was also happy to let Charlie spend some time out with somebody aside from herself and John. She considered herself lucky to have such a kind neighbour and friend in Marin. In the back of her mind she was also grateful to have the distraction from what had happened in her bedroom, *in her bed*, the night before. *Not real*, she tried to tell herself, but was not buying it. She knew she was not all that convincing, so distraction would be her best weapon for the time being.

"What's up?" John asked with a hint of concern in his voice.

Emma hesitated, then sent Charlie off to brush her teeth, with only mild protests and accusations of talk which she knew she was being excluded from. She was quick to pick up on their *tells*.

They listened to her sing her way all the way to the bathroom to brush her teeth and begin the job of combing out her wildly tangled hair, before her mother would intervene and take control of the messy situation. Max trodded along after her, to sit and watch her get ready for the day, as he was wont to do, so they found themselves completely alone.

"I hope you do not mind," Emma began, and she could see the muscles in John's face tense up, though he quickly regained his stoic composure, "but I'm meeting here with Marin's uncle Felix this morning while she takes Charlie to the museum. I'm hoping he can tell us something about your aunt and maybe about the house itself. I hope you do not think I'm being disrespectful. I could cancel if you want." *She was not sure if that was the truth.*

"What is it you're hoping to find?" He seemed somewhat defensive to her.

"I do not know," she responded truthfully. "I'm just curious if I'm honest. We do not know anything about her and here we are living in her house. We do not know anything about the history of this place and I think we're here for the long haul, so it might be nice to know what things were like in the past here."

John looked deeply into her eyes, as though he were searching for any ulterior motive she might be hiding. She was mildly offended, as he did not trust what she was telling him. He put his arms around her waist and smiled. "So you're not like, obsessed or something?" He was teasing her now. She decided to leave out the fact that she had been having a creepy feeling about their new house lately, especially after last night, but he knew her well, and she could not help but wonder if he did have some suspicion that something was not quite right with her.

She worked harder to come across as nonchalant. "No. A little bored maybe. Mostly just nosy."

He smiled and pulled her in close for a hug. "Me too. Be sure to tell me anything juicy you learn." He kissed her on the head and they said their good-byes as he headed out the door for his day.

We'll see, she thought absentmindedly, as she started cleaning up the kitchen in preparation for her special guest. She did not often have company. She was actually quite excited that Felix was coming to her house specifically, as she'd had a sneaking suspicion that Marin was going out of her way to avoid coming into the house. Now, with Marin's beloved uncle coming for a visit, she was sure it had just been her imagination.

After she was finished with tidying the house, she quickly made her way upstairs to get herself ready for her company. She could hear Charlie in her bedroom, conversing with herself in a voice which swayed from singing to talking, whispering to giggling, all without apparent cause, outside of the little girl's imagination. Charlie entertained herself long enough for Emma to get dressed in a bright red, wide-strapped, v-neck tank top and a pair of her darkest blue jeans. She put her hair up in a loose ponytail, knowing it was expected to be a hot day and that she could already feel the house quickly warming as the sun rose higher in the clear blue sky.

Emma finished dressing Charlie in her favourite pink t-shirt and flower-embossed shorts and packing up her backpack for her visit to the museum and any other adventures she might encounter on her day out with Marin. It contained all the indicators of an overprotective mother: sunscreen lotion *and* spray; bug repellant, also including both the lotion and spray options; a container of trail mix; an extra double-insulated water bottle; and even a first aid kit, as though they were heading into the forestry, and not two towns down the road to the local museum. It seemed that the moment she had Charlie's shoes tied, Marin was knocking at the door. The woman had perfect timing.

Charlie pulled the heavy door open and excitedly bounced around as she invited Marin and Felix into the house. Marin made quick introductions all around and eagerly herded Charlie out the door before she bounced off the walls with her enthusiasm. Emma waved them off out the door and welcomed Felix into the kitchen where they sat at the table and she poured them some strong fresh coffee and served up some homemade chocolate chip cookies. Marin had not lied, her uncle devoured the cookies and Emma had to fill the plate twice more before their conversation ended.

Felix was tall and slim, with bright white hair and piercing blue eyes in a pale and deeply lined face. Though he confided in her that he was about to turn *the big nine-o*, as he put it himself, he was still handsome and had an air of distinction, though he was also approachable and down-to-earth. They shared some desultory conversation to break the ice before they started talking about the house. Emma offered to take Felix on a tour, but he said there was no need, as he had been in the house more than once over the years, and was sure he still remembered where everything was, though he was curious about the cellar.

"Do you have any plans for it? Cold storage, or maybe even a wine cellar?"

"I'm not sure. We've considered a few options. We're not in any rush to decide. Still settling in, you know."

"A priest lived here a long time ago, believe it or not. He used to make and store the wine here in your cellar. Good wine too! Let's just say he did not use it all for the holy sacrament!" He laughed heartily as he sipped his coffee and wolfed down another cookie.

Emma was surprised at this curious revelation. "Really? How long ago was that?"

"Well, let's see." He paused for a moment to consider. "That must have been the fifties. There have been lots of people who have lived in your house, including Father Bailey, your aunt, and a nice family called the Walters, just to mention a few."

Emma was dumbfounded at the breadth of information Felix seemed to have. "How do you know all this?" Was all she could manage.

"Born and raised in the Pass, just behind here in Hillcrest actually. You know everything about everybody when you've been in one place for that long. What else is there to do but fish, hunt, drink and gossip?" He winked at her good-humouredly and continued. "What I do not remember myself, I remember from my mother and my aunts talking about the past." He grew serious, a dark shadow falling over his kindly features. "And your house does have a past miss Emma, I'm sorry to say."

Emma had not realised how close she had been drifting toward her guest across the table until he said this and she started, as though she had been hypnotised. She sat straight up in her chair from the slouching stupor she had fallen into while listening to the lulling cadence of his deep voice. A chill ran from the crown of her head, down her face and neck, spilling over her shoulders and down the length of her body. She had *known* this somehow, but she had not expected to have it confirmed. From the moment they had moved in she had felt differently, as though there was something she needed to know. It was as though there was something the house was trying to tell her, or maybe keep from her, she was not sure which. It was crazy thinking and it scared her deeply, so she kept it to fleeting thoughts and denied it vigorously to herself any time her mind strayed in this direction. A house was just a house after all. Emma had never considered anything else.

"We can stop right here if you want to, you know," Felix said softly, in response to the distant expression on her face and in her eyes. "I do not need to say anything more. Maybe I've already said too much. You should have the chance to live here in peace."

Emma looked at him as though she was not sure what he had just said, as though he were speaking some foreign language she did not understand. She was in a bit of a fog, but then she emerged to reassure him. "Absolutely not! I so appreciate you doing this for me. I want to know the truth. Tell me everything you know okay. That's why I asked Marin in the first place after all. If there's something you think I should know, please tell me. Even more importantly, if there's something you think I should not know, then definitely tell me. I'm a big girl, and I've got my daughter to consider. I grew up in the city, and not in the nice parts of the city either. I'm sure there's nothing you can tell me about this place which will be that shocking."

Felix looked at his hands as he wrung them and rubbed them, the tan age spots standing out against his thin white skin, blue veins standing out against sharp bone and sinewy muscle. "Maybe you're right," he agreed. "But I would not count on it. do not say I did not warn you."

"Okay Felix. I'm listening."

"Put on a fresh pot of coffee first, young lady, while I make use of your facilities. I've been about ready to burst for the last ten minutes. Once you get to my age your bladder's about the size of a pinhead." Emma laughed and automatically gestured to show him which way to find the bathroom but he waved her off, reminding her that he'd been there before. Breathing deeply, she focused on making a good, strong pot of coffee for the two of them to share. She had the feeling they were in for a long afternoon.

Once Felix had returned and Emma had refreshed their coffees and the plate of cookies, he gave her a long hard look, as though he were deciding something about her, or about what he was about to tell her. Finally, he spoke. "Well, I guess the best way for you to understand what happened with your poor aunt Helen, is to first understand the history of this place, so forgive me if I start back at the beginning, which is a little vague, and quite frankly, second hand for me, but I will tell the story the best I can. I hope you're in for the long haul," he warned. " This is a very old house. Even older than me!" He laughed in his jovial way for the last time that day.

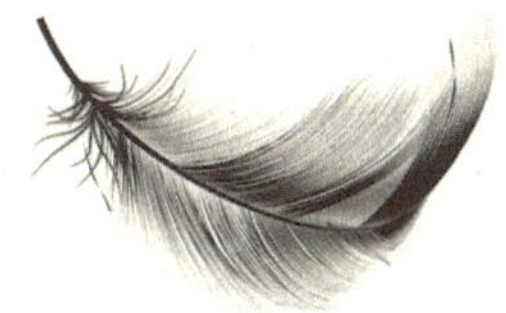

CHAPTER TEN

The house was not originally built where it now stood. It had been hauled by a strong team of horses from the diminutive town of Lille, now a ghost town. Only the foundations of the buildings and the hand-crafted, custom-built coke ovens from Belgium remained visible for hikers and adventurers who walked the gentle slope and curve of the mountain, crossing over Gold Creek along the way. The hike was an easy one, even for the least-skilled of hikers, as there was a clear road making its way to the town, which could easily be missed by the careless wanderer, had they not known where it had once led. The town was officially dismantled in 1913, ten years after the tragic Frank Slide, and the house was moved to its current location, near the eastern edge of the Pass, alongside the Crowsnest River, a tributary of the Old Man River.

The early history of the house was somewhat vague, though it had likely been just a few years over a decade old when it was moved, as Lille had not existed much longer than that, having boomed and died with the fluctuation of the coal which it had been born upon. It was unclear whether the owner of the house in its new location had also owned it in Lille, or if it had been sold to a new owner, a widower who had lost his wife and young daughter years before in the Frank Slide. It was also not completely clear what the man's name had been, as nobody from that time was actually still alive. However, it was generally agreed upon by local amateur historians to be *Mr. Harris*, though this was not official. Instead, it was for the sake of convenience and agreement in the details of local lore.

Mr. Harris kept mostly to himself. He was not an old man, as he had been fairly young when he had lost his family. Most of the ladies of the day agreed that he was indeed handsome, but fiercely intense. It seemed he was always deeply lost in thought, and he carried a heavy burden of sadness for his loss wherever he went. He never married again and seemed to prefer to be alone. Most said he seemed incredibly lonely, a deep unanswerable loneliness which he seemed to choose. Though how much choice an individual has over such matters is debatable.

The reclusive man had ironically chosen to live in a place so near where the worst loss of his life had occurred. He was a great mystery to his neighbours and acquaintances. He really had no friends to speak of, except perhaps his dog, who seemed to always be at his side. No one visited him and he spoke only with the neighbour who lived immediately next door. The old man recounted the stories, of course, which seemed to become more intense and bizarre over time, to his closest friends in the area. This meant that most of the town was aware of everything which happened in poor Mr. Harris' house, or at least what he chose to tell his poor choice of confidante. Of course, it was nothing personal, not really, just the typical bored gossip of a small town, meant to fill the hours between work and sleep.

The house had been standing at its new location for barely a week when Mr. Harris had his first unexplained experience. He had just had his evening tea, sitting on the back porch gazing up at the dreadful mountain which had taken those he had loved so much. He came inside, got ready for bed, and quickly fell asleep. He awoke in the night to the sound of running water coming from the tub in the bathroom, the same old clawfoot which still sits there now. He pulled on his housecoat, armed himself with a heavy pewter candlestick which he kept on the bedside table, and made his way to the bathroom.

Strangely, the door was closed. There was only Mr. Harris in the house at the time, at any time really, and there was no reason to shut the door as he lay asleep in his bed. He hesitated briefly before trying the polished white porcelain door knob, but had to push violently on the door before it gave way into the room, where it seemed there was nothing unusual in nature. The deep tub was completely empty and dry. The faucet was silent and still. Mr. Harris splashed some cold water on his face, stared at himself in the mirror until he was convinced that not only was he awake, but that he had actually been asleep when he had first heard the sound of the water. He could not recall when the sound had stopped, but in his mind he had been convinced that he could still hear it when he had forced the door open. He knew he must have been wrong.

Things were routine in the house for a few days after that, but then Mr. Harris was torn from his sleep once again, at the same time, so late in the night it was closer to morning. Once again he heard the water running, though this time he left the candle holder on the bedside table in his bedroom, quite sure that he would not encounter any unwelcome strangers creeping through his house late in the night. Again he had to force his way into the bathroom, but this time, the water was running! In fact, it was spilling over onto the floor and quickly spreading like an overfilled pint of beer.

Mr. Harris raced to shut off the taps to stop the flowing water. He reached deep into the tub and pulled the metal beaded string for the stopper and the water slowly and noisily drained away. He had to use all of the towels he had to mop up the mess. He himself was soaked through and had to change into fresh bedclothes. He struggled to sleep for the rest of the night, questioning whether he had somehow left the tap running himself, but he could not convince himself that this was the case. He knew it to be untrue.

For weeks after this unsettling event, there were no further disturbances. Mr. Harris nearly put the overflowing tub out of his mind and returned to his daily tasks of work and leisure. His work was a management position with the local coal mine. His leisure time consisted mostly of long walks, which ended in long days of fishing. There was nothing else which could come as close to putting aside his misery over the loss of his family. When he fished the streams and battled the currents, he thought of nothing else. He could put his wife, who had perished in the prime of her life after having mothered only one beautiful child; and his precious daughter, who had not even been to school yet, almost out of his mind. They were never far from his thoughts. Even when he worked he found himself drifting off in important meetings and sometimes mumbling to himself when he thought he was alone. Yet when he fished, he could almost find some semblance of contentment. There was no happiness, but at least for a time, there was also no torment.

Mr. Harris' wife and daughter were never far from his mind, yet it still startled and shocked him when he was on the stream one bright and sunny day, the summer following the migration of the house to its current place, when he heard a snapping twig and looked up expecting to see his faithful dog, but instead glimpsed a young girl. She turned to run further down the path which ran along the stream and deeper into the forest which followed along the path of the water. He was physically shaken and immediately reacted, tripping and falling into the cold mountain stream as he screamed for the girl above the roar of the rapids. It had been a miracle that he had heard the snap of the twig at all at such a loudly running rapid. It was difficult to hear above even the calmest sections of the river.

As he stumbled to the riverbank and hauled himself up he reminded himself that this could not be real. *She is gone,* he told himself, as he could never bear to say that she was *dead.* That she had been crushed under the mammoth rocks that raged and spilled their way down the face of the mountain to where she lay sleeping, never suspecting a thing, as it had happened when most were still deep in the throes of sleep. But there had been no mistaking the dark curly hair, like her mother's, flowing long and free down her back. The profile, even at a glance as she had turned, was the same: cherubic and fair, with a slightly pointed nose, just like her father's. He had even seen the curl of her dark eyelashes and the pink of her lips and cheek. No detail had escaped him. *Am I just seeing what I want to see,* he asked himself, as he ran as quickly as he could, trying not to trip over the many bare roots of the mountain aspens which crisscrossed the path like a tangled web of knotted varicose veins.

The forest path was short and he quickly found his way to the clearing at the other end of the trail, pushing his way through the thick green foliage of Chokecherry and Saskatoon bushes, wild grasses, and impressive weeds which lined the path. Emerging near the stream once more, Mr. Harris could not see his daughter anywhere, so he continued on around a curve in the path, up a small hill, moving away from the water and closer to the railway tracks. The loyal dog kept close at his heel and was eager to follow where his master was leading at such an unusually quick pace. Once he cleared the trees at the top of the hill he was on a barren flat of gravel, which flanked the tracks on both sides. From here he could see far off in both directions, but there was no sign of the girl. He called her name feebly, then heart pounding, adrenaline roaring, he fell to his knees in the sharp gravel, though he barely felt it digging into the flesh beneath his pants. He sobbed so deeply it came out as a moan. She had not been here. It had been a trick of the mind. It had been so believable that when he thought about her running away from him, his broken heart shattered all over again. Even her dress had been so familiar now that he'd had time to absorb what he had seen.

A great deal of time passed, along with several very nearby trains, each screaming their shrill whistles as they passed him, before he could pick himself up off the ground. He brushed away the gravel which had embedded itself into his knees after he had collapsed with his own misery, his dog never once leaving his side, though surely the poor beast must have been bewildered to see its master in such a state. Mr. Harris picked up his rod, which he had carelessly discarded when he had fallen to the ground, and made the trek back home. He no longer had it in him to fish and he could barely sleep that night.

When he finally drifted off, his sleep was not restful, but fitful. He found himself watching his daughter running away from him over and over. But in his dream, the warm sunny day was replaced with a cold and dreary one. He could almost feel the drizzle on his face when he was startled awake by a scream, one short but loud scream, which seemed to come from the bathroom. He quickly threw off the covers, which were drenched in his own sweat, likely the mind's cause of the drizzle in his restless slumber. His dog lay on the braided rug beside the bed, the hackles high on his back as he looked out into the hall and half-whimpered, half-growled.

Mr. Harris instinctively grabbed the candle holder and made his way quietly to the bathroom. Strangely, again, the door was closed. He wrestled with the porcelain knob, his clammy hand slipping as he forced the door open. The tub was running over again, but this time, the water spilling onto the floor had become a crimson pool of blood. He screamed shrilly, slammed the door shut and stood shaking in the hall, barely able to grip the candle holder in his quivering hands. His mind could not register what it had just seen and he was frozen in place for what seemed like an eternity.

Mr. Harris felt like a child standing there in the hallway, unsure what to think, unsure what to do, but he could not shake the feeling of terror which filled every cell in his body. His body, which felt ten years older than it had just this morning when he had started off on his day of fishing. He had time to think, *How strange, what happened today, and now this,* before he realised that the house was silent. Unable to hear the water or *blood* running any longer, he still was unsure of what to do. The fact that it had now stopped was equally as terrifying as the fact that it had been running in the first place. The fact that it had now stopped meant that there must be someone *or something* in there to stop it.

Be a man! He scolded himself, but it was still some time before he could muster the courage to slowly crack open the door, armed with a candlestick held high above his head, unsure of what was awaiting him. But there was nothing. There was no one. There was no blood, no water even, to be seen. He looked closely at the tub, which was not exactly sparkling, but it was essentially clean, and definitely free of any blood.

Shaken, Mr. Harris backed slowly out of the room, still holding the candlestick defensively, waiting for something or someone to jump out at him, but it did not happen. He made his way back to his bed, which was now chilled with the exposure of the sweaty sheets to the cool night air, but he did not notice. He huddled down into the bed and pulled the covers up over his head.

Like a child, he cried himself to sleep that night, alone and afraid. Questions and dark thoughts ran circles inside his head, driving him mad until the light of morning crept its way into his bedroom. *Was I dreaming? Was it real? Am I mad?* When he considered what had happened during the night, it seemed most likely to be the first option: that he had been dreaming it all along and was walking in his sleep. In fact, it would have been easy to convince himself that he had probably never even gone into the bathroom at all, that he had just stood there dumbly in the hallway, drooling, hanging on tightly to a heavy candlestick, dreaming everything he had witnessed. However, when he considered what had happened when he was fishing earlier in the day, coupled with the evening's traumatic experience, it seemed that he was mad, and hellbent on torturing himself. After all, what else *could* it be? The clean tub had said it all. None of it had actually happened and he would soon find himself locked up somewhere, probably in a softly padded room in a shabby, once-white straightjacket, worn grey by years of overuse. By the time he rose to get ready for the day, he was exhausted and feeling shaken.

But it did not end there. It seemed that whatever was out to frighten Mr. Harris was not quite done with him yet. For a while he continued to think that he was losing his mind, and so he did not say anything to anybody. But after so many sleepless nights and tortured waking hours, he had to unburden himself to someone. He spoke with his neighbour, the closest thing he had to a friend, and told him what had happened.

"Has anything else happened since?" The curious neighbour inquired, seeming to withhold judgement regarding Mr. Harris' sanity. He knew he must have seemed quite frail, with his pale clammy skin, his wildly tired darkly-circled eyes and his dishevelled hair, so unlike his usual well-kept self.

"No," Mr. Harris replied, "nothing since, but still, don't you think it's enough?"

"It was probably just something you ate," the neighbour kindly reassured him. "Or maybe you had a touch of the flu or something. You never know how these things work." Seeing he had Mr. Harris' rapt attention, the man continued. "Considering nothing's happened since, I would just put it behind you and forget about it."

Mr. Harris grabbed the man's shirt collars and pulled him uncomfortably close. But his face was not angry, it was terrified. "But I can't *sleep*!" He moaned desperately. "Why the hell can't I sleep?"

The man pulled Mr. Harris' grip from his shirt, firmly but kindly, and took him by the shoulders. "You need to pull yourself together man. You can't be going to work like this. They'll sack ya'. Think on what I said and I bet you'll sleep just fine tonight. You just got a little shook up is all. Things will seem better after you get a good night's sleep. And make sure you're eating too. Would you like to come for dinner with me and the missus?"

Mr. Harris seemed to be miles away and took several moments before finally turning down the offer and assuring the kind neighbour that he would indeed be sure to have a good dinner, a hot bath, and hopefully, a badly needed rest. "I'm sure you're right," he agreed jovially with the man. "If something else was going to happen, it probably would have by now. Thanks so much for listening to my rantings. You must think I'm crazy, or *lying*."

"Certainly not, Mr. Harris," the man was solemn. "You're about the most serious and put-together man I know. I'd sooner believe you were being haunted than think you were crazy, or lying for that matter. My grandma would tell us stories that would curl your toes! Not that I believe in ghosts, mind you, it's just that I'd believe in a ghost before I'd believe you were off your rocker."

"Well we are both of the same mind then." Mr. Harris laughed along with the man, a foreign sound to most ears, including his own. "Except I'd sooner believe I was mad than seeing actual ghosts." In that moment, Mr. Harris showed another side of himself rarely seen by others, though more familiar to himself. He welled up, his eyes shining with unspilled tears. "I, I just miss my little girl so much sometimes you know. All the time really."

"I can't imagine your suffering sir."

"My mind must have fabricated her there. I just wanted to see her so badly."

"I'm sure that's all it was."

"Thanks again for listening. It was good to get things off my chest." And he really meant that, as he was already feeling less anxious than he had for days, and truly was looking forward to a nice, hot bath. He had not been able to manage one after seeing the dark deep crimson blood overflowing onto the white-tiled floor, though he knew he was being foolish. It had just been a dream after all. It was time for a good wash; he was beginning to notice his own sour stench, a sickening concoction of stress and poor hygiene. Mr. Harris and his neighbour wished each other a good evening and went their separate ways, the kindly old man looking on with concern as the younger man hesitated at his front door, then disappeared inside without another glance.

Surprisingly, he found that the talk had done him well after all. It was amazing how unburdening one's soul could work such wonders for the spirit. He felt a hundred pounds lighter, as though a great weight had been lifted from his shoulders. He had a soothing and relaxing soak in the tub and was pleasantly surprised when he drifted off to sleep without worry or the constant fixations which had kept him up for so many nights.

Again he dreamed. In the dream he rose from his bed when he heard his daughter calling him from the backyard. He eagerly pulled on his robe and made his way to the window to see her standing near the back gate, smiling her milktooth grin and waving at him as she had done in life when he would return home from his work at the mine. She gestured for him to come down to where she was. The sun was shining brightly and the details stood out in vivid clarity, though something at the back of his mind told him this could not be real. He pushed the thought away and made his way downstairs to the garden, but she was already gone. The heavy feeling of dismay awoke him from his dream, and without thinking, he jumped from the bed and went to the window.

Unlike his dream, there was no bright sunlight, but the full moon lit up the mountain, the horrible rockslide with its pallid broken face, like the moon itself. And there in the backyard, stood his daughter, calling him down, just like she had in the dream. He pinched himself to be sure it was true. He closed his eyes and opened them again, and there she stood, still beckoning from the garden gate. His heart leapt with delight. This had not been a bad omen after all; she had come back to him. It was why he had come here in the first place. As morbid as it might seem to others, he had wanted to be near her and had to be near the place where she had *disappeared* in order for that to be so. And now, for reasons he could not understand, here she was and he would not have to live in misery any longer. He ignored the warning bells clanging loudly in his mind, as they chimed in tune with each beat of his lonesome heart.

He raced down the stairs and out the back door into the garden, his dog at his heels. The gate was just clicking itself shut. She had not been patient. He thought of the angry river, only steps away, and his beautiful young daughter now outside the gate in the back lane which led to a deep pool, immediately followed by quick and rocky rapids. His heart dropped. He could not lose her again.

He ordered his dog to stay put, raced into the lane and looked in both directions. He caught a glimpse of her white dress, and realised it was her linen nightgown, the one he'd bought her for her birthday while he had been on a business trip to Calgary. She had worn it every night after, until her mother would demand she relinquish it for cleaning. He heard her giggle as she disappeared into the shrubs which lined the river's edge. She did not look back when he screamed her name, though he was screaming loudly enough to wake the entire neighbourhood. He did not care. All he could think of was his her. She was still so little, as though no time had passed at all.

He cleared the thick bushes and stumbled onto the grassy plateau beside the pool. A mammoth of granite rock overhung the pool with a menacing darkness, casting a shadow on the water to block the reflection of the moonlight. The stream was shallow near the edge. To the left were the rapids, the rocks glinting silver in the moonlight, black water engulfing the underwater path. In front of him and to the right the pool spread out in a deep fan which encircled the granite rock and undercut it, so that it resembled a rounded abstract of *The Thinker*, hunkered over the pool in deep contemplation.

His daughter was in the water, her white gown glowing in the moonlight, dark curly hair flowing down her back, and the black water engulfing her in deep darkness. She walked as though in a trance, deeper and deeper into the pool, ignoring the pleas of her father to come back to him. She did not turn his way. It was as though she could not hear him at all. He did not falter, but plunged into the frigid night water, intent on stopping her before she was swept away in the current or pulled under into the depth of the dark pool. He dove in to hasten his pace, but when he came up she was gone. He panicked and searched the pool until his teeth were set to shatter from the chattering, as he grew colder and colder in the water. He finally could take no more and pulled himself up onto the bank, sobbing deeply and rolling on the grass as though he had been kicked in the guts. He felt as though he had been.

Making his way back to the house, he was still crying loudly in the quiet night air. Shivering violently from the chill, he was soaked through. When he returned to the house, he had somewhat pulled himself together, and had stopped wailing, though his chest still hitched unpredictably and his dog peered up at him with visible concern. He thought it best to make his way to the bathroom to remove his wet nightclothes and dry himself with a towel.

He undressed slowly, having to peel the clothing from his waterlogged skin, and dried himself as thoroughly as he could, still shivering hard enough to snap his back. He looked at himself in the mirror, eyes puffy with tears, skin white with shock. Then he saw and sensed a movement to his right. The curtain hanging around the tub had twitched. He stared at it for a long time, until he was sure that it had just been his imagination. He shook his head at his own skittishness and looked back to the mirror to another great shock.

His own reflection had been replaced with that of a woman, a dark featureless silhouette. Transfixed, he stared into the dark void in the mirror, drifting closer and closer, as though he might be able to make out her face if he just got close enough to her. He was only inches away from the mirror when the shadow lunged at him, howling a terrible cry and reaching out to grab him. He scurried away to the corner of the room, reduced to a blubbering mess, and put his arms up defensively to shield his face.

The phantom screamed something at him, something he could not understand because it sounded as though she was underwater and trying to speak. When he gathered the courage to face his fate and uncover his eyes, she was gone. The room was empty except for poor Mr. Harris, literally frightened out of his mind. He did not sleep that night, but sat up in his bed, the covers pulled tight around him like a shield, unsure of what to do except occasionally succumb to a fresh round of tears.

The next day he informed his neighbour once again of the night's events. He held nothing back. It seemed to the man that he was in some sort of shock, as he mumbled the details monotonously. The terror in his eyes was real, and the way he told the story had a ring of truth, though it was obviously insane. Mr. Harris was well aware that his well-meaning neighbour likely considered him to be a candidate for the madhouse, but he did not care anymore.

Things went on like that in the house and around the house until Mr. Harris began missing work and eventually, not going at all. He would wander the woods, his dog at his side as always, both with their heads hung low, the world around them invisible. The poor sad dog, from time to time, would glance up at its master, as though it were waiting for the day the man it had known would return to replace this whisper of who he had once been.

The neighbours would watch when the pair left in the evenings, and mark the time, as their wanderings drew longer and longer. They felt it foolish to wander the forest at such late hours, as the wild animals were most active at those times, but Mr. Harris seemed not to care, or perhaps, to not *understand* the dangers of his recently new neighbourhood. The kindly neighbour assured everyone that they were wrong, because Mr. Harris was an accomplished fisherman and hunter, so he was well aware of the dangers in the mountains. He suggested that perhaps the man felt prepared to take on any eventualities which arose, especially with his loyal and ever-present dog at his side. He also hinted at the possibility that poor Mr. Harris was simply losing the plot, so to say, as he no longer slept and barely ate, insisting that he was being subjected to nightly terrors. He grew more and more pale as the days grew long, despite the time he spent out of doors in the sunlight.

The evening walks grew longer as the summer rambled on, until they grew so late that most of the neighbours no longer took note of when they returned to the house. Until one evening in late August when they did not come back at all. The next morning Mr. Harris' neighbour took his own dog on the same trail, climbing the hill slowly, as he was considerably older than Mr. Harris, and could only trudge along at a slow and steady rhythmic pace.

He was concerned that he had not seen or heard Mr. Harris or his dog return the night before, as unlike the other neighbours, he continued to count the passing time until the tormented man and his faithful companion returned.

Once he crested the low rocky hill and caught his breath, he lit a hand-made cigarette and made his way along the river. He did not have to walk far before reaching the deep dark pool which lay just before the stretch of fast-moving rapids of *The Wall.* Beside the pool to the west was a small patch of tall Cottonwood trees, spreading their dancing foliage over the river like a lacework umbrella. The bright morning sun glinted off the pool, blinding the old man. He shielded his eyes and turned away from the sun, facing the tall trees. Suddenly, he stumbled back, his dog barking and jumping at the foot of one towering tree which seemed to be the keeper of the rest, as it sprawled its limbs and roots into each of their spaces.

"Jesus Christ Almighty," he whispered, his cigarette hanging from his bottom lip, ready to drop onto his lap. "Mr. Harris…"

High above his head hung poor Mr. Harris, his face contorted and purpled, his tongue bulging from his mouth, his eyes bulging from his head. There was no trace of the refined, handsome man he had once been. He swayed gently in the morning breeze, a rough noose around his neck. Three opportunistic crows had gathered in the tree around the corpse, surely preparing to feast on the remains before their find could be taken from them.

When the poor old man finally gathered his wits, he struggled to his feet and went to gather his dog, which was worrying over something just behind and beneath the massive Cottonwood. When the dog would not come when he used his gruffest voice, he went to investigate what held his attention. It was the dog, Mr. Harris' dog, shot once in the back of the head, surely by his master, before he did the horrible and terrible deed he had done to himself.

The man pulled his dog away and made his way home more quickly even than he had come, and informed his neighbours of the horrors he had discovered on such a beautiful August morning. The discovery was grossly incongruent with the atmosphere of the day, and that detail seemed to bother the poor man as much as the gruesome discovery itself. They said he was never the same after that day, and that he never again took his daily walk along the river, opting instead to head in the other direction, toward the road which had been cut through the devastation of Frank Slide.

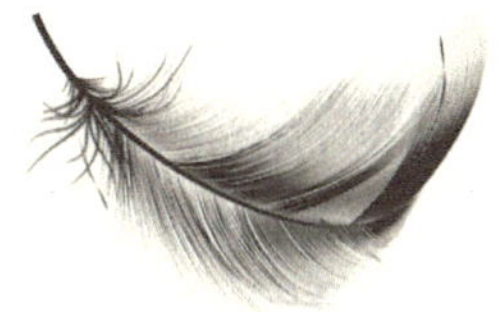

CHAPTER·ELEVEN

Emma felt a chill run up her spine and she instinctively pulled back from Felix, as she had been transfixed, and was drawn out by shock. "That's horrible," she barely whispered. "It can't be true. Is it?"

"There are some who have said they have seen poor Mr. Harris and his dog, if that really was his name. No one was really sure, but they thought it *might* be," Felix paused and sipped his coffee slowly. Emma felt that he might be hesitating. She waited patiently for him to continue. He looked her straight in the eyes, his face serious, his brow furrowed. "There are those who swear he haunts the river and the woods, alongside his little girl who died in the slide. Most do not believe in the story though, because only a few claim to have seen him."

"*Who* said they saw him? And why do they think it was *him*? There are lots of guys who come down here to walk their dogs along the river. They park right at the bottom of the hill and walk to the old collieries, or the beach and back. We take Max there ourselves." Emma sounded strangely defensive. She did not like the idea of a past owner of her house having committed suicide, but it was not *that* farfetched. Still, she did not want to believe it and preferred to think of it as local folklore, probably made up by bored kids and passed down through the generations as "history".

Felix pressed on persistently. "Strangely enough, those who have claimed to see Mr. Harris and his loyal companion have all been the inhabitants of his own home."

Emma sat back in her chair and let out her breath, as she had been holding it unknowingly as she listened to and processed what the old man was saying. "Why though? Why only people who live *here*?" She gestured to the house around them.

"Maybe he targets people who try to live in the home he bought to be near his daughter, the same home which caused his own demise," Felix theorised.

Emma interrupted him with her own theory. "Maybe it's the psychological suggestion of what happened to him that caused them to think like that. There's nothing like the power of suggestion."

"The only problem with that theory," Felix contradicted her gently, "is that although all of the people who've claimed to see him have lived in his house, not all of them knew of Mr. Harris before asking about his presence." He put his hand, cool and deeply lined by time, over hers, "I'm not trying to scare you, okay? I just thought you wanted to know."

Emma was reminded that it was she who had wanted to know about the history of the house in the first place, so that she could learn more about her husband's mysterious aunt, she had just had no idea where it would lead. She took Felix's hand in a gesture of friendship. "I'm sorry. You just caught me off guard. That's quite a creepy story! I did want to know. I want to know everything you do."

"Are you sure about that?"

"Yes." She did not hesitate. "I'm positive. We love this house. I want to know everything you can tell me."

Felix nodded and Emma could see that he had grown tired. She was reminded of his advanced age and asked if she could ask him just one more question for the day. "If the story is true, why do you think he did what he did? Mr. Harris, I mean."

"It's unclear why he killed his poor dog and took his own life. Clearly he did not want his dog to have to live without him. Maybe he hoped to bring the dog into the next life along with him." He paused and seemed to be thinking. "It is possible that he could no longer live with what he thought he saw in the forest; at the river; in his house."

"Maybe he hoped to join what had become of his beloved daughter," Emma offered up.

"She too is seen by some, not all, who live in her father's house. So perhaps he was not crazy after all."

Emma visibly flinched. Felix continued on quickly. "Who's to say who's crazy in any case?"

Emma smiled and raised her cup to Felix. "Maybe it was a bit of both." She sipped her coffee, peering at him over the rim of her cup then explained her point. "Maybe he went over the edge because he saw something that pushed him that way."

Felix smiled goodnaturedly. "It sounds like you believe in ghost stories after all."

"*I* never said I did not," she reminded him.

"I'm sorry if I'm overstepping here, but you seem a little distracted. Is there something you're not telling me?" Felix searched her face for a clue, "Have you seen anything yourself?"

She was careful not to hesitate with her lie. "Me? No. Nothing."

He looked at her suspiciously and she changed the subject to talk about his childhood in the Crowsnest Pass. Before long Marin was at the door to collect her uncle. Charlie was holding onto Marin's hand with one hand and rubbing her eye sleepily with the other. Emma could see she was destined for a long afternoon nap.

"Did you have fun honey?" Emma asked her daughter, though she was pretty sure she already knew the response.

"Yes!" The tired girl perked up at the opportunity to relay the day's events. "We went to the museum and the playground and for lunch at Chris' Diner and I had dessert too." She said this last bit in a hushed, conspiratorial tone, as though she were letting Emma in on a secret.

"I hope you do not mind," Marin said with a blush in her cheeks. "I know some parents these days are pretty strict about sweets and whatnot, but I figured it was kind of a special occasion since it was our first time out together."

"A date!" Charlie piped in.

Emma laughed and hugged her neighbour reassuringly. "Of course I do not mind. Thank you so much for spending some time with her so that your uncle Felix and I could talk."

"Were you telling secrets?" Charlie inquired curiously.

"No, silly." Emma felt like she was somehow lying with this remark. "Felix was just telling me some stories about our house. We did not want to bore you, that's all."

"Were they real stories or pretend ones?"

Emma looked from her daughter to Felix, who was watching her with kind eyes. "I guess that remains to be seen." An understanding passed between them. She knew there was more to be told, probably on both of their parts, assuming she ever decided to tell Felix the truth about the things she had already seen and felt.

They agreed to get together again in a few days so that Felix could continue with the history of the house. Emma kissed him on the cheek and hugged him carefully to show her appreciation. He blushed fiercely and told her he looked forward to more of her homemade treats.

As she watched them go, she found herself watching the hill which led to the path where she had seen the man watching her just yesterday. Emma shuddered involuntarily and wondered if it could be true. She could not deny that a big part of her felt that the man she had seen, along with her dream and the story she had been told were all one in the same. But that was illogical thinking, and illogical thinking was long behind her now. Perhaps she was jumping to conclusions and making associations where there were none. That's not how it felt though. It felt real. Of course, the problem with any mental distortion is that it always seems so real, therefore making it difficult to confront or deny. But she would try.

CHAPTER TWELVE

Lille, Northwest Territory, 1899

Fisher and Olivia endured their first winter in the mountain pass in the fledgling town of Lille. Fisher worked long hours building and maintaining the important rail lines which connected the towns of Frank and Lille, a pivotal role which presented him with great responsibility in their new community, as he had already progressed in his status at the company to carpentry foreman. He was known for his honesty and dependability, as well as his willingness to work alongside his men for even the most trying of tasks. Though he could have easily delegated difficult work, he refused to put any man in a position he was not willing to put himself in.

Olivia had a difficult pregnancy, followed by a difficult childbirth. When the time came for the baby to be born, it had started in the middle of the afternoon and had been intense from the outset. Because it was in the middle of the day, in the middle of the week, Olivia was at home alone when her water broke, followed by intense contractions which seemed to emanate from her back. She sat at the kitchen table, trying to find strength and a moment without pain, so that she could seek help.

After what seemed an eternity, she finally had a moment to breathe normally and to think lucidly. She gathered herself and stood to make her way outside, but as soon as she stood up her vision grew dark and her legs turned to water beneath her. She fell to the floor, in a half-faint, though she did not lose consciousness completely. The fierce pains returned to her back and she called out in agony, begging for help, though no one could hear her. That is until by some great fortune, Fisher's supervisor, the mine manager, Mr. Callum Hollis, came by to extend a dinner invitation to one of his best employees through his exceedingly beautiful and very pregnant wife, Olivia.

He had not even reached the door before hearing her cries for help. Instinctively, he barged through the front door to find her curled up on her side, her hand twisted around to her back, and her face sweating, red and grimacing in pain.

Without hesitation he went to her and took her hand as he took charge of the situation. "I'm going to go get the midwife," he reassured her immediately. "Can I help you up? Do you think you can get to the bed?"

Olivia shook her head furiously, and again he acted before thinking, scooping her up easily off of the floor into his strong arms before she had time to protest. He moved lithely and placed her quickly on her bed, reassuring her that he would be right back. She grabbed his arm with a furious strength, her fingers digging into the muscle with a power she did not know she had. She managed to find the words. "No, *please* do not *leave* me!" She was begging in desperation, terrified of the excruciating pain which was wracking her body and driving her mind from her.

"I'll be right back," he promised, but she tightened her grip on his arm and screamed a blood-curdling wail that told him he would not be going anywhere.

"Nooooo…" she howled desperately, "I think the baby is coming *now*!"

"Right now?"

She nodded wildly, sweat pouring profusely down her face, plastering her long dark hair to her forehead. "Please help me," she managed. "You have to help me."

"I will," he assured her, though he had no idea what he was going to do next.

She started to moan lowly, progressing to a crescendo of a scream. Instinctively he hiked up her dress, careful to be as respectful of her dignity as he could be under the circumstances, and told her that he could see the baby's head. She did not respond, but pushed herself up on her elbows and started to bear down. Before he knew it, the baby spilled into the midday light of the tiny house. He was the first to hold her before he put her into her mother's arms.

Olivia seemed exhausted, but was through the worst. Mr. Hollis left them together and went for help from the midwife, who was only one street over, literally only a minute or so away. Once he found her and sent her to the house, he went on to find Fisher, to let him know that he was now the proud father of a beautiful, and by all accounts, healthy baby girl.

When the two men returned to the tiny house, they found the midwife cleaning up the wailing infant and Olivia laying back in the bed with her arm draped across her forehead, straining to see her new daughter. She smiled when she saw Fisher and he came to her first, taking her in his arms and crying into her hair.

"Are you okay?" He asked. "I'm so sorry I was not here. Mr. Hollis told me you had a pretty hard time of it."

"It all happened so quickly," she explained. "I could not even go for help. I was in so much pain I almost passed out. Luckily Mr. Hollis came by for some reason and found me. He ended up delivering the baby."

Fisher looked back at his supervisor, an unidentifiable expression on his face. He stood and made his way to the man, who was still standing near the front door. and stuck his hand out. "Thank you so much Mr. Hollis. I do not know what would have happened if you had not come by. I'm so grateful you did. You're a real hero by my standards."

The men shook hands. "I think with all we've been through you can call me Callum," he insisted. "It was just dumb luck really. I was just coming by to invite you both to dinner, to thank you for all your hard work. Things have been running very smoothly since you've come on board and it hasn't gone unnoticed."

"Thanks so much. And thank you for everything you did today."

"We'll put a rain check on that dinner invitation," Callum suggested. "I imagine you two will have your hands full for the next while." He turned to Fisher. "Take the rest of the day and stay with your family. Your wife's been through a lot."

Fisher nodded in agreement and thanked him again.

"You're a lucky man," Callum mused. "I'd give anything to have a family of my own. My ambition's gotten in the way I guess. I'll soon be too old for any decent woman to take an interest."

"I doubt that very much," Olivia chimed in. "Any woman would be fortunate to have such a level-headed man. You were amazing today. I owe you everything."

"We'll see, I guess. My mother's hoping to have a namesake someday, but she might be waiting a while at this rate!" Callum laughed heartily.

"Oh? What's your mother's name?" Fisher inquired.

"Her name is Grace, but like I said, she could be waiting a while." He grinned, shook Fisher's hand, and let himself out to leave the new family to themselves.

Later that evening, when Fisher and Olivia were alone, their precious new baby snuggled safely in arms, they made a decision. The next day, Fisher went to see the man who had helped his wife and child in their time of need. Handing Callum a bottle of red wine, he shook his hand heartily.

"It's nothing fancy; it's from my own reserve. I make it myself. Kind of a hobby of mine. I just wanted to say thanks again. I hope you like it. Most people say it's pretty good. I don't mind saying I like it myself!"

"Thanks a lot Fisher," Callum said with genuine appreciation. "I'll put it away for a special occasion."

"I'd like to invite you to the baby's baptism as well," Fisher announced proudly. "Both Olivia and I would really like it if you could make it. It'll be in Frank and we'll be having a reception afterward at the Frank Hotel. Olivia's sister and her husband own the place."

Without hesitation, Callum replied, "I'd be honoured. Can I bring anything?"

"Just yourself. It'll be this Saturday at two o'clock." The men were becoming true friends.

"I'll be there."

Fisher thanked him and left for his workday. There was a damaged trestle which was threatening the stability of the bridge which ran along the mountain, climbing its way to Lille. The repair needed to be done quickly because the trains could not run until the repairs were made, halting progress at the mine. Another hands-on job for Fisher. Another typical long day at work, but he made his way off with a smile plastered across his face that could not be shaken for the entirety of the day. He was a man who had everything he wanted and everything he needed: a smart and beautiful wife, a precious daughter, a great job, and a home in the mountains. He could not be happier.

That weekend a small group of friends and family gathered at the tiny wooden church in Frank to see the baby baptised. When the priest poured the water over the child's head, eliciting a series of whimpers which threatened to become cries but never did, he announced that her name was Violet *Grace* Standen. Olivia and Fisher both turned to see the expression of surprise and pride on Callum's face.

Later at the reception, he approached the family together to show his appreciation. "I can't tell you how surprised I was to hear your daughter's name," he began with deep emotion. "What made you decide to do it?"

Fisher replied with confidence and conviction."We owe you everything for what you did for Olivia and Violet. We'll always be indebted to you."

"Well consider the debt paid. Your friendship is enough payment. Not to mention the relief this will earn me with my mother. She might even lay off of the marriage comments for a while." Callum grinned widely and motioned for the baby. "Can I hold her? Would you mind?"

"Not at all," Olivia assured him and put the baby into his arms. He was a natural. He spoke soothingly to the child and she calmly gazed up at his face.

The group enjoyed the afternoon together, then everyone made their way home. Things were good for a while, till the quiet was disrupted, and everything changed.

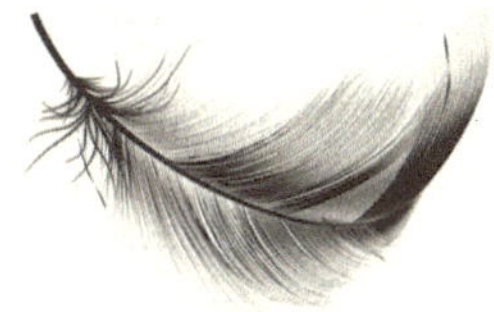

CHAPTER THIRTEEN

Emma spent the rest of her day after her visit with Felix trying not to think of what he had told her about her house and its former inhabitant. Her mind kept finding its way through the maze of chores she had intended to busy herself with, returning constantly to the feel of that strange touch on her skin. *Did I imagine that? I must have. I was probably still half asleep.* But it did not matter how much she reassured herself, she knew that she had felt it. *Something,* or *someone,* someone not her husband. The persistent memory gave her the creeps, but her mind continued to betray her and lead her back to the last place she wanted to be.

After Charlie helped her to make a simple dinner of salad and sandwiches, along with an icy jug of homemade lemonade, Emma sent her into the garden to play with Max. Her true motivation was to get some time alone with John so that she could tell him what Felix had told her about their new house. She did not want to say anything more in front of Charlie. It would not be wise to frighten her little girl with stories she did not even want to know herself.

"Do you think it's true?" John asked when she relayed Felix's story about the past owner. "Please tell me you do not. Nothing's happened to us. Maybe you should not meet with this guy again."

Emma felt he was being ridiculous, not to mention dismissive and condescending. "I do not know what I think to be honest with you. I do not know if Felix believes it himself. He was just telling me what I'd asked for. I just did not realise how disturbing it would turn out to be. I'll be honest, I do not think it's going to be easy to fall asleep tonight thinking about it."

"And that's why you should leave this alone and let the old guy be."

She wrapped her arms around his waist and pulled him close teasingly. "Do I detect a hint of jealousy, dear husband? You have nothing to worry about."

He was suddenly serious. "I worry about you. You and Charlie and that's it. You two are my whole world. I do not want you feeling all anxious about our house now. You won't want to live here anymore."

"That's not true," she reassured him, though she was not sure if it was more herself that needed the reassurance. "However, I do think I'd be *less* anxious if I knew more."

He peered into her, trying to read her mind with his uncanny ability to do so. "I know you *think* you'll feel less anxious, but what if there's more that's not good? How will you feel then? Have you considered that?"

"I'm sorry, but I feel like I need to know. I feel, somehow, *compelled.* I want to know what happened to your aunt's daughter. Don't *you* want to know?"

"On the one hand, maybe," he agreed, "but on the other, this is a Pandora's box. You do not know what you might find, and I worry about you." This time when he stared deeply into her eyes he was not trying to read her. Instead, it seemed to her that he was sending her a message, a warning.

Emma ignored his tone and his insinuation and released her grip on John. "No need to worry," she said woodenly. "They're just stories after all. It gives me a chance to get to know the neighbours. I know you would not want me feeling lonely and isolated out here. It would not be good for my mental health."

John winced when she said this and took the point to let it go. They both stared away from one another awkwardly, trying to navigate through the tainted moment and on to forgetting about the exchange. Max took care of the situation for them as he howled loudly in the garden. They both immediately flew to the back door, throwing it open and racing outside to see what was causing the commotion. Max normally never made a peep, so the unfamiliar sound rang alarm bells for both parents. Their thoughts were one in the same: Charlie.

They came onto the back deck just in time to see the back gate closing. Both registered the fact that their young daughter was too small to even reach the latch on the gate. *Someone* had let her out, possibly even *lured* her out. It was not like Charlie to leave her beloved dog behind, especially as he continued to wallow in misery, letting the whole neighbourhood know that something was seriously amiss. John followed quickly behind and Emma went to the dog to try and calm his wails. He either sounded like he was in great pain, great sorrow, or great terror, perhaps all three. She could barely get him to quiet until John returned to the garden holding Charlie's hand.

Emma ran to Charlie and embraced her, then pulled away and looked her in the eyes, "What were you doing going outside the gate?"

"Following my new friend," Charlie replied matter-of-factly. Emma's heart jumped into her throat and she felt faint. Her mind went to the man who had been watching her and she was furious with herself for not telling John earlier. She had kept it to herself because she had been worried about what he would think.

"Which new friend?" Emma demanded, panic edging into her shrill voice.

"I can't remember her name." Charlie's face contorted in concentration. "I do not know if she told me or not."

"It was a *she*?" Emma asked, with only a trace of relief in her trembling voice.

"It was a nobody," John interjected. "When I got out into the alley she was standing in the middle of the lane all by herself, staring at the ground. I do not know how she got the gate open."

"I did not," Charlie insisted with annoyance in her voice. "My friend did. And you did not see her because she can do *magic*. That's how she opened the gate, even though she's little like me. She said she could show me the fish under the water."

Emma looked at John with a look of horror, then turned to her little girl, holding her gently but firmly by the arms, and looking fiercely into her eyes.

"Listen to me Charlie. do not *ever* follow anyone outside of this fence again. I do not care who they are. You know you are never to go to the river without Mommy or Daddy right?"

Charlie nodded. "I forgot," she said innocently and started to cry, the spittle on her lower lip reflecting like a mirror. "I wanted to follow my friend, but I forgot the rules."

John interjected with a voice of reason once again. "There was no friend. There was nobody there. Now tell me how you got outside the gate or go to your room." Emma was surprised that he was raising his voice, but she understood that he was just as shaken as she was over the whole ordeal. The river was so unforgiving, and they had explained this bluntly and thoroughly to their daughter so that she was aware of the dangers in her own backyard.

Charlie stopped crying abruptly, stuck out her lip in a stubborn pout, crossed her arms over her chest and sneered at her father defiantly before turning on her heel with the dramatic flair of a four-year-old and making her way inside the house. Without looking back at her father she slammed the back door to show her feelings about his ultimatum. Emma could see her making her way up the stairs, and although she would have expected her to be stomping her way up to her room, she seemed instead to be moving very slowly, as though she were slowly floating upward. She stopped at the window and stared out at her parents, though only Emma was watching and seeing the blank expression on her daughter's face that chilled her and made her throat tighten. Once Charlie turned away from the window and continued her slow ascent up the staircase, Emma turned her anxiety on her husband. "That was smooth," she sneered sarcastically. "Maybe it's just another imaginary friend. It would not be the first."

"It's the first to lure her out to the river," he snapped back. "So excuse me if I overreacted, but I do not want her going where she should not go."

"I know honey," Emma tried to calm the situation. "It's just not like you to get so angry."

He looked at her earnestly and his face relaxed. "You're right," he sighed. "I'm sorry. I'll go talk to her and apologise. Maybe the gate was already open and her imagination got away with her."

"You're probably right," Emma agreed, but on the inside, she knew she did not believe it. Though her first reaction had been relief when she had heard her daughter had not followed some strange man into the alley, her mind focused on the detail in Felix's story about the man seeing his deceased daughter in the garden.

As she watched her husband climb the stairs, she whispered to herself. "There's no such thing as ghosts." However, her heart still lurched when she turned away from the house and out of the corner of her eye she saw the garden gate just being pulled shut. She cleared the lawn in two seconds and flung the gate open, but there was no one there. *Must be a faulty latch*, she told herself, but she did not believe it. Not even a little.

CHAPTER FOURTEEN

Three days after their first visit, Felix came to see Emma once again for coffee and storytelling, or historical education, depending on one's perspective. This time Charlie stayed home and spent the first part of Felix's visit interrogating him for information. She wasted no time to play shy, as this was the second time this elderly, and seemingly kind man, had come to visit with her mother.

"What's your name?" Charlie asked, though Emma was sure the girl already knew.

"My name's Felix, young lady, but most people call me *Uncle* Felix."

"*Uncle* Felix," she repeated in a whisper. "How old are you, Uncle Felix?"

"Charlie! do not be rude!" Emma scolded.

"Oh, I do not mind dear. I'm not worried about getting older. I'm much more worried about *not* getting older!" He chuckled at his own joke and winked at Charlie, who winked back, struggling to keep one eye closed. "I'm almost the big nine-o! That's eighty-nine and then some to be kind of exact."

"Whoa," Charlie said with reverence. "That's super old! Like almost a hundred or something!"

The little girl said this so seriously that Emma and Felix could not help but laugh. Charlie refused to join them, as she had not intended to be funny. Instead, she patiently waited them out as they finished snickering at her expense. "Are you gonna tell my mom some more stories about our house today?"

"Well," Felix clearly hesitated, "that's what I'm here for after all."

"Can you tell me?" she asked excitedly.

Emma interjected before Felix had a chance to respond. "I do not think so, shortcake. You would not like these stories anyway. They're pretty boring to tell you the truth."

"That's not nice. Now look who's being rude!" Charlie responded quickly to her mother's comment. "You should say sorry to Uncle Felix for being mean about his boring stories."

Once again Emma and Felix laughed and Charlie scowled, because again she did not see what was so funny. Once he finished laughing, Felix told them that he actually did have a story about one little girl who had lived in their house.

"She was about your age, maybe a little older. This was quite a long time ago now. I remember she used to wear frilly dresses and sell lemonade right out in front of the house here to fishermen passing by on their way to the river. I bet she made a real killin' too. Her daddy was considered to be one of the best fishermen around, and I guess he passed that on to her. She caught one of the biggest Brown trout I ever watched anyone catch around here, in one of her frilly dresses and all. She was something else."

"Do you know her name?" Charlie asked.

"I sure do," Felix said with a nostalgic tone. "Her name was Lorraine."

Emma glanced at him, her eyebrows raised. *Did he mean Helen's Lorraine?* Felix answered her question when he told Charlie, "I believe she was related to you by your daddy. You two would have gotten along just fine if you had grown up together. She was a sweet girl."

"And what other stories do you know that you can tell me?" Charlie interrupted.

"That's all for now," Emma interrupted again. "It's time for some adult time. Which would you like to choose for your time? A movie? Or, would you like to carry some of this tea party up the stairs to share with your toys?"

"Tea party!" Charlie shouted eagerly. "I can do it Mommy. I do not need any help." She took the tray her mother had put on the table for Felix's visit. She pilfered two cookies from the plate Emma had set out and got a couple of juice boxes from the fridge, then smiled at them both and marched up to her room for a tea party, humming a private melody to herself.

"Are we going to talk about Helen today?" Emma inquired.

"Not yet," Felix deferred. "I thought I'd tell you about the stained glass window in your bathroom and the man who made it."

"Really?" Emma was excited. "Did you know the man who made it, or did you just hear the story?"

"This man I actually knew. He was the local Catholic priest I mentioned to you before. He made the wine here and stored it in your cellar. It probably hasn't changed much down there since then."

"I remember you mentioning that. It's weird to think a priest actually stayed here. When did he live here?"

"Why don't you top up my coffee and I'll tell you everything I know about Father Bailey, alright?"

"Sounds good." Emma was eager to hear something a little less disturbing than the story of poor Mr. Harris, though she knew she should not make any assumptions at this point. She poured them both a refill and settled into the chair across from Felix to learn the story of Father Bailey.

CHAPTER FIFTEEN

Father Bailey, a portly and smallish middle-aged man of Irish descent, moved into the house from Lille in the fifties. It was the location, being so near to the Crowsnest River and Turtle Mountain, which first drew him to the house. It was the cellar which had sealed the deal. Though thoroughly devout in his faith, the father did indulge his vices: wine and cigarettes. He was not drawn to the location for the fishing. Instead, he enjoyed the peace of the ever-babbling river, which seemed to get even more insistent during the dark hours. And he loved that the river drew every manner of bird, as birds were also a great weakness for the simple man of the cloth as he considered them one of God's greatest creations. He had ample room in the cellar to produce and store his wine in the perfect environment, as the temperature was cool and consistent.

It did not take long for the priest to become well-known in the community, as he was seen as a kind and wise man, yet was thoroughly down-to-earth and approachable. His kind nature was demonstrated once again when he moved his ailing mother into the house as well, so that he could take care of her when he was not attending to his duties in the local parish. His mother had always been proud of him. She had been supportive when he had decided to take the vows, and was so pleased with his position now in the community, though she was too frail to go into the world herself any longer. It was a great stress on the priest whenever he had to leave his mother on her own, and so the congregation found a way to employ a young nurse to attend to her needs whenever he was away. This put his mind at ease and once again his life fell into its normal rhythm, as one's life does once all the bugs and kinks are worked out.

Father Bailey was also well-known for his artwork, in particular, his work with stained glass. He spent painstaking hours repairing and restoring the church windows to their original glory. But he did not just repair the work of others. In fact, he much preferred to create his own. His calling had taken him around the world, and in each of the homes he had lived in, he left his mark somewhere in the form of an intricate and delicate piece of glass art. In the house from Lille, he decided the subject of the window should be a bird of some sort, as this was his favourite part about his peaceful new home. The difficulty was settling on the type of bird to depict, as there were so many beautiful species in abundance, from the wrens and hummingbirds in the warm summer months, to the chickadees in the winter. He often encountered the eagle in its swooping flight along the river, its sharp eyes trained for prey.

In the end the answer was obvious, considering where he was now living, and the fact that the crows were indeed his favourite birds because of their cunning wiles and purposeful wit. They were the most intelligent of the winged variety as far as Father Bailey was concerned, though perhaps not the most beautiful. When he was a boy, his father would tell him that crows were reincarnations of fishermen, though he realised how blasphemous this was now. Ironically, his own father had never been a man of God. Had the man lived long enough, Father Bailey was sure he would not have supported his son's decision to become a priest. Still, the thought of his father always came to mind whenever he encountered a crow, especially when they were loitering near the waterways and *speaking in tongues.*

The true inspiration came to him when he was on his way from the Pass to Pincher Creek to meet with the local priest in that community, Father Gough. They made the habit of meeting, taking turns coming to one another, at least every few weeks for a meal and a few drinks. Father Gough was openly envious of Father Bailey's impeccable cellar and his finely fermented wine. They had been drunk together on more than one occasion, often thanks to that very wine. On his way to Pincher, he passed by the Burmis Tree, which was still alive at that time, as it had survived until the 1970s, when it lost all its needles at a tender age, somewhere between its sixth or seventh hundred years. Sitting on the gnarled old Limber Pine were three conspiratorial crows. Not only was he reminded of his father's words, but he sensed that they were seeing him somehow, watching him. He felt it as he passed them and as he drove away, the eyes following his blue Impala as he made his way east.

Driven to distraction while enjoying dinner with his friend, he finally admitted to Father Gough that he was suddenly artistically inspired to create the image for the window which he had been pondering for months. Father Bailey cut the visit short, foregoing the usual aperitifs, which often led to heavier spirits or wine of some sort. He was eager to make his way home and begin work on his project and had to remind himself to focus on the highway more than once. The road was even more narrow than the highway which replaced it in later years, and the dusk did not help with his efforts of being vigilant for deer wandering onto the road without warning.

Once he was home, his back stiff from the drive, he sent his mother's respite caretaker on her way and went to check on her himself. The frail woman was sleeping so soundly and peacefully that he stood and watched her for a time, thinking of how kind she had always been to him when he was growing up and becoming a man. She was there for him even when he went through his own difficulties, sowing his wild oats, so to speak, which involved a lot of drinking and breaking of hearts of many undeserving lovely young women. His nonchalant and cruel attitude hurt many beautiful and often inexperienced ladies, until the *second*-last one he had spent time with. He had wished so many times that she had been his last, that things had gone differently. But they did not.

They had been seeing each other for a few months, and though she was committed to him, and he had claimed to be committed to her, he had known all along that he did not feel the same, not *really*. In reality, she was just the next in what would likely be a long line of beautiful women, used up and tossed aside like trash. She was not the first and she would not be the last. He was not sure why he treated women the way he did. Though really he had never bothered to take much time to consider why he was the way he was, until Meredith.

He remembered that her favourite thing to do was to spend the entire day at the beach together with some friends, sometimes stretching the days into fireside nights under a dark blanket of dazzling stars. She would ask him to walk alone with her on the beach so that they could hold hands and kiss under the stars as the water lapped at their ankles. Meredith was a beauty, with a sexy bob of platinum blonde hair and naturally red lips which begged to be kissed. All she wanted was to be with him and to make him happy. All he wanted was to break her, though perhaps not consciously, and he set about doing so during one of the parties she loved to throw at the edge of the summer waves.

Although she had planned the get-together and invited all of her friends, Meredith said she was not feeling herself early on in the evening, not long after they had finished having dinner around the fire. Deciding to go home early, she insisted that her boyfriend stay and have fun, as she was not up for anything but a good night's rest. After half-heartedly offering to go with her to take care of her, he finally succumbed and agreed to stay behind, as the evening was still young and *he* was feeling fine after all.

After a few drinks they broke into song, as they always did, and flung their arms around one another's shoulders, swaying back and forth in unison to the harmony of the tune they were attempting to carry. He looked to his left and smiled broadly at his dear friend, who was one drink away from finding himself face-down in the sand. He looked to his left to see Meredith's sweet younger cousin, Suzanne. She did not return his gaze or even notice that he was watching her. He marvelled over the simple beauty of her profile, how her little nose curved up just at the end, how her dark eyelashes curved above her deep, dark eyes, and how the dimple in her cheek remained, even as she belted out the tune with the rest of them. And she was truly belting it out.

When the song was over and everyone clapped and cheered for themselves, all feeling the effects of the drink, he kept his arm draped over her shoulder and finally caught her attention. She looked at him with some confusion, but did not ask him to take his arm away and did not move away from him. Instead, she looked straight ahead, gazing distractedly into the flames as he lowered his arm and rubbed his hand along her side and her lower back. Still she stared ahead, though she occasionally glanced at him from the corner of her eye. He knew that she could see, could *feel,* his desire. He wanted her, but knew what she was thinking: this was her cousin's boyfriend and he was far too old for her, but he also knew how forbidden attention could be so enticing.

Leaning toward her he whispered something only she could hear. A few moments later he got up and left the fire, though his friends did not even seem to notice, or care, as they were too inebriated to even worry about themselves, let alone keep an eye on him. Suzanne looked about her, as though she were searching for someone, or like she was scared someone was searching for *her*. Finally, when she felt like no one was paying her any attention, she too got up from where she was sitting and slowly started sauntering in the direction she had seen her cousin's boyfriend heading.

Suzanne did not have to go far from the fire before the darkness was upon her like an invisible weight and she felt scared. So when his hands grabbed her from behind, it was a small miracle that she only let out a little yelp which only the two of them heard. Before she even had time to say anything he put his finger to her lips and led her away from the beach, back to the parking lot where they could have a little privacy. Here he could actually see her under the one light the town had installed only a few years before in an attempt to modernise the local beach. He pulled her over to his car and lifted her onto the hood. He held her young and pretty face in his hands and stared deeply into her eyes, confirming what she wanted from him, and him from her in that one long look. He moved in close to her, kissing her softly at first, then deeply and fiercely. He was kissing her neck and running his hand up her leg and under her skirt when he heard his name, but it was not coming from Suzanne's lips. He knew the voice. It was Meredith.

Emerging from the shadows, Meredith gasped when she saw her own cousin's face and realised the gravity of the betrayal. Suzanne was horrified. She pushed him away and ran off after Meredith into the darkness, calling her name. He returned to the beach, knowing he had messed up another relationship, but not particularly caring. The evening continued on and they shared a few more drinks and sang a few more songs, allowing him to practically forget what he had done and the pain he had caused.

The next morning he awoke to someone banging violently on the door. When he answered it, it was Suzanne and her face was red and swollen with an exaggeration of tears. He immediately regretted what he had done, knowing he should not have involved Meredith's cousin. He considered that perhaps he had gone too far this time.

"She's dead!" Suzanne screamed in his face. "She's dead and *we* killed her!"

"What are you talking about?" He asked incredulously.

"Meredith! She took a handful of pills last night after she found us. My aunt found her this morning. We did this!" She was still screaming.

"Meredith's dead?"

"YOU did this! WE did this! How can I ever live with myself?" Suzanne was screeching and wailing hysterically. He could not console her. There was nothing he could say. She was right.

He did not sleep for weeks after he learned of what Meredith had done and why. He would lay awake at night, and just as sleep would prepare to take him, his vision narrowing to a dark tunnel, she would emerge from the darkness. Her once beautiful face was bloated and pale, her hair stringy about her heart-shaped face, her once red lips a ghastly white. He would start at the edge of a scream, sometimes having to physically stifle himself in the middle of the night.

As if it was not already terrible enough, she had left a note to explain why she had decided to take her own life, spewing the vile truth in her final moments so that everyone would know what a monster he was. He drank heavily, but it only seemed to make it worse. He would hear her whispering to him when he was alone and he thought he would lose his mind.

Poor Suzanne had already been shipped off to God-knew-where to take some space and deal with what she had done, as apparently she was not doing well. All of her friends and most of her family turned on her when they discovered the part she had played, that her name had actually been mentioned in Meredith's final note, and in such a degrading and sinful way. It was such a shame. It was all his fault and he knew it. Suzanne was mostly innocent. He had lured her, seduced her, and he had known she was young, inexperienced and naive. He really *was* a monster.

When the drinking did not work to take Meredith's ghost away, he finally turned to God, unsure of why he had not considered it before. He begged for mercy and prayed for Meredith's soul to rest, not only so he could get some peace, but mostly for her. He truly wished to atone for what he considered to be the darkest mark he could have against his soul. After one night of prayer he awoke renewed. He knew what he had to do, and it led him to his calling.

Ironically, he was drawn to a belief system which avowed damnation for those who took their own lives. He had considered his actions to be the darkest mark on his soul, but truly, it was her decision which left the deepest cut for them both, wounding him and damning her for eternity. At times when the guilt crept back upon him as it sometimes did when he was least prepared for it, he felt that he had subconsciously chosen the Catholic faith so that he could blame Meredith, though he could never blame her. But it felt sometimes like a betrayal he could not help, because no matter what he felt, his faith was real, and there was nothing he could do to deny it.

He had awoken a new man and now he was *Father* Bailey. And he would never forget why he had ended up where he had. He also remembered that in all of it, it was his mother who had stood beside him, who had never wavered in her love and support for him. She stood up against those who put him down and reminded them that he had not made the choice for Meredith, that she had done that herself. He knew she meant it. She deserved the best in return from him.

After he checked in on her and found her sleeping soundly, he pulled her door so that it was almost shut, but not completely, as he did not want to bother her while she slept, but liked to be able to hear her if she called out in need. He went into the dining room and looked up at the mountain from the table and stared at it for a long time. He rarely thought about what had happened only fifty years before, when its face was torn away as it went bounding and crashing a path of horror and destruction on the unknowing people of Frank. He usually saw the beauty in the mountain, despite its history, but on this night it was menacing. It seemed a thing alive which was considering his fate. He shook his head in dismay, as these were not the thoughts of a devout Catholic, these were the thoughts of a pagan.

He turned away from the mountain which was alight from the powdery moon hanging in the sky. The moon could not be seen yet from where he stood at the window. He draped a large sheet of paper, akin to the size of the window hanging in the bathroom now, so that he would not have to rework the structure of the wall to change the window. Although the scene he had observed earlier in the day on his trip to Pincher Creek was alive and bright, the image in his head on this night was ominous and dark, though he did not even realise it until the whole thing was done, right down to the last piece of glass.

Father Bailey worked the picture for weeks before setting out to find the appropriate colours of glass in his well-organised collection. He needed to order the black for the crows, as he wanted them to glisten iridescently, as their true feathers do. Once he had the glass he needed for the window he set about assembling it. He finished it in record time, though that was likely the result of the fact that he seemed fixated from the time he started it, in a way he had never been with any other piece. His nights were nearly sleepless until it was finally done. He was so pleased that he hung it at once.

The effect was astounding. The light was muted by the dark shades of glass, though it passed more freely through the opaque shades of grey in the moody sky. Everyone who came to his home loved the beautiful window, which was a tall rectangle divided into four panes, so that the tree twisted from one pane to the next. It was reaching upwards in a gnarl like an old man whose back has been bent from a lifetime of heavy labour, and was supporting the weight of three crows, their silhouettes cast against the gloomy sky. The tree was an intricate mosaic in shades of charcoal, navy blue and purple, slivers of glass painstakingly cut into the small hours of the night.

Because it was directly behind the tub, whilst sitting in the bath one had the distinct impression that the crows were not just watching, but *conspiring.* Though he had worked so diligently and lovingly on the incredible piece, Father Bailey could not bring himself to enjoy it. It gave him a feeling he struggled to put into words and he was almost ashamed at how much of his focus had gone to the window during its production. The time was almost a blur and he had the distinct impression that he had somehow let down the people who depended on him: his congregation; his darling and frail mother.

The window gave him a feeling of guilt, and he regretted putting it in such a necessary room, as he could not avoid it while at home, as this was the only bathroom in the house. He hated the feeling it gave him when he bathed in the tub, as it seemed the crows were intently watching. He went to the extent of covering the damned thing while he bathed, not that it accomplished much to dissipate the feeling. Bathing became perfunctory, rather than a rare moment of relaxation.

Father Gough was impressed with Father Bailey's interesting creation, but he sensed the feeling of unease it seemed to create in his dear friend. "Is something bothering you, Father?" He finally asked out of concern, noticing the tired dark hollows of his friend's eyes.

"What do you think of it? The window?"

"I think it's beautiful. A real work of art. You've really outdone yourself, especially considering it's an original piece. Why do you ask?"

"How does it make you *feel*? Do you have any kind of emotional reaction to it? How do you feel about the crows?"

Father Gough looked closely at his friend, as though he were examining his face for clues. "I guess it evokes a sense of gloom, but it's beautiful nonetheless. Why do you ask? How does it make *you* feel? What aren't you telling me?"

"It makes me feel angry, sad, paranoid, *disturbed...*" Father Bailey looked at the window and looked back at his friend. "*Sometimes terrified.*"

"I do not understand. Why don't you just replace it if you despise it so much? Though I do not understand why a man of God would feel so strongly about such a benign piece."

"That's the strangest thing," his voice quivered. He sounded as though he was on the verge of tears. "I can't bring myself to get rid of it. I can feel myself avoiding it. I can feel the effect it has on me, but the last thing I want is to be rid of it right now."

Father Gough examined the lines of worry in Father Bailey's face. His friend's worries were real to him, though they seemed a trivial detail to the old priest, who had heard the fears and worries of men for many years of his life, most of them seemingly more pressing than the design impact of a stained glass window. "Perhaps this has nothing to do with the window really. Maybe that's why you do not really want to get rid of it," he suggested. "Because you know it's not the real issue, but something you've subconsciously chosen to fixate on."

"Why would I do that?" Father Bailey retorted defensively.

"Guilt," Father Gough replied with a blunt tone.

"Guilt? Why would I feel guilty?" The moment he asked this Meredith's face, pale and hateful, loomed before him in his mind's eye.

"Well, you spend all your time caring for others in your life," Father Gough began. "Perhaps you feel guilty about needing some care for yourself. Maybe you just need a break, some time away from everything to collect your thoughts so that you can feel yourself again."

Father Bailey shook his head. "I could not," he insisted. " I have my mother to think about, and my congregation."

"I could stay here with your mother. And if you were to leave on a Monday, you could take some time for yourself for almost a week before returning to deliver your sermon the following weekend. What do you think?"

Father Bailey was silent for a long moment, as though he were considering what his friend had suggested. Then he shook his head and smiled reassuringly. "No, that won't be necessary. I'm fine, old friend. I'm sorry if I worried you. I guess I've been burning the candle at both ends. I'll take it easy this week. I'll be back to my old drunk self in no time."

"Are you sure? What about the window?"

"I guess it just did not turn out how I expected. I was disappointed. I'm sure it'll grow on me. The next time you return I'll be taking back everything and telling you how much I love it."

"But you seemed, I do not know, genuinely *frightened* for a moment there."

Father Bailey laughed off his friend's concern. "I think I frightened myself for a moment there. I just need some sleep, I assure you."

The rest of their evening together was somewhat forced and awkward, as it was difficult to think about much else after the conversation they'd had and Father Bailey regretted his emotional overreaction in front of his friend. Though he had not been lying about any of it, he knew it was not wise to share such things with others, even the closest of friends. That night he had fitful dreams, though he could not recall the details in the morning, nor did he care, as he did not regard dreams as anything of importance. But he could not shake the strange feeling which followed him out of his bed that day.

After preparing a simple breakfast of hard boiled eggs and toast with tea and cream for himself and his mother, he decided on a walk along the path which ran along the river, up the hill between the water and the railroad tracks. He needed some fresh air to clear his mind, as his conversation with Father Gough the night before had not been a dream. He was supremely embarrassed at his confession to his dear friend, and concerned that the poor man might think he was losing his mind altogether. After all, it was just a window, a stupid object, one he had made himself even! It held no power.

He wondered if perhaps he should reconsider Father Gough's offer after all. He could make his way west, deeper into the Rocky Mountains on the British Columbian side of the border and take a well-deserved rest, or badly-needed if not deserved. Just the thought cheered him a little. He looked around and noticed that he had wandered through the forest path and had already made his way to the tiny beach on the other side, just beyond a small meadow clearing, and somewhat hidden behind robust bushes. He had barely noticed his surroundings as he had considered his potential holiday.

At the beach he noticed a large crow perched across from him, sitting on a dwarfed pine tree growing out of the side of the bank which sloped steeply to the river. He smiled at the bird, which seemed to be watching him with some curiosity before it cawed loudly three times, looking back at him, beak open to cool itself. Another crow arrived, perching in a taller tree a few metres above the first; then another came and steadied itself on the riverbank just below the dwarfed evergreen. Again he had the sense he was being watched, and found that the feeling was unwelcome. He decided to leave and make his way back home.

The crows took flight just as he lumbered his way through the tall bushes and back to the forest path, which was a narrow and twisting tangle of wild plants and trees overhanging an ancient deer trail which had since been appropriated by fishermen and nature lovers like himself. About halfway through the short path, a crow, possibly one of the three he had encountered at the beach, perched itself on a low branch in a tree directly in front of his line of sight. He had to pass near to it, and as he did, it screeched aggressively, making him jump and even yelp a little. It flared its black obsidian wings and hunched like a vulture, watching him with a menacing glare.

Father Bailey hurried his way through the path and tripped over a twisted tree root which had worn its way through the hard packed dirt. He tore the knee in his pants, scraping away some of the skin beneath and cut himself quite deeply on the palm of his hand. He picked himself up and continued on, the crow still squawking behind him. He tried to slow his pace to avoid another fall, and yet another crow perched itself in a tree overhanging the end of the pathway. It seemed to be glowering at him, daring him to pass beneath. He had no other choice. He expected it to take off once he got right up close to it, but it held its perch on the long and drooping branch, which made a natural arch over the entrance to the forest path. He ducked his head and the crow screamed at him angrily, flapping its wings offensively, but not flying away. It was making the point that it was not afraid of him, but that *he* should be afraid of *it*. He thought of his father's words and pushed them aside, aiming to get himself into the open clearing toward the safety of home.

As he gained ground, breaking into the open air of the bright morning, he let a rush of air out of his lungs, as he had been holding his breath in fear. Why he had suddenly developed an irrational fear of crows he did not know or understand, but he wanted to put a great distance between himself and them. But it was not to be, as they took flight again, the third swooping up from the riverside and joining what seemed to him a pursuit. Though he tried to find a sense of reason, he failed, and quickly found himself running, the crows following above at a calm and steady pace. He was no match for them; he kept glancing back over his shoulder, his face a picture of unabashed fear.

They suddenly flew ahead on the road and perched upon the aspen directly across from his house before he even got there, as though they knew where he was headed and making the point that they could and would get there first. He kept looking back over his shoulder at the sinister winged stalkers as he struggled to unlock his front door. Though he felt a little better once inside, he could not shake the creepy feeling sitting in his gut. He would check from time to time, hiding himself behind the gauzy white curtains in the front windows, and they remained for the entirety of the day. Even as darkness fell, he was convinced that he could see the shadows of them in the towering tree, that he could *feel* them there, watching, waiting.

He helped himself to an exorbitant amount of the wine and poured himself into bed. The drinking had been medicinal, an attempt to calm his shattered nerves, so that he might have some semblance of sleep. He had aimed for the dark, heavy sleep of the drunkard, too deep on the other side of life even for dreams, but had failed. In fact, he had dreamed, and remembered it vividly, as though it had really happened, though like most dreams, it made no sense to him.

In the dream he had opened his eyes to find himself in the cellar. Though he did not know how he had got himself down there, as he was sure he had been quite drunkenly passed out in his bed upstairs, he did not trouble too much with such a seemingly trivial detail, as one tends to accept such details in dreams. The cellar was dimly lit, the rock walls glinting an orange glow from a source of candlelight. This too was a nonsensical, if still trivial, detail, as the cellar had electric lighting, and he did not even keep candles, or a lantern even, as a result. Again, he did not concern himself with these things, though he would ponder them later. It was because of the flickering dark glow that he had not noticed her at first. A woman, standing in the corner, her head in her hands, as though she might be crying. He was startled at first, and should have been more frightened to find a strange woman in his home, where his beloved and elderly mother slept just two floors above, but he felt no fear, though he knew there was something strange about her.

He took a gentle approach, assuming she did not know he was there, and not wanting to startle her, he quietly whispered, "Miss? Are you alright?"

She did not respond, but went on weeping quietly into her hands, hiding her face.

He persevered, “Miss? Can I help you? How did you get in here? If you need guidance, I’ll have to ask you to come to the parish. This is my *house*.”

She dropped her hands to her sides abruptly as she leaned against the wall, he assumed for support, which cast her face in shadow so that he could make out her shape, but not her features. Father Bailey felt that she was staring at him, and though he could not see her eyes, he could *feel* them. He sensed that she was making a decision, perhaps a decision as to whether she should reveal herself and her intentions. As he waited for her to respond, to say something, or to *do* something, he felt his heart pounding in anticipation and a budding fear.

After a painfully long silence, she finally spoke. He sensed it was a great struggle to say what she had to say. “This is not *your* house any longer, it’s *his*. You’ve let him in, Father. You’ve welcomed him home with open arms.” The mysterious woman shook her head in dismay and put her hand to her unseen mouth, stifling a moan.

“I’m sorry miss, but you can be sure that I do not know what you mean. Is there someone else here?” A sense of panic arose in him as he pictured his dear mother asleep in her bed.

“He stays so I stay.”

“I do not understand. Who is *he*?”

She hesitated. “The man who thinks he owns this house.” Her words dripped with disdain. “He has corrupted you. I saw what you made for him.”

Suddenly he understood. “The window,” he whispered.

“The window,” she replied. “The harbingers.”

“The crows?”

“He inspires them. They inspire you. Now he watches the place he has cursed with his own sickly hands. He is reaching out to you. He wants your mind. He wants your *soul*. You must resist.”

"I did not mean… I mean, I did not know… It can't be real."

"What is real?" She smiled at her own question. "He's coming for you, priest. He does not want you here. Get on your knees," she hissed. "You had better say your prayers."

"The hangover I'm going to be sporting tomorrow, that's real. This, whatever *this* is, is not real. Am I dreaming? How did I get here?"

In that moment, Father Bailey became truly lucid and the dream melted around him, though the shadow of the woman remained burned into his vision, as though he had been staring into a bright light and could now only see a silhouette of darkness. Then even she faded away and he awoke in a cold damp sweat in his bed. Though it was still very early, and he was sure that he was still a little drunk, he made his way to the kitchen and made a steaming pot of tea.

Staring listlessly out the dining room window at the fallen face of the mountain, he tried to make sense of the dream while simultaneously trying to banish the damned episode from replaying again and again in his mind like an eight millimetre home movie reel cast in a dead sepia tone. He whispered a memory from the dream: *harbingers*, without even realising it, and was startled by the blood-curdling scream coming from the master bedroom, his mother's room. He dropped his cup where he stood and it shattered to the floor, cutting his foot as he ran over it on his way to his screaming mother. At first her screams were aimless wails, then she started barking orders at someone to get away and leave her alone. It seemed she was not alone.

Father Bailey bounded the stairs with a vigour he did not know he still had. He threw open his mother's bedroom door in a defensive stance, suddenly aware that he had not brought anything with him as a weapon in case he might need it. But his concern was quickly abated by the fact that, aside from his mother, who was sitting up ramrod straight in her bed and staring at the window with a look of wide-eyed horror, she was alone. He followed her gaze to the window and was shocked to see a large black crow sitting on the ledge, pecking at the glass.

He had seen this before at the church, when some boys had thrown an egg at one of the windows in the rear office, and an assortment of crows and pigeons had worked vigorously to remove some of the dried mess from the glass. They had nearly frightened him half to death the first time they had done it, as he had not realised it was there. It had stopped as soon as he had used the ladder and a bucket of soapy water to deal with the mess. But this was different. This crow was not just tapping on the window, it was pounding, to the extent that Father Bailey was worried it might smash its way right through the old lead glass.

He ran to the window to frighten it away but it did not fly away immediately as one might expect a skittish wild bird to do. Instead, it held its place, and though it quit pounding, it lowered its head and gave the poor old priest such a sinister stare it seemed as though the animal was trying to send him a hateful message. To confirm his thoughts the bird uttered one final loud screech and flapped its wings wildly on the window, draping the room in darkness under the cover of its prismatic black feathers.

As soon as the terrible bird flew away, Father Bailey turned his attention to his poor, distraught mother. She was still sitting up straight in her bed, her blankets pulled up close around her shoulders in a poor attempt to shield herself from the menacing creature which had threatened her in her own room. The look of horror which she'd had when her son came to her room was the same and she stared transfixed at the window, where small specks of rain were starting to peck the glass, leaving what looked like miniscule sparkling commas. Before long, the small specks turned to a drizzle, which was to become a relentless pouring sheet of rain for the remainder of that gloomy day.

He went to his mother and held her in his arms as she wept as though she were a little girl once again. Her frailty in body and spirit terrified her loving son. She grew weaker and tinier with each passing day it seemed. He gently coaxed her to lay back down in her bed. The exertion and adrenaline had quickly exhausted her and she grasped at her chest in pain then reached instinctively for the pills which her doctor had given her for such occasions. Father Bailey gave his mother her medication and helped her to sip her water. She choked feebly as she swallowed as she was still sobbing and shaking in fear.

Once she was breathing more calmly and could speak with clarity she gripped her son's arm with a force he did not know she still had. In a moment he was reminded of the woman she had been, the woman who had raised him and loved him. She had been strong both in physical stamina and in character. Though she had been firm, she had never been cold. He had always known unconditional love from this woman. To see her so frightened, trembling as she held onto him, was devastating for him. He had never seen her this way before.

"He told me it was time to go," she started in a whisper, still fighting back her tears. "He told me I did not belong here, that I'm not *wanted* here." The old woman could not hold back any longer; she uttered a low shaking sob.

He did not want to press her, she was clearly already too upset, but he could not stop himself from interrogating her. "Who said it was time to go? There's nobody here Mother."

She pointed a long spindly finger, gnarled with arthritis, toward the rain-streaked window, and whispered hoarsely, "Him! Didn't you see him?" She seemed almost delirious with terror.

"See who?" He did not understand. Nobody had been in the room, he was sure of it.

She gripped his arm even more tightly and pulled him closer to her so that she could stare directly into his eyes. "The crow! It was the crow! He means to harm me."

"No mother. Consider what you're saying! It's not possible! It's *blasphemy*!"

She laid back on her pillow and stared at the ceiling, tears rolling down her cheeks and whispered, "Go away, go away, go away…" over and over again.

Father Bailey backed away from his mother's bed, his hand pressed tightly to his mouth to stifle the sobs which threatened to escape as he groped for the door knob. He pulled the door closed as his mother continued her haunting mantra. He was not sure if she was telling him to leave, or repeating what her horrific vision had insisted she do. It did not matter, as either way he was terrified that she might be taking full leave of her senses, and if that happened, it was unlikely that he would be able to continue to care for her, and he could not imagine what his life would be without her. Even more terrifying was the idea already forming at the periphery of his consciousness, despite his efforts to push it down and prevent it from forming at all. But there it was and he could not deny it, that a big part of him believed that what his mother claimed could be true after all. Just the consideration of the idea was a sin, an affront to God, and he was ashamed for thinking it. He was again reminded of his father, and of the dream he had awakened from less than an hour before this waking nightmare had occurred.

The next day Father Bailey spent the entire day at home, unwilling to go anywhere for any amount of time considering the state his mother had been in. When he finally had the courage to check in on her to see if she was ready to take her breakfast, she was sleeping fitfully. The rain continued its tapping on the window, reminding him of last night's strange and traumatic events. As he closed the door, he saw a flash of black at the window. A crow! He threw open the door, slamming it against the wall, waking his exhausted and frightened mother in the process. But it turned out that there was nothing there. It had been a mere trick of the imagination. He apologised for waking her and for scaring her and brought up her breakfast, a meagre piece of lightly buttered toast with a boiled egg which he had already lovingly shelled for her, and a cup of steaming hot tea. She did not have anything more to say and neither did he, so he ate what he could and spent the rest of his day deep in thought, or perhaps trying to avoid the train of thought which had infested his brain.

The woman in his dream had told him to say his prayers, but he found this to be a struggle, yet failed to see the danger in the fact. It was not late in the day before he had his first drink. By mid-afternoon his already frayed nerves were shattered and he pounded the first two drinks before slowing to a respectable sip. He kept a steady pace until dinner, so that preparing his mother's evening meal had been a practice in balance and hoping for small miracles that he could at least avoid cutting himself and starting up a whole new drama to deal with. It was all for nothing anyway; his mother was sleeping once again, and he did not have the heart to wake her. He put the tray on her bedside table and lovingly stroked her bright white hair then kissed her on the forehead. She stirred lightly but did not wake.

That night he drank himself into a stupor, unable to cope with the possibilities which his own mind had posed. He awoke with a shuddering chill. He had passed out on the couch in the living room. Standing on shaky legs, he looked around the room to orient himself, then saw that the back door was wide open to the cold night. Quickly, he stumbled across the dining room to the back porch and closed the door against the rain, which had slowed, but was now blowing with a howling, chilly wind.

With the turn of the lock he scolded himself for drinking so heavily. Clearly he had opened the back door for some reason and left it open to the stormy night, with no consideration for his own safety or that of his poor dear mother's. His mind turned immediately to his mother and he made his way as quickly as he could on unsteady legs up the stairs and to her room. He slowed on the stairs and his heart began to pound when he saw that her bedroom door was left ajar. He was sure he had closed it. Had he returned to her room in his drunken state and forgotten to shut the door behind himself? His guilt weighed more heavily than it usually did.

He hoped to find her sleeping peacefully, but instead faced the shock of an empty bed. In the moment it took to register that she was not where she should be he imagined all of the horrible possibilities. He swore to himself that this would be the end of his nights of drinking alone, perhaps of drinking altogether, as long as he could find his mother safe and sound and return her to her modest, simple bed. He checked the floor on the far side of the bed to see if she had fallen out in her sleep and was perhaps unconscious and out of his line of sight, but she was not there. He was mildly relieved but still in a state of shock, confusion and growing fear. If she was not there, where *could* she be?

An instinct he did not recognize drew him to the window. Though it was difficult to see through the drizzling rain being blown against the panes in the darkness, there was no mistaking his elderly mother's form running, stumbling and crawling in the back garden. She was wearing the white flannel nightgown he had given her for Christmas. He could see that she was in distress, yet for a moment he remained frozen on the spot, as a dark swooping form descended on his mother. One crow, then another.

Shaking himself from his momentary shock he set off to the stairs, bounding down with no concern for his lacking balance. He felt much more sober than he had when he had first been awakened by the howling wind and rain. This feeling was doubled upon when the cold wind and rain struck him in the face. He ran to his mother, who was on her back in the garden, one skeletal white arm draped fearfully over her terrified face, the other clutching desperately at the front of her night gown. As he lifted her clumsily from the ground to carry her inside to escape the chilling rain, one crow dripping with rain, swooped at him. Another followed, then another, as though they meant for him to drop his frail and ailing mother. He needed to get her inside quickly. By the way she was desperately clutching her chest and gasping for air he knew that his time was short.

As the crows swooped overhead, he lost his footing on a slippery patch of muddy grass and his legs flew out from beneath him. He crashed onto his back and his mother landed with a thud on top of him. What a sight they would have been, splayed out in the rain on their backs. The situation would have been comical if it had not been so desperate. He somehow scrambled to his feet and pulled his mother up into his arms once again. He carried her inside and left her on the couch in the living room as he bounded up the stairs to collect her medication.

By now he was shaking so badly that he knocked the precious bottle to the floor, and because the cap had not been securely in place, the tiny brown pills poured out over the floor, rolling and skittering this way and that. He swore and got down on his knees, quickly recovering one of the pills. Pulling himself back up to his feet, he made his way back to the living room. He had to fight against his mother who was sopping wet and tiny as a bird now, so that she would take the medication which it seemed would be her only chance. Her body was writhing and it seemed as though she was a swimmer, swept up under the waves, fighting to come up for air. When she did, her gasp was deep but rattly and immediately mixed with gagging sobs of terror and helplessness.

She grabbed him by the collar and pulled him close, so that he could smell the sour stench of fear on her breath. "Go away. He said I do not belong here. I need to go away. I do not belong here!" She repeated this desperate plea in a whisper as he somehow found the strength to take her back to her room, to her bed, where he changed her into a dry nightgown and smoothed her thinning white hair, dishevelled by the rain, as he tried to reassure her that she was indeed safe, though he did not really believe it himself anymore.

After weeping turned to exhaustion, she was finally sleeping, though Father Bailey was sure she was still whispering the same thing over and over again, even in her fitful dreams. She did not sleep for long, so he did not sleep for long either, and though he had hoped things might be better in the morning, they were not. In fact, from that time on, she only became worse. She struggled to eat, insisting she felt sickly all the time.

Terrified that she was being watched, she initially refused to bathe unless he used a sheet to cover over the stained glass crows. Eventually she refused to bathe in there at all. With God's good grace she did not repeat the same disturbing phrase any longer, as he feared she might for good, though she did in the rare moments when she slept.

In time Father Bailey had to admit that he could no longer keep his mother in the house. It seemed she was wasting away before his very eyes and he had no choice but to take action or lose her, and bear the guilt of it for the rest of his life. He could not bear to have yet another guilty weight on his conscience. He knew it might crush him altogether. He requested a transfer to another parish, even though the thought of leaving would have made him miserable only months before. He loved his congregation, and the mountains, and the friendships he had fostered. But now he felt relieved that his transfer had come through and he had only one week left before they could leave.

The exhausted priest invited his good friend, Father Gough, to the house one evening to enjoy a few final glasses of wine from the cellar. His latest and last batch was just now ready. It was a sad occasion, as the two men had grown close and would miss one another's company. They agreed during their visit to stay in touch by letter. They shared a humble, but well-cooked local duck, given to Father Bailey by Mr. Grimes, a man who had sought his counsel after he had found himself drawn to a woman who was not the lovely Mrs. Grimes. Of course Father Bailey had been supportive and understanding, and in the end, Mr. Grimes, with the support of his holy father, had overcome and maintained the sanctity of his marriage vows. The men had been friendly ever since, as the young man had seen the kind nature of the priest, and came to count him as one of his friends. The duck was a gift, hunted just for this occasion. Father Bailey cooked it with care, stuffing it with a fresh orange, a rare indulgence during that time, especially in such an isolated place.

The meal was splendid and the company easy, though they avoided discussing why the goodbyes were necessary at all. After several attempts, Father Gough had finally accepted that his good friend would not discuss the nature of his concerns, though he was sure it had everything to do with his mother's ailing health, and nothing at all to do with sinister crows lurking outside her window. Not that he was even aware of this possibility, since Father Bailey had kept that particular story to himself, having learned from his friend's understandable reaction to his thoughts about the window.

When it was time for his friend to leave, Father Bailey saw him off at the door and watched him drive off into the darkening evening. There was still enough light though for a nice brisk walk along the river. He grabbed his coat and hat, and after checking in once again on his sleeping mother, he made his way out into the fresh evening air, growing heavy with dusk. The sky was a bizarre mix of pink and orange on navy blue, painting the surrounding landscape in a reddish hue, making it appear strangely alien. *It looks like Hell,* he thought, and tried to banish the horrible thought before having it, but it was too late. But it *did*, in a way. Not the flaming inferno described in his own teachings, but like the landscape which had appeared in his nightmares from time to time, when his own mistakes had tortured him to sleep and followed him into his dreams.

There he would see a young woman, waiting in the distance, not looking at him, but waiting for him nonetheless he knew. There was something not quite right about her, he knew this too. But on this walk he was not dreaming, and Meredith's ghost was not there to haunt him. He had come a distance without even realising it. It was amazing how quickly he could get lost in his anxieties these days. He stopped and stood still for a moment, his eyes turning to the towering tree near the bend in the river, then beneath the tree to the figure standing there in stark contrast to the surroundings. He caught his breath, though he was not sure why, as it was not unusual to see another person out for an evening stroll. It was a man. The man faced away from him. Something about him did not seem right, something about the neck. His attention was drawn to the silhouette of a dog which was crouching in a menacing stance, near the bushes which skirted the giant tree. He could not see much of the creature, but he could tell it was watching him. He could *feel* it. The hair stood up on the back of his neck.

Time to go back, he told himself, cutting his walk unexpectedly short. Father Bailey was trying to deny the terror rising in his mind, ignoring the danger which his heart was screaming out as it tried to pound its way out of his chest. His feet felt frozen in place, his eyes glued to the man in the near distance. A bead of sweat trickled down his wrinkled brow, making its way to the corner of his eye, but he did not feel the sting; he was transfixed on the figure before him.

The man, his neck twisted at an unnatural angle as he surveyed the stream, began to turn slowly toward the terrified priest. The terror of this reality finally put his aching old feet in motion. He turned before he could see any more and made his way run-walking back to the house. On his way down the hill he crossed paths with a teenage couple who had been holding hands when he had crested the hill, but they had quickly dropped their innocent embrace when they saw him.

"Good evening Father." The young man practised his best manners. "A beautiful night isn't it?"

Father Bailey mumbled incoherently, something about watching out for the dog, though he made no further effort to ensure their safety, and instead hurried on toward the house in a panic. Something in his mind was whispering that he should not have left his vulnerable waif of a mother all alone in the house. Perhaps he had been drinking too much once again, more than he had realised. He stumbled over the front steps and fumbled with the keys, his hands shaking so much with fear that it seemed a lifetime before the key finally found its way into the lock and he forced his way through the door. He slammed the door behind him and pulled his coat and hat off in a flurry, throwing them onto the sofa.

Sweating profusely, he crept up the stairs to his mother's room, hoping to find her sleeping peacefully in her bed. But she was not. His heart skipped a beat to see the covers thrown back and only the shape of her left behind in the mattress, after too many months of laying in the same spot. He felt ill. The room was dark. His eyes adjusted and travelled from the bed to the window, where she stood looking out, her hands gripping the white wooden sill with all the strength she had left in her failing body.

"Mother! Why are you out of bed?"

It seemed to him that he rarely saw her out of bed since the night in the storm, when the crows had threatened them both. He crossed the simple room in three strides and was at her side, his hands automatically going to her wrists, to firmly but gently take her away from the window and back to the safety of her bed. But the moment he touched her she screamed and pulled away from him so abruptly that he gasped, fearing she might actually break the window and cut herself. She started to bang on the glass with a strength he was surprised to see she still had, as she had wasted away to nothing over the past weeks while he awaited the news of his requested transfer and the arrival of his replacement.

This new priest, he too would live in the same house, the *Lille* house. This knowledge had given Father Bailey both a sense of dread and guilt, though it did not change his mind about leaving the godforsaken place. There was still a part of him trying to deny the darkness he felt lurking in the corners, in the shadows of each dingy room. It was a sin to think a house could hold such sway, but in his heart he knew, and this tortured his conscience. He told himself he had to put his dear mother first, but he knew this was a coward's excuse. He owed the priest an explanation. He decided he would speak to him frankly, and in earnest, when he arrived, and though he would surely think the old man crazy, at least this course of action might allow for some semblance of sleep for the compassionate priest. At least he would know that he tried and did not hide behind his cowardly reasoning.

As he wrapped his arms around his mother to stop her banging wildly on the glass, she began to whisper, which grew to a shout. "Go away, go away, go away!"

As he tried to pull her back from the window, that's when he saw it, saw *him*, the man from the river. Again the man was facing away from him, the same dangerous, unnatural twist in the neck. A sense of dread fell over him and he almost dropped his mother, who had grown limp in his embrace.

Father Bailey backed away from the window, dragging his mother in his arms, desperate to move away from sight before the man could make his sickening about-turn to face him. It was only now that the priest realised the dog lurking in the shadows at the man's side. Again he could not make out the dog's features, just as it had been at the river, but it was darker now too. It had suddenly become night as he stood here transfixed in a state of sheer terror at the window. He did not know how long he stood there, frozen in the unseen gaze of that hellhound, before it melted into the night before his eyes.

He looked up to see the man, but he was gone. Everything was suddenly silent and still. The darkness of the night was heavy in the room, as heavy as the weight of his precious mother as she lagged in his arms. He was holding his breath. All was silent.

A cold hand rested on his shoulder, and he heard a woman's raspy voice whisper closely in his ear. "Stay Father." Her breath was stale ash, like the old embers of a long-forgotten fire. He somehow knew the voice, like something he had heard in a dream. Only this was not a dream as far as he knew, though that would make everything a lot easier, as nothing was making sense any longer in this cursed house. He almost leapt out of his skin and again almost dropped his dear mother in a moment of shock. He suddenly became very aware of her weight and he dragged her to her bed and hoisted her, with difficulty, onto the bed. He decided that he must be beyond tired, as he knew his mother was not heavy at all. She was a mere whisper of a woman.

He tucked her into her bed. She was suddenly sleeping so peacefully, as though she did not have a care nor a fear in the world. And that was because she no longer did. As he took her hand to kiss it in reassurance, both for her and himself, he drew back in horror at the icy coldness of her skin on his. He could feel that she was already growing stiff in her stillness. *How long had he stood* there, the idiot son, gripping her dumbly as she slipped away and grew cold in his arms? There was something immoral in the thought of it. He knew she had been well, stronger than she had been in a long while, when he had pulled her back from the horrid image which had seared itself upon their gaze and upon their very souls. He had no doubt.

Had he hurt her? He was sure he had not, but at the same time he was completely unsure. He was not a strong man, but she had been so weak, so frail, like a bird which could be so easily broken in hand. No. He knew it was not true, or he *needed* to know it at any length. *How long had he stood there, holding her corpse?* He did not want to know. It was an abomination, an affront to God. He could not remember how long he had been there.

Now that he was consciously considering it and focusing on the detail, he realised that he had felt the day darken, that he had felt the time shift and had felt frozen in fear, transfixed first on the man with the twisted neck, and then on his sinister shadow dog. And in his hypnotic state, with this terror which insulted his love for his creator, he had missed her languishing, and had therefore been absent in the final moments of her being. Moments of terror, though he had held her in his arms for what had likely been hours.

Father Bailey was sure that he was losing his mind. Surely the horror of what he had seen, coupled with a subconscious awareness of his mother's death, had sent him into a state of shock which took hours to recover from. He had not recovered, even now, though he was coming to enough to realise the horrors of his mother's final moments in life. He had loved her more than anyone, and she him, and he had been such a good son to her, and she a good mother to him, and in the end, he had failed her. She had died alone, there in his arms.

With all that had happened, Father Bailey waited until the morning to head into Blairmore to report that he had come in to check on his mother in the morning to find that she had died peacefully in her sleep. A lie. She had died alone and terrified and likely wishing for more than just sleep. He was a terrible son. Truly, when he considered it, he probably always had been. For all his trying, for all his noble efforts, in the end, he kept his ailing mother with him out of more than a sense of obedience, but in a wish for some sort of atonement for things which could no longer be atoned for. Because Meredith was dead and now his mother was dead. And when he thought about it and was honest with himself, both of these things were directly his doing. He should not have brought his sickly mother to this foreign place out of some whim to satisfy his own boyish curiosity. And even worse than that, his never-ending need to run away from what he had done and who he could never stop being: a bad man and a selfish son.

It was in this tortured state of mind that Father Bailey found himself on his last night in the house. He should not have stayed, he told himself, but he could not think of a reason to tell the local hotelier why he could not remain in his own home until young Father Curtz had actually arrived. His sleeps were fitful, as they always were now, and he struggled to tell the difference between when he was awake and when he was dozing off. He had been in a thick fog for days. And so, he was unsure if he had been awake or asleep when the woman came to him, but the room was dark and he could only make out her silhouette against the moonlight. He was startled, but not afraid, although he did not know why, because he should have been. She came toward him, and even as she came into the light, her face remained in shadow. He had the sense that she had once been beautiful. *Once.*

He closed his eyes as she drew near and he heard her whisper, "Stay."

He knew he could not, but then again he knew that he could not in good conscience allow his successor to live in the house without warning him of all that he had experienced in the house. He would tell him the entire truth and leave it all behind him. He kept his eyes closed until he no longer felt her watching him closely.

The horrible woman left him alone for the rest of the night, as did the man with the twisted neck and demonic dog. He was unsure if this was because they had shown him mercy for his final night in the house, or because he had drunk himself into such a stupor that he would not have known if they had visited him anyway. He got both a sense of terror and satisfaction from the possibility. The idea of these horrible phantoms hovering around him, begging for his attention as he drunkenly snored his way through the night. In fact, he could not remember the last time he had slept so well in the terrible house.

When Father Curtz arrived in the morning on the first train in, Father Bailey was there to collect him. After some brief introductions and smalltalk, Father Bailey stayed true to the oath he had made to himself and told the young priest everything he had experienced. As he had expected and feared, the naive young man disregarded his concerns and assured him that it was all the stress of losing his dear mother and that with time and distance he would once again regain his composure to feel himself again.

Father Bailey thanked him for his kindness and for listening to his wild tale. He bade him not to keep the story a secret in defence of the priest's reputation, but to share it with anyone who considered spending time in the house in the future, for the sake of both of their souls. Father Curtz agreed. He stayed on at the house and shared the story before he moved on himself after having only lived in the house for a matter of a year. It is unclear if he too left because of direct experiences with some kind of supernatural force, but one would assume that his short-lived presence in the house, coupled with his willingness to share Father Bailey's story, would suggest just that.

Nobody really knows what came of Father Bailey after he left the Crowsnest Pass. Some say he left the priesthood for a woman, others claim it to be true that he left the order, but not over a woman. Some say that his experiences in the house broke his spirit and drove him to madness, his days ending in sorrow and despair, locked in an institution. Others say his experiences in the house and the loss of his mother drove him to be more devout than ever. They claim that he ended up in a monastery somewhere in Europe.

The most common claim is this: that he drank himself to death, still telling the awful tale of his time in the coal-dusted mountains of the Crowsnest Pass, in the shadow of the terrible Frank Slide, smack dab in the middle of *Disaster Alley*. Regardless of which ending one believes to have been the fate for the man, the one thing everyone can agree on is that he was never the same again.

A part of him remains in the house still, in the glittering glass, delicately placed to illustrate a scene depicting three crows on the branches of a single tree. Although most see it as merely a thing of beauty, as it really is quite beautiful, a true historic piece of art, over time, it seems to give an ominous sense of dread to *almost* every resident of the home in time. Strangely enough, despite its bad reputation, or perhaps because of it, no owner has ever removed it and it remains a prominent piece in the house even still.

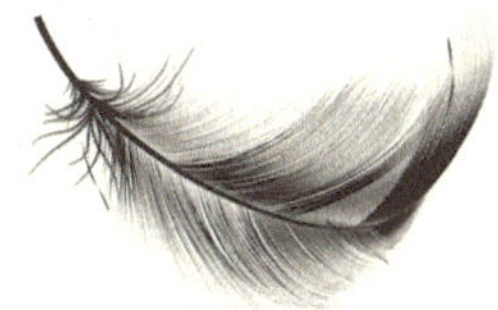

CHAPTER SIXTEEN

Emma was dumbfounded. So much for her hopes for a *less* disturbing story. She found herself feeling a little defensive, as though she had to stand up for the house her family had inherited, but found that she could not. She did not know enough. This man certainly would know a lot more than she did, having lived around the area for so long, but he had not lived in the house and she had. So what was her argument? That everything had been great? That she had not noticed anything odd or off in their new house? She could not claim those things after all.

Felix struggled to make eye contact with her. She could read the guilt on his face regardless. Finally he broke the ice. "Maybe I should not be telling you these things."

"So why are you?" Emma interrupted. She saw him visibly flinch, as though she had slapped him. She drew back. "Sorry, but *do* you have a reason for telling me these things?"

"You mean, aside from the fact that you asked me to?"

Now it was her turn to flinch. "I deserved that. Sorry. I did ask you, but I certainly was not expecting anything like this. Do you really think these things happened in our house? Is that what people believe?"

"First of all, *I'm* sorry. I should have warned you more strongly about what I had to tell you. I do not really believe these things myself; at least, I do not *think* I do. But I still felt like I had an obligation to tell you since you *had* asked. As far as what other people believe, there are some vague notions of ghost stories, but for the most part, these stories are old and forgotten by most."

"I'd have to say I agree with that. Most of the locals I meet here in the Pass, the people who grew up here anyway, ask where we live and when I tell them, the response is pretty universal: they used to party here when they were growing up. I guess it could not have all been bad, if they used to throw parties here and the local kids actually wanted to come."

Felix chuckled. "Good point! I do remember those days. I guess you could say that those were the heydays of this house."

"There, you see," Emma interjected reassuringly. "It can't be that bad."

Felix smiled and sipped his cold coffee. As she watched him, she saw his smile fade to a frown as he seemed to drift off to somewhere, or sometime, else. Then he snapped back to the moment and flashed her a thin smile.

"Another story?" Emma gently prodded.

"Another time."

Charlie came downstairs to say good-bye to *Uncle* Felix. She appeared dishevelled, as though she had enjoyed an impromptu nap, interrupted by her mother's summons. He promised to return very soon, as there was still so much to tell her mother, but that would be for another time. They said their good-byes, and he made his way next door to Marin's.

They enjoyed what was left of the day together and made John's favourite: beef stroganoff, for dinner. They ended up having dinner without him, as they often did, because Charlie was usually ready for an early dinner and John always had lots to wrap up at work, so that an early dinner was usually impossible for him. However, whenever they wanted to see him badly enough, it was a ten-minute trip to the cafe to enjoy some delicious sandwiches together, made with John's signature fresh-baked whole wheat bread. They did this on schedule at least once a week. Most evenings though,

Charlie ate at home with her mother, and John enjoyed the leftovers when he arrived home, famished, despite being surrounded by food all day. He insisted that he preferred Emma's cooking to his own, but at times she suspected that it was a subtle form of surveillance, a way to keep tabs on what she was feeding Charlie. This was paranoid thinking of course. John was not the type to be controlling or untrusting, but he did have a tendency for being overprotective and insisted that he always wanted what was best for his girls. Just thinking about it gave Emma pangs of insecurity, as though she did not deserve his love. As though he was out of her league.

The phone rang while she was reading a book with Charlie about a boy who lived in a peach with an assortment of overgrown bugs. Emma kissed her daughter on the forehead. "Raincheck madam?"

"Why certainly, beautiful lady. Can I have a cookie?"

"Whoa, that was quick!" She picked up the phone and saw her mother's number and answered Charlie as she answered the phone. "Sure honey. Just one." Charlie gave her a quick high five and ran off to the kitchen with a squeal. "Hi Mom. How are you?"

"I'm good honey," Charlotte replied in a faraway voice. "Just missing my girls."

"We miss you too Mom."

"Good. I'm glad to hear that. So you'll be happy to see me for a visit? I was thinking about coming out there next weekend. I thought I would give you a little notice so that you can get the house in order for company. What do you think?"

"That would be fantastic! Charlie will be thrilled! I can't wait to see you." Emma walked into the kitchen to check on her daughter as things had grown a little too quiet for her liking. She found Charlie sitting on the pantry floor, sharing her cookie with Max, a guilty look on her face, her long dark curls peppered with cookie crumbs. Emma shook her head and silently ordered her out of the pantry. She let her mother share the good news directly and the little girl squealed with delight.

"I can't wait to see you and your mommy and your daddy, Sweetie."

"You almost forgot Max, Nana."

"Oh dear, of course, and Max. How could I forget? He must be getting pretty big."

"No silly. He's a kind of dog that won't get big. He's still little." They went on like this for ages before Emma finally broke it off when she heard John's truck pull up outside. After he was finished eating he spent some time playing with Charlie before Emma whisked her off for her bath. She had wasted no time in announcing that her grandmother was going to be visiting soon, quickly followed by a discussion about what they would do while she was here, then reversing course to discuss how on earth her grandmother could have forgotten Max. It could be dizzying to keep up with the four-year-old at times.

While Emma was bathing Charlie she found herself distracted by the crows which were cut and soldered into the window. More than once she caught herself on a different planet while her daughter got progressively more frustrated, realising she did not have her mother's full attention. Finally, she had enough, and called her mother out for ignoring her, "Why do you keep staring at the window Mommy?"

This caught Emma's attention and she apologised for being so distracted. "I was just admiring the crows, little miss. Uncle Felix told me a story about the man who made this window today. His name was Father Bailey."

Instead of the expected barrage of questions, Charlie responded with a silent stare, locking her mother's gaze before mumbling in a low, seemingly angry voice. "I know. They do not like you looking at them like that." She was serious and her expression was flat as she stared long and hard into her mother's eyes.

At first Emma was too shocked to say anything, then she asked, "How did you know? What do you mean?" But Charlie just shrugged indifferently and went back to playing with her little blue whale and pink fish, engaging in an imaginary battle with full sound effects, which involved copious amounts of spitting. Emma was grateful the child was in the tub. She let her play for a while then she gently washed her hair. Charlie laid back in the bath so that her mother could rinse her hair in the quickly cooling water. She held her hand under her daughter's head as she gently scooped the water over her hair to rinse it. Once again, she became entranced by the crows, feeling almost as though they were watching her, perhaps *plotting* against her.

Charlie finally snapped Emma out of her daze when she screamed at her mother. "LET ME UP!"

Emma responded quickly, so that she almost lost her grip on her daughter, causing Charlie to cry even harder than she already had been. "I'm so sorry sweetie," Emma pleaded, frightened and upset. "I must have gotten distracted again."

"Why wouldn't you let me get up?" Charlie continued to shriek. "I want to get out *now*!"

Emma grabbed the towel and quickly pulled her out of the deep tub. She shivered and cried as Emma patted her down, her long hair dripping water everywhere. Emma was on the verge of tears herself, but was trying to hold back so as to not make the situation worse. The next thing she knew, John was at the door to see what all of the commotion was about.

"Mommy was holding me down in the tub," Charlie cried to her father. "I told her to let me up, but she would not listen to me Daddy!"

John looked at Emma with a look of shocked concern. "What happened?"

"I was just rinsing the shampoo out of her hair," she explained in a timid, confused voice. "I just got distracted and she got upset. It's okay."

"It's NOT okay!" Charlie shouted, her choked sobs renewed.

"Sorry honey, I meant *you're* okay."

"I'm *not* okay!" She wrapped her arms around John. "I want to go to bed Daddy. Can you take me to my room?"

"Of course I will. It's okay," he reassured her. "You just got a fright. You'll be okay."

They left Emma standing in the bathroom on her own. She pulled the stopper from the tub to let the water drain and started to clean up the towels and toys left over from Charlie's bath. She found herself gazing at the window once again, and the cursed crows stared back at her.

After he finished reading Charlie a story and settling her down for sleep, John joined Emma for a cup of tea downstairs. He told her that what had happened was no big deal and that Charlie had overreacted, as four-year-olds can and will do, and that she should just let it go. She agreed, but the rest of their evening was punctuated by uncomfortable moments of awkward silence, so she made a lame excuse about needing to finish something up when it was time for bed, so that John went on without her. She sat quietly for a while on her own then made her way upstairs when she was sure he would be sleeping. There was no doubting he would be, as he had no problem drifting off after a long day at work. Hearing him breathing slowly, she came into the room. She snuggled in beside him, and after a long time of staring at the ceiling and counting backwards in threes, a trick she used when she struggled with insomnia, she finally drifted off.

When she awoke in the night she instinctively looked at the glowing red numbers on her bedside alarm clock: *4:10.* She was reminded of the sleepless nights she had before moving to this house, when she awoke at the same time for nights on end. She never knew what to make of it, except that her body was on some kind of strange internal timer which seemed intent on waking her up at the usual time of 4:10, which was almost two hours before her alarm was actually set to go off, just early enough so that she could enjoy a coffee with John before he had to head out for the day.

Feeling like she was being watched, she looked toward the bedroom door to see Charlie leaving the room, her nightgown and dark hair trailing out behind her as she darted out of sight. "Charlie?" Emma got up from the bed and quickly followed her daughter into the hall, looking both ways just in time to see the same white nightie turning the corner to head down the stairs. "Charlie!"

The little girl did not respond. Emma was confused and worried, still half asleep, and wondering what her daughter was up to so late at night that it was almost time for the next new day to begin. As she reached the foot of the stairs, she thought she should be right behind the girl, but instead she was just in time to see the front door closing, she assumed, because Charlie had just gone out into the darkness.

"Charlie, no!" Emma shouted, but the door was already closed, so she ran across the main floor and out the front door, which slammed shut behind her. She did not notice, as she was sick with worry for Charlie, and followed her into the dark night. Looking all around she could not see her daughter anywhere, even though the near-full moon had the landscape around the house lit up so that every tree and bush stood out in stark relief.

Emma started to shiver. Still screaming her daughter's name, she ran across the road into the forest. It was much darker in here, where the tops of the trees blotted out the light of the moon. Just enough light shone through the trees to cast a ghostly glow across the forest, painting everything a surreal and nightmarish alien green, blotted with dark shadows. She found that she had stopped screaming Charlie's name without meaning to, and the night air was silent and heavy around her.

At first she could see nothing beyond the forest landscape, until in the distance she saw movement which stood out as something different from its surroundings, though the shadows of the forest blurred the distant features. At first a sense of relief washed over her, but it was quickly followed by a growing, sinking terror, as the person coming towards her in the woods, though still at a distance, was clearly too tall to be Charlie. She had mistakenly envisioned her daughter at first, seeing the long dark hair and the gown, glowing a greenish white in the moonlit night. But this was not her daughter. Her heart sank, and as the figure drew nearer, features still unclear, moving with an unnatural gait, her terror grew. But she was transfixed, and could not move.

"Emma!" John shouted as he ran toward her through the tall grass and overgrown bushes, "What the hell are you doing out here? You should not be out here in the middle of the night! It's dangerous!"

Emma glanced quickly in his direction, then looked back toward the menacing figure, but it was no longer there. It was gone, vanished into the night. She looked all around, but could not see the apparition anywhere. John reached her and grabbed her by her shoulders, "What were you doing Em? I woke up and you were gone. I did not know what to think. You scared the shit out of me. Answer me!"

"I… I," she stammered, unsure what to say. Then she remembered why she had come running out into the forest at such a late hour, past four in the morning, in the first place. Before she had been frozen in terror by the darkness and the person she was so sure had been there, coming toward her, with that unnatural jerky movement. Emma shivered involuntarily. "I was looking for Charlie. Oh my god, where is she? Charlie!" She began screaming again.

"Emma stop! You're going to wake the whole goddamn neighbourhood! Charlie's in the house. She's still in bed."

"No," Emma insisted vehemently. "I followed her outside. She was in our room, then she ran downstairs, and I followed her, then she went out the front door, and I chased her outside, but I could not find her! She was gone!" She started to cry. "She's gone! We have to find her, John!"

"Charlie is in her bed fast asleep, Emma. I checked on her myself thinking you might be in there when I came looking for you. Max is with her. She's safe and sound, which is more than I can say for her mother right now. Let's get inside."

For a moment, Emma stood frozen in place, as she struggled to understand what John had said. How could Charlie be sleeping in her bed? She had just followed her out here. Who else would have been watching her sleep? Who else would have been in their house? She was positive that it had been Charlie, wearing a white nightgown, her dark hair streaming behind her like the river at night. She was still sure of what she had seen as she let John lead her from the forest, across the road, through the front door and up the stairs to Charlie's bedroom. She felt like she was walking in a dream. Her feet and head felt heavy.

When she saw her child sleeping peacefully, she was overwhelmed with emotion. She was desperately relieved that she had been wrong, that Charlie was here sleeping safely in her bed. She had not seen her since her father had put her to bed after the terrible bath incident, and now she noticed that she was not wearing a white nightdress, in fact, she was not wearing a nightie at all. Charlie was wearing her dark blue pyjama pants and top, her favourite pair, because of the sparkly silver stars which curled over her shoulder, encircled her tummy and trailed halfway down her right leg.

The outfit was unmistakable and definitely not *white*, and her hair was not down. Her father had braided it in his usual clumsy style. Emma suddenly felt ill. What had she seen? Who had she seen? She had been so sure that she had followed a child out of her room and out into the night. Had she been sleepwalking? It had all felt so real.

John led her back to their bed and tucked her under the covers. He climbed in next to her and put his strong arms around her, holding her tight as his knees tucked into the back of hers as they laid on their sides. She was a perfect fit beside him. He kissed the back of her head. "I'm a little worried about you honey. Maybe it's time to take it easy on the visits with your new buddy, Felix? I do not know what he told you today, you did not say anything about it when I got home, or when Charlie went to bed. Something's got you rattled. Do you want to talk about it?"

A tear trickled down the side of her cheek, but she did not let John see and she stopped herself immediately. Emma thought carefully about what she should say before responding. She did not want to hear anything else about her house that might be upsetting or frightening either, but a bigger part of her wanted, no, *needed* to know more. There was clearly more to know, and she had indeed opened that box and felt now that she could no longer shut it. She had to see it through. But if John started worrying about her, started thinking that maybe she was feeling unwell, there would be no way he would stand by and allow her to continue on the path she had been on.

"You do not need to worry, love. I had a good visit with Felix today, and Charlie really likes him. It's nice to see her meeting new people, even if they are almost a century older than her. It's good to see her making her life here. And yes, he told me more stories about the house, but it's not like I believe this stuff. I'm just enjoying the company. He's totally harmless. I'm just overtired. I haven't been sleeping well lately. I'll work on getting to bed earlier and I'll be right as rain."

"Are you sure? I'm still worried about you."

"do not be. I'll be fine. I just need some sleep. So why don't you shut it now and let me do that." She paused dramatically for a response, trying to make things light between them, and after a moment he allowed her to. He poked her side teasingly and nibbled on her neck playfully.

"Brat," he whispered, then he breathed deeply into her hair and kissed the side of her head. "I love you."

"I love you too. Now go to sleep."

"*You* telling *me* to go to sleep. I just chased you outside at four o'clock in the morning and you're telling *me* to go to sleep. The *nerve*!" He teased her, kissed her again, and pulled her in close. After a short time he was asleep again, breathing deeply in her ear, as she laid silently staring at the bedroom door, envisioning the strange sight she had seen in the forest.

CHAPTER SEVENTEEN

Instead of the usual coffee visit, a few days after her nighttime forest excursion, Emma invited Felix to accompany her on her daily walk along the river with Charlie and Max. She had not seen anyone or anything out of place since that awful night after their last talk. At first she struggled with John's assertion that her visits with Felix and his stories about the house were having a detrimental effect, but once the rationality of a few days had passed, she once again found herself curious to know where Felix had gone after she mentioned the popularity of the house for local teen parties. She assumed correctly that this was before John's Aunt Helen had owned the house.

Being direct with the elderly man about her curiosity, Emma asked if there was something he wanted to tell her about the parties that went on in the house. He admitted to being distracted and admitted to what he had been thinking about. "I'm sorry, it's just that you reminded me of the family who had lived here then, back when it got the reputation of being the 'party house'," he began. "They were good people, the Walters. Mrs. Walters was a hardworking widow who wanted nothing more than to make her boys happy."

"When did they live in the house?"

Felix stopped and scratched his chin thoughtfully, and after a moment he snapped his fingers and smiled. "It was the mid-seventies when they lived in your house. That was about forty years ago now."

"How old were the boys?"

"They were in their teens then. Maybe sixteen and seventeen."

"What were their names?"

"Even after all these years I still remember somehow. Probably because they both worked at the local lumber yard and at that time I was deep into renovating an old jalopy of a house. Their names were Luke and Bobby. They were nice boys."

"So what happened to them anyway? While they were living in the house I mean."

"I was trying to get around to that if you'll let me. Or were you planning on playing twenty questions instead to try and guess your way around it?"

Felix gave her a sideways grin and for a moment she stood, mouth agape at what he had said to her, then she turned to him and punched him gently in the arm. "Felix, you really are a crotchety old bastard aren't you?" She grinned.

"It's about time you got to know the real me. I figure I've earned it after all these years on this lousy planet. Now, are you ready to hear this story or not?"

"I think so. I hope it's nothing too terrible, but I want to hear it one way or the other." She kept a close eye on Charlie and Max as she and Felix walked and talked. Emma called to her daughter and reminded her from time to time to stay close so that they could see and hear one another at all times. Close to home or not, this was still a wild place, full of beauty *and* danger.

"I thought you might say that."

CHAPTER EIGHTEEN

Carol Walters, a thirty-seven-year-old widow, moved into the house in the seventies, many years after the departure of Father Bailey and his successor. She had two boys to raise on her own since the loss of her husband less than a year before she moved to the Crowsnest Pass and into the old house by the river. Having married her high school sweetheart after they had grown up together in the small mountain town of Fernie, which although it was in the next province, was still less than an hour's drive from her new place in the Pass, she had started her family at a young age. Though she did not feel young at the time. She had felt ready. What she certainly did not feel ready for was to be raising them on her own before they were men. But she was a strong woman and did everything she could to make her boys happy.

Having lived in the city for most of their lives, they were surprisingly content with the idea of moving to a small town in the mountains. Carol felt it was because they loved outdoor pursuits, and there were so many opportunities for them to go skiing on the weekends in the winter, then camping and fishing in the summer. She also suspected that it was an opportunity to escape what they had known of their old life, the life they had shared with their father, which they likely hoped might be easier to leave behind with a new home and a fresh start.

Luke was the older of the two boys. He was a serious young man with big plans for the future. He wanted to be an engineer and was dedicated to his studies to make it a reality. This was not an issue for him anyway, as he was a born bookworm. He was also a great athlete, and was a star on the school basketball team. This, coupled with his charming good looks, made him an instant hit with the girls. Typically, this would have caused him problems with the local boys, out to defend what they saw as their turf, but he was so charming and forthright that it was impossible not to like him. Even though he had every opportunity for a girlfriend, he opted to be friends instead and vowed to stay focused on his goals for after school.

His only obstacle to being his mother's beacon of boyhood perfection was his younger brother, Bobby. Although he was a year younger than his older brother, he was taller and broader than Luke. He too was an athlete, but preferred to use his stature to his advantage playing football. Handsome like his brother, he was also popular with the girls, which, unlike his brother, he took full advantage of. Though he could be sweet, he could also be an annoyance to Luke. There was not much that he took seriously in life, which had always been his style, but his brother felt this mindset had grown worse since the loss of their father. He seemed to have a "live for the day" approach to life, which Luke could sometimes empathise with.

The loss of their father had been sudden and shocking, and they had all learned how quickly life could change in significant and permanent ways. Bobby took it as a licence to live life on his own terms. He was often impulsive, failing to think about the possible consequences of his actions, and usually really not caring even if he did. Even though he was only sixteen, he was already in a habit of drinking and smoking cigarettes and sometimes pot with his buddies, and though Luke would have liked to pride himself on not engaging in these things himself, he often found himself sucked into the vortex which was his brother. Sometimes he just needed to cut loose, and living with someone like Bobby could make that so easy.

Their mother announced on a Wednesday that she would be spending the night in Fernie on the coming Saturday, hoping that the short notice would put a damper on any potential party plans Bobby might cook up. Of course, she had underestimated the planning and social network capabilities the boy possessed when the payoff was a good time. Carol had known for months now that she would be gone for that day and night, as it was her twentieth high school reunion in Fernie. She had contemplated not going; it would be so difficult without her beloved husband. The thought of having to listen to the pitying comments and the repetitive questions had horrified her at first, but as time passed, so too did her perspective, and she saw the opportunity to remember him anew.

It would be refreshing to talk about him. It seemed her family did less and less lately. She felt the boys pulling away and moving ahead. Carol felt that she was not really ready, but she could not put her own needs before theirs. So she relented, and decided to go, even renting a room so that she could stay overnight after attending the buffet dinner and dance party. She figured that way she could cut loose, enjoy some drinks and not worry about how she was going to explain herself to the boys. It did not take a genius to know they would appreciate the break from her too and enjoy the opportunity for some independence. It was a chance for them to show her that they could be trusted as mature and responsible young men. Of course, if that were really the case, she would not have felt the need to delay telling them her plans for the past few months.

The boys had been supportive and excited for her, not even questioning why the news had come up so suddenly. They seemed to assume that it had been a spontaneous decision. If they were eager for her departure, they did not show it. This made her proud of their growing maturity and sure that her decision had been the right one. They were good boys. They could be trusted.

She left to make the short trip to Fernie on Saturday morning. Her hair was freshly cut and curled and she was even wearing some makeup, for the first time in a long time. The boys both took notice and hugged her tightly as they saw her off after Luke made them all a simple breakfast of fried eggs, overcooked bacon and toast made from Carol's fresh homemade bread, which he always struggled to cut thin enough to actually fit into the toaster, often leading to a smoky kitchen.

They stood on the front step and waved her off. As soon as she was out of sight, Bobby gave Luke a pat on the back and draped an arm over his shoulders. "Well big brother," he said with a grin, "we'd better get ourselves prettied up for the ladies because there's gonna be a party tonight! Oh yeah!"

"Oh no," Luke protested weakly. The proposition had not caught him completely off-guard; he had figured his brother might pull something like this and was not totally against the idea himself. However, taking the time to contradict the idea might buy him some leverage to say he had tried to stop his little brother's plans if their mother happened to find out, which she likely would. She had a way of finding these things out. He might also be able to use the information to extort future favours from Bobby, so a little protest was worth it before caving in and helping out.

"Oh yes," Bobby insisted. "Besides, I've already let everyone know."

"Everyone? Who's everyone?" Perhaps he should be more concerned. This was Bobby after all. He did not want to have any part in wrecking the house or pissing off the neighbours. Then his mother would be sure to find out. With all that she had been through in the last year, he could not stand the idea of disappointing her, though he did not want to be a stick in the mud either.

"Calm down man, just the usual crew and a few girls from school. I'm not looking to draw attention, just to cut loose and have a good time. Celeste said she might come by."

"Since when are you into Celeste? I thought you liked her cousin, Jocelyn."

"*Since when have I been into Celeste?* Ever since I saw her, loser. I know you probably won't understand this, since you're allergic to women or something, but a guy can think of more than one girl at a time. Celeste is hot and I think she likes me, so why pass up on the opportunity?"

"Slut."

"Just giving the ladies what they want, brother. Just giving the ladies what they want. Now let's get ready. We've got a lot to do before tonight."

After showering and tidying the kitchen, they spent the rest of the day getting ready. They had to make a trip to the store to get chips, drinks and various other forms of junk food, as their mother would surely notice if they raided the cupboards for a small squadron of teens. They also had to go to

Randy Squires' place to pick him up so that they could drive him to the liquor store. Every kid in town knew he was the man to see if you needed some booze, and his finder's fee was relatively reasonable, considering he was the only easy option around.

The guests showed up generally around the same time, as most of them were carpooling. Bobby had not lied about the invites. The Pass was such a small place that their list of friends was becoming very predictable, which was fine with them. Celeste showed up and Luke could tell that his brother had been right about how she felt about him. She and Bobby spent the evening openly flirting as they all danced to vinyl records and played drinking games. So they were all well past the line of sobriety when Celeste's cousin Jocelyn, the first object of Bobby's so-called affection, dug into her ridiculously deep macrame purse and pulled out a thin rectangular box containing a ouija board.

"Creepy Jocelyn," complained Celeste. "Your mom would kill you if she knew you had that thing! Where'd you get it?"

"I bought it a while ago. And who gives a shit what my mother would think? Are you planning on ratting me out?"

"Well, no, of course not."

"Then shut it and come play this thing with me."

"Forget it, there's not a chance in hell I'm touching that thing."

"Chicken," Jocelyn teased, before turning her sights on Bobby. "How about you big boy? You're not afraid are you? It's just a little fun."

Celeste sneered at her cousin, having been fully aware that Bobby had pined away after the girl for months. She had not let that get in her way, having known from the start that Jocelyn had not been interested, not really anyway. Her cousin had quickly supported Celeste's efforts to make it known to the boy that she was the one who really liked him, and tonight had been evidence that it had worked after all. Now that her chance was within reach, here was Jocelyn flirting with him right in front of her. This was what led her to intervene in the moment which would have seen them staring into one another's eyes as Jocelyn asked ridiculous questions in a smoky voice, their fingers close enough to touch on the planchette used to point to the letters on the board.

Celeste could not risk it, not when she was so close to the prize. "Fine. I'll do it," she insisted as nonchalantly as she could. When she saw the knowing grin on Jocelyn's face, she knew how easily her closest cousin had manipulated her using her affections for this boy against her.

Everyone gathered around after someone cut the music and the lights, leaving the room lit only by the dim candles which were near to their ends after burning all night. Jocelyn and Celeste placed the board on the coffee table and sat facing one another, their long blonde hair glowing golden red in the candlelight. While Jocelyn sported a confident smile as she listed off a dramatic monologue of rules as they attempted to contact the *spirit world*, Celeste was clearly nervous and possibly regretting her decision to go along with her bolder cousin. But it was too late to back out now. She wanted to look cool in front of Bobby. She was desperate for him to see her in the same way that had first drawn him to her cousin.

The girls moved the planchette softly around the board as Jocelyn asked creepy questions then answered them herself, as far as everyone was concerned. It was just another party game after all.

"Has anyone ever died in this house?"

The planchette swirled slowly around the board, then moved to the "yes" at the top of the board. A fleeting look of worry flashed across Jocelyn's face, so quickly that it was gone before anyone could notice. She pressed on.

"How many people have died here?"

The little heart-shaped piece of wood circled the board and moved fluidly from letter to letter, spelling out "too many". Celeste jumped and pulled her hands away from the board. Jocelyn snapped at her. "Do not forget the rules! Keep your hands on the board till I say we're done, or you could invite something evil into this house."

Celeste hesitantly put her hands back on the board.

Jocelyn continued, "Is there anyone here with us now? Anyone we should worry about?"

Suddenly Luke spoke up. "Maybe we should put this away now. This is kind of a downer wouldn't you say?"

"What's the matter Luke? Scared of a little party game?" Bobby taunted his brother in front of their friends.

"No," Luke replied with irritation in his voice. "Just bored shitless Bobby."

The planchette suddenly moved quickly around the board but did not settle on any letters. They all turned back to the board in unison and there was a unanimous gasp when the little piece of wood flew from the board and across the room, knocking over the vase the boys' father had given to their mother for the last anniversary they'd had together. It had been sitting on the mantle above the fireplace where she could always see it, as she treasured it so much, and now it was shattered in a kaleidoscope of splintered glass.

"Holy shit," Bobby whispered in awe.

"Son of a bitch," Luke replied to no one in particular. "Mom's going to kill us. Shit. Put this thing away now! Maybe we should start cleaning this place up. I'm not much in the mood to party anymore." He was visibly upset and did not care who knew it. Only Bobby knew the significance of *why* he was so upset.

"Come on man," their friend Robert whined. "You're overreacting. It's just a vase. Put another one there and your mom will probably never notice the difference if she's anything like my mom."

"It's okay Luke. I'll take the blame. You've got nothing to worry about," Bobby consoled his brother.

"First of all, you *should* take the blame because *you* are the one to blame for planning this party in the first place. Second of all, this may be a foreign concept to you," Luke poked his finger into Bobby's chest, "but I do not give a shit about getting blamed. I was actually concerned about how Mom would feel. You know how much this means to her."

"For someone who's so pissed off about having a party, you sure didn't put up much of a fight."

"Asshole."

"You fuckin' mama's boy. You're drunk. Why don't you just go to bed and let us have a good time?"

"Maybe I will."

"Good."

"Great."

Leaving their awkward exchange at an impasse, Luke stomped off to bed. The party continued on without him, but things weren't the same. The atmosphere was spoiled and everyone was a little too drunk now anyway. The dancing turned to lounging in various positions around the room and polishing off the snacks the boys had picked up earlier. The ouija board was abandoned in the corner for the rest of the night.

"I think I need some fresh air," Jocelyn announced as the night grew late. "Can you come outside with me Celeste?"

By now Celeste was wrapped up in Bobby's arms, as they groped one another, oblivious to their friends. "No thanks. You should stay inside. It's too late and too dark to go roaming around here at the river bottom."

"*Please.*"

Celeste responded by shaking her head mid-kiss and flipping her cousin the middle finger.

"Bitch." Jocelyn slurred, then threw on her jacket and someone else's shoes, which were too big, so she was clunking and dragging them across the floor. Grumbling to herself as she left the room, she headed to the back door to go outside in the garden. She stopped in front of the dining room window, which faced the back garden, and screamed, scaring everyone sitting in the living room. Celeste and Bobby both instinctively jumped and ran to the window to see what had frightened her so badly, but there was nothing there.

"What the hell, Jocelyn? You scared the shit out of me!" Celeste's voice was shaky and she was still rattled. "Why did you scream like that?"

"I…I…" she stammered. "I saw a man out there!" She started crying uncontrollably. "There was something wrong with him. There was something wrong with his head, or no, his neck. Like, it was twisted or something. He was just standing there, staring at the house, and he had a dog! It was snarling at me, like, right *at* me!"

"Are you sure?" Bobby asked, though he did not doubt her reaction. He could see that she was genuinely frightened. "Maybe it was just the moonlight in the trees or something. The night can play tricks on your eyes."

"No," she insisted. "I saw someone! He was there! He was looking at me!"

"Well, maybe I should go take a look," Bobby tried to sound brave.

"Oh no you do not," Celeste scolded, sounding as though they had been an item for the past year, instead of the past hour. "You're not going out there on your own. What if there's some deranged lunatic?"

"I'll go with you man," Robert volunteered. "And if someone is out there, he'll have to take the both of us," he bragged.

"Somehow that does not make me feel much better," Celeste complained. Bobby squeezed her hand then put on his shoes and jacket. The boys went out together into the dark garden. After a few tense moments they returned, having found nothing outside.

"I want to go," Jocelyn announced. "It's getting late." She was visibly shaken. "Are you coming Celeste?"

"Uh, no, I think I'll stay here a while longer." She glanced surreptitiously at Bobby, who was noticeably concerned with Jocelyn.

"But you're supposed to be staying over at my place."

"I know. You'll vouch for me, right?"

Jocelyn was irritated with her cousin, but Celeste's only concern was Bobby. "Fine, have it your way," she snapped as she made her way to the front door to leave. "I hope that creepy guy doesn't show up back here again."

"I'm sure that was just your imagination."

"Whatever."

Without any further drama, Jocelyn left. Soon after, most of the other guests departed as well, leaving only Robert, who was passed out on the couch, and Celeste, who was eager to have some time alone with Bobby, now that he was finally taking notice of her.

Bobby suggested they head to his room. "We don't have to do anything," he insisted. "I just thought it might be nice to have a little privacy." He was suddenly self-conscious. "Actually, never mind. What was I thinking? I really like you Celeste. I don't want to…"

She cut him off mid-sentence, "I'd love to hang out in your room. Let's get cosy together, somewhere a little more private." She threw a look over at Robert who was snoring loudly now.

"Are you sure?"

"Let's go." She stood up and took his hand then let him lead her upstairs. When they got to his room she positioned herself on the bed while he closed and locked the door.

They talked and kissed and did not do much more before they fell asleep, snuggled into one another on top of the quilt Bobby's mother had made for him for Christmas the year before. They slept like that for a few hours, drunk on booze and infatuation. It was dark in the room when Celeste opened her eyes, feeling that she was not alone. Her concern turned to delight when she remembered where she was. She could feel Bobby's chest rise and fall as he slept deeply.

The soft whisper of his breathing was suddenly interrupted by an ugly, ragged breathing, which caused her to pull away, startled, before she realised the hideous sound was not coming from her new boyfriend. As she turned her head slowly toward the foot of the bed she became aware of someone standing there, barely visible in the darkness. It was a woman in a long white gown. Celeste was so terrified, she opened her mouth wide to scream, but no sound came out. The woman took a step forward, her face still a blur of shadows, and opened her dark hole of a mouth, as though she were mimicking the young woman in abject terror on the bed.

"You should go," she whispered in her wet, ragged voice. "He's coming for you."

The sound of the voice broke the spell and Celeste let out a scream to wake the dead. Bobby jumped up beside her and she looked at him with horror, having almost forgotten that he was there.

"What the hell! What's wrong?" Bobby demanded after being scared awake.

"There's a woman in here!" Celeste cried and pointed to the foot of the bed, but the spectre was gone. "I swear, she was right there! Check the room! Oh my god!"

As Bobby checked the small room he assured her that he had locked the door and that nobody was in there with them. "Maybe you were just having a bad dream," he suggested.

"No," she cried. "I saw her! She was here! She even spoke to me. I should have listened to Jocelyn and went home with her. Your house is fucking creepy. I don't want to stay here anymore. Can you take me to Jocelyn's place? Please?"

Against his better judgement, as he was still feeling the effects of the alcohol, he agreed. Always the opportunist, he tried to kiss her before she jumped out of the truck, but she was in no mood. She barely looked at him when she told him she would call him soon and headed inside her cousin's place. Bobby made the quick trip back home and went back to bed. It was a weird end to what had been a weird night. He figured he had better get some shut-eye so that he would have the energy to clean up in the morning before his mother returned home.

That night was the first and only time either of the girls saw anything at the Walters' home, because they never returned. Although neither one of them spoke much about it after that night, it was clear that it had rattled both of the girls. The shared experience seemed to pull them apart, which was strange, as they had been close, like sisters. Even they were not sure why there was this new expanse between them, but both suspected it might have something to do with denying and forgetting what they had seen and felt that night. They also cut ties with Luke and Bobby, much to Bobby's dismay, as Celeste wanted nothing more to do with him, even though she had been so enamoured.

The boys had not seen anything strange or odd in their house that night, aside from the flying planchette, but it did not take long for the onslaught of rumours at school to get started. There were whispers about the girls seeing ghosts at the house after a seance with a ouija board. Luke was furious, concerned that this might get back to his mother, who so far was none the wiser about the party.

At first the talk was minimal, but then stories started spreading, including one about a priest who was tormented in the house and another about a man who had seen a ghost there and hung himself near the river. Before long, the boys found themselves isolated, their friends ignoring them in class and failing to mention plans. The worst was when someone started a particularly mean line of mythology, which implied that because of the untimely death of their father, the boys were somehow cursed, and had likely awakened some sort of evil which had been dormant in the house. Others suggested it had never been dormant at all, that those who had not reported anything while living in the house had simply chosen not to say anything because they did not want other people knowing about it. This, after all, would explain why no one ever seemed to live in the house much more than a year or two.

Both Luke and Bobby had hoped that moving to this new place would remain as positive as it had started. They had never seen any reason why it would not. It was the social isolation which was the worst for Bobby. He became withdrawn and depressed, brooding for long hours in his room alone. Luke was most hurt by the mention of his dear father in the gossip of his peers. He hoped and prayed that this would never get back to his mother, no longer because he wanted to avoid trouble for having the stupid party without her permission, but because he did not want her to feel how he was feeling, which was completely miserable.

A dark cloud descended on the house. Carol was concerned for her boys, but assumed that this retreat into themselves was a normal part of the extended grieving process, that they would go through their ups and downs in life, but that they would overcome, as they always had. Besides, she was so busy with keeping the house afloat and working at her new job to focus too much on the teenage drama which was a normal part of having two boys only a year apart. It was because she was so busy with her normal day-to-day life that she did not feel the depth of the darkness which descended on the house, settling itself in the corners and sealing them all up in their individual rooms, alone and away from each other.

A few months after the doomed party, after what had been a long day at work, Carol made a quick dinner of grilled cheese sandwiches and canned tomato soup for herself and the boys. Eager to take over the bathroom for a nice long soak, she warned the boys that it would not be available for at least an hour, which was a concern, as it was the only bathroom in the old house. They both assured her they would be fine and that she could take as long as she needed; they would relieve themselves in the backyard if things got desperate enough.

"Don't you dare," she warned them both.

"I do it all the time," Bobby teased. "I'm an outdoorsman."

His mother glared at him but he just grinned in response. She reached up to mess up his hair. He was more than a foot taller than her now and he was not done growing yet. He pulled away but then swooped in for a big hug and she embraced him back, happy that he was the kind of boy who was still willing to hug his mother on a whim. She kissed the side of his head and he let her head off to take a much-needed rest in the old clawfoot tub.

With her housecoat and towel ready beside the tub, along with a small glass of red wine and some matches to light a candle to read by, Carol slipped into her long-awaited bath. She preferred to leave the lights out when she bathed; it was more relaxing, though the low light made her eyes tired as she read. As she lay in the tub, enjoying her reading and the quiet, it occurred to her that it was *too* quiet. She listened for the typical sounds of the boys in the house, but could hear nothing. The house was silent, except for the occasional *plip*, *plip* of the dripping tub faucet.

When the clock downstairs chimed it startled her and she jumped in the tub because she had been listening so intently to the quiet of the house. Clutching her chest she laughed at her own foolishness. Dipping her hair in the water she laid back in the tub, which sloped nicely, so that she could lay back comfortably to read. She sipped her wine and picked up her book, flipping to the page she had marked when she sensed movement from the corner of her eye.

Instinctively, she turned her head, wincing at the thought of a spider dangling from the ceiling above her, but there was nothing there, only the window, with the crows perched in their tree. They looked different in this light, she noticed for the first time. Fire flickered in the obsidian black of their glass feathers. She understood now why she had sensed movement, as the fire provided this effect, dancing on the ebony birds and breathing life into them. She shook her head at herself but did not laugh this time. Cautiously, she returned to her reading, but found herself constantly distracted by the birds, so that she put her book aside, dropping her arms and hands into the water to warm them.

Carol was suddenly chilled with the notion that one of the crows had somehow changed its position on its perch. Not in any obvious way. It was subtle, but enough to make her question whether it had faced in this particular direction, toward the wall behind her. She could have sworn it had faced the wall in front of her. She was creeping herself out thinking about it when a loud bang on the bathroom door scared her enough to make her jump in the tub. After gathering her wits about her she demanded, "What? Who is it? What do you want? I'm taking a bath! You scared the life out of me!"

The response was that oppressive silence she had noticed earlier. On her knees now in the tub, gripping the sides, her knuckles were the colour of the white enamel. The water dripped off of her hair and down her back, making her shiver involuntarily. Then came another loud banging on the door, which again caused her to jump and almost slip down in the tub. She decided to get out, trying to ignore the terror rising in her throat with the acid taste of bile.

Carol put on the angriest mother voice she could muster, but it came out sounding much more meek than she had intended. "Whichever one of you boys is there, you will be facing some consequences! I told you I was going to be in the tu..."

Bam! Bam! Bam! She was cut off by another series of loud bangs at the door. Throwing on her housecoat, she rushed at the door, where the intensity of the banging was literally shaking the door in its frame. Carol grabbed the knob and threw open the door, a wild look of terror and fury on her face, only to find that nobody was there, though the banging had persisted until she had opened it. She stood there gasping for air before pulling her housecoat more tightly around herself and stomping down the hall to the boys' rooms. Starting at Bobby's, as he was the most obvious suspect, his room was sitting empty, so she made her way across the hall to Luke's room, where they were both sitting. Luke was on the bed and Bobby on the floor, as they played on the new Atari she had bought when they had moved to the mountains. They both stopped playing, shocked to see her.

Their smiles turned to frowns, as she burst through the door with that wild look on her face, shaking her finger admonishingly as she accused them. "Which one of you was banging on the door, huh? I told you I was taking a bath!" Her voice came out shaky, but not as timid as it had been when she had heard the banging on her bathroom door.

"What are you talking about Mom? It was neither one of us. We were both right here. We've been playing this game since you got in the tub like, over an hour ago," insisted Bobby.

"An hour ago? That can't be right. I just got in there. I barely read any of my book, and then someone started banging like a lunatic on the door. It had to be one of you!" She was on the verge of tears now. Her sons could see how confused and shook up she was.

"Maybe you just fell asleep in the tub," Luke suggested. "You probably just had a nightmare."

"True," Bobby joined in. "They do say you should not go in the water right after you eat, you know."

"You numbskull. That's for swimming, not taking a bath," Luke interjected.

"Oh gee, I didn't know that Einstein. Thanks for clearing that up for me," Bobby replied sarcastically. "Later on I'll give you some pointers on how to take a joke. But don't worry, I know to keep my expectations low."

Luke punched his brother in the shoulder then turned his attention back to Carol. "Are you okay, Mom? Do you need me to do anything for you? You look pretty tired."

Having been in a daze she reacted slowly to his questions. "Huh? Uh, oh no. I'm fine. I just need some rest. I think I'll hit the hay early."

Although she went to bed, Carol did not expect to be able to sleep at all, but she actually drifted off quickly, exhausted from her long day and her strange and scary experience. The room was much darker when she awoke and turned to the clock on the bedside table to see that it was 4:10 in the morning. There was a sound at the window. When she looked, she could make out the silhouette of a crow, which was pecking gently at the glass. She climbed out of bed to scare the big black bird away. It remained perched on the sill until she approached the window, then startled her as it flew off, even though she had expected it to. The flurry of black wings beat at the window then the crow melted away into the darkness.

As she drew the blind over the window, she noticed a figure standing in the backyard. It was a man, standing in the shadows, a dog at his side, and although she could not make out his features, she could feel his cold glare. There was something wrong with the way he was standing there, something *unnatural.* With a sense of horror she realised it was his neck, which appeared to be twisted at an odd angle from his shoulders. She was frozen in place for a moment then the dog moved forward snarling and it set her off.

Without even thinking, Carol broke into a run to Luke's room, as he would be able to see the man from his bedroom window. Running into his room she stopped dead in her tracks when she saw a woman standing over his bed, bending down to stroke his cheek as he lay sleeping, unaware that she was even there. She had long dark hair hanging down over a white gown which seemed to glow in the darkness. Her face was turned to Luke, so that Carol could not see what she looked like, aside from her hair and what she was wearing.

"Get away from him!" Carol shrieked, her mind steeped in sheer terror at the thought of her son being hurt. Luke shot up straight in bed at the sound of his mother's terrified voice. The woman had somehow melted back into the shadows, but Carol still searched the darkened corners of the room to find her, though something inside her already knew that she would not. Still, it made no sense to her.

"What's going on Mom?" Luke was stunned. "What time is it?"

Carol was reminded of why she came into her son's room in the first place. She went to the window to see if the man was still there, but he was not. "He was right there," she whispered, more to herself than to Luke.

"Who was?"

"The man," she whispered, far away now. "He had a dog with him." Then she turned her gaze to Luke. "There was something wrong with his neck, like it was twisted or something. *Broken*."

Luke sat stunned on the bed, staring at his mother, who seemed miles away. Saying nothing more to him she turned and left his room, her shoulders slumped, seeming dejected. He laid back on his bed, wide awake now, though it was still too early to get up. He laid there thinking about what his mother had said about the man with the dog, the man with the twisted neck. He had heard the story many times at school now.

Things were different in the Walters' house from then on. Carol was constantly searching out the window for something, or *someone*. She slept little, up searching in the night and checking in on the boys to make sure that they were safe, and *alone*. She became distant with her sons, not knowing how to confide in them about what she had seen and what she was feeling. They too were wrapped up in their own issues and did not want to trouble their mother for so many reasons: because of how the rumours had started in the first place, at the party they had thrown while she was out of town for the night; because the notion of it was ridiculous and childish anyway; because they did not want her feeling creeped out in her own house; but most of all, because they could read their mom, knowing her well, and she was in no place to hear about such things. Her sons could see how preoccupied she had become. They would all sit together at the dinner table, worlds away from one another, wrapped in the anxiety of their lives, the house at the centre of it all.

It was because of Carol's new affliction with insomnia that she found Luke the night he left the house. It was what happened that night that finally made her decide to leave the godforsaken place and never look back.

It was early fall and the weather was turning colder by the day. It took a long time for some things to change in the tiny mountain community, but the weather and the seasons were not included. It seemed to go from summer to winter overnight. Luke awoke in the middle of the night to a sound in the hall outside his bedroom. He had taken to leaving the door open when he went to sleep at night, so that his mother would not constantly wake him on her nightly security rounds, which had been going on for some time now.

As he listened closely, he thought he could hear footsteps, which he at first took to be his mother's, but before long was convinced that something was different. These footsteps were much lighter and less purposeful, as the padding sound made him think of someone dancing about in the hall. He got out of bed and glanced into the hallway from his room and was shocked to see what looked like a little girl with long dark hair and a white dress, her tiny hand curling around the bannister as she raced down the stairs, so that he only saw the back of her as she ran away giggling.

"Hey, wait!" Luke called after her as he raced across the hall and down the stairs. "Who are you? How'd you get in here?"

He reached the foot of the stairs just in time to see her run out the front door and into the night. Instinctively he followed after her, though he was shirtless and barefoot and the night was bitterly cold. His breath was floating in front of him as he slammed the door behind him before chasing off after the little girl, who he could see was now headed in the direction of the river.

The slamming door woke both Carol and Bobby and they met in the hall with their housecoats. Carol instinctively ran to Luke's room and found him gone. She shrieked in dismay and ran back into the hall, "He's gone! We have to go find him Bobby!"

"Let's go," he responded without hesitation.

They raced down the stairs and out into the night, unsure of where to go. Bobby looked down and noticed that his brother's footprints left in the frost on the front steps, turned to head toward the river. So that is where he went, with Carol following behind. They reached the river, which was black in the darkness, and could see nothing, until suddenly Luke surfaced, flailing wildly in the water. Again, Bobby did not hesitate. In an instant he was in the river, grabbing onto his older brother and pulling him to safety as Luke continued to cast about, seeming to be searching the water in a panic.

"Where is she?" he cried as they pulled him up onto the grass beside the stream.

"Where is who?" Carol cried as she held her son, who was shivering uncontrollably.

"The li-little girl," he chattered, "sh-sh-she was in th-th-the house. I followed her and watched her f-f-fall in the river. I tried to save her but I c-could not find her anywhere!" Luke was shaking and sobbing hysterically as he tried to tell them what had happened.

"Let's get him inside!" Carol took control. "He's going to end up with hypothermia if we don't get him warm right now."

They brought him in and wrapped him in blankets and sat with him in his room. He was insistent that they call the police to look for the little girl.

"I don't think there *was* a little girl," Carol replied.

"*What*? You don't believe me?"

"I believe you *think* you saw a little girl, but I don't think she was really there," she began. Carol finally shared what she had seen and felt in the house and they finally confessed to all that they had been through with the kids at school. To their surprise she was not angry, but she was convinced. "We're not staying here anymore. This is not a good place."

"Do you mean the Pass?" Bobby asked.

"No, I mean this house. I don't think it wants us here, and I have to say I am not about to put up a big fight to stay. So how about it?"

The boys agreed and they spent the day packing up. They stayed at the local motel, frequented by truckers and seasonal workers, at a weekly rate until they could find a new place. They never slept another night in the house. Carol was convinced that if they had, the thing which had become fixated on her oldest son might succeed in using his good nature to lure him away from her once and for all. And that was not a chance she was willing to take.

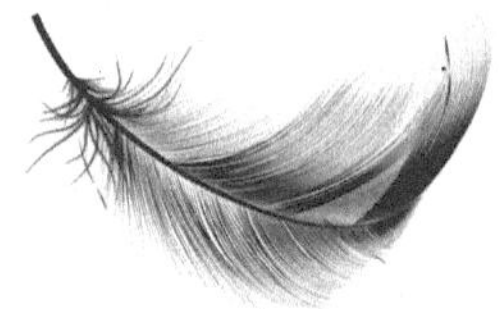

CHAPTER NINETEEN

There was a small rocky beach alongside the river where Emma and Charlie always took Max on their walk because it was easy for Charlie to throw sticks to the little dog there. Charlie was already hunting for the choice sticks as Max trailed closely behind her, eager to start their favourite game. As Charlie distracted herself, Emma turned to Felix, a look of dismay on her face that she could not hide.

"What is it?" Felix pressed. "What's wrong? I'm sorry. I should not be telling you these things. I can see how much it upsets you."

"No, it's not that. Well, it's kind of that, but not how you think."

"I'm not following you, sorry."

Emma made a spontaneous decision to be honest about what had happened and what she had seen. As she described chasing who she thought was her daughter into the night, then seeing the strange woman in the forest, she was reminded of the fear and confusion she had felt. In the hopes of normalcy, she had pushed these thoughts away for the past few days, but Felix's story about Luke following the little girl to the river brought it back full force for her.

"I don't know what to say. What did John have to say when he found you wandering around outside in the middle of the night? He must have been terrified."

Regarding this detail, Emma decided to be less honest, holding back what John had surmised about her meetings with her elderly friend. "Let's just say he was not impressed, but he got over it. Once I saw for myself that Charlie was still in her bed, it was like it was a dropped topic all of a sudden. We did not come back to the fact that I had seen someone, even if it wasn't Charlie. Which means someone was in our house. I think he just chalked it up to sleepwalking and left it at that."

"You're probably right. I doubt he would have jumped to the conclusion that there was a ghost poking around in the middle of the night."

"Is that what you think is going on here? Do you think I'm being haunted?"

"If I'm honest Emma, I don't know what to think. I have told you these stories because you asked. The fact that you asked I guess means that something was already tugging at your mind for attention. Likely just pure curiosity. The fact that you've had these experiences since we've started talking could simply be the power of suggestion. You might be looking for something that isn't really there. You could be under stress perhaps. Or, maybe you were just sleepwalking and making a whole lot of something out of nothing."

"Do you think so?"

"I meant what I said: I don't know what to think. I'd like to just put it all to bed and say that ghosts don't exist but," he paused, lost in thought, watching Charlie throwing a stick half the size of herself into the river.

"But what?"

"But, the other part of me wonders, if none of it's true, why the stories in the first place? This is not the only story here in the Crowsnest Pass, I'm sure you know. Between the slide and the Hillcrest Mine disaster alone, this place is ripe for spooky legends. Even before it was an established settlement, the Blackfoot people in the area refused to stay near Turtle Mountain, insisting that it was cursed ground, always moving. I guess they were right in the end.

Whether you believe in them or not, this area is full of ghosts. It's a matter of whether you take them figuratively or literally I guess."

"So are you saying that there are other houses in the Pass rumoured to be haunted?"

"Well of course. In a place like this, with so much tragedy embedded in the local history, there are plenty of stories about old houses suspected of being haunted." He hesitated. "But your house is different somehow."

"What do you mean by that? Different *how*?"

Felix was quiet for a moment as he reflected on what he meant before replying, "The other stories, well, they're just as creepy, just as believable, *or unbelievable*, depending on how you look at it. I guess the difference is that it seems like with each of those, the story never changes, the same families live in the same houses for generations and they *live* with the ghosts they claim to be haunted by. Nothing ever really happens or changes from what I can tell. Even people who report ghostly experiences when they visit for the Bellevue Mine tour and have an encounter get to continue on with their lives, as though it never happened. Sheer entertainment. But then there's your house. It seems to continue on with the story, changing and continuing with each family who lives in it. Until your Aunt Helen came along, nobody ever stayed for long."

"You think something about the house affected them somehow?"

"I didn't say that," Felix responded defensively.

"You didn't have to." They were both quiet for a few moments, distractedly watching Charlie as she and Max explored the rocky beach together. Emma broke the silence between them. "So let's say it is haunted, my house, what does it mean?"

"What does *what* mean?"

"The little girl. Why did she lead me outside in the middle of the night? Was she trying to hurt me? Should I be worried?"

Felix considered for what seemed a long time before answering her. "I won't tell you what to think or feel, especially considering I don't know what to think or feel for myself. But I will tell you this: it never hurts to be careful, especially when you have everything in the world to lose."

They both turned back to watch Charlie and Emma knew exactly what he meant. She was reminded of the day when Charlie had left the back garden, claiming to be following her *friend*, a little girl. She was suddenly chilled and wanted to turn back. "Thanks Felix, that's good advice." She called to Charlie that it was time to head back and the little girl happily followed, as they had already been gone a long time and she needed something to eat. Emma did not say anything to Felix about what had happened with Charlie, sensing that he would refuse to tell her anything more if she revealed the whole truth.

When they got back to the house, Felix asked if she wanted to meet again. "I would understand if you're not interested in hearing any more stories about the house after our discussion."

"Honestly Felix, what I'd love to hear about next time we get together is Helen. It's been good to hear about the history of the house, but that was what this was all about in the first place. Would that be okay?"

"That would be fine by me. I guess it's time now anyway. I just wanted you to know a bit about past incidents before I told you about your aunt."

"John's aunt," she corrected him, "not that he knew her any more than I did."

"Next time then," he said and he took her hand. "I really am sorry if I've caused you any stress."

"You really haven't Felix." Emma wrapped her arms around his neck and kissed his cheek. "You have been a great friend. I'm looking forward to seeing you again."

"Ditto kiddo."

On the day Charlotte arrived, the weather was dreary, but everyone was in good spirits to be together again. John was able to take some time off to spend with his mother-in-law, but knew to give his wife some time with her mother without him around, so he was still able to focus his time at work, which was good, because the weekends tended to be his busiest days. The word was getting out amongst locals and visitors alike about the cafe and he was on the verge of needing to hire more staff, assuming the momentum held out through the colder months, which was the true test of endurance in the little destination town. The traffic slowed considerably during the winter and businesses often slowed to a crawl. To survive it was important to have a strong local core of customers and an atmosphere unique enough to warrant an occasional winter drive for those who found themselves on the treacherous highway in the cold.

Charlie was thrilled to have her grandmother stay with them. She had always been around since she had been born, and the distance had been a huge adjustment for the child. Her grandmother smothered her with attention and bowed to her every whim, including letting Charlie act as her make-up artist, which left her looking like a bizarre crazed clown. Despite this fact, she smiled when she saw her reflection in the hall mirror and complimented her granddaughter on her artistic flair. When John got home he jumped when he saw her, which took Charlotte by surprise, having forgotten what she looked like. They had a nice, quiet evening together, letting Charlie stay up an hour past her usual bedtime, until her head began to droop as she snuggled up on the sofa and read with her grandmother, who had finally removed the make-up disaster and was looking like her old polished self.

After Charlie went to bed John stayed up long enough to share a drink with his wife and her mother. He was buzzing with excitement as he described the roll-out of the business and the warm reception they had received so far. John excused himself early to give Emma and Charlotte some time to catch up, *and* because he was exhausted from another long day. He kissed them both on the cheek and said 'good-night' before dragging himself upstairs for a shower before heading to bed.

They spent time reminiscing and Emma explained what things had been like so far adjusting to life in a small town with a little one. Most of what she said was positive, yet her mother's face was marked with a look of concern. Charlotte finally asked her, "So, what do you think of your new house?"

"It's alright. It's another thing to adjust to."

"So you're not having any second thoughts?"

"No, no second thoughts. I get lonely sometimes for the life we had in the city. We moved here to be immersed in nature, but we barely get any time for fishing or hiking. John's been so busy getting the new business off the ground. I don't really know many people here yet, so that can be a bit isolating at times I guess." Emma trailed off, seemingly lost in thought. "But don't get me wrong, I really do love it here. I think it'll be a great place for Charlie to grow up."

"Maybe I should stay a little longer and give you some time to yourself. Give you and John some time alone. What do you say?"

"No, it's fine. I wasn't looking for sympathy or anything. We're okay. *I'm* okay."

"Nobody's saying you're not okay Emma. I just want to do this for you." Charlotte leaned in close and took Emma's hand. "Besides, now that I'm here I realise how much I've missed you all. Two days won't be nearly enough time."

"You can stay as long as you like Mom, but don't do it because you think we need your help or something. We've been doing just fine. We've been super busy is all, and adjusting of course."

"Of course honey. I just want to help you take a load off for a little while. I've been feeling completely useless at home on my own all the time. It's been hard having you gone."

"Sorry, Mom. I'd love for you to stay for a few extra days. You're right. Two days isn't enough for anything. And I'll definitely take you up on your offer to watch Charlie while I get some fishing in, assuming the weather clears up soon enough. But do not be disappointed if John can't take much time off right now. He's just been so super busy. I miss him, but I don't mind."

"I'm sure John can take the time. It was his idea after..."

"What?"

"Oh nothing. I just meant he would have come up with it himself if he knew I was staying."

"Have you been talking to John?"

"*No.*"

"That sounded more like a question than an answer. When were you speaking to him?"

"Just right before we spoke last and I told you I was coming to visit."

Emma eyed her mother suspiciously. "Did John *ask* you to come here?"

"Don't say it like that."

"He did! Why? I don't understand. Why are you guys talking behind my back?"

Charlotte looked like she had been backed into a corner. She had not meant to break John's confidence. She was clearly choosing her words carefully. "Well, first of all, let's dial down the paranoia a notch or two there dear. John is my son-in-law, who I happen to be very close to, and I'll talk to him when I like. He felt like the two of you could use some 'couple time', to go on a hike or something. Not exactly my kind of date, but you know, to each his own."

Emma crossed her arms over her chest defensively. "And?"

"And what?"

Emma scowled at her mother. "And what is this really about? What did John tell you?"

"So you admit there's something to tell?"

"Aha! Guilty! Tell me what he said dammit!"

"Calm down now." Charlotte scolded her daughter. "You'll wake Charlie."

Emma started to pace the room, concocting all kinds of reasons for why John would go behind her back to talk to her mother about her. Why was he so worried? Maybe he did not trust her. Charlotte interrupted her thoughts, "He told me about this old man you've been meeting with, this *Felix*."

"Felix?" Emma was visibly surprised at her mother's response. She had not expected her mother to even know about Felix.

"Yes, Felix. John says he's been telling you all kinds of stories about your house. He thinks it's been freaking you out. He says you haven't been yourself."

Emma was dumbfounded and did not know what to say.

"Well? What's going on? Have you not been yourself lately?"

"John shouldn't have said anything. He's blowing it out of proportion."

"Really?"

"Yes, really."

"How can you explain him chasing you out of the house in the middle of the night then? I can understand why he might be concerned. Can't you?"

As she always seemed to be able to do, her mother had somehow wiggled her way out of the confrontation by using the truth to turn the tables on her. Emma had assumed that because *she* blew off what had happened that night, that John had just let it go. Obviously he had not. She should have known better. He had suggested she quit meeting with Felix, and even then she had made light of his concern and gone behind his back to see Felix again. She had made light of it all because it was all so ridiculous and because her main motivation was simple curiosity. It was not like she took it seriously. The moment she had this thought her ears burned hot pink. She knew it was not true. She knew she had taken it all quite seriously. After all, some strange things had happened, or at least it had *seemed* that way at the time. Maybe John was right. Maybe she needed some perspective.

In that moment she decided to tell her mother what had been going on, although she could not quite bring herself to reveal the stranger details, the things she had seen and felt for herself. Instead, she relayed the stories Felix had told her, as they moved from the house and into the backyard for some fireside wine. Charlotte listened carefully, interjecting on occasion to ask a question, but otherwise remaining silent while Emma recounted the history of the house and the distraction it was causing her.

"I think I'll be able to move on once I know what John's Aunt Helen has to do with all of this. I feel like Felix has been leading up to this for some reason and I'm anxious to know why. We really don't know anything about this woman and we're living in her home."

"I'll point out that you're making a big deal out of a minor detail. Most people don't know the people who lived in their house before they did. It's a pretty standard thing."

"Yeah maybe, but most people don't have those strangers give them that house either. It just makes me curious is all."

"Are you sure that's all?"

"Well," Emma hesitated and glanced across the flames at her mother, "maybe I'm a little creeped out too. I mean, who wouldn't be?"

"I certainly would be. I'm not all that thrilled about heading to bed if I'm honest. It's bad enough knowing that I'll be sleeping beneath that cursed mountain. I don't know how you do it all the time. My nerves would be frayed."

"Sorry mom, maybe I should have told you what was going on before you came."

"You certainly should have," Charlotte scolded. "Not that it would have changed my mind about coming. I just wish you could feel like you could talk to me about these things, even if it has to be over the phone."

"Sorry mom."

"Quit saying 'sorry'. You have nothing to be sorry about. I just want you to know that I'm always here for you honey. You can tell me anything you know. It's between me and you, just like it's always been. I do not like hearing that my girl is feeling anxious in her new home; that's not how it should be. It's not good for you and it's not good for your family either. Maybe it is time you took a step back from this Felix person and focus on making your life here. It's what the two of you have wanted since you got together. Just let yourself be happy."

"I know mom, I will, I just need to know about Helen, that's all, and then I will let it go okay?"

"It's not like it's up to me anyway Em. Although if it was, I would tell you to just let it go and move on *now*. I don't like where this is going. It's not good for you. You should be taking better care of yourself."

"I'm fine mom."

Charlotte crossed her arms and stared across the flames into her daughter's eyes. "Are you really, though, Emma? Are you really? Because if you're not, I'd hate to think…"

"Okay mom," Emma interrupted her. "I think that's enough for tonight. You asked me what was going on and I told you. Now I'd appreciate it if *you* would let it go and move on. I'm okay. I need you to trust me on this. Now let's let the fire burn itself out and head in for the night; it's getting late."

She gathered their glasses and the empty wine bottle and headed for the house, her mother following behind her across the darkened lawn.

"Fine, but don't forget Emma. You can tell me anything. I'm always here for you."

"I know mom." Emma smiled at her mother sheepishly then glanced up to take in the stars, which grew more intense as they drew away from the fire, but she saw a movement of white in the darkness of Charlie's bedroom window. Her head snapped back to do a double-take, and there in the window, was the face of a child, a little girl, but not Charlie. This little girl had long dark hair, but her face was deathly pale and her eyes were enveloped in darkness, so that Emma could not tell where the little girl was even looking, though she felt like the child's gaze was directed right at her.

After being frozen in place for a split second, which to her seemed an eternity, Emma snapped out of it when the little girl, dressed in what looked like a dirty white cotton flannel nightgown, smiled an impish grin which seemed to tear at the corner of her tiny mouth and spread out in a web like a cracked white porcelain plate. Emma tore open the back door and ran into the house and up the stairs to Charlie's room. Charlotte was following closely behind, demanding to know what was wrong as Emma screamed her daughter's name. She woke John, who came stumbling from their room wiping at his eyes, hair flattened on one side of his head, his bare chest heaving with fright.

Emma ignored his and her mother's pleas to know what was wrong and bolted into her daughter's room without hesitation. Charlie sat up in bed, and was visibly frightened. Emma swept her daughter into her arms. "Are you okay sweetie? Mommy's here. Where is the girl? Did she try to hurt you?"

Charlie's face contorted in an attempt to stop her tears but she failed. She cried and pushed her mother away. "What girl Mommy? You scared me! Why were you screaming? You woke me up!"

Emma's jaw dropped, "Sorry honey, I… I thought I saw something in the window."

Charlie cried even harder and struck out at her mother. "Go away! You're scaring me! I want Daddy!"

Emma backed away in tears as John came in, swooping past her as though she was not even there, and taking Charlie in his arms, trying to console her as she wept into his shoulder. Charlotte took Emma by the hand and led her away, back to her own room. She wiped at Emma's tears, like she had when she was a little girl, and asked her why she had reacted the way she had. Emma did not have the strength to lie, and she knew she could not make anything up which would sound any less crazy than the truth, so she told her mother what she had seen in the window. "I can't be certain, but I think it's the same little girl I chased out of the house that night that John found me out in the forest."

"You didn't say anything about a little girl," Charlotte interrupted.

"I know Mom, I'm sorry. I still don't even believe it myself. My imagination is just on overdrive with all of these ghost stories buzzing around in my head. I didn't want to burden you with something we both know isn't real."

"So you're saying you thought you saw a ghost, *twice*, but you don't believe it's real?"

"Yeah, I guess that's what I'm saying. Because I did think I saw something, but I know that's not the case, and so there's nothing to worry about and no need to say anything to John, right?" Emma was reaching now, hoping that her mother would keep what she had revealed in confidence to herself, though she immediately knew it was hopeless.

"So what you're saying is that you've been seeing things, seeing *ghosts* to be specific, which have you running in and out of the house at all hours of the night, but you do not think that warrants informing your husband? I don't think it's a good idea for you to be keeping anything from him Emma. Need I repeat myself? He's your *husband* and you owe him the truth. I think he deserves to know that his wife has been seeing things."

"Oh for fuck's sake Mom! You make it sound like I'm losing my mind or something. I just thought I saw something and I overreacted. The first time it happened I was probably just dreaming, so can you please just let it go?"

"I love you very much Emma. You are my one and only child. But let me make something crystal clear: you might be willing to keep this from John, but I'm not. You might want to make light of what's been going on, but I'm no fool, and I know that you have been affected more than you've been letting on, and probably even more than what you've told me now. So, either you tell him, or I will."

Emma put her head in her hands and rubbed at her temples. She was furious with her mother, but knew her well enough to know that there was nothing she could do to change her mind, so she gave in. "Fine, I'll tell him tomorrow, when it's just the two of us. Then we'll have lots of time to talk about how I need to be locked up or whatever."

"Emma, do not…"

"Fine, fine." She waved off her mother. "Tomorrow. I'm sure it will make for great date material."

"Please don't be mad. I just want what's best for you, for all of you."

Emma softened, knowing that she was being unreasonable, knowing that what her mother said was true, that she was just looking out for her family. She knew that she needed to tell John everything, that it was long overdue. She took Charlotte's hand and pulled her close in an embrace. "I know Mom. I want that too. I'll tell him everything tomorrow, I promise. I'm sorry I put you through all this tonight. It's not fair. I was really looking forward to having you here and now I've ruined everything."

"Don't be silly," Charlotte reassured her. "That's what moms are for, right? We've got lots of time for a great visit, and I thought it was pretty great so far anyway."

"Except for my hysterics maybe."

"Had to happen. Now we can put everything out on the table where it belongs. It's always for the best Em."

"I know Mom. Thanks for listening."

They said their good-nights and went to bed. John pulled away, pretending to be sleeping when Emma tried to snuggle into his back. She turned over with a sigh, knowing that tomorrow he would know everything, and it would all go one way or another.

CHAPTER TWENTY

After an awkwardly quiet family breakfast, John and Emma loaded the car with their backpacks, which were full with the necessities for an easy hike, and their fishing gear, so that they could take advantage of the small, but locally famous creek which flowed alongside the trail they would be taking. After arranging for Charlotte to spend the day with Charlie, and for his small staff to cover for his absence, John had given Emma the option to choose what they would do for the day. After some thought and research, she decided that they should take the easy hiking trail to Lille, the site of the ghost town where their house had first stood, before the closure of the local mine ended the tenure of the town. Apparently there was not much to see at the old historic site, but the old coal coke ovens which had been shipped from Belgium at the turn of the century, the remains of the local hotel and the grass-covered foundations of the buildings which had stood for a brief period in history in a tiny valley at the centre of the Mist Mountain Formation.

Along the trail to Lille ran a slow and steady trickle of water known as Gold Creek. Though the fish, which were mostly Rainbow and Cutthroat trout, were visible to even the most untrained eye in such a crystal clear mountain stream, their striking visibility also meant that the fish too could see what was above the water with equal clarity. So catching them was a near impossibility for even the most sly and sneaky fisherman. This did not put Emma off. In fact, this detail just made the challenge all the more interesting. John had shared in her sentiments and was glad that she had chosen to do something outdoors, as his opportunities to take advantage of the beautiful mountains they had chosen to move to were limited as a result of his busy schedule.

Of course, they had known this would be the case when they chose to make the move. The hope was that with an investment of time and money, and a commitment to finding the right staff to train, the place would eventually run itself and they would have more time to spend in their other, more personal pursuits. For now, they would take the opportunity of having Charlotte staying with them to get away for a badly-needed day alone together.

They did not have to go far, after travelling by the old Frank road, directly through the heart of the rockslide on the old, pocked gravel road, in the shadow of what remained of Turtle Mountain. They turned right onto the highway which connected the towns of the Crowsnest Pass, and quickly made a left just past the gas station and fast food burger joint, turning uphill at a sign which advertised the interpretive centre for the slide. Though they had been to the building to check out the historical artefacts and details of the mountain under which they lived, one of the greatest disasters in history, that was not the destination for today. Instead, they pulled off the main road about halfway to the centre and parked at the start of the trail which led to Lille. They quietly geared up for fishing and shared some bug spray before heading into the forest and up the mountain.

Emma wanted to say something, anything, to break the tension between them, but she could not think of anything. She was not sure how John was feeling, but his silence frightened her, bringing back all the old insecurities. They were past all that, she told herself, but it was so easy to slip back into the same intrusive thought patterns that had plagued her even after things had stabilised between them. It had taken longer for her to steady herself, to believe that John was not going anywhere, that he still loved her. That he had never *stopped* loving her, despite everything that had happened.

Watching him as he walked away, Emma knew that her life would never be the same without him in it. She knew from experience that love was such a fragile thing. It suddenly struck her, the gravity of what she had been doing, the risks she had been taking, the games she had been playing with her relationship. Her mother had been right. Keeping things from John could only lead to problems. She realised that she had shut out the one person who could have helped her to navigate this craziness that she found herself somehow a part of, without intending to, and she could not even explain why. But that was a lie. The truth, the real deep-down truth, was that she was afraid that he would not believe her and that he would think that she was truly losing it. *Hell, he probably already thinks that anyway with the way I've been behaving lately*, she thought to herself.

"Are you coming?" John interrupted her train of thought. He had turned to face her as she stood transfixed, lost in her own anxious thoughts.

"Uh, yeah, sorry," she stammered in surprise.

He shrugged and started to turn away from her and back to the trail, when she gained the courage to break her silence. "Can we talk? I do not want to waste this day together. It's so rare for us to get some time alone like this these days. I know that I have been acting like an idiot lately and I'd like to explain."

The expression on her husband's ruggedly handsome face softened and he walked back to her and took her hands in his and kissed them, as he stared into her eyes. Then he pulled her close in an embrace and kissed the top of her head. "I'm sorry I've been quiet. I've been a jerk."

"No you haven't! I can't blame you for feeling pissed."

"I'm not pissed," he said with obvious surprise.

"You're not?" Emma was equally surprised.

"No, I'm not. I'm worried. I can tell when something is going on with my wife, but you won't let me in these days. I'm starting to get jealous of a man nearing a hundred years old for god's sake. I have the feeling you've been telling him more lately than you've been telling me."

"I'm so sorry honey. I wasn't thinking. I want to tell you everything. I guess I just thought that you would think..." Emma trailed off and did not finish her thought.

John was a good man, so he did not push her. Instead, he offered a pause on the subject for the time being. "How about we just put this aside for now and enjoy the hike and the fishing. When we stop for lunch you can tell me everything. Sound good?"

Emma smiled appreciatively and agreed to his suggestion. They took their time enjoying the hike and stopped on occasion to take turns at fishing the more promising parts of the stream with little success. Before long they came to a beautiful pool with a small yet beautiful waterfall spilling over into the clear stream. They could see the fish darting in and out of sight as they snapped up the aquatic bug life. Emma unhooked her fly from the eye on her rod and pulled out enough line to start casting. She aimed to land her fly just left of a large angular rock jutting out from the water's surface, just above the fall, hopeful that it would momentarily mimic a fly falling over the waterfall into the pool below before the well-educated trout realised the scam. Her first three attempts ended in a water-logged fly with not even a sniff from the hungry and waiting fish. The fourth attempt landed exactly where she had aimed, shimmied back and forth across the surface of the rippled water, and slipped quickly over the flat rock which overhung the pool. It landed perfectly for just a moment, bobbing back up in the gush of water after getting pushed under the current for a split second.

Emma barely had time to react before her line was being zipped quickly from her reel by what appeared to be an impressive specimen of a fish. Her light rod bent over with the weight of the fish so that she thought she was either going to lose it or it was going to snap her rod in two, but she quickly tipped her line to the side, momentarily disorienting the fish so that she could reel it in quickly without too much of a fight. John recorded the encounter for prosperity on his phone as she brought the fish in, then she waded into the water to release it from the hook and let it go after a quick photo op. Careful to keep it in the water, she was mindful to upset it as little as possible after the commotion which had seemingly cleared out the stacked pool. Once she had released it, John put his phone away and they grinned wolfishly at each other before sharing a high five.

"Well, I'm going to say that's going to be the biggest of the day," Emma bragged.

John turned to her with a boyish smile. "You know, you don't always have to take the opportunity to be such a *bitch* about it."

She laughed explosively, loving it that he could still catch her off-guard. "Oh, but I do. I really, really do."

He reached out for her, touching her arm lightly with his fingertips as he gazed longingly into her eyes. His touch electrified her and she felt a deep longing for him. She knew the feeling was mutual. There had been too much space between them for too long. They kissed one another fiercely and were nearing taking things to the next level as John unbuttoned the first two buttons on her shirt. She wanted him so badly, she did not even try to make him stop.

"That must have been quite the catch!"

They both jumped at the sound of the old man's voice. They looked around to see an elderly couple watching them from the trail, with backpacks on their backs and huge smiles plastered across both their faces. Emma was grateful that they had not found them in a more precarious position.

"It sure was!" John laughed and kissed her again. The couple laughed with them and then waved goodbye and carried on. John started to pull Emma closer again and tried to pick up where they had left off but she had regained her senses.

"Let's leave that for later. This isn't exactly a private spot."

"Come on!" John pleaded playfully, knowing his chance had already passed.

"How about lunch?" She suggested.

John suddenly looked sheepish. Emma wondered how much he really wanted to actually know about what had been going on with her. She was ripped back to the reality of what she needed to tell him and she found that she suddenly did not really have much appetite for lunch anymore.

By the expression on his face, he seemed to read her mind and took her hand. "That sounds like a great idea. I'm famished!"

They unpacked some peanut butter and jam sandwiches, baby dill pickles and cheese, some orange juice boxes and a pair of apples. As they sat on the pebbled beach in front of the tiny waterfall pool and shared their lunch, they avoided the topic which they had agreed to discuss and instead focused on reliving the moment of the big catch and the moment of being caught. Emma knew that they both appreciated the lighter subject matter, but once they finished their lunch, she also knew that they both knew it was time to have the talk they had been waiting to have for some time. She took a deep breath and began. She told him everything, sparing no detail, from Felix's recounting of the history of their house, to her own strange experiences, to the feeling that she needed to somehow protect Charlie from harm, but that she was not even sure why. She just knew how she felt, and something was telling her to heed that intuition.

When she had finished, John was quiet for a long time before finally speaking up. "This is a lot to take in Em. I mean, it's kind of hard to believe really."

"I knew you would think that. You think this is in my head."

"I didn't say that, but I won't lie and say that I'm not a little worried about you."

He suddenly fell quiet, but she knew that he had not said all that he needed to say. She knew him well enough to know that, so she pushed him to be completely honest with her in return for her trust in him.

"I have to tell you Em," John started and hesitated again before going on, clearly distressed with what he had to say, though she already knew what it would be. "It makes me a little nervous that you would bring Charlie into this. I mean, it's one thing to indulge in these ghost story sessions with Felix, but the moment you started worrying about our daughter, you should have told me. *It makes me think of before...*"

"This isn't like *before*," she retorted with more vehemence than she had intended, and so she softened her approach. "I promise you, it really isn't. I would have told you long ago. I promise you that. I *promised* you that."

When he finally looked her in the eye, she could see that he was holding back tears, but she no longer could. She held onto him and cried into his shoulder as she whispered to him and to herself, "I promise, I would tell you. This is *different*. Please tell me you believe me. This is different."

He rocked her gently and assured her that he believed her, but she was not sure if *she* believed *him*. She knew that in the end, she really had no choice. When she finally pulled away from him she sat facing the waterfall, wiping the last of her tears away. This was not how she had intended for the conversation to go. However, she had figured that the past would likely come up, and understandably so, but she had been hopeful that it was a subject that they would simply avoid for the rest of their married lives.

That was how things were for the most part as it was, just carrying on as though nothing bad had ever happened and moving on with their lives. It was a good tactic for the most part, because Emma knew that dwelling on dark things could be a toxic habit, but so too could avoidance of those dark things. She knew too that it was the airing of those dark things which was one of the only releases for the mind and soul. Much of her struggle with insecurity came back to the mistakes of the past, things she would always regret but could not change any more than she could the rising and setting of the sun. She could feel John's eyes on her, as though he were trying to figure her out, but she kept her eyes averted, and focused on the diamond-dappled ripples of water darting away from the white foam of the fall. She was pretending to be transfixed.

"I'm going to try to keep an open mind, Em. That does not mean that I'm not still worried. But I'm willing to listen to reason."

"There's not really any reason to this though is there? I was between a rock and a hard place in this situation. I knew that what I was thinking was outlandish and that you would either think that I was losing it and that you should be worried, or that for some reason I was lying to you. And I think that would probably be an even bigger problem. How could I tell you all this when I knew it was crazy myself? But I don't think it's crazy. I don't think this is all in my head, and that has got me truly scared now, because the alternative isn't much better. I just didn't know what to think anymore and so I knew I had no choice but to tell you what was going on. And, if I'm being completely honest, and I might as well be, Mom did not leave me much choice last night after I told *her* what was going on."

"You told your mother before you told me?" John sounded genuinely hurt.

"I think I needed a warm-up. This is all pretty fucked up John. I was not exactly excited to tell you. Telling my mother did not seem as risky I guess. I don't want to lose you."

John put his head in his hands, clearly exasperated, "You aren't going to lose me Emma. I love you too much." He took her hand and made her look him in the eye before going on. "Besides, it would be pretty shallow to leave your wife because she might believe she's living in a haunted house, don't you think?"

"Maybe for the average person, but with everything that's already happened in the past, it's a little different, I'd say. Besides, I didn't say that I necessarily believe the house is haunted, I'm just finding it harder and harder to ignore the creepy feeling I have, like I'm being *watched* or something."

"I think we both can agree that there is every chance that listening to these stories from Felix has had an effect on you. The question is, has it affected your perception so that you're seeing things that aren't there, or are you just more aware of and maybe open to something which really *is* there? I think that's what we need to figure out, because I believe that *you* believe in what you've seen and felt."

"And if it's all in my head?"

"Well, then that will be good for you to know so that you can put your fears to rest."

"One set of fears maybe, but then I'd have a whole other problem to deal with?"

"Depending on how you look at it I guess."

"What do you mean? There's only one other way to look at it: if the house isn't," she hesitated before she could say the word, "*haunted*, then it's all in my head. And as much as I would be grateful to have a ghost-free home, I can't say that I'd be thrilled about finding out that I'm out of touch with reality."

"I think that's a bit extreme," John interrupted.

"Do you really?" Emma shot back.

"Really," he insisted. "Because if it is in your head, then I would say it is totally understandable considering all of the things that Felix has been telling you. In fact, I would say that it would be a pretty normal reaction under the circumstances. This has nothing to do with anything else."

Emma sat quietly and tried to absorb what he was telling her. Not only had she not expected this response from John, but she had not even considered it herself, when really, it was the most obvious answer. She had to consider that maybe he was right, that maybe her recent experiences were merely a normal reaction to some spooky stories about an old house which was new to her. Still, she could not shake the feeling that it was not just all in her head. There was something about Felix's demeanour during their last visit which had spurred a concern in her, that maybe he knew more than he was letting on and that she had more to be worried about than he had warned her of. All she wanted now was to know the truth about the place where her family was living their day-to-day lives. She needed to know they were safe, and she felt that Felix might be the only one to have the answers she was looking for.

When she did not respond, John continued. "Maybe we should both try looking at this with our minds as open as possible. Let's consider the possibility that we may have actually inherited a haunted house from my Aunt Helen. Where does that leave us now? What are the important questions we need to answer?"

"I don't know. I guess, maybe *who* is haunting the place?"

"And *why*?"

"And most importantly, are *we* in any danger?"

"Well, and I guess it would be good to know if there is anything we can do about it."

"If it's a danger, then we'll move out of course."

"Could we afford to do that?" He was returning to the voice of reason now.

"Could we afford not to?" She reminded him that they had a lot at stake, a sentiment Felix had just shared with her recently. "I am curious to know what your aunt has to do with all of this. It's been eating me up actually, like I'm becoming fixated or something."

"Maybe she has nothing to do with any of it," John suggested hopefully.

"That was not the impression I got from Felix. When I told him that it was soon time for him to tell me about her, he said that he agreed, so obviously, there is *something* to tell. I just don't know what. But it seems to me that it must have something to do with all of this, otherwise, why would he bother to tell me all of these things before finally getting around to telling me what I came to ask him about in the first place?"

John was pensive for a moment. "Okay, maybe you've got something there. But let's not jump to any conclusions. Maybe Felix is going to tell you that he told these same stories to Helen and that she didn't take it well. Maybe she never asked, so he never told her anything. We have no idea."

"I thought you wanted to be completely open-minded."

"I do. I just don't want to make more of something than we should. So let's try to deal with the things we know for now, based on what Felix has told you. And when we know what happened to Helen, then we can add that to our paranormal investigation. What do you think?" He winked at her flirtatiously and she was reminded of why they had come.

"I've got an even better idea. Let's put all of this aside for today and enjoy the rest of our day together. We won't have a free babysitter every day after all. Let's finish the hike to the town site. I heard that since it's a historic site, there are some markers with information about the town and even some pictures from when it was still inhabited. Maybe we can find where our house was before they brought it to where it sits now. What do you say, *Mulder*?"

"I say it sounds like a plan, *Scully*. We can get back to the case over a glass of wine later on. I guess we can even get your mother in on the discussion and make it a party, since she already knows everything."

"So would she be *Skinner*, or the *Smoking Man*?"

John cast her a sideways smile. "She's The Lone Gunmen: totally on our side."

"So true."

They chuckled quietly at their nerdy joke as they packed up the remnants of their creekside picnic and continued on with the rest of the hike to Lille. The walk was much as it had been, the trail wide with forest on either side, though the hike was getting steeper. When they levelled out it was a short walk to what remained of the once bustling coal town, now a near-invisible ghost town in the heart of the mountains, stripped of almost everything it once was.

The first thing Emma noticed was the beautiful view. They were in a bowl-shaped valley, with hills on all sides, except to the left of the trail, where they saw the ruins of the old Belgian coke ovens which the ghost town was best known for, as there was not much else to see. They took photos of one another standing inside the stone arches of the old ornate ovens. Though they came from Belgium, the architectural style reminded her of Italy, where she had gone with some friends soon after graduating from college, just before she had met John.

There was a sign marker near the oven to explain where it had been built, how it had been shipped and why it had been left behind, when everything else had been moved from the town when it had shut down in the early twentieth century. They made their way into the bowl of the valley and found other informative signs with pictures of life in the town when it was a busy and living place. There were grainy black and white images of the tiny school, with several children standing out front, smiling for the camera where the school was once located. There was a marker for the miner's living quarters, a neighbourhood of tiny identical houses.

The photograph for this part of town showed a team of men and horses working together to pull the houses to their new resting places, but this was not an image of their home, as it was considerably smaller than theirs. There was another for the bank and one for the local hotel, which still had a part of the front lower brick wall standing to mark where it had once stood. Finally they came to a sign for the mine manager's home, which was clearly a picture of their own house, modest, yet larger than the miners' homes.

The stone foundation was still clearly visible, though overgrown with wild grass. Emma and John first walked around the perimeter of what was once where their home stood, then as though the walls still stood, they circled back to the front and entered through where they knew the door to be and roamed through the rooms. Emma mapped a picture in her mind of the image she would see through the front room, the kitchen and the bedrooms from where the house would have stood in this location. The view was beautiful and wild from all angles, though the presence of the town would have lent some measure of domesticity to the close-up mountain view.

"I have to admit, ghost stories or none, this is pretty cool. We didn't actually have to go that far to see where our house used to stand. How many people get to say that? It's pretty cool." John repeated himself as Emma moved about the rooms of the house, acting as though the walls were still closing her in and imagining what it would have looked like so long ago.

"Eerie," she whispered in reply.

"I need to go and water some weeds," John announced. " I'm going to have to head back over to the woods near the coal ovens. There isn't a tree around in this valley except for the ones growing up on the hillsides, and I'd rather not make that journey just for a little privacy. Will you be alright here on your own while I go do that?"

Emma nodded silently in response. She had become fixated on an indentation in the ground near the inner wall at the back of the house. It was so subtle, like a tiny gravesite depressed into the long grass, that she was surprised that she had even noticed it. She felt herself pulled, a moth drawn to flame, to the depression in the ground, so that she barely heard anything John said to her before he left her and made his way back toward the forest at the entrance to the valley.

Although she felt surprised, anyone near her would never have known that is what she was feeling at that moment, as her face had taken on a slack-jawed, droopy-eyed look, as though she were sleep-walking or hypnotised. A tiny spittle of drool escaped her bottom lip as she dropped to her knees and mindlessly started digging at the depression in the ground. First she tore at the long grass, until it was low enough to start digging into the dirt. The sharp stubble of the grass slid up under her finger nails and cut the tender skin to the quick, a torture she would suffer later on, but which she seemed to be immune to in the moment. There was no thought in her mind at that moment, only a singular purpose: *dig*.

As she dug furiously, she was sending the hard dirt flying in all directions, creating a cloud of dust all around herself like a cyclone. When John returned she was still digging, a pile of dirt gathered around her, her hands filthy, bruised and bleeding, and what appeared to be a dirt-caked, small wooden box open beside her. In the box was what appeared to be an old leather-bound book. Emma had tossed it aside and had continued to dig, tossing dirt and gravel in every direction. John, clearly shocked, grabbed her and pinned her arms at her side as she fought to continue with her mission. He pulled her away and they both fell to the ground, his arms still holding her tightly. She was cocooned in his careful grip.

"Emma, are you okay? What did you do? Why did you do this?" John asked her with concern.

"I, I…" she stammered in response, as she choked back her tears, "I don't know. I can't remember."

CHAPTER TWENTY ONE

When they got home, Emma headed straight to the bathroom to clean up as she was still a terrible mess. She was glad that her mother and Charlie were in the back playing in the garden with Max so that they would not see her in such a state. John brought their things in while she carried the book she had found. She had not put it down since she had unearthed it, but she had not thought to open it either. There was no doubt that she intended to, after she made herself presentable and spent some time with her daughter. The secrets of the buried book would have to wait. It could be full of blank pages for all she knew, though something told her that was not the case. Why, after all, would someone go through so much trouble to bury something which was void of words? In fact, for someone to even bother, there must have been something rather scandalous they wanted to keep to themselves.

Emma tucked the book away in her night table on her side of the bed before making her way downstairs and outside, to where Charlie was chasing Max in circles in pursuit of the toy she was keeping from him for the sake of the chase, and John was standing with her mother, a look of concern on both of their faces. The way they looked at her when they noticed her presence said it all: they had been talking about her. She was sure John had told her mother about how he had found her, sitting in the dirt, her fingernails bleeding from digging. This was not going to help her case. Though she was infuriated at the thought of them talking about her behind her back again, she knew that she had to keep her cool and put on her best face.

"Why so serious?" Emma asked casually.

John's response caught her off-guard. "It's Felix," he said, his tone serious. "He's had a heart attack."

"Your neighbour, Marin, stopped by while you were out and said that she thought you would want to know. She said that he's in the hospital and they've got him stabilised."

Emma was shocked. This was not what she had expected them to say. "Is he going to be okay? Can I go see him?"

"They *think* he's going to be okay. They got him to the hospital quickly, but he needs to recover, so he's not taking any visitors just yet," John responded calmly.

"Marin said she'd call you or stop by when she knows more," Charlotte added. Her concern for Emma was written all over her face. "Are you going to be okay, Em? I know you've become pretty close with Felix since you've been here."

"I'm okay," Emma responded absentmindedly. "Does Charlie know what happened?"

"I didn't say anything to her. I wasn't sure if the two of you would want her to know. I don't know how much of it she'd really understand. It's up to you. Are you going to tell her?"

In a glance Emma knew that she and John felt the same and so she replied for them both. "No, let's wait and see how things go. We will tell her, but I don't want to alarm her unnecessarily. Hopefully we'll be sharing some good news in a few days."

"I'm going to make us all a pot of coffee. I think we could probably use it." Charlotte headed inside and motioned for Charlie to follow. "Come on, sugar bun. Let's go make an afternoon snack. You look like you might need a cookie fix."

"Cookies! Yeah! And for Max too, right?"

"Of course for Max too. Let's go."

Without saying anything, John wrapped his strong arms around Emma and held her tight to his chest. She could hear the slow rhythm of his heart as she buried herself in his embrace. He kissed her head softly and wrapped his arm around her shoulders as they made their way inside to tell Charlie about their day, or the part they felt they could share with her anyway. For now, it went unsaid that they should keep what happened to themselves, though Emma was not sure if John might still tell her mother what had happened when he had a chance, as it seemed they had been confiding in one another quite regularly lately.

She wondered if she should beat him to the punch and tell Charlotte about it herself. She had hoped that she could discuss it with her husband alone to see where his head was at with it before they shared it with her mother. Wanting to trust him and knowing that she should, there was something that would not let her, something that felt like a wall of silence that had been building up between them. She had been keeping her concerns about the house from him, and in turn, he had been keeping his concerns about her to himself, until he felt he should confide in her mother about what was going on.

Later that evening, they were still waiting on some news about Felix. Emma was feeling unsettled and did everything she could to distract herself so that she did not sit and stare at the clock, wondering when she might hear from Marin. Although she would have appreciated the distraction of giving Charlie her bath before bedtime, her mother had been insistent that she do it and encouraged Emma to relax after what had turned out to be a long and difficult day. John had decided to take Max out for an evening walk before it got too dark, but Emma had opted to take the lazy option and stayed at home on the couch watching a fishing show on the television.

Although she was feeling high-strung, she was also exhausted, and was fighting to keep her eyes open. She had dozed off when she was suddenly awakened by her mother's screams coming from upstairs. Disoriented, she jumped up from the couch and raced up the stairs before she even had time to wonder what her mother was screaming about, so it took a moment to register what she was screaming outside the bathroom door.

"Charlie! Let me in, Charlie! Are you okay in there?" Charlotte sounded nearly delirious with panic as she pushed and pounded on the closed and seemingly locked door. "Charlie!"

As she watched her mother's panic, Emma saw her step back and look down at the floor outside the closed door. Water was quickly spreading out from under the door and pooling in the hall. An image of long dark hair fanning out in the water stabbed through Emma's mind; she gasped at the thought. Eyes wide, Charlotte began to scream and pound harder and Emma shook herself into action to run up and join her in her efforts to open the door. As soon as she touched it, the door flew open, causing the two women to nearly fall into the room.

Charlie was sitting in the tub, a mountain of bubbles piled on top of her head in a makeshift bouffant, her favourite bathtime hairstyle, talking softly to her doll as she dipped her wiry hair into the water. She jumped in surprise when her mother and grandmother spilled into the room. "What are you doing Mommy?" Charlie asked innocently. "You scared me! Nana, why are you crying?"

Charlotte rushed forward and hugged Charlie while she was still in the tub. Emma could see that she was clearly confused at what all the commotion was about. It suddenly dawned on her that there was no water on the floor, and that the tub was at the usual low level they used whenever they were bathing their little girl.

Finally Charlotte was able to let go of her granddaughter and she too was clearly confused with the whole situation. "Did not you hear me, sweetie? I was asking you to open the door. I was afraid."

"No Nana, I didn't hear anything. I was just playing mermaids with my doll and then you and Mommy came bursting in and scared me because I didn't hear you." She looked like she too was on the verge of tears now. It was clear that she was sensing their panic, so Emma stepped in to defuse the situation.

"It's okay honey. Nana just got scared, that's all, because the door got stuck, and you know we don't like you in the tub all by yourself." Emma intervened for her mother.

"I'm sorry, I was in here with her, and then I thought I saw someone in the hall, but when I went to see, there was nobody there, and the next thing I knew, the door slammed shut and I couldn't get in. It doesn't make any sense."

Seeing the look of concern and confusion on Charlie's face, Emma quickly took control of the situation. "I'm sure you were just pulling the door instead of pushing it. We do that sometimes too, hey Charlie? I bet Nana just gave herself a fright when she forgot which way to open the door. Silly Nana!" She shot her mother a look that told her to go along with the story and Charlotte finally snapped out of her state of shock and realised what Emma was trying to do.

"That's right," she agreed. "Silly me!"

Charlie looked slowly between her mother and grandmother then smiled widely and giggled. "Silly Nana!"

Emma offered to finish up bath time with Charlie so that her mother could get her bearings and Charlotte quickly accepted. She was still visibly shaken from what she had seen, or what she *thought* she had seen. The rest of Charlie's bath was uneventful, and the little girl seemed to brush off any concerns she had felt about her mother and grandmother's strange behaviour. Emma tucked her into bed and read her current favourite: *The Paper Bag Princess*. But Charlie was softly snoring before she could even finish. Closing up the tattered book they had read a million times, she watched her daughter drifting off peacefully, seemingly oblivious to the strange happenings which were going on in the house around her. She knew too though that it would not be long before she would sense that something was wrong with the adults in her life, and that they had a responsibility to figure out what was going on for her sake and for theirs. They had moved to this place for a more peaceful life after all, and it had been anything *but* lately.

By the time she got downstairs to check on her mother, John had just returned home from his walk. He and Max were both wet, as it had started lightly drizzling while they were on their way home. He took off his jacket and boots before turning to them. "It's not raining much out there, but I'm soaked to the bone! I'm just gonna go upstairs and..." John paused as he took in the expression on Emma's face, then turned to see a look which was even more startling on Charlotte's ashen face. "What's going on? What did I miss? Wait," he turned to Emma. "Did you tell her what happened today?"

"What do you mean? What happened today?" Charlotte seemed confused, and Emma knew she had been focused entirely on what had just happened with Charlie.

"I'll tell you everything," Emma assured her mother. "But first, I think we should fill John in on what just happened here."

"What do you mean? What happened?" John was clearly growing concerned.

Emma convinced him to go get changed into some dry clothes and that they would all have a drink and talk about everything that had gone on that day. She followed him to their bedroom, and while he changed, she retrieved the old leather book from her night table and quickly left the room to get back to her mother. Charlotte had poured them all a stiff drink, and Emma was grateful, knowing that they might need another by the time their conversation was done. She put the book on the coffee table in front of her and took the drink that her mother had made her, finishing off almost half of it in one swift gulp.

Charlotte showed no surprise, and did the same with her own. When John joined them, Emma first asked her mother to describe what had just happened upstairs. Charlotte explained in detail and was clearly hesitant to share about the water coming from under the door, and yet none being anywhere on the floor once they opened the door. Or perhaps, once the door opened *for* them it had seemed. "It must have been in my imagination I guess. I just panicked."

"Except that I saw the same thing when I came upstairs," Emma interrupted. "So what does that mean?"

Nobody had anything to say, so Emma continued on with her own account of what had happened on their hike. She was honest about the feeling of being *compelled* to dig, that she had noticed the depression in the grass and had been desperate to know what lay beneath. She remembered the sheer feeling of relief when John said that he had to go for a while so that she could be alone to do what she knew she had to do. She told them that when she had finished, and had found what she knew was there all along, that she had felt confused and exhausted, but also exhilarated.

"So what does it say?" Charlotte asked. "What is the book about?"

"I don't know," Emma replied. "I haven't opened it yet."

"Well," John interrupted, "maybe it's time we did that."

"Before we do," Charlotte stopped him before he could go any further, "I need to apologise, or I won't be able to live with myself."

CHAPTER TWENTY TWO

Lille, Northwest Territory, 1900

After what seemed like ages of living the difficult life in a mountain mining town, Olivia and Fisher settled into a content, if not comfortable, life in the bustling little community. They made many dear friends amongst the townsfolk, and counted Callum Hollis as one of the dearest. Callum doted on little Violet like a wealthy bachelor uncle, and could often be found at the Standen house for a weekend dinner or a weeknight drink with Fisher after a particularly difficult day.

Fisher enjoyed the challenges that came with the responsibilities of his position, but it was difficult on both he and Olivia that the days were often long and he was typically exhausted by the time he stumbled through the door for dinner. He rarely complained, and instead made the most of the time he had with his treasured girls. Violet adored her father and followed him relentlessly when he was finally home. Fisher did not mind, and the adoration was mutual. Though he and Olivia were open to another child, they were in no rush, as Violet was still so young. It would happen when it was time.

It was nearing the new year when Olivia visited her sister Margaret at her home in Frank. She had accepted a ride with the neighbours who were going into town to visit with friends for a few hours, but had planned to spend the night so that Violet could spend some time with her older cousins, who loved to lavish the busy toddler with endless attention. She and Margaret rarely got to see one another it seemed, even though their towns were very near to each other. Family life was a busy life, and making time for even the closest of sisters was not always easy, so both women were as giddy as schoolgirls on a long-awaited sleepover.

Once the children had been put to bed, Margaret emerged from the cellar with a bottle of wine, chosen especially for the occasion. She poured a deep, rich red glass for them both and handed one to Olivia before throwing herself onto the settee. "So I know it's short notice, but Harold and I want you to come to the New Year's Eve party at the hotel again this year. You can bring Violet here for the night with our childminder. I figured you wouldn't need much notice, since it's kind of becoming a tradition."

"I really appreciate the invitation, but I'm going to have to pass this year, I'm afraid." Olivia paused for a sip of wine. "Callum has invited us to a party at the Lille Hotel for the company. I know it's important to Fisher that we go. I'm sure we'll be able to resume the tradition next year, I promise."

"Callum huh? Seems pretty comfortable to be on a first name basis with your husband's boss. Are you sure this party is a good idea? I've heard some things about your Mr. Hollis, and they're not all good." Margaret's tone was calculated, as though she had been waiting for the opportunity to discuss this particular subject matter for a while.

"You are such a gossip!"

"How dare you," Margaret replied with mock offence. "You say that like it's a bad thing."

"Some would say it is," Olivia smirked at her sister. They had never kept a secret from one another in their lives and they both knew it.

"Well, in this case I would say there is cause for concern on a number of fronts."

"What do you mean by that?"

"First of all, the rumours I've heard are that this Mr. Hollis is a nasty piece of work. He cares more about money than he does about the men working for him, and it's not even his money really. I mean, he's really just a manager, not an owner. But I digress, that is beside the point. I've heard more than one person say that he's put the lives of men at risk for the sake of a dollar."

"That does not sound like the man I know. You should see him with Violet. He's like family. He did deliver her, after all. The connection is understandable."

"*Is* it though? He was in the right place at the right time, thank heavens, but does it have to be any more than that? *Should* it be?"

"I don't see the harm."

"You are being blind as well as foolish then," Margaret chided her sternly.

Olivia was stunned at her sister's tone. They never spoke to one another with such harsh words. "How dare you speak to me that way!"

Margaret took her sister's hand and apologised. "Forgive me, Liv. I didn't mean for it to sound that way. I'm just worried about you, that's all."

"I don't understand. What is there to be worried about?"

The older sister seemed to be searching her thoughts for the right words, though it was clear she had been thinking about this for a while. Finally, she explained her concern. "For one thing, as Fisher's superior, he spends too much time in your home. This kind of thing can lead to unforeseen complications and unwanted consequences as a result." Olivia started to intercede, but Margaret held up a hand to stop her and continued on with her thoughts, clearly eager to get them out once she had started. "For another thing, he is a bachelor, and an undeniably handsome one at that."

"Oh for heaven's sake! I hadn't noticed."

"What? That he's a bachelor or that he's good-looking? You might be a married woman, Olivia, but I know you're not blind."

"No, just not looking. I love Fisher. There could be no one else."

Margaret hugged her sister. "I know you do, Liv, but that doesn't mean that would stop a man like Callum Hollis if he got it in his head that he wanted what Fisher had. You are a beautiful woman, and you said it yourself that he already adores your child. It would not be that much of a jump for him to turn a wistful eye to her lovely mother as well, don't you think? Some men are used to getting everything they want. From everything I've heard, he's one of them."

"I think you're being a little paranoid and very unfair. There is nothing to suggest that Mr. Hollis has any designs on me. He is a great friend to Fisher and has been since we came to this godforsaken place. He has been a good friend to us both." Olivia stuck out her bottom lip and raised her eyebrow as was her custom when she was growing frustrated with a conversation. She was a truly loyal person, whether it was as a sister, a wife, or a friend, and she was growing defensive for Mr. Hollis. "Perhaps you should trust your sister and your brother-in-law over the opinions of the local gossips. Do you really think we would allow anyone around our daughter if he did not have our absolute trust?"

With a heavy sigh, Margaret relented, as it was clear that this conversation was going nowhere. "Just promise me you'll be careful. I would never want anything bad to happen."

"Enough! Nothing bad will happen. What *could* happen? You worry over nothing."

They both agreed to let it rest, but not until Olivia assured her sister that she would be vigilant, though she felt there was really no need. They spent the rest of their evening on lighter subjects, including the idiosyncrasies of their dear husbands which drove them mad and the amazing feats of brilliance displayed by their perfectly imperfect children. They dug through Margaret's closet, which was more well-endowed than Olivia's, so that they could choose the perfect outfits for their upcoming New Year's Eve parties. Olivia chose a lovely scarlet dress which her sister proclaimed was a surefire method of turning every head in the room.

"Thank you sis." Olivia smiled and took Margaret's hand, looking directly into her deep, dark eyes. "For *everything*."

On the night of the party, Olivia took her sister up on her offer and arranged for Violet to stay with Michael and Angela, even though they weren't going to be going to the party at the Frank Hotel. They planned for Margaret to bring Violet back to Lille the next afternoon while the men were at work. The women would have a late lunch with the children and swap stories about the highlights of their evenings as a way to ring in the new year together to make up for the missed opportunity to attend a rare soiree together.

Although she felt a little guilty about leaving Violet at her sister's for the evening and for not attending Harold's party, Olivia was glad that she and Fisher had decided to accept the invitation to attend the party at the Lille Hotel instead. They had spent the night dancing, drinking and talking with friends. She and Fisher had not been so carefree since they had become parents, likely because they did not have to worry about getting home to their daughter, as it was her first night away from her parents overnight.

It did Olivia's heart good to see her husband having such a good time. It seemed sometimes like all he did was work, for her, for them. But still, it was good to see him looking like he did when she had first seen him that night at her cousin's wedding. She had never seen him before, and was struck by how the mere sight of him sent a warm flush up under her collar. Nervous to meet him in case she might burst into flames, or at the very least, that he would notice how much he affected her with his mere presence, in the end, she brought their meeting on herself. He felt the heat of her eyes boring into him from across the room and once he took notice of her, the way *she* had of *him*, he too was instantly smitten.

Fisher had not hesitated to approach her and had asked her to dance. Olivia, of course, had said *yes*, and before they knew it, they had danced the night away. This night felt like that one in many ways. The way he looked at her made her feel warm all over and she could not wait to get home alone with him and feel his hands on her body. The excitement of the new year and a fresh start enveloped the room in an atmosphere of good cheer.

Margaret's words of warning resonated in her mind, and though she had no intention of concerning herself with her sister's needless worries, she could not help but pay closer attention to Callum. More than once she had turned to find him in the crowd, only to find him watching her. She told herself that it was because she'd had too much to drink and was feeling a little tipsy. It was more plausible that she was misreading the situation. As she had told Margaret, he was a good friend, and nothing more. Still, something in her was suddenly on guard, whether she wanted to admit it or not. Whether it was justified or not.

Having lost track of the time and her husband as the night advanced, Olivia found herself searching for him at the strike of the clock to mark the midnight turning of the calendar year. She pushed through the tightly packed crowd of partiers in search of Fisher. Instead, she ran directly into Callum. She found herself crushed against him and apologised as she looked for an escape route.

"Sorry," she shouted above the crowd.

As he bent down so that he could be closer and not have to shout at her, she could smell the faint sting of whisky on his breath. "No need to apologise." He smiled sweetly. "I'm glad we ran into each other."

Without warning he leaned in and kissed her, so that she had no time to react. It was a brief kiss, but it was hard and intense, meant to convey a strong message in a fleeting moment. She felt his lips on hers, and then he was smiling conspiratorially, gripping her arm as he stared longingly into her eyes. As he leaned in close again she jumped back defensively, though she was still pressed in against him by the crowd, still revelling in their mutual cheer. But he did not kiss her again, as she feared he might, but instead whispered in her ear, "Happy New Year, Olivia."

She mumbled, "And to you too," and pulled away from his grip. "I have to go. I have to find Fisher."

Callum nodded and smiled knowingly. As she pushed her way through the crowd she felt like she was fighting the need to hyperventilate. Instead of searching for her husband, she now found herself searching for the exit so that she could get a dose of the freezing night air of the mountain winter. She was feeling as though she might faint and needed to get out and away from the gregarious crowd.

In her panic, she did not see Fisher, who had just come in the way that she was making her way to leave. She did not see the look on his face, a look which said that he had seen it all, a kiss he would never be able to banish from his mind's eye. He was a good man and a trusting man, who knew his wife loved him and their family. But that kiss had not meant nothing, he could feel the heat of it from where he stood across the room. Still, he would not jump to conclusions. Surely Olivia would tell him what had happened when they were alone together at home and they would decide what to do from there.

In the cold darkness of the winter night, Olivia stood stock still and in shock, running through what had happened and whether she should have seen it coming. She had been watching him all night. Perhaps he had misread that and assumed that she had been watching him because she had discovered some source of feelings toward him. Perhaps she was to blame for what had happened. But no, she had not asked him to do it, she had not seen it coming, and she had no chance to even react. *But a part of you liked it*, she accused herself. *No!* She answered herself with immediate vigour, but she was not sure of herself anymore.

When she and Fisher returned home they were unusually quiet. She assumed he was tired, but he was merely giving her the chance to tell him what had happened and how it had happened. He knew he could trust her, but as the night wore on and they found themselves in their bed together and she had still not breathed a word, he could not help but wonder if his trust was misplaced after all. He did what he could to explain it all away, but it seemed his wife would be no help in that area.

When they finally turned in for the night she caressed his arm and moved closer to him, but for the first time in their marriage, he turned away from her. Though she was shocked, she tried not to read too much into it, assuring herself that he'd had too much to drink and that he would likely be waking her in the early morning before heading to work for his shift. Despite her own assurances, she found herself choked with guilt. Still, she decided at that moment that she would say nothing to Fisher until she talked to Margaret and got her advice on how to handle the situation. She hated keeping anything from her husband. She knew how much he trusted her: as much as she trusted him. But she was not even sure what she would say and what he could even do about it. Really, she might just be putting him in the difficult position of having to confront his boss about what he had done, when they could not afford to put his job at risk.

Margaret had been right all along; personal relations with the boss were too complicated and not a good idea. She would find a way to distance herself, but realised it might be very difficult because Callum was both Fisher's boss and a good friend, or so she had thought. But she was already questioning her own assumptions and how much of what she had felt in the moment was the result of her sister's suggestion. Perhaps it was just an innocent and platonic new year's kiss, which meant nothing, and she was just overreacting. If that was the case, then Fisher need never know, because it would only serve to hurt him, and unnecessarily so. As she pondered her query, in the darkness, her husband pulled further away from her, but she was too lost in thought to notice.

The next morning, she awoke, but Fisher was already gone. She was hurt at first, wondering why he did not wake her up to take advantage of their time alone, but then she scolded herself for assuming the worst and assured herself that he was just letting her sleep off last night's party. Again she was reminded of what a good husband he was and how fortunate she was to have found a man like him, even if they did not have the lifestyle she and her sister had grown up with and her sister still enjoyed. Those things did not matter to her, as long as she had Fisher's love and devotion.

Olivia was reminded again of why she would be keeping what had happened to herself, except of course for talking with Margaret, who she could trust just as much as talking to herself. Now she found herself torn about whether or not she should confront Callum on her own, or simply move on as though nothing had ever happened. She had smelled the whisky on his breath, after all; it was probably fair to assume that he'd had too much to drink and was either already regretting what he had done, or did not even remember it anyway, in which case a dramatic confrontation would be nothing short of mortifyingly embarrassing for both of them.

And so she decided that it would be best if she kept her thoughts to herself on all fronts and tried to forget that the moment had ever happened. Sparing Fisher the details would avoid unnecessary hurt and concern over his boss' intentions. In the light of day, with a decidedly clearer head, she decided that surely Callum had not intended anything by it and that she herself had made it all up in her head: the way she had seen him looking at her over the course of the evening, the way he *kissed* her.

The seeds of paranoia had been planted by her wary sister. When she thought about it, she felt embarrassed for her overreaction and she was glad to have let the night pass before deciding what to do about it. She moaned aloud when she realised that he had probably been wondering himself why she had kept looking at him so strangely all night. What kind of a message might she have unwittingly sent?

Olivia tried not to think about it any further while she prepared for the arrival of Margaret and the children. She swept the floors as she did every morning as the coffee began to bubble on the formidable cast iron stove, the delicious toasty aroma filling the tiny house. Once she had the kitchen clean she quickly prepared some biscuits for her visit with her sister but realised that there was no butter in the ice box. The thought of serving her sister dry biscuits in her tiny kitchen embarrassed her even further, so she quickly threw on her wool shawl and warm hat and went out into the brisk January morning. She knew she could make it to the Lille General Store and back well before her sister arrived.

The town was sleepy, though many of the men were still at work. Coal mining did not take a day off. In fact, most of the businesses in the tiny town were still open for service on New Year's Day, unwilling and unable to miss the opportunity to make a dime or to provide a necessary service. The only days off were Sundays and holy days, unless you were a miner, in which case you had no holidays, unless you were fortunate enough to be in line for the privilege. For the miners, every day was like the last, a prayer before going into the darkness of the deep and a *Hallelujah*! once emerging from it. Down in the depths of the earth, there were anything but holy words from the mouths of the men, who were as hard as the rock they toiled and died for. They lived hard, they worked hard, and they often died hard.

When Olivia turned the corner onto the road which her house was on, she found herself face-to-face with Callum Hollis. He smiled at her sheepishly. *He came here hoping to run into me.* The thought came to her at the sight of him. She forced herself to smile back with as little awkwardness as possible. She hoped that he would not bring up the night before.

"Good morning, Mr. Hollis."

He feigned hurt feelings, and teased her. "Good morning, *Mrs. Standen.* I see we stand on formality today. I had hoped we were beyond that."

"Sorry, I…" Olivia stammered, caught off guard by his nonchalant swagger, unsure of what to say. But he interrupted her and took away the need for her to reply.

"No need. I'm only kidding." He grinned wolfishly. "*You* can call me whatever you want, *Olivia.*" Before she could say anything, he took her hand and kissed it, while he gazed deeply into her eyes. Though he was a difficult man to read, he made no effort to conceal how he felt, though it was difficult to know what that meant exactly.

He knew that she was a happily married woman. She could not imagine what he was thinking. His behaviour was so inappropriate that she did not know what to say, but pulled her hand away from him and smiled curtly. "Thank you so much, *Mr. Hollis.* I'm sorry, but I have to be getting home. Violet will be here with my sister any time now. It was nice to see you."

"It was lovely to see you Olivia. Be sure to say hello to little Violet for me."

Olivia nodded and hurried away blushing. She found herself wishing that this man had no connection to her or her daughter. What if they came to regret letting him into their lives? She found that she no longer trusted him the way she once had. It was hard to believe that she had considered him to be a friend at the same time just the day before. As Margaret's warning voice came to her again, she heard herself reply so stupidly, so *naively*, and she blushed even harder.

Olivia reached her house without even realising she was moving toward it, her feet moving automatically over the short path she took so often to the main street of town. As she went to turn into the pathway to her front door, she glanced back and gasped in a breath of icy air when she saw that Callum was still standing and watching her. A chill ran over her entire body and she bolted quickly through the front door, throwing off her hat, but pulling her shawl closer before moving to stoke the fire she had left behind while on her trip to the store.

She blew into her hands and warmed them by the fire. Once she was warm, she pulled her rocking chair closer to the wood stove and tried to rock herself steady, to calm herself and think through all that had transpired since the night before.

Lost in thought, the time passed and the fire almost died down, so that when Margaret rapped on the door before letting herself in with the children, Olivia jumped out of her chair and filled the stove with more fuel to burn. Violet settled happily into her mother's arms, her little cheeks red with the chill of the frosty morning air. Even her little red lips were cold as her mother planted a loving kiss on them.

"Brrrrr, it's chilly in here," Margaret complained loudly. "What have you been doing here sister? Certainly not keeping the fire lit from the look of things."

"Good morning to you too sister," Olivia replied, arms crossed. "So good to see you."

"Sorry, but it's true, the poor children are already half frozen. Did you fall asleep by the fire? A bit of a wild night last night perhaps? Feeling a little under the weather today after all of your gallivanting?" Margaret was relentless with her teasing, but her sister's response, or lack thereof, quickly changed her tune.

"I guess you could say that. I was not thinking, but I definitely had a lot on my mind. I guess I was distracted. I'm sorry you had to come to a cold house. It should warm up quickly. One of the few benefits of such a small place."

Margaret looked at her sister sidelong with concern and curiosity. It was obvious that something was on Olivia's mind. Something was bothering her. She also knew better than to bring it up around the always-listening ears of the children, so she suggested that they have their snack so that Violet could go down for a nap while the children went down the street to visit some friends they were eager to see, as trips between the towns, as close as they were by miles, were sparse. Life was too busy for frivolous trips on most days of the year. Olivia agreed, as she warmed the coffee and the biscuits on the stove.

Once they had finished their snack and were thoroughly warmed, the children headed out into the sunny winter day and Violet put her head on her mother's shoulder as she carried her off to her bed for a much needed nap. She had hardly sat back down at the table before Margaret started in. "What happened last night? I know you, Olivia. You aren't yourself this morning."

Unsure of how to start, Olivia started at the beginning and told Margaret how she had listened to her warning and had been vigilant throughout the night, paying attention to Callum's every move. "Maybe I brought this on myself," she worried. "Maybe he got the wrong impression."

"How could he get the wrong impression if he didn't know you were watching him? Why, he'd have to be watching *you*."

Olivia looked into her sister's eyes and Margaret understood at once. "But that's not even the worst of it," she continued. She told Margaret about the kiss and about how Callum had behaved so strangely when she had run into him on her way home this morning, admitting that she had felt uncomfortable with the way he looked at her, the way he touched her, the way he kissed her again, if only on the hand.

Margaret's face showed her clear disgust with what this man had put her sister through and her response was swift. "You are not to blame for this beast's despicable actions. He is fully aware that you are a married woman! He claims to be a friend of your husband's, but clearly, he is nobody's friend. Fisher must be livid!"

The shock and confusion on Olivia's face at the mention of Fisher was obvious. Margaret gasped. "You haven't told him? Olivia! You have to tell him!"

Olivia shook her head in disagreement. "No, you're wrong. What can Fisher do? This is his boss we're talking about. It's not like he can quit his job. Why would I put him in that position? What is there to be gained?"

"No, *you're* wrong, dear sister. There might not be anything to be *gained* in this situation, but let me warn you, there is plenty to be *lost*. With a man like this on the prowl, Fisher should already know. What will you do if he brings this Mr. Hollis here to your home again?"

The perturbed look on Olivia's face showed that she had not considered this. She had assumed that Callum would keep his distance once he realised that she did not harbour any affections toward him. But she knew that Margaret could be right. He might use his relationship with Fisher as a means to get closer to her if his motives were unscrupulous, and she was beginning to believe more and more that they were, especially now that she had voiced her concerns aloud and listened to the worry in her elder sister's voice.

Margaret took Olivia's hand and smiled reassuringly. "Everything is going to be okay Liv. You just need to be honest with your husband. You know I'm right. Fisher would never prioritise a job over his wife, and nobody is saying this needs to affect his work anyway. If he knows what has happened, then at least he can keep the man at an arm's length from now on and spare you the attention of this, this…"

"Don't say it," Olivia interrupted her. "He's not worth it. I know you're probably right, and I promise, I will think about telling Fisher, but give me time. I need to consider the possible consequences of the situation before I do anything. I know that honesty is important in a marriage…"

"It's not just important! It's everything! Without it, you have nothing."

Olivia sighed heavily. She hated it when her sister insisted on being right. She knew she was not really being listened to, but carried on trying to explain herself anyway. "I *know* it's important, but so is supporting your husband in his dreams and endeavours. You did not hesitate to move out here, away from the city and the life you loved, to make your husband happy. You and I both know that the hotel was *his* baby, not yours. It was *Harry* who had this dream of living in the heart of coal country, in the shadow of the mountains, not *you*."

"I do not see how you can compare the two situations. I'm not keeping anything from my husband, but you are, and from the sounds of it, you do not have any intention of changing your mind about that any time soon."

"I didn't say my mind was made up. I told you that I would consider what you had to say and I meant it, but this isn't an easy situation for me. I need some time to think."

"This decision should require very little time and thought, because it really isn't a decision at all if you're wise, dear sister."

"Enough Margaret! Please let it go now. I will take all you have said into consideration, but I still need time to think."

Margaret crossed her arms and pouted. Unable to ever allow her sister to have the last word on a subject, she gave one last warning, "Fine, I'll let it go, for now, but do not take too long contemplating what you should do about Callum Hollis, Liv. These things have a way of spiralling out of control more quickly than you might imagine. There's no telling what could happen with a man like that."

When the children returned from their visit and Violet awoke with the excited voices of her cousins telling their mother about their time with their friends, the conversation between the two women was officially over. Before long, Margaret was piling the children into the carriage sleigh to head back down the mountain to Frank. Olivia and Violet stepped out into the cold day to wave good-bye. Shielding her eyes from the white glare of the sky, Olivia warned her sister. "Be careful, but be swift getting home. It looks like the weather is threatening to turn ugly today."

Margaret shielded her own eyes and looked to the west, where the clouds were advancing quickly and turning a menacing shade of charcoal grey. "I think you may be right. We're off then. Don't forget what we talked about, Olivia. Don't forget how much I love you. I only want what's best for you."

"You'd be wise to get ahead of the storm that is surely coming." Olivia changed the subject with a curt smile.

"I will say the same to you, dear sister. Make sure you get ahead of that storm yourself."

After threatening for the rest of that gloomy day, the storm finally took hold in the evening after dinner. Absorbed in her own thoughts of confusion and guilt, Olivia remained oblivious to the distant mood which had overtaken her usually warm and passionate husband. She did not notice how instead of coming to their bed, he would fall asleep in his reading chair beside the hot stove, though in reality, he slept very little in those days following the party and the scene he had encountered there at midnight, the incident his beloved wife had still to inform him of.

Fisher had always assumed that the trust and loyalty between them could not be broken. He had assumed and still knew that nothing was going on between them, at least not from Olivia's side of things. But he had also assumed that she would waste no time in telling him what had happened, so that he, as her husband, would know not to trust this man who he had trusted as a friend. No friend of his would have ever kissed his wife the way that Callum Hollis had kissed his wife that night. He had seen the way that he had looked at her, however brief the moment, and knew the meaning behind that look.

He had assumed that Olivia would have told him, if not on the short trip home from the Lille Hotel, then at least when they arrived home and were finally alone. Now after days had passed, it was clear that she had no intention of saying anything about it. He could not help but wonder why, and the distance grew between them. She did not notice the space he was taking from her, further and further each day, as she was so wrapped in the feverish blanket of her own thoughts. But he had noticed her lack of attention to his sudden change in demeanour, and grew even more wary still about the state of his marriage.

He was stirred from his restless sleep in his increasingly uncomfortable chair by a loud rapping on the wooden front door. It rang loudly through the house in the darkness and Violet began to whimper in her bed. Fisher sprang to the door to prevent the interloper from disturbing the peace any further. Standing in the raging storm, his greying hair plastered to his forehead, as he had foolishly removed his cap in the blowing snow, was Emery Clark, his partner on the opposite shift. It was not like Emery to disturb Fisher when he was not on shift, highlighting the gravity of the situation.

"Emery, come in! What brings you here so late?"

Emery paused briefly as he visibly registered the fact that Fisher was fully dressed, as though he had never been to bed, though it was already on the morning side of the night. Finally, he blurted out what he had come for. "It's the storm; she's knocked out one of the trestles on the train bridge. Mr. Hollis says it needs to be repaired immediately. He says any delays in getting the trains in could spell disaster for the mine and the town. He told me I needed to get down there now to shore up the damage."

"Jesus," Fisher swore without thinking. "Sorry Emery. What do you need?"

"Well, it's not me really."

"What do you mean?"

"Well," he hesitated again, as though it pained him to say what he needed to say. "I mean, I told him that I wouldn't do it tonight. I told him the storm is too wild. It's not safe for anyone to be up there on that bridge in this. It's madness!"

Fisher seemed surprised and impressed with the old man. "So what did he say to that?"

"He demanded for me to come and get you. He insulted me, Fisher. Said if I was not man enough to do it, maybe you would be. Said that he'd prefer a young man on the job anyway. I told him that I wouldn't bother you at this hour of the night for something that could wait for the morning. And he said that I would if I wanted to keep my job. He really is a dirty bastard, that one. Pardon my language."

Fisher shook his head and chuckled. "We'll call it even."

"You're not going to do it are you? It's storming too hard out there. You wouldn't be able to see your hand in front of your own face." Both men turned to see Olivia, standing in the bedroom doorway in her nightgown and housecoat, listening to what they had been discussing.

Fisher's face changed slightly and Olivia finally noticed the hardness that he felt toward her. Without answering her he turned to Emery. "Well, I guess I'd better get going. The boss won't be kept waiting from the sounds of it."

"Fisher no!" Olivia protested and Emery was clearly uncomfortable, but Fisher was unmoved. Olivia begged him to reconsider. "It's too dangerous. Please don't leave us here alone!"

But her begging fell on deaf ears. Fisher said nothing as he dressed for the frigid night. He ignored Emery when he said that he agreed with "*the missus*" and that it was too dangerous to attempt in the dark, howling storm. Fisher headed into the night without another word, only taking a moment to glance in the direction of his distraught wife. She could see in his expression a deep hurt that she did not understand. With the slamming of the heavy door, he went out into the night with the old man ahead of him, awkwardly apologising to them both as he was herded out the door.

Returning to her bed was a pointless endeavour. Olivia could not sleep for even a moment. Every time she thought about the look on Fisher's face, a look like he was regarding her as a stranger somehow, her heart pounded fiercely and she flushed furiously. There was something to it. *Could he know? No. But, why not?* It's not like Lille was a big city. It's not like the kiss didn't happen in front of anyone who might have happened to look in their direction at that moment. *Anyone...*

Olivia was suddenly struck by a deep terror that in fact Fisher *did* know what had happened at the party that night. Perhaps, horror of horrors, he had seen it all for himself. But why wouldn't he have said anything? He would have said *something.* She searched her memory of the past few days since the party and saw the signs that had been so obvious: the long nights away from their bed, the half-eaten meals, the quiet between them. Could it be? She wished that she had listened to Margaret and told him everything right away. If he had known, if he had *seen,* then he would have been waiting for her to talk to him. And all he would have gotten on her part was silence. She was furious with herself and vowed to tell him everything when he got home.

Olivia stoked the fire in the stove and put a pot of coffee on to brew. A mixed feeling of hope, relief and dread hung over her heart as she waited for the day to begin. Though she feared what Fisher would say about what had happened, and even worse, the fact that she had kept it from him for so long, she was also relieved at the thought of having it over with and getting her marriage back to where it should be.

Olivia knew she could never love another man. There was never any doubt about that. She had given up a life of comfort and security to be Fisher's wife, and never regretted it for a moment. He was a good man and a good husband. He was worth any sacrifice she had ever made to be with him. Though she struggled to see the life she had left behind as a sacrifice. She was much happier with the unreserved affection she shared with this good man and would not give it up for anything. Theirs was a special relationship, based on true love and respect for one another. She knew how fortunate she was in love, with a wonderful husband and daughter, even if they did not have much else.

It was hard to believe that one man could cause so much havoc with so little effort. It had not been so long ago that these thoughts were nothing to her; they did not exist. She wished it could be that way again. Perhaps, once she told Fisher the truth about everything, it could be.

She was sipping her coffee, which was almost too strong to drink, when there was a soft knocking at the door. Outside, the hint of morning light had still not arrived, and here was someone at her door. A feeling of dread fell so heavily over her heart that she waited for the second knock before slowly rising to answer it. Standing with his hat in his hands and tears in his almost-white grey eyes, at a wholly ungodly hour for the second time in a matter of hours, stood Emery Clark. He sobbed as he told her. "I'm so sorry missus, it's your husband, it's Fisher..."

Before he could say anything more, Olivia collapsed to the rough wooden floor. Emery sat beside her, panicked, until she came to. She barely had time to gather herself before Violet began to cry in the next room. The old man tried to go on explaining. "I told him not to go up there missus, but he would not listen to no sense. It was blowing too hard and the ice had gathered up on the trestles. He lost his footing up there. He fell. I tried to help… I, I was already too late. I'm so sorry. I told him not to go up there."

She found herself in the impossible position of reassuring this old man at the worst moment of her entire life and felt she had no other choice. "It's not your fault Emery. I heard you. We both tried… I need you to go now please. I need to be alone with my little girl. I have no idea what I'm going to tell her. I have no idea what I'm going to do."

"I'm so sorry. I'm *so* sorry."

Olivia nodded and guided the distraught man to the door, then quickly made her way to the bedroom to her daughter. She wiped her tears and did her best to gather herself. It was no lie, she truly had no idea what she was going to do. Walking into her daughter's room, she was as pale as a ghost. In her heart, she felt like she just might be one.

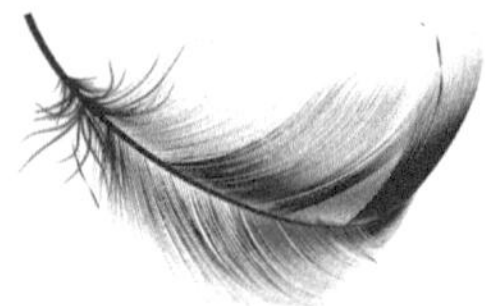

CHAPTER TWENTY THREE

Charlotte insisted that they all sit before she explained why she needed to apologise to her daughter. Emma had a sense that she might actually already know, and that she would rather just leave it alone. She had tried to press the sentiment with her mother, telling her that she had nothing to be sorry for, but Charlotte would have none of it. Of course John already seemed to know as well, since clearly he had been talking with her mother about his concerns before she had come to visit. Though she had been frustrated and annoyed, she also understood his concern, and knew that she had given him every reason to worry, so her feelings toward him were unwarranted.

"When John called me," her mother began hesitantly, "and explained what was going on with you, I assumed that you might be heading down the same path you had years ago. I'll admit, I was scared. Scared for you, scared for your family, especially Charlie. The last thing I wanted was to see you go through all of that again, to see us *all* go through it again I guess, if I'm being honest. Maybe it's selfish, but I did not think *I* could handle it again."

Emma felt herself welling up as she took her mother's hand. "I understand Mom. You don't have to explain."

"But I do," Charlotte insisted. "I want you to know that I didn't just take it on what John had to say. I needed to see for myself, so I asked if I could come visit. And with everything you told me, then the way you acted that night when you ran into the house in a panic, well, I really did think that you were in trouble again. I thought..."

"I know what you thought, and I can't say that I blame you. My behaviour hasn't been very rational lately."

Charlotte shook her head in disagreement. "From what I witnessed myself tonight, I would say that your behaviour has been totally understandable with what's been going on. Any doubt I had about," she hesitated briefly, as though she were seeking the right words, "your *mental state* is gone. Whatever you're dealing with here, it's not in your head. That means that whatever is going on here, it's real, and we should be taking it seriously."

"I have to agree," John chimed in. "If you both experienced the same thing, it has to be real. I'm sorry for jumping to conclusions. I was just so worried about you."

"Okay, now please let me speak," Emma interrupted. "I appreciate you both apologising for what you thought was going on, but like I said, I do understand why you felt the way you did. I just want to let it go now. I am completely exhausted. I think I'm going to head to bed early tonight. Would you mind if we left the book till tomorrow? I'm eager to take a look at it together, but I'm spent right now."

They said they understood and that the book could wait. It was still early, so John and Charlotte were still going to stay up. Emma kissed them both good night and made her way upstairs. When she was ready for bed she laid alone and stared at the ceiling, trying to push away the memories which had been brought to the surface by the discussion with her mother and John. She groaned and rolled over, trying to physically turn away from the intrusive thoughts she fought so hard to avoid, but it was too late. Unwillingly, she was returning to that time years before, when Charlie was still an infant and everything had gone so wrong.

Her pregnancy had not been easy. In fact, the entire reason she had found out that she was pregnant was because she had been so inexplicably ill. It had happened so quickly that she was in a panic by the time she reached the clinic to ask if they could see her. Emma had been so sick for two days that when they asked if she could come in two days' time to see the doctor, she burst into tears and begged them to give her a flu shot or an anti-nauseant, as she had progressed to the point where she could no longer even keep a few sips of water down. She had not been exaggerating when she cried and begged for help, fearful that she might die if she waited another two days. After putting her on hold for what seemed like a lifetime, the receptionist came back on and told her that she could squeeze her in to see her doctor that afternoon.

While sitting in the waiting room in the clinic, she had to keep a waste basket between her feet for all of the horrendously loud vomiting. She could feel the others in the room trying not to look at her and everyone involved was thoroughly relieved when she was led into a private room to wait for the doctor. When the doctor asked if she might be pregnant, she reacted with shock, then had a creeping realisation that she just might be. After taking a quick test, she was informed that she was indeed pregnant. She was still quite early on, which she had already realised, since she had barely even registered that she was late that month.

The doctor encouraged her to make a follow-up appointment for a thorough exam when she was feeling a little less green around the gills and prescribed her an anti-nauseant so that she could carry on with her life, even though she knew this would change everything for her and John. They would have a lot less freedom, but the progress forward was at exactly the right time in their relationship. They were happy and they were financially sound. There was no reason not to be thrilled for the new baby; she could only bring joy to their lives.

Emma stayed on the treatment for her nausea for a full five months of her pregnancy, which was longer than she had hoped, but there were no other options. Even with the medication she suffered with morning sickness, just on a more reasonable level so that she did not have to fear for her well-being and that of her baby. Once the sickness passed, she gave in to every craving she had, which included fairly normal choices like spicy chicken burgers and excessive amounts of pickles and chocolate milk. Of course, there were the less conventional cravings as well, which included strange combinations like fresh-cut lemon wedges with mint chocolate ice cream.

Before she reached eight months, she was put on a special diet, as her love of all things chocolate and her unwillingness to deny any of her cravings after five months of virtual starvation, had led her to borderline gestational diabetes. By the final month of her pregnancy, she was suffering from hypertension and was ordered to bed rest, which was fine with her, since her feet were terribly swollen. The worst of it was the extreme boredom of being stuck in bed alone all day. Thankfully, John was amazing throughout the pregnancy and catered to her every whim. Her mother was also the picture of maternal support, and her best friend Joni stopped by almost daily, even if it was just for a few minutes. Really, she had to admit that she had been quite spoiled at the time.

When the time finally came for the baby to be born, the birth was difficult and dramatic, but after more than a day of labour, Charlie was finally born. Emma and John were immediately smitten with their perfect little girl. When they went home, John spent the first week away from work so that he could give Emma time to rest while he helped out with the tiny new baby. When the time came for him to return to work full-time, Charlotte made a point of stopping by each day to lend a hand. But the time came that Emma was on her own, and despite her crippling fatigue, she had to live up to her maternal responsibilities.

Emma could tell that something was not right, but she could not tell *what* or *why*. Though she loved Charlie desperately, she found herself constantly afraid that something was going to happen to her, although she was not sure why she felt that way. She felt an overwhelming need to protect her daughter from any harm, which at first meant that she struggled with being overly picky about her daily care, when she ate and slept, when she was changed, even if she did not need to be. Before long her fears kept her at home, away from others who could not be trusted with her most cherished little girl. By the time that Charlie was four-months-old, Emma found herself constantly watching John when he was with her. Overly critical of the way he held her, the way he bathed her, the way he rocked her to sleep and burped her when she was done eating, it seemed there was nothing he could do right. John took it all in stride, knowing that his wife was exhausted, and that she did not mean to be so nit-picky. He assumed she would outgrow it as she got used to being a mother, but in fact things only seemed to grow worse over time.

Emma became so controlling, that finally, she seemed unwilling or unable to even let John hold his daughter. His patience was growing thin, though this just pushed her further away from him still. After an especially vicious fight over Charlie and the fact that John had bought the wrong diaper cream at the pharmacy that day, he returned home from work to find her gone. Charlie's baby bag had been packed and so was Emma's overnight bag. Though he tried to be calm about the situation, when the clock passed eleven and there was still no response to the messages he had left for her, John began to panic. He reluctantly called Charlotte, not wanting to worry her about the situation, but by now he felt he had no other choice. She immediately came to the house to console her son-in-law and to figure out where her daughter and granddaughter had gone. When she arrived, she was able to deliver the good news that she had heard from Emma and that she and the baby were at a motel.

John had been bewildered and horrified at the thought of his wife and new baby in some seedy motel, that she would rather be there than with him. Then it had occurred to him that she was willing to stay in such a place with Charlie, by choice, finally illuminating for him the possible depth of the problem. John started to backtrack and examine his wife's behaviour since she had become a new mother. There were subtle changes which added up to more severe shifts in behaviour over time: how she had grown more and more paranoid over the baby, how this had equated to her becoming overly controlling, making him feel like she saw him as less of a parent than she was. He was finally able to see so clearly what was really going on. His wife was in real trouble, and he had let it get worse than he could have ever imagined. John had no idea what he should do and simply fell apart. It was his mother-in-law who stepped up to do what needed to be done.

Charlotte got John to sit tight while she set to work on convincing Emma to come and stay with her until she knew what she wanted to do. She even took time off work to stay at home with Emma and the baby. It wasn't long before John's suspicions were proven to be true: Emma was suffering from postpartum depression. Although it took time and patience, Charlotte was able to convince her daughter to see a doctor. When he admitted her to the psychiatric ward at the local hospital for six weeks of treatment, Charlotte and John were both shocked. They had not expected that she would need such an intense level of support. They visited her as much as they were able, and though they brought Charlie to see her every time, Emma missed her infant daughter desperately, and was willing to do whatever it took to get well and get home to her family again.

Even when she was finally able to return home, she needed continued medication and therapy. Though she was over the worst of the acute bout of depression, caused by a severe imbalance in her hormones after the birth, she was still struggling to cope with the sometimes crippling anxiety that came with what had happened when she was at her worst. She had cut John out. She had taken his daughter away from him and belittled him as a father and a husband. There was a part of her that was convinced that there was no way that he could ever forgive her for what she had done, that it would be a black mark on their marriage.

John was tireless in rebuilding trust with his wife, which seemed backward in her mind, as she was the one who had shown she could not be trusted. But John was too reasonable and loved her too much to give in to this kind of thinking. He knew that she had to learn to trust him, regardless of what she had done. She had not been herself at the time, and he was not going anywhere. They would not give up on their family.

Over time, with the love and support of her family and close friends, things had grown better, *she* had grown better. It took work and patience before she felt confident as a mother, and even longer to regain her confidence as a wife. But as always, John was strong and stood beside her every step of the way. Though things had been good for a long time now, Emma still had moments where she felt anxious, sometimes even panicked, where her marriage was concerned. She knew that she could trust John at his word, that he had truly forgiven her long ago, but a part of her was convinced that at some point he would come to realise that she simply was not worth all that she had put him through. And now, it seemed, continued to put him through with all of the issues she had conjured up with their new house. Her anxiety was building and she convinced herself to calm down, taking slow deep breaths and counting backwards in threes from three-hundred to clear her mind of the racing thoughts which were plaguing her once again. *Two-ninety-seven, two-ninety-four, two-ninety-one...* She found herself losing track of her countdown and having to start over as her mind continued to fixate on the problem at hand.

As was often the case when Emma used the countdown trick to calm herself, her constant stops and starts eventually served the purpose to finally put her to sleep, though it was shallow and fitful. She awoke to the realisation that she had fallen asleep and that some time had passed because it was considerably darker in the room. Looking at the clock she was surprised to see that it read *4:10*, and though it sparked a momentary sense of deja vu, she was too tired to pay the feeling any notice.

Remembering at once what she had been trying to forget as she counted herself to sleep, she was relieved to feel John's arm draped over her waist. She moved her hips and pushed back into him and he stirred, pulling her closer and kissing her neck as she softly moaned. Then he pulled away from her and laid back in the bed as he ran his fingers down her back. Emma smiled to herself, and though she was still more asleep than she was awake, she was not about to turn him away after the night she had experienced. Before turning to him, she pushed herself up onto her forearm to take a sip of the water she always kept beside the bed.

As she turned to him she was smiling coyly, but her expression quickly turned to one of sheer horror when she realised that she was in their bed alone. She slapped her hand to her mouth to stifle the scream which would have shook the whole house awake. Throwing back the sheets she practically fell out of the bed and twisted her ankle when she hit the floor at an awkward angle and again had to stifle the urge to cry out. Without realising it, she was silently crying, a mix of frustration, pain and terror.

When a hand reached out from under the bed, grabbing her by her twisted ankle, she hollered out in excruciating pain, but the fear overwhelmed all. Emma pulled her foot away from the dead grey hand as she shrieked uncontrollably, crawling to the door and pulling it open as she fell into the hallway.

Looking back over her shoulder, as she lay sprawled on the floor in the hall, she could see that there was nobody under the bed. It occurred to her that the house was quiet and still, which surprised her, as she had made so much noise. There was no way the closed door could have stopped the rest of the house from hearing her.

Crying, she pulled herself up and limped down the hall to Charlie's room to find her sleeping deeply. Next, she checked in on her mother who was also fast asleep. Emma was baffled at how they could have slept through her shrieks of terror. She found herself wondering where John was when he should have been sleeping beside her.

Descending the creaking stairs, she expected to find her husband sleeping in some uncomfortable position on the sofa, as she had more than once when he had fallen asleep in front of the television. But he was not there. She looked out the front window, and out the back, but he was nowhere in sight. Her senses tuned like a frightened cat, she turned automatically to a nearly inaudible noise coming from the cellar door, which she now realised was askew, something they were always careful about, in an effort to keep Charlie out of the cellar, where she had no business being. Emma was sure that she could hear someone whispering down there, but it was so quiet, she could not be sure that it was not just her imagination.

The light in the cellar was out, and she turned it on before carefully making her way down the wobbly old staircase. It only lit so much of the room, but she could make out a shape standing in the far corner. Tentatively, Emma made her way toward the figure and was hopeful when she whispered, "John?"

There was no response. He just went on standing there, staring into the corner. Emma slowly approached him from behind. As she placed her hand on his arm she whispered softly again, "John, are you okay? What are you doing down here?"

Her touch seemed to jolt him and he turned to her, surprised. She could see that he was in his pyjamas, so he *had* come to bed after all. So what was he doing in the cellar? Again she asked, "Are you okay?"

He looked at her with a confused expression as though he was sorting out what exactly was going on. After a moment he finally responded, "I, I don't know. I must have been sleepwalking or something I guess."

"I don't think you've ever done that before have you?"

John simply shrugged in reply.

"Come on," she had to guide him up the stairs like he was a little boy in her care. "Let's get you to bed."

John nodded silently and allowed himself to be led up to their room. Emma hesitated for a moment at the door, remembering why she had left the room in the first place. Then she shook it off and led her husband into the room, put him in their bed and pulled the covers up around him. He was sleeping before she could even lay down beside him.

"What is going on?" Emma whispered to the darkness, as she lay on her back, hot, angry tears slipping down her cheeks and into her hair. "What the *fuck* is going on?"

Emma stayed there in the bed beside her husband, like an early morning watch, but she did not even try to sleep again. She was not sure if she wanted to. Her mind had been made up: the house was not to be trusted.

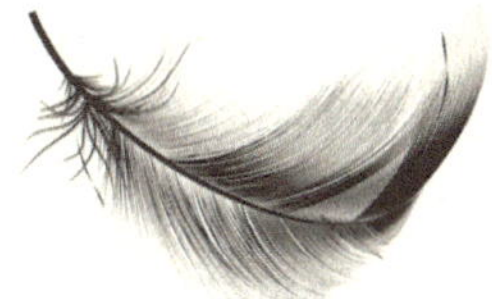

CHAPTER TWENTY FOUR

In the morning, Emma was still tired, but she had decided that she should tell John and her mother what had happened the night before. John had no recollection of going to the cellar or of being led back to bed. He was horrified at the thought that someone or something had been in bed with his wife, posing as him, and apparently not for the first time. Emma recounted the first time it had happened, when she had felt the hand on her arm then realised that John was not actually in the bed with her. As she told them what had happened, she watched over Charlie and Max as they played, blissfully unaware, in the backyard.

Begrudgingly, John had to head off to work for the day. They could not afford for him to take any more time away. He took solace in the fact that Charlotte was there, but suggested that they should get out of the house for the day. They promised him they would and agreed to stop by for lunch during their travels. He kissed Emma and hugged her intensely before heading out to say goodbye to Charlie and to let her know that he would see her for lunch. He waved at Emma and Charlotte through the window before heading out through the gate.

After they had both showered as quickly as possible, their nerves still raw from the experience with Charlie in the bathroom, Charlotte and Emma were both ready to head out for the day when the phone started ringing. "It's the landline," Emma remarked. "Maybe it's the hospital."

Much to her surprise, it was actually Felix on the line. She was thrilled to hear his voice, though she could tell he was not his usual chipper self. He assured her that by some miracle he was fine, and that he was indeed on the mend, despite his advanced age. "I guess the world can't get rid of me just yet," he joked darkly. "I've got some unfinished business to attend to. Will you come see me?"

Emma was surprised, but touched. "Uh, sure, of course," she stammered. "When are you allowed to start having visitors?"

"Can you come today?" He asked with a sense of urgency in his voice.

"Are you sure you're up for that Felix?" Emma glanced at her mother and could see her look of surprise at the mention of his name. "Maybe we should wait until you're feeling a little better. I'm not in any rush."

"But I am," he interrupted her. "I *need* to see you. Please, say you'll come today."

Emma could tell that there was no thwarting his plans. It was clear that the idea that she might not come to hear what he had to say was very stressful for him, and she did not want him feeling that way. Whatever he had to say, he clearly needed to get it off of his chest as soon as possible. She agreed to come and see him right away as her mother nodded in agreement, signalling that she would take care of Charlie on her own while Emma was gone. When she got off the phone with Felix, Charlotte assured her that they would carry on with their plans for the day, outside of the house, and that hopefully Emma would be able to join them in time for lunch with John.

"And if you can't make it in time," Charlotte added, "I'm sure John will understand. He'll be happy to hear Felix's coming around. I assume he's feeling better, since you're able to go and see him."

"I think so. He sounded tired, but who wouldn't? I should probably get going. I'll let Charlie know."

Emma turned to look out the window into the back garden. To her surprise, Charlie was standing in the middle of the lawn, looking back at the house with a frown on her face, slowly waving as she stared at Emma through the window, as though she already knew that her mother would be leaving. Max was crouched on the ground in front of her, barking and whining, in what seemed an attempt to get Charlie's attention, which was fixated on the house and on her mother. Something in her expression chilled Emma and she stepped back from the window with a gasp.

"What's wrong?" Charlotte asked and came to see what Emma was looking at.

Emma turned to her and said, "It's Charlie." When she turned back Charlie had gone back to playing with Max and Max had gone back to bounding around her cheerfully, as though they had never been how she had seen them just a moment before.

"Charlie?" Charlotte asked, panic in her voice. "What's wrong with Charlie?"

"I… it's…" she stammered. "Nothing I guess. I thought… I don't even know. She just didn't seem like herself, and Max was barking at her for some reason."

"But Max doesn't even bark, let alone bark at Charlie."

"I… yeah, you must be right. But…" she looked at her mother thoughtfully for a moment. "Just promise me you'll get out of here for the day okay? Don't stick around here too long after I leave. I don't want you guys here alone."

Charlotte smiled with concern and hugged her daughter reassuringly. "We'll take off right away. I promise. We'll have lots of fun, and hopefully we'll see you for a nice lunch."

"Okay."

"*Okay*?" Charlotte sought reassurance from her daughter.

"Well, hopefully I will be soon. For now, I'd better get to the hospital." She hugged her mother again and went out to let Charlie know that she had to go see Felix.

"Can me and Max go and see Felix too Mommy?"

"Sorry, honey. He's only allowed to have one visitor for now. But hopefully he'll be able to come and visit us again soon."

"*Prob'ly* not though Mommy," Charlie said matter-of-factly.

Emma was shocked by her daughter's eerie response. "What do you mean by that sweetie?"

"He *prob'ly* won't get out of the hospital any more silly."

"Don't say that Charlie!" Emma felt ill. "Why would you say something like that?"

"I don't know," Charlie whined apologetically, realising she had upset her mother. "That's what my friend said."

"Which friend? Who are you talking about?"

Charlie looked at her long and hard, as though she were considering the best way to help her mother to understand what she needed her to know. Finally, she smiled wryly and leaned in to whisper in Emma's ear, "It's a secret Mommy." She hesitated, still leaning in close as she breathed heavily in the way that children do when sharing a secret up close. "But she said I can say she thinks you're *really* pretty."

Shocked, Emma fell back from her daughter. She could not make sense of it. Why would Charlie say such strange things? Before she had time to think or respond, the little girl threw her arms around her mother's neck and hugged her emphatically before running off in a sudden game of tag with her little dog. Emma was dumbfounded and could do nothing but get up, brush herself off, and leave to head to the hospital.

In a daze for the short drive, she realised when she pulled into the hospital parking lot that she could not remember the trip because she had been so distracted by how Charlie had behaved. She pulled herself together and checked herself in the rearview before heading inside the squat, red brick building. Inside the atmosphere was quietly busy, as hospital staff and the occasional patient milled about in the receiving area.

She approached the main desk and the receptionist gave her directions to Felix's room after questioning her about their relationship and her reason for visiting, which Emma felt had more to do with small town nosiness rather than hospital protocol. She made her way through the wide hallways, following the arrows which she had been instructed would lead her to Felix's wing of the hospital. It did not take long before she found herself at another desk, where a visibly distracted nurse pointed her in the direction of room 307.

Felix was leaning back on his bed, which was propped up so that he was almost sitting. His eyes were closed and looked deeply and darkly bruised in comparison to the ghastly white paper skin which hung on his sharp cheekbones. Emma gasped inaudibly, but Felix seemed to sense her presence anyway and slowly opened his eyes. He smiled widely with little effort and despite the condition he was in, he suddenly looked like himself again. He reached out his hand to her and she quickly crossed the room and embraced him awkwardly as the wiring which hooked him to the machinery at his bedside tangled between them. She carefully untangled herself and apologised, but he insisted that there was no need and she knew he had meant it. Emma pulled up the visitor's chair from the foot of his bed and put it at his bedside so that she could sit with him and hold his hand as he told her what he needed to say.

"How are you? And do not bullshit me Felix," Emma tried on her best scowl, as a telling smile twisted at the corner of her mouth. "We know each other too well for that now."

Felix laughed a deep belly laugh, which caused him to cough and wheeze. Emma apologised again, but he waved her off. "I thought you said we were too close for bullshit, so that goes both ways young lady."

"Okay, alright," she smiled and squeezed his hand. "But seriously, how are you feeling?"

He shrugged nonchalantly and replied, "Like shit."

She burst out laughing in surprise at his vulgarity and scolded him jokingly. "Felix!"

"What? You started it. But seriously, I've been better. They say I'm going to be okay though, whatever that means. I'm not sure they even know what they're talking about in this one-horse-town. If the food is any clue to go by, I might be in trouble."

"I don't care what they're feeding you, as long as they're making you better."

"Does that mean you won't be bringing me any of your husband's fancy sandwiches or gourmet goodies?"

"I'll have to ask the nurses, but if it's okay with them, I'll make a daily delivery if it helps."

"It could be a matter of life and death. I heard a rumour there's meatloaf on the menu for tonight. I think they might be trying to kill me!" He laughed heartily at his own joke and set off on another coughing fit.

Emma stroked his hand and encouraged him to quiet down, as the man in the bed beside him stirred behind the curtain. She could hear him snort and groan as he shifted in his sleep. Felix assured her that he would be sleeping for the next few hours, as he had just come in from surgery and would still be feeling the effects of the anaesthetic for a while. Eager to get on with why she was there so that she could get Felix back to some badly needed rest, Emma asked why he had been so eager for her to come.

"There are things I still haven't told you," he began, "about your house… about your aunt. With everything that has happened, to you and to me, I realised that I should have started there, because maybe that would have changed things for you."

"Are you sure you're up to this Felix? I'm sure it can wait until you're home, or at least further along down the recovery road…"

"No, it *can't* wait," he interrupted her insistently. "I should have told you the first time we met. I don't know why I didn't. I guess I was worried that you might not take it seriously if you didn't know more of the history, but it was still stupid of me. I'm afraid I've let you down, and now nothing is going to stop me from telling you everything today. I won't be taking any chances, no matter what they say. I've already had one heart attack. I won't risk having another and kicking the bucket before I've told you Helen's story." He gripped her hand so tightly she almost pulled away, but the desperation in his pale blue eyes stopped her. He whispered hoarsely, "I'm afraid you and your family could be in *great* danger."

Emma instinctively let go of Felix's hand and sat back in her chair, dumbfounded, though the information was not necessarily a shock to her. She already knew that something sinister was going on, though she did not know what. She hugged herself tightly; although the room was warm and she was wearing her jacket, she felt a distinctive chill creeping through her bones. She looked Felix in the eye and plucked up her courage, saying, "Tell me everything you know."

CHAPTER TWENTY FIVE

Most people in the Crowsnest Pass who knew Helen, really did not know anything about her at all. She was known to be a recluse, keeping to herself and avoiding social contact as much as possible, even when she had no choice but to venture into the public eye. People believed she was strange, and she was, but that had not always been the case. Anyone who had endured her tragedy would likely be seen in the same light: someone who was somehow missing a vital piece, and she was.

Some people in town said she was a spinster, having never had any interest in a relationship with a man, let alone marrying one. Those same people surmised that Helen was indeed too much of an odd duck for any kind of meaningful relationship. Others insisted that she had in fact been married, and that she had become a widow at a young age. The story behind the loss of her husband depended on who one was talking to. The younger people in the small community turned her into a real life legend, a local witch figure they could make up fantastical stories about.

Some said that because she could never have a child, her husband abused her viciously and she finally had a mental breakdown. While she was locked away in an asylum, her husband divorced her and ran off with her best friend, leaving her with all of his debts and a house she swore to never leave, whatever it took. Those same people proposed that the reason she clung so desperately to the old house was because she could still pretend that nothing had changed in her life; she could set the table for two and carry on with her days as though her husband had not actually run off with the only friend she thought she had left.

There were others who swore that the reason Helen was a widow was because she had made it that way herself. They claimed that she had never been a stable woman, and that despite her strange ways and apparent disconnect from reality, her husband had truly loved her and had done everything he could to give her a good life. Although most would have thanked their lucky stars for such good fortune, Helen could not see how much he adored her.

In time, seeds of suspicion and doubt about why he had chosen to be with her, spurred on by the whispers of the local gossips, bloomed into full-blown paranoia. Driven mad by her own insecurities, she confronted the only man who had ever loved her, demanding that he tell her the truth about his motives. When he could not tell her what she knew to be the truth, she murdered him in cold blood.

Some said the crime was one of great passion, a bloodbath not seen in this part of the world since the days of the rumrunners. Others insisted that the killing was in fact *dispassionate*, that she had done the deed with utmost efficiency. Because although she knew she could no longer trust him and that he therefore had to die, she still loved him deeply. She knew his affection for her was all a ruse to ensure her own imminent demise. In the end, it had to be her, or him. For Helen, though difficult, the choice had been obvious.

Those same people who believed that she had killed her husband, also claimed different scenarios for her punishment and eventual release back into society. Some said she was locked in an institution for the criminally insane in Ponoka, which was up north past Red Deer. After years of medication, therapy and good behaviour, she was allowed to return home. Once she had regained her independence, she immediately quit taking her medication and proceeded to become the town pariah, though this was likely the case as soon as she returned.

Helen never really had a chance in the community, and would have been better off somewhere where nobody knew anything about her, if she had not been so hellbent on staying in the old house she still owned, which many claimed to be haunted. That detail never really added up with her insistence on staying in the house though. After all, why would a mentally ill woman who had killed her beloved husband in a fit of paranoid delusion want to stay in the place where the murder took place, especially if she then had to contend with the resident poltergeists? It did not make any sense.

Others said that she never suffered any consequences for what she had done, as she had managed to get off on a technicality, even though everyone had known that she was guilty. With belligerent boldness she had stayed in the house, infuriating anyone who crossed her path. Eventually, the glares and stares caused her to stay home, away from the judgmental and cruel community which had always shunned her. Over time, most people moved on and forgot why they crossed the street when she was coming from the other direction. All they knew was that they did not have time in their day for the awkward moments brought about by merely being in her presence, and so, they avoided her, even though over time they forgot why they were doing so.

The truth of the matter is that she would not have wanted to talk to any of them anyway. They had nothing to fear. She avoided talking to anyone, and was a master at sidestepping unwanted conversations. But on the odd occasion that she was cornered, and asked, she felt the need to share her version of the truth, as unbelievable as it might be. Helen insisted that she would not tell a lie to anyone who took the time to ask her for the facts, but that they might be better off not knowing the things she had to tell them about her lonely existence. In the end, most people never asked, they simply crossed the street and carried on with their own lives.

If a person was truly interested in who Helen was and why she seemed so strange, it was best to talk to the old-timers. Although an elderly woman's memory might be short on what she had intended to pick up at the store, as she was standing in the parking lot racking her brain, it could be heavily relied upon for memories of local lore and gossip. The men were no different. The oral tradition of storytelling stayed alive and well in the scruffy clubhouse pubs with wooden panelling adorning the walls, asbestos tiles chipping away on the floors, and washed up miners drinking cheap beer as they shared their own versions of the local myths with anyone who cared to listen.

People loved to talk, and they thought they knew it all, but really, when it came to Helen, even most of the old-timers did not know the whole story where she was concerned. Most of them knew that she had been quite different, more friendly and approachable, when she had first come to town with her husband, Leo. Most of them also knew that she and Leo had a little girl, Lorraine. They knew that Lorraine was the centre of the universe as far as her parents were concerned, and that when they lost her, their whole world fell apart. Leo left soon after and Helen was never the same again. They could not fathom what would possess her to continue living in the house where she had lost everything, staying there to wallow in her misery until her dying day.

But Felix was different. He had known Helen and her husband when they first moved to the Crowsnest Pass. Knowing that she had nobody to turn to in her time of need, he had been the one to be her friend, her confidante. Out of kindness and patience, he never asked her anything about why she chose to stay, until finally he felt that enough time had passed and he was able to muster the courage to broach the subject with her over a rare drink one evening. He did not have to wonder how she would feel about him sharing her story with Emma. He already knew. Helen would approve.

When Helen and Leo first arrived in the Crowsnest Pass, they were thrilled with their new life on the eastern slopes of the Rockies. Leo worked as a pharmacist in Blairmore and was quickly welcomed into the tight-knit community. Truth be told, Helen was a rather plain woman; the latest trends in fashion never interested her and she had never cared to busy herself with her outward appearance too much. She never wore make-up, regardless of the occasion, and could not see the point in wasting her time on painting her fingernails. Having been raised by strict and pious parents, she prided herself on class and cleanliness, but no one would have ever called her vain.

Because their daughter was so young, Helen and Leo decided that Helen would remain a homekeeper, at least until Lorraine was ready to start school full-time. With Leo's pay they could afford for her to stay at home, but it did not leave much room for anything extra. Still, they were happy. Their little girl was healthy and they had everything they needed, if not always everything they wanted. The move back to Leo's hometown had been a good choice it seemed, at least for a while.

They had lived in their new home beside the river for almost a year before anything strange had happened, or at least that's what they thought at first. Looking back, Helen had recalled seeing an unknown man in the distance, walking his dog beside the river, almost as soon as she had moved to the area. It was nothing strange, as many people chose this area to walk their dogs and perhaps even take in some fishing, though she never noticed him with any fishing gear that she could see from such a distance. And although she met most of the locals who came to walk their dogs, she could not claim to have met them all, and so it was not really strange that she had never spoken to the man, but her sightings of him grew more frequent over time.

What *was* strange was the *feeling* that washed over her every time she saw him, sending a shiver of prickles across her skin, even on the hottest summer day. Even though he was always too far away to make out his specific features, she had a sense of familiarity when she saw him which, instead of putting her at ease, always put her on edge. It was like a sense of deja vu, a premonition, or a warning instinct of some kind.

Although he was at such a distance, she had a sense that if she saw him up close he would be handsome. Helen also had a sense that there was something intrinsically wrong about the man, though she knew her instincts, as strong as they were, lacked any sense of reason and therefore were likely to be completely incorrect. Helen was sensible and self-aware enough to know that her fears of the man likely came from her insecurities about the unknown and an over-active imagination resulting in too much time spent in the company of a young child and not enough time amongst people of her own age.

In time her instincts were proven to be dead on, when she saw the man more than once standing in her backyard, staring maliciously at the house, at *her* in a way that told her that she should be afraid. And she had been afraid, but it seemed any time she tried to tell Leo about the man, she was at a loss for what to say. She finally said something when the man appeared in the backyard the first time, as now she knew that he was somehow a threat to her and maybe even to her family. Leo had been furious that a stranger had defiled the privacy of their property for no apparent reason, except to spook his wife.

"I know he gave you a fright," he tried to reassure her, as he pulled her to his chest and held her tight. "But there's no need to overreact. It's not like he did anything more than standing in the backyard grinning at the house like an idiot. He probably didn't even see you standing there."

Recoiling from his patronising tone, she pushed him away, and refused to back down. "No, you didn't *see* him. He was looking right *at* me, *glaring* at me, like he wanted to *hurt* me." Leo tried to interrupt her but she was not finished with what she had to say. She knew if she did not say it at that very moment, she might never get the courage again. Finally she blurted out the whole truth of what she had seen, almost screaming as she said it, "You don't understand! It wasn't just that he was here in the yard, it wasn't just that he was staring at me like some sort of psychopath! He's been watching me from afar since we got here! I just didn't know it yet till he showed up here." Again Leo moved to speak, but she held up her hand firmly to stop him from interrupting her. "That's not even the worst of it. I knew all along there was something wrong with him, I just couldn't place it until I saw him here tonight!"

She seemed on the verge of hyperventilating and Leo held her by her shoulders and gave her a gentle shake to help her focus. "What is it? What's wrong? What did you see?"

Helen covered her mouth with her hand as though she might be ill, then found the last ounce of courage she needed to tell him the thing she was most afraid to tell him, out of concern for how he might look at her. He might just think *she* was the one who had something wrong with her. But she had no choice; she was mortally terrified of what might happen next and she knew she could not face it alone, so she told him. "It's his *neck*," she almost whispered, as though they were in public, and not in the privacy of their own home. "I don't know how, but I think it's *broken* somehow. I don't know how he's standing there grinning at me like that. I'm no doctor, but I'm not an idiot; with an injury like that, he shouldn't be alive. So how *is* he alive?" Again, her voice rose in a crescendo of fear. "*Is* he? I can't stop thinking about it! I can't get the horrible picture out of my mind."

"Is he what?" Leo asked hesitantly.

"Is he *alive*? I know it sounds crazy, but I have a feeling that there's something wrong with this place, with this house, that maybe that's why he's here. Maybe he doesn't want us here. I don't know why, but lately I've been feeling like an intruder in my own home. Can't you *feel* it?"

"Feel what?" He moved her to the sofa as she gripped his arms, pleading with her eyes for him to believe what she was telling him, to *understand* her.

"That we don't belong here. That we aren't *wanted.* Please Leo, tell me you believe me. Tell me that we can find a new house and start again." Helen was crying now, and she could see the sympathy in his face. It made her hopeful that he knew how serious this was, that even with no proof that something was going on, he was wise enough to trust his wife's intuition and help her with her plight.

He brushed away a fresh tear from her cheek and held her chin in his hand as he gazed into her eyes. "I believe that *you* believe there's something sinister going on here. I really do. But think about what you're saying. Are you really suggesting that there's a dead man stalking our house? Does that make any sense to you?"

Helen did not respond, she just stared helplessly at her husband, knowing what would come next.

"Besides, we still owe years on this mortgage. We've just barely started paying on it. We'd lose our shirts if we pulled up stakes now. And where would we go? We had a hard enough time finding this place, I'll remind you." He pulled away from her now, contemplating his own words and reminding himself that he was the man, the breadwinner, and that his word was final, regardless of how his wife felt. She could see the wheels turning in his head. He had not really heard a word of what she had said.

"So that's that I guess," she said curtly as she wiped the last of her tears away. Her fear had turned to hurt and was now quickly souring to anger, an emotion she had rarely felt toward Leo in all the years of their marriage. But this one time when she had really needed him to listen to her with love and understanding, he had failed.

"That's that," he retorted coldly, with an air of authority, as though he were talking to his daughter and not his wife.

"Well, I'm glad we had this talk," she said sarcastically.

He either missed her tone or ignored it, replying in the same condescending tone, "Me too. But let's keep this between us. I know this was just your imagination acting up because of some jerk who put a bad fright into you, but others might not see it that way. We don't want the whole town talking behind our backs. It wouldn't exactly be good for my career."

She stood looking at him, mouth agape, as though she were seeing her husband for the first time, and she did not like what she saw. He went to kiss her but she pulled away and turned her head, making it clear that she was not interested. Leo ignored this gesture too and moved on to asking what she had planned for their dinner, as he was famished after a long day's work.

Helen kept things to herself after that, knowing not only that Leo would not take her seriously, but that the comment he had made about her sanity was likely a reflection of his own feelings, rather than a concern about what others would think. If he felt that she was losing her mind, as a man of medicine, there was no telling how he might react. Would he try to have her locked up? If so, there would be no one to protect Lorraine, and she did believe that her beautiful little girl needed protecting somehow. Her family was under threat, and if her husband was not able or willing to see it, then it fell to her to keep them safe.

In time, the incidents surrounding the house became more frequent and more severe in nature. Helen had seen all manner of terrors, writing her experiences in a journal she once shared with Felix to help him to fully understand what she had been through. At first he had doubted her assertions, but in time her vehemence and insistence on staying in a house she despised and feared convinced him that everything she was saying was true, or at least, it was true to her.

Helen's journal revealed that there was more than one entity involved in what she believed to be the haunting of her house. Her first experience was with the man, who came more than once to torment her with his malicious and terrifying grin, which seemed to transfix her when he would show himself to her. His mangy mutt was always close at his side, fur matted, bearing its horrible teeth in a permanent vicious sneer. In time his appearances caused her to stay within the confines of the house more and more. She isolated her daughter from the outside world, terrified that if she ventured outside on her own, the man might appear and Lorraine would be alone and vulnerable.

Before long, she started to experience other disturbances in the house, usually in the evening and seemingly directed at her. She had documented a feeling that there had been someone in the room with her, possibly even in the bed with her, when Leo was not there. She could have sworn that someone had touched her, though this was still early on, and she was not sure that it was not a bad dream. In time she became convinced otherwise.

One night she had heard sounds coming from Lorraine's room and went in to check on her daughter. Lorraine was sitting up in her bed, looking intently at the foot of the bed. When her mother came into the room, Lorraine had looked at her and asked where the lady had gone.

"Which lady?" Helen asked with some fear, though she knew the child had most likely been dreaming.

"The lady with the long dress," the little girl had replied matter-of-factly. "She told me she was so happy to see me. She said I didn't have to be afraid."

Helen's heart began to pound. Lorraine seemed so sure. Still, she was not convinced that there had actually *been* someone there. She could not deny however that her daughter's insistent tone gave her a chill. "I'm sure it was just a dream," she reassured the child. "Why don't you lie back down. It's very late."

"But it wasn't a dream, Mommy," Lorraine protested. "The lady was really here. She went away when you came in."

Helen laid the little girl back on her pillow gently and kissed her forehead. She was about to insist that it had all been in her head, or had been a dream, when she heard a loud rap at the window. When she turned she saw a crow at the window, pecking at the glass. It had frightened her and made her jump, which had made her laugh at herself in the moment, as she had felt rather silly. That is, until it started to peck more insistently on the window, finally beating a furious drumming rhythm which terrified the woman and the little girl both, so that by the time the windowpane cracked, they were both in hysterics, holding tightly to one another.

In the moment that the glass cracked, the menacing bird disappeared into thin air and Leo, having been awoken by the commotion, came rushing into the room. He demanded to know what had happened, and the little girl had blurted a flurry of details from the ominous experience which served to confuse him only further. Helen pushed him out of the room and insisted that she calm their daughter first and get her back to sleep and that she would tell him what had happened. He hesitantly agreed, and it had taken a while to get the child back to sleep, but when she did she had stayed true to her word and told him what had occurred.

He was silent and incredulous, though he could not deny the state he had found the two of them in, nor could he deny the state of the broken window. She could see that despite the evidence and all that she had told him, that his mind was still seeking a stronghold to find some logical explanation for what she was claiming. Her frustration with him grew even more, for now she felt he was willfully denying what she felt was a direct threat to their precious daughter's safety. She felt trapped with a man in denial, in a house she could not trust. She had nowhere to turn.

Soon after this experience, Helen awoke in the night to a sound in the hall outside her bedroom door. Being on edge, she immediately went to see what it had been and saw Lorraine as she was heading down the staircase. Helen followed, shocked when the child ignored her calls and made her way out the front door and across the road into the forest. When she entered the forest, she swore that the girl had vanished. She was horrified and searched the woods in vain. Before she came back to the house to wake Leo and tell him what had happened, she saw a figure in the woods. She knew it was not Lorraine - the figure was too tall, and it seemed to be moving toward her. Her mind flashed back to the man who had been outside her house and she raced inside to get help, terrified to lose a second to help her daughter. She came flying through the front door, screaming and crying and calling for Leo, who awoke immediately and came running to the top of the stairs.

"What's going on?" he demanded as he brushed his hair back from his forehead in exasperation. "What in God's name are you screaming about at this hour? I have to work in the morning!"

"I don't care about that you idiot!" She screamed in response. "Lorraine just ran outside into the forest. I can't find her, and I think there's someone else out there! You need to come now! We need to find her before *he* does!"

"Before *who* does?"

"Before..."

She was interrupted then when Lorraine came to join her father at the top of the steps, tiredly rubbing at her eyes. "Why are you yelling Mommy? You woke me up," the little girl grumbled sweetly. Helen could not believe her eyes. She had no doubt that she had just followed a little girl out into the night, but now she could clearly see that it had not been her little girl after all. She did not know what to say.

"Sorry sweetie," Leo soothed the little girl as he shot Helen a frustrated glance. "It was nothing. We'll get back to bed now. Let's get you back to yours first, though." She let him lead her back to her bed as Helen stood frozen and flabbergasted in the living room, the front door still hanging wide open to the night.

After soothing Lorraine back to sleep, Leo returned to bed without saying anything to Helen. He did not need to. She could feel the tension between them, like a third person in the bed, when she turned in to try to get back to sleep herself. Her sleep was fitful and filled with dreams where she found herself roaming endlessly through the forest as the figure she had seen earlier in the night pursued her. Though she could not make out her stalker, she had the creeping sensation that it was growing ever closer to her, so that she was afraid to turn around. She continued to run through the trees, which seemed to be fighting against her, so that despite her efforts, the nightmarish figure would soon be upon her. She could hear and almost feel its ragged, gasping breathing.

By five-thirty in the morning Helen had given up any hope of a decent sleep and carefully crept out of bed, as Leo was still lightly snoring and would not stir for at least another hour. It was still dark outside, though a hint of the morning dawn glowed behind the black hills to the east. She made herself a strong coffee and stared through the front window at the forest on the other side of the road. Although she was eager to explore the area she had been drawn to the night before to see if there were any clues about what or who had led her there, her vivid and tormenting dreams were enough to keep her curiosity at bay until the light of day kissed the tops of the eastern hills, revealing a diamond blade edge sparkling across the tops of the lower mountains. It was almost six o'clock and she knew that Leo and Lorraine would be up and about soon, and she did not want Leo questioning her about what she was doing wandering around in the forest at the crack of dawn. After last night's drama, she knew that she might as well keep her concerns to herself, as her husband was surely beginning to question her sanity with her recent rash of seemingly paranoid behaviour. She could feel the space growing between them as he did what he could to maintain the sane and peaceful life they had once enjoyed, and she suffered alone with no one to turn to at a time when she felt she might break under the relentless pressure. Her family was being threatened and there was little she could do about it but no one who would help her.

Pulling on a light jacket as she quietly closed the front door behind her, conscious to avoid waking her family, Helen made her way tentatively across the road to the forest, where she had followed a vanishing little girl just the night before. As she walked she wondered whether it had all been a dream. Perhaps her husband's concerns about her state of mind were founded. Maybe she was the real problem, letting her imagination get the best of her, as though she were the child in the house and not Lorraine, who seemed mostly unbothered by her mother's recent antics.

When she entered the still of the forest the air seemed to grow cooler and quieter around her. Although she could see her surroundings just fine in the morning gloom, she found herself wishing that she had still brought a flashlight to reassure her in the shadows of the woods. She wandered aimlessly, careful to watch her feet as she silently explored the small tract of trees, so as not to trip over a fallen tree or an old stump hidden by the carpet of overgrown wild grass. Making her way toward the east where she had seen the figure the night before, she would stop for a moment to see if there was anything telling in the forest, any clue left behind to indicate what she had seen the night before. She desperately needed some semblance of reality to reassure her that she was indeed *not* losing her mind. Having searched the forest fruitlessly, Helen decided that the search had been for nothing and turned to head back toward the house.

As she turned around she came face to face with a woman, but she was no normal woman. She had come out of the shadows and stood directly behind Helen without making a sound. Her hair was long, dark and stringy with dampness. Her eyes were deep hollows of darkness set in a ghastly white face. Every ounce of Helen's mind and body wanted to scream, to run, but she was frozen in place, unable to will herself to react to the horror in front of her, except to stand there staring into the abyss of those black eyes which seemed to stare right back into her. The horrific face twisted into a grimace of what felt to Helen like deep sorrow and pain. A blackened rotten tear fell from the corner of the apparition's black eye and Helen could feel it, or *her* fighting to speak. The mouth opened and a rush of foetid grey water spilled over the front of her rotting white dress. The woman's deathly white hands reached out to grab onto Helen's hands as she spoke, but there was no substance to them.

The ghostly woman whispered only five raspy words which she seemed to choke and gurgle to the surface of her throat. "Go." She twisted and wrenched in a frighteningly unnatural twitching manner and fought to say more. Her next words came out in a desperate screaming whisper, as though she was frightened she might run out of the strength to say them "Don't ever come back!"

With the final word the apparition vanished before Helen's eyes and she was immediately released from the invisible hold which had frozen her in place while the woman had said what she needed to say. Helen remained frozen in place for a moment as she dealt with the shock and horror of what she had just seen and felt. There was no doubt, standing here in the growing morning light in the forest that she had just been face to face with… *something* or *someone*.

Still, her mind struggled to accept what had just occurred. Finally, the shock broke and she covered her mouth for fear of screaming and waking the neighbourhood. She looked all around her to see if she was still alone, and when she saw that she was, she could even *feel* that she was, she turned and ran back to the house. Though the distance was short, she reached the front door panting and sweating as though she had just gone for a morning run, which would make an excellent excuse for Leo if he happened to be up and noticed that she had gone. Not that she was typically a woman who would ever run by choice, but there was always a first for everything, and the stress of the night before would surely make a good excuse for that.

As she weighed out her excuses for Leo, she realised that once again she had decided to keep this from her husband. She knew that she did not have his support. He would not understand. Helen knew that he would not even believe her if she told him anyway. It was much more likely that he would declare her crazy and commit her, taking her child and her life in the process. And she *knew* she was not crazy. The *situation* was crazy, but she was not.

There had been no need to worry after all, as she could hear Leo in the shower, getting ready for his day. She made a fresh pot of coffee and sat down at the kitchen table, staring out at the forest. Though she was afraid, a feeling of curiosity also gripped her. She could not make sense of what the apparition's warning had meant, though she was sure that it *had* been a warning. What she could not be sure of was what she was being warned against. Did the woman mean that she should stay out of the forest? Though she wished it were that simple, she had the sense that it had meant more than that. In her heart she knew that the warning had been about the house, that it was somehow dangerous for her family to stay there, and yet, she also knew that Leo would not hear any talk of them leaving. She felt like a trapped animal. A sense of panic began to set in.

Her mind was racing; she wondered whether the ghostly woman meant her harm. Yet, how much harm could she do if she could barely speak or even be *there*? Helen had a sense that the woman was not warning her about what *she* might do, but about what the horrible man with the broken neck might do, given the chance. Still, she knew better than to rely on her instincts alone in this situation. She would trust nothing and do everything she could to protect her family, although she had no idea just how she would do that without Leo's support. By the time he was dressed and had come downstairs for his morning coffee and breakfast, Helen had grudgingly decided to tell him what had happened in the woods.

After asking him to agree to hear her out before interjecting with his thoughts, she relayed what had happened in as matter-of-fact a tone as she could muster. She did not want to leave room for him to question what she knew she had experienced, though she knew in her heart that he still would. For years in their marriage she had always appreciated his scientific and analytical stance on the world, as it had conformed to her own way of thinking. Her first instincts in this situation were to deny what was happening, which was why she had not even noticed anything amiss for at least a year after moving into the house. She knew that if she had any hope in keeping them safe, she would need Leo behind her. When she had finished the story, they both sat in a tense, awkward silence as Leo stared ahead, transfixed on the forest outside the window. His brow was furrowed and she could see that he was worriedly chewing on the inside of his cheek.

When he finally spoke he kept his eyes focused outside the window. Helen was hopeful that he might finally be seeing sense, as he seemed deep in thought, searching for the right response. He seemed to choke out his words with a forced sense of calm, though Helen sensed a simmering anger just beneath his controlled veneer. "Am I supposed to take this seriously? Are you *actually* losing your fucking mind?"

Helen flinched when he used such vulgarity, as he had never spoken to her so coarsely. Sensing that she was at a loss for words, Leo continued with his abuse. "I can't believe you're pulling this shit right now. Things are going so well for me… for *us*, yet it's just not enough to make you happy. Making up these outlandish stories! Either you're craving for attention, maybe because I've been so busy, or you really do have a screw loose. So which is it? Why are you doing this? I don't know who you are anymore!" His voice rose as his anger built to a crescendo and she began to cry.

"Please, Leo," she begged as she sobbed. "I'm not lying, and I'm not losing my mind. I know what I saw. I know it's hard to believe, but I need you to try. Something evil is going on here and it's got its sights fixed on our little girl! I can't pretend it's not happening and I'm not going to let you bully me into acting like I can for your sake."

"God forbid you do anything for *my* sake! It's not like I give every spare minute of my time to provide you with a comfortable life. I work all day and then I get to come home to this lunacy. Today I get a special surprise with an early dose of crazy to last me through my day."

"Why don't you just leave then?" she snarled. "You're clearly not going to listen to a word I say anyway."

"I'm not so sure I should," he snapped back. "Maybe I shouldn't be leaving Lorraine with her mother when she's clearly becoming *unhinged*."

"You son-of-a-bitch! I suggest you get out right now before I say something I might regret. That little girl is my whole world, and you know it. I'll do whatever it takes to protect her, even if that means pissing you off. Now get the fuck out of my sight!"

"Mommy?" Suddenly Lorraine appeared, leaving Helen to wonder how much she had overheard of their fight. "Why are you and Daddy yelling at each other? I heard you swearing. That's bad." Her tiny lip quivered as she fought to hold back her tears.

Helen rushed to her and took her in her arms, kissing her quickly on the cheek and reassuring her as she shot Leo a threatening glare. "It's fine baby girl. Mommy's sorry for swearing. I lost my temper, but everything is okay now, right Daddy?" Helen turned to her husband for support.

He threw his head back and gulped the rest of his coffee as he tossed his jacket over his shoulder. "I'm leaving. I'll see you at dinner," he said coldly. "Don't cry LuLu… everything's going to be fine," he added half-heartedly as he shot a frustrated look at Helen before leaving and slamming the door. Helen shook her head and soothed her daughter, distracting her with ideas for breakfast.

Things actually calmed down for a few weeks after the confrontation that morning. In fact, things were so quiet, that Helen actually began to question if perhaps it had been her imagination, or if perhaps her husband had been right and that she had experienced some strange sort of mental lapse. Though at first she had not trusted in the sense of peace and quiet that settled over their lives once again, she quickly fell into the normalcy of their daily routine which seemed to have returned for the most part. Things were still a little tense between her and Leo, as they had both spoken to one another in a way they never had before and there was no taking back how they had treated one another in the heat of the moment. However, they were both making the effort and it seemed that things would heal themselves.

That all changed the night of the storm.

It had started gradually, a pattering of rain common in late springtime. Then the sky grew a threatening slate grey before the lighting cracked the sky like a shattered plate and thunder rumbled in the near distance. When the rain started coming down in sheets, the power went out soon after. Helen and Leo found the drawer containing the flashlight and candles and melted some candle wax onto a few plates to make impromptu candle holders so that they would not have to sit in the dark. They sat quietly and watched the storm, sitting in matching armchairs looking out the front window. As the storm quieted to a steady rain, Helen saw that Leo had drifted off in his chair, his head tilted to the side, as though he were trying to rest it on his own shoulder. She looked back out at the rain and gazed at the candlelight as it flickered on the windowpane. Submerged in the hypnotic atmosphere, Helen drifted off to sleep in her own chair, sitting beside her husband.

It was difficult to tell what time it was when she was jolted awake by a loud boom of thunder which seemed to almost shake the house. She was surprised when she looked to her left to see that the noise had not awoken Leo, who now had his head resting over the back of the chair, so that he seemed to be gazing at the ceiling with an open mouth. Helen yawned as she stretched, just as a streak of lightning splashed across the dark sky.

For a split second the world outside was fully lit up and Helen could see everything where just a moment before the dark blanket of night had concealed everything. She could see the deep puddles forming on the gravel road in front of the house, exposing the many potholes pock-marking the street like a sponge. She could see the rain still splashing wildly in the puddles, ensuring that Lorraine would have an unlimited supply of mud and water to play in for days to come. She could see the tall trees swaying in the wind and rain. And in that split second, when the world was bright and everything was vibrantly white and clear, she could see a little girl in a nightgown from behind, just as she stepped into the forest.

"Lorraine!" Helen gasped as the horror struck her that as she and Leo slept uncomfortably in their chairs, their little girl had somehow left the house without their knowing, and was now about to roam into the forest, in the dark, during a lightning storm. It occurred to Helen that the child had to be sleepwalking.

Leo awoke and looked around the room in startled confusion. "What? Where am I? What's going on?" He scratched his head and looked to Helen for an answer. The world outside was dark again and Helen could no longer see her daughter.

"It's Lorraine!" She cried as she threw open the front door calling back behind her. "I just saw her! She's in the woods!"

"Why would she be in the woods during a storm in the middle of the night?" He glanced at his watch and grumbled. "It's just after four o'clock in the morning. You must have been dreaming or something."

Helen ignored him and ran out into the storm with no jacket or shoes. She was in a panic, though there was nothing particularly dangerous about the woods, which was really barely a patch of forest, not even enough to get lost in, even if one was not familiar with the area. *That woman's in the woods*, her mind warned her. She had grown complacent in the new quiet of her life, but she had not forgotten that horrifying ghostly face and did not want the fiend anywhere near her daughter.

Helen stumbled into the forest but could not see anything in the darkness. The clouds had covered any source of light she might have had. She groped her way through the forest, calling for Lorraine over the noise of the storm. Before long, Leo appeared at her side with the flashlight and walked with her through the forest, but they soon realised that they were the only two there.

"Let's head back inside," Leo shouted over the rain. "She couldn't have come out here. You must have been dreaming. I bet she's still in bed. We'd better get back. She'll be scared if she wakes up and she can't find us."

Helen grudgingly let him guide her back through the forest. Though she knew he was right, that there was nobody there, she could not accept his theory that she had been dreaming. She had been wide awake when she had seen Lorraine heading into the forest. When they came out onto the road she looked around to see if the child had roamed out of the forest without them noticing, but the road was empty. Lorraine was nowhere to be seen. Helen tried to relax and reassure herself that Leo was right, but something in her was still holding onto the feeling that her little girl was in danger. She could not let it go.

As soon as they got back to the house, Helen ran to the stairs, needing to see immediately that her little girl was indeed sleeping peacefully in her bed. She tripped on the dark stairs, as the power was still out in the neighbourhood, leaving it darker inside and out than it would normally be. The shadows on the staircase were ominous as she pulled herself back up, nursing a sore knee, as she had banged it on the edge of the stair when she tripped. She barely noticed and continued on with a limp up the stairs and into Lorraine's room. Because she had forgotten to bring the flashlight with her, she had to grope her way to the bed to check on her daughter. To her horror, the blankets were thrown back and the bed was empty. She stifled the urge to scream, knowing the little girl might be in the bathroom, though it would be strange as she would have wanted her mother to be with her in the unfamiliar darkness. Still, she did not want to overreact to her own fears and frighten the little girl.

As she was about to leave, the lightning flashed across the sky again and lit up the backyard. In a moment of vivid clarity, she could see that the back gate was open, swinging back and forth in the wind. Her breath caught in her throat, but still she tried to hold her panic, trying to assure herself that Lorraine was still in the house and that the wind had simply blown the old gate open.

Leo was standing at the top of the stairs when she emerged from the empty bedroom, shaking her head, though she was not sure if he could actually see her in the darkness of the hallway. Although it was strange to see the bathroom door shut in the darkness, something Lorraine would typically never do, as she was afraid of the dark and certainly would not want to be in a dark bathroom by herself, Helen was still reassured, as it signalled that the girl was still in the house. She was likely still half asleep and did not even realise that the house was so dark.

When she tried the door she was startled when the doorknob would not turn. It seemed to be locked. She looked at Leo who was equally surprised, so she started to bang on the door and call out to her daughter. When there was no response, Leo pushed her out of the way and tried to force the door open.

They both jumped back when a pool of water came spilling out from under the doorway. For a moment they stood in quiet confusion, then the reality of the situation hit them both simultaneously and they began to pound on the door and scream Lorraine's name. The door suddenly flew open and they almost fell into the room. At the same moment, the familiar sound of power came on in the house and they quickly threw up the light switch to illuminate the room. They stood in dumbstruck confusion as they realised they were standing in an empty room. Then they both seemed to notice that the floor was perfectly dry.

"What the hell is going on here?" Leo whispered.

His quiet voice shook Helen out of her stupor and her mind went immediately to the sight of the gate in the backyard, open and swinging in the wind. She turned to bolt out of the room, but Leo stopped her and asked, "What is it? What's wrong?"

"It's the gate," she cried. "The gate is open in the backyard. What if she's out there?"

Leo said nothing but his eyes grew wide and he quickly ran out of the room and down the stairs with Helen at his heels. They ran out the back door, slipping and sliding through the water-logged yard to the muddy back lane. To the right the lane led to the road back to the bridge which was the only way out of the neighbourhood; to the left the lane led to the river. Leo and Helen looked at one another, then without saying a word, instinctively ran to the river.

Even in the darkness, they could see her there, floating facedown in the water as the rain continued to fall. Her long dark hair fanned out around her head, her tiny arms and legs were spread-eagle, her nightgown flowed around her. For a moment they were frozen with the shock of the horrible sight, then Leo threw himself into the water and scooped up the little girl in his arms. He brought her to the shore and demanded that Helen run back to the house to call the ambulance, but she stood there, transfixed on a horrible sight on the other side of the stream.

Already in the distance, walking away into the forest which divided their town from the next, she could see a man and a dog. She had seen them before. What she had never seen before was a little girl with long dark hair, following behind the man and his mongrel. In the moment before they disappeared into the rain-soaked woods, the girl turned to look back. They were too far away to see her face and the darkness was still deep, but she had the feeling that she was looking at her own little girl and she wanted to swim across the river to follow them. But she knew it was too late, that she could never get to them now. She began to scream and wail uncontrollably.

"Helen!" Leo's shouting snapped her out of her trance and she turned without another moment's hesitation and ran back to the house to call the ambulance. She was shaking so violently she almost could not dial the number. As soon as she had told them where to go, she hung up the phone and ran back to the river. By the time she got there, she could already hear the sirens approaching. They did not have a very long way to go in such a small place, so they were always quick to respond to an emergency. Even so, they were too late. Helen was too late. Leo had been too late. Their little girl was gone.

The days that followed the storm were a blur for Helen. People came and went with their condolences and casseroles, but she could not remember a word any of them had said, nor could she remember responding to any of them. Somehow the funeral had happened. Leo must have arranged everything alone, despite his own suffering, but she could not bring herself to care. In her mind it did not make sense that she should see her baby buried, so she wanted no part of it. Looking back, she could not be sure how long things had gone on before she finally spoke a word to Leo. He had been careful and patient with her misery and had seemed to need the time for himself to come to terms with what had happened anyway.

In an attempt to cope with the tragedy, he suggested that it might be best if they considered selling the house, "There are too many bad memories for us here now. If we ever want to move on with our lives, I don't think it's going to be here."

Helen turned to him, a look of reserved surprise on her face. "You want to leave *now*?" She said it so quietly that he almost did not hear her.

"Well, it might take a while," he reflected, encouraged by her response. "It's not exactly a hot housing market. But yes; we should leave once we sell it and start over again. There's nothing but sadness for us here. That's all that will *ever* be here now."

Time ticked by as she stared ahead, seeming to be lost in thought over what he had suggested. Leo waited patiently for her response, but from the look of shock on his face, it was clearly not what he had expected. Her voice never rose to much more than a whisper, but her tone was severe. "You want to leave *now*," she repeated her question as a statement. "I begged you to leave here but you wouldn't hear of it then. But now…"

"You can't blame me for that. I could not have known…"

"Shut your stupid mouth," she snarled. "This is all your fault. I told you we were in danger, that our *baby* was in danger, but you wouldn't hear it. You were too busy thinking about yourself and your money and your precious career. Well now you can do whatever you want, but I won't be going anywhere. I'll be staying right here and waiting."

"What are you waiting for? What is there to wait for anymore?" He was in tears but she was hardened to his feelings.

"I'm waiting for my daughter," she replied matter-of-factly, as though it were the most normal thing to say. "I intend to be here when she returns. If you want to go, you know where the door is. You won't be missed here anyway. But I'll be staying right here in this hellhole until my little girl comes home."

Leo stood, his mouth hanging open. After a prolonged silence, his shoulders slumped and he left the room to head upstairs. After a long while he came back downstairs with his suitcase and travel bag.

"I'm leaving," he announced. "If that's what you really want."

"I don't care what you do. Like I said, you won't be missed here."

He hesitated for a moment, as though he were considering what he might say, then his shoulders slumped and he shook his head in frustration. "I just wanted to take care of my girls, you know," he said with tears in his eyes. "I know that you're suffering, but I'm just as devastated as you are. I could not save her for God's sake! How do you think that makes me feel?"

She turned to him one last time with hatred in her eyes, "You could have saved her though, but because you wouldn't listen to me, you chose not to instead. So now you can live with yourself, because I don't *want* to anymore. I can't stand the sight of you for one more day. You would be doing me a favour if you left me here alone."

His face contorted into a look of complete devastation; he was utterly broken. There was nothing more he could say, so he turned, opened the door and left. She did not see him look back at the house. She did not see him drive away. She had already walked away.

Helen stuck to her word and stayed in the house until her death. Though she had never intended to stay for so long in a place she hated so much, she was not willing to leave until her daughter returned. Tragically, she never did.

She heard from Leo through his lawyer a few years after he left. He was ready to move on and get married again, to start a new family and a new life. The house would be hers to keep if she was willing to sign the papers without contesting the divorce. She was happy to sign them and glad that he could move on with his life in a way that she knew she never would.

Helen had hoped to sign the house over to the Crowsnest Pass Historical Society, to ensure that nobody else would ever be put in the situation she had been but she never actually got around to writing her will. Her life had been one of waiting, but when her time had come, she had not been ready at all. Because she never got around to doing what she had intended, the house went to her next of kin. She would have been devastated to know that not only did she fail to protect another innocent family from the torment of her cursed house, but she in fact failed once again to protect her *own* family from the tragedy that might await.

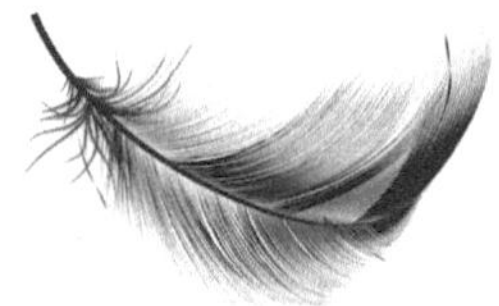

CHAPTER TWENTY SIX

Emma sat in silence after Felix finished recounting the tragic details of Helen's life in the house. Felix had tears in his eyes as he remembered his friend and the sad existence she had endured.

"I should have told you all of this right away," he said sorrowfully, his guilt overwhelming his words. "I wasn't sure if you would believe me if I didn't explain the different events that have happened in your house first. I thought maybe if you knew what had gone on there before, you could maybe accept the possibility that what happened to Helen's little girl was no typical accident, not as far as her mother was concerned anyway. I wasn't sure I believed it myself, despite the stories about the house and how convinced she had been that it had all been the work of some supernatural force. It was just so unbelievable. At the time I remember thinking that if a silly ghost story helped her to make sense of her loss, then there was probably no harm in it. But there was great harm for Helen." Felix sniffed back fresh guilty tears. "She never moved on with her life. She lived in that house she hated, waiting for her little girl to come back and never got what she wanted. Besides, I've never been able to make sense of what she did want. Was she hoping that sweet little girl would come back from the grave to haunt her? Is that what she wanted?"

"It would be better than knowing that she would never see her daughter again," Emma interjected, breaking her silence. "I can't imagine what she went through. How could you move on after losing your only child?"

"She never did move on. That was the sad part. I don't think Lorraine would have wanted the mother she loved to waste her life waiting for something that could never be."

"Maybe not, but we don't get to choose how people will react to tragedy. For Helen, maybe the waiting is what kept her going. The idea of seeing her little girl someday might have been the only thing that kept her putting one foot in front of the other each day."

Felix nodded in agreement. "You're probably right, but all of that is beside the point now. Helen is gone, but you're still here, and I worry you might be in danger. *All* of you. I'll admit, I've always believed that Lorraine's drowning was an accident, but with what's been going on, I'm not so sure anymore. I certainly wouldn't take any chances where your little girl is concerned. There was nothing I could have ever done to save Lorraine. I wasn't even in the picture when that happened after all, but I'm not totally helpless in this situation. I can warn you. I can beg you to listen to what your instincts are telling you, because I'm pretty sure I have a good idea of what they're trying to say."

Emma squeezed Felix's hand. "I won't let anything happen to my little girl, I can promise you that. Thank you for telling me everything Felix. I know that wasn't easy for you. I can see how much you cared for your friend."

"I'm so sorry I didn't tell you sooner," he cried.

"No; you were right Felix. I don't think I would have taken you as seriously without the whole picture. It's a pretty crazy story, but I've been living in that house long enough now to know that just because something *seems* impossible, doesn't mean it is. Now that I do have the whole picture, I need to talk to John and see where we go from here. I should probably get going. I'm supposed to meet Mom and Charlie at the shop for lunch. If I get there a little earlier than them I might get a chance to talk with John alone. He and I have some important decisions to make."

"Take care of yourself Emma, and take care of your family."

"You know I will Felix." She leaned over and kissed him on the forehead. "Thank you for everything. I don't know who I could have ever turned to if you hadn't been willing to talk to me about everything you know."

"It was nothing. I was happy to spend the time getting to know you all this time. It's not easy to make new friends at my age, you know, especially young pretty ones."

"It was not *nothing,* old man? It meant a lot. Because of you, my family will be safe." She kissed his hand affectionately and left with a wave.

"I sure hope so," Felix whispered to himself as he watched her leave.

Emma raced her car along the highway back to Bellevue to see John and tell him Felix's final story as quickly as she could. If she could get there soon enough, she might be able to convince John that they should leave the house right away. She was hoping that things would be slow at the shop so that he could take the time to talk.

When she got there she was grateful that John's was the only vehicle there. He smiled widely when he saw her and came around the counter to give her a quick hug and kiss. "Where are your mom and Charlie? Is it just the two of us for lunch today?"

"No, I said I'd meet them here," she began. "I'm glad I got here a bit early. We need to talk."

"I don't like the sound of that. What's going on? Is everything okay?"

"Everything is fine. I just went to see Felix at the hospital. He called me after you left this morning."

"Wow! Really? How's he doing? What did he want to see you for?"

"That's what I wanted to talk to you about, before Charlie gets here. He finally told me about your Aunt Helen." She held his hand and led him to the lunch counter. "I think you'd better sit down while I tell you what he said."

When she was done telling him everything Felix had told her, she revealed what she had really come for. "I don't want Charlie to stay in that house any longer. I think I should pack up some things and go back to the city with my mother. Charlie and I can spend some time there while we figure out what we should do."

John reacted as though he had been jolted. "I don't want you to go and take Charlie away," he blurted before catching himself.

Emma flinched; for a moment she wondered if this was an issue of trust between them. "I'm not taking her away. I'm just bringing her to my mother's for a little while. I don't want her staying in that house any longer, John."

"No; you're right, it's no big deal. I'm just going to miss you girls. I'm not sure what we're going to do, but I can see that no matter what, you could use some time away from this place."

Sensing a different tone in his voice, Emma pulled away to look him in the eyes. "This isn't just me, you know. I'm not losing it or something. I thought you were on my side with this. I thought you believed me." There was a rising sense of panic in her voice.

"Stop Emma. You're being overly sensitive. Of course I believe you. That's why I think you need to get away from here, regardless of what we decide to do. Go and relax. Let your mother fuss over you and Charlie for a while. Get out and spend some time with your friends; it's been a while since you were there. Try to leave this stress behind for a while. Okay?"

Emma eyed her husband suspiciously. "Do you mean it?"

"Of course. I'll miss you. I really don't want you to take Charlie away, but I know it's for the best. Maybe you should stay one more night and give yourself time to get ready."

"I'd rather not;" she blurted. "Sorry."

"Okay. Whatever you want, boss lady." He kissed her on the lips and hugged her tightly when the welcome bell jingled as the front door opened.

Emma turned and smiled, sure that it would be her mother and daughter coming through the door to meet her for their planned lunch date, but it was an elderly couple she vaguely recognized as repeat customers. She caught herself in a frown then forced a smile as John introduced her as his wife to the man and woman. Afterward their names were immediately a fog to her. The clock ticked loudly and she looked up to see that it was already twenty minutes past the time when she had expected her mother and Charlie to arrive. Though she considered ordering ahead, she became too antsy with worry about why they might be so late. When John returned from the table where he had seated his regulars, she could no longer tolerate the worry and told him that she was going to go back to the house to see what was keeping her mother. She was not sure if the concern on his face was for them, or for her.

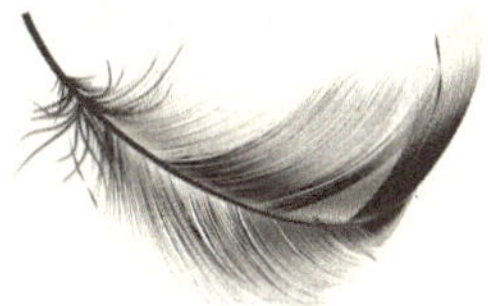

CHAPTER TWENTY SEVEN

Lille, Northwest Territory, Canada, 1901

Months passed and things only seemed to get worse. Olivia knew that the mine had extended their kindness for longer than what was typical, letting her stay in the house that she and Fisher had shared. It had only seemed fair at the time, as Fisher had lost his life on the job, unnecessarily as far as most were concerned. The small savings that they had accrued was quickly disappearing now, despite her frugality, and the time was nearing that she would have to make some decisions about what she and Violet would do and where they would go next.

Margaret seemed to know what was going on, despite the fact that Olivia had not breathed a word to her about it. Not for a lack of effort on Margaret's part, as she was constantly trying to pry into Olivia's situation, asking how her funds were holding out and surmising about just how long she would be able to remain in the house reserved for the employees of the mine and their families. After months of beating around the bush, she finally got to the point and started pushing Olivia to leave her home and come to stay with her sister's family until she could get her feet under her. Though she had insisted that it was what she and Harry both wanted, not to mention how wonderful it would be for Violet to stay with her cousins, Olivia could not accept that she would not be a burden to her sister and a weight around her family's neck, dragging them down to the depths she was sinking to. And so, she continued to deny her sister's wishes, and had remained in the town of Lille, alone with her daughter and the loneliness which plagued her days.

The day was warm when she ventured out for a walk with Violet to get some much needed air. They neared the space in the trees where the townsfolk typically went to enter the forest, as a path had been carved out by the local deer and further cleared by human feet. Just before they disappeared into the woods, a familiar voice called her name and she visibly flinched at the sound of it, though she quickly righted herself and forced a reserved smile.

"Good morning Mr. Hollis. Fine day."

"It sure is," he agreed. "And made all the better by seeing you lovely ladies out enjoying the beautiful sunshine. Where are you headed?"

Olivia breathed deeply and forced herself to respond congenially. Though she had no use for the company of Callum Hollis after what had happened to Fisher, following his strange advances on New Year's Eve, she had to behave according to one who has been living on the charity of others. It was becoming increasingly difficult to avoid him without locking herself and her child up like prisoners in their tiny home.

"Just going for a walk in the forest. We've been holed up for too long and it's a nice enough day, so I thought I would get Violet out for some fresh air before lunch." She did not inquire as to where he was heading, as she did not want to prolong the conversation unnecessarily.

"Well, would you mind if I joined you?" He asked, ignoring her subtle rudeness. "I've got something I'd like to discuss with you."

She hesitated visibly, not wanting to spend time with him, then it occurred to her that he likely needed to discuss her moving out of the house. It was likely that it had been needed for another family for a while and the time had come for her to leave. She had no choice but to accept his offer, "Of course. You're welcome to join us. We weren't planning to go far though I'll warn you."

"That's not a problem. What I have to say won't take long."

Her heart began to race. This was what she had dreaded. Now she would be forced to decide what she was going to do next. Would she have to accept her sister's offer? She loved Margaret and Harold so much, the last thing she wanted to do was to burden their marriage with the troubles of a grieving widow with a small child to care for. Would she have to turn to her parents for help? That prospect seemed even worse.

A sense of fear began to creep over her, pricking her skin so that she suddenly felt a chill. Would she end up homeless and destitute? What would happen to Violet? Would she have to give her up? If only she could get past her own pride. She knew that she had options, but she did not want the charity of her family, or anyone else for that matter. She would have to come up with a plan to support herself and it would have to be quick. The time of grieving and ignoring the situation that she and her child were in was over. It was time to face reality and make a choice.

Their walk started with small talk, mostly Callum filling her in on how things were progressing at the mine. Olivia listened intently, though she really did not care about the mine or anything this man had to say. Finally, she'd had enough of his rambling and pushed him to get to the point. "I'm sure you did not join us to discuss your business Mr. Hollis."

"Callum," he interrupted.

She nodded curtly. "What did you want to talk to me about?"

"Well," he began, ignoring her refusal to revert to a first-name basis with him. "I have been waiting for a while to discuss this with you, but obviously I wanted to be sure that a decent amount of time had passed. I know that losing Fisher has been trying for you to say the least."

Olivia smarted at the sound of her husband's name coming out of this man's mouth. She had to work to hide her distaste. But of course, it made sense that he would bring up the loss of her husband, as this was why she had been allowed to remain for an extended period in the house. Nobody would be callous enough to support the eviction of a widow and her young child so soon after the loss of her husband, but nobody would mourn Fisher as long as she would, and they would move on and expect her to do the same. She would have to move on. Still, she kept her thoughts to herself and Callum continued.

"I know that you've been distant with me after what happened between us at the party that night."

"Nothing happened between us," she interrupted. "I had no idea what you were going to do and I wouldn't have agreed to it if I had been given the chance, but I wasn't. I'm a married woman."

"You *were* a married woman," he corrected her coldly. "You're a widow now and you have this beautiful little girl to think of."

"I don't need *you* to tell me that. I have been thinking of nothing else."

"No, you haven't Olivia. Be honest. Since Fisher died, you've only been thinking of yourself."

"How dare you!"

"Please don't take me the wrong way. I'm not trying to be critical. Anyone in your position would be the same. How can you think of anything except what you've lost? I know that you saw a life laid out ahead of you that included Fisher, and now that can never be. It must be devastating. But you're not the only one who has lost him. This little girl will have to grow up without a father now, unless you do something about it."

"What are you talking about? There's nothing I can do about it now. Fisher is gone and he's never coming back." Olivia fought back her tears, refusing to share such intimacy with this man who dared to talk to her about such personal things. "Violet will have to grow up without him. That is no fault of *mine*," she added venomously. He ignored her implication and continued with the point he had been getting to.

"You can marry *me*."

His words fell through the air and almost struck her to the ground, they were so unexpected *and* unwelcome. Dumbstruck with shock, she could not find the words to tell him how she felt. Callum took the chance to forge ahead and deny her the chance to respond to her emotions in the moment.

"No other man will feel the way about you that I do. No other man will love your daughter the way that I already do. No other man will love you enough to accept that it will take time for you to move on from the love of your life. I will, because I know that if you give me a chance, in time, you might just come to love me too. Don't answer me now. Take time to think about it. I know you have a lot to consider."

Before she could say another word he turned and left her standing in the forest, surrounded only by the trees and tittering birds. Her thoughts were so clouded in disbelief, she had to sit for a while to fend off a wave of dizziness. It seemed as though the world were tilting sideways. Taking deep breaths to steady herself, she finally regained the sense to carry on and return home. After a light lunch she laid Violet down for an afternoon nap; after her time in the fresh air she immediately drifted off to sleep.

Feeling exhausted herself, Olivia went to her own bed and curled up on her side. Though she tried to push away the hurricane of broken thoughts that raced through her mind, she could not find any peace. It seemed there was no way out for her. After crying herself to sleep, she awoke with a resolution.

The next morning Olivia awoke early and packed a bag for a day trip to Frank. Violet squealed in delight and babbled incessantly over the joy of seeing her cousins unexpectedly. It was clear that she was delighted and this made Olivia smile genuinely for the first time in a long time. When they arrived in Frank they stopped first at the hotel to see Harold and to make sure that Margaret was at home. He was surprised to see her, but happy as always. She sensed a hopefulness in him. Perhaps it was because her surprise visit might mean that she had made up her mind about coming to stay with them, but she also wondered what he might be hoping for: that she would agree to come and stay, or that she would decline. There was no point in asking him directly, as she knew he would never tell her if he did not want her to stay.

Eager to see her sister, Olivia and Violet said their good-byes to Harold and continued on to Margaret's house. They did not have far to go and Violet was buzzing with excitement when they arrived at Margaret's doorstep. They both knocked loudly which made the little girl giggle uncontrollably. When Margaret answered the door, clearly shocked and elated to see them, they both cried out, "Surprise!"

"Come in! I wasn't expecting you two. What a wonderful surprise! Wait till your cousins see you young lady." Margaret tickled Violet, who giggled again. Olivia reveled in the sound of her daughter's laughter. She kissed her sister and handed Violet over so that Margaret could bring her to see the children and they could have some time alone to talk.

Making herself comfortable in the kitchen, she marvelled at the lovely belongings her sister had accumulated over the years. Margaret's life was not perfect by any means, but it was enviable. A part of Olivia felt at home here; she was with her family after all, which was so much nicer than being alone and lonely. Another part of her felt like an intruder, an imposter, someone who did not belong. She remembered all she had done to escape the grips of her parents and their disapproval at her abandonment of the life she had grown up with. This was the life Margaret had. It seemed so ironic to Olivia that the only options available to her now meant returning to the life she had once gladly left behind to be with Fisher. She was trying desperately to be honest with herself about how she felt about it all, though in the end it did not seem to matter, as she would never have what she wanted. She could *never* have her old life back.

Margaret glided into the kitchen, filled the kettle with water, and set it to boil on the massive cast iron stove. Then she came and sat directly across from her sister, gazing at her with curious eyes, likely trying to discern for herself why Olivia might have come, hopeful that she was here to accept her offer.

"So, to what do I owe the honour of this unexpected visit from my favourite sister?"

"I'm your *only* sister."

Margaret playfully waved away the assertion. "Moot point. Why are you here? Have you finally come to your senses? Are you going to leave Lille and come to stay here with us?"

Olivia looked away from her sister and bit her thumbnail as she searched for the words to tell her what had happened. She decided to get right to the point. "Callum Hollis has asked me to marry him."

"That snake!" Margaret erupted ferociously. "He knows you're still in mourning. He's got no class! No class at all. I hope you put him in his place."

"I didn't have a chance," Olivia admitted. "He told me he wanted me to think about it and disappeared before I could respond."

Margaret narrowed her eyes as she tried to peer into her sister. "You do plan on saying no I assume. There's no reason for you to feel like you have to resort to such a desperate act. You have your family."

"I know. Believe me, Callum Hollis is the last man on earth I would want to marry, but I don't know if that's any worse than hoisting all of my problems onto you and Harry. It wouldn't be right. You aren't my parents. I'm not your responsibility, and neither is my daughter."

"Nobody is trying to parent you Olivia. I think you know me better than that. I might not be your mother, but I am your sister, your *family*. There's nothing I wouldn't sacrifice for you."

"Not even your marriage?"

"Why would I have to sacrifice my marriage? You're being silly. You know how much Harold loves you. He considers you his family too."

"Maybe so, but things change. He might not feel so affectionate once he realises the financial burden of taking in a single mother and her young child. How long is this supposed to go on? It doesn't really seem like a sustainable solution to me."

"It can go on for as long as it needs to," Margaret replied. It was clear that she was growing frustrated with Olivia's hesitance. "Besides, I've spoken with our parents and they've agreed to help with the financial side of things if need be. You have nothing to worry about."

Her words stunned Olivia into silence. It had not occurred to her that her sister would betray her in such a way. Margaret knew how she felt about accepting anything from her parents after how they had treated her and

Fisher when they had told them that they were going to be married. She had not forgiven them, as she had seen it as a verification of the cold and heartless people she had always suspected them to be.

Growing up in their house had been stifling. Their demands had nothing to do with sense, or even with being happy. The only thing they ever cared about was their image and what others might think of them. The fact that she had dared to marry such a common working man had disgusted and humiliated them and they made no secret of it to her *or* to Fisher, telling him that she was miles above his station and that he was doing her a disservice to pursue her hand in marriage. She had been mortified and horribly embarrassed with their crass views.

Many men would have relented to their cruel demands and left her, but it did not phase Fisher in the least. He had made it clear that he would marry her with or without their approval and he did just that. She had not spoken a word to her parents since and had not had the desire nor the need. Though she had known that contacting them for help was an option she could consider, she had quickly rejected the idea, knowing she could never live with herself if she ever had to sink so low. Now here was her sister telling her she had gone and done just that in her place. She was almost as humiliated as she had been when her parents had openly abused the man she loved. The only difference was that a part of her had expected that behaviour from her parents. The betrayal from her sister was a shock.

"So you thought it would be okay to go behind my back to decide my fate with our parents? What would possess you? You know how I feel about them," Olivia sneered.

"Yes, of course I do. You never let me forget after all." Margaret sighed in frustration and looked to the heavens for the patience to say what she clearly needed to say. "But has it ever occurred to you that what you're doing is just as cruel as what they did to you? They've never met their granddaughter for goodness sake."

"How can you say that when you know how they treated Fisher? I will defend him, even when, no, *especially* when he's not here to defend himself."

"And what is it that you need to defend him against? Me? You know how much I loved him. I loved the two of you together. And with Violet, well, it seemed you had the perfect life, even if you didn't have much money to throw around." She hesitated and looked to Olivia for understanding. "But Fisher's gone and he's never coming back. Do you really think he would want to see you and Violet go without when it's not even necessary?"

"Well, we certainly wouldn't go without if I accept Callum Hollis's offer. I imagine even our dear parents could approve of his financial position."

"I can't believe you would even say such a thing after everything that man put you through. You're the one who's been blaming him for what happened to Fisher. Do you seriously think you could share a bed with the man you hold responsible for your late husband's death?"

Olivia replied as honestly as she could. "You know, I've been asking myself that very question ever since he proposed marriage. At first I thought, *absolutely not!* But to be honest with you, I'd rather subject *him* to my misery than you, and I have no interest in taking handouts from our parents. I was done with them a long time ago and that hasn't changed. The fact that you even went to them confirms my concern that my presence here would not only be an emotional burden for your family to bear, but a financial one as well. If not, you would have had no need to seek their assistance and would have given me your own charity, as I had assumed that was what was being offered all along. Now that I know that was not the case, I feel like I have no other choice but to accept his offer."

"Are you really that stubborn and prideful that you would rather marry a man you despise than turn to your family for support?"

Olivia looked her sister in the eye as she stood. "Please get Violet for me if you would. I should get going if I want to be on time to catch the coach back to Lille."

"You can stay here Olivia. We'd be happy to…"

"I'd rather not. I have some business to attend to with Callum Hollis. I intend to accept his proposal."

CHAPTER TWENTY EIGHT

When Emma got to the house her mother's car was still in the driveway. There was an eerie quiet as she unlocked the front door and made her way through the house calling out to her mother and Charlie. But there was no response, except for Max's quiet tail-wagging greeting. She checked upstairs in case they had not heard her, but they were not there. Her heart began to pound but she did her best to control her breathing and told herself that they were likely gone on a walk along the river, which would explain why they had lost track of time. That made the most sense, as the car was in the driveway, so they were obviously nearby, though it was a little baffling that they would leave the dog behind.

There was a chill in the air as she made her way up the hill which led to the path they always took to walk the dog along the river. The wind started to blow as she crested the hill and she pulled her jacket tight to her body. Surprised that she could not see her mother and Charlie from her vantage point, she knew that she would have to make her way to the woods. It finally occurred to her to call her mother's cell phone, but she found herself starting to worry once again when there was no answer. Quickening her pace as she traced her way along the river, she almost tripped a number of times and had to slow down to watch her feet as she walked. When she turned into the woods and there was still no sign of them, she started to call out, as the path was not much longer before running out at a barbed wire fence beside the railroad tracks.

After calling their names she stopped to listen for a reply, but all she could hear was the sound of the wind whispering in the trees, the relentless rumbling of the river, the panicky sound of her own breathing. After receiving no response to her cries, she continued on, hoping that they had just not heard her, or that she could not hear them calling back over the ambient noise of the forest. After climbing the low hill to the railway tracks which ran along a sheer rock face of slate, she had to accept that they were not there. There was no way for them to go but back from where she had come, and no opportunity for them to pass her on the trail without them seeing one another. The familiar sense of panic began to set in and she turned back at a trot through the forest, trying to control her emotions so that she could take the necessary care to make her way along the trail, which was beset with searching poplar roots covered by long stalks of fallen grass.

The cawing of some crows in the trees up ahead broke the quiet of the day. Emma looked up at them and had the creeping sensation that they were watching her. Normally she would have berated herself for being so foolish, but she had no such inclination with everything she knew. The sight of the mysterious black birds put her on edge and she knew she had to be on guard.

Just before the last turn on the trail which took her out of the forest and back into the open air beside the river, she heard the telling crack of a branch behind her. Instinctively, she turned with a smile, assuming that she had in fact passed by her mother and daughter without noticing and that they had seen her and decided to follow. But they were nowhere to be seen. She stopped in her tracks, listening for another sound, sure that she had heard something. There was a *snap* and although the hair was standing on the back of her neck, she started to walk back along the trail to see if someone or something was following behind her. As she turned back around the corner she had just passed, she was able to see back to the far end of the trail from where she had come.

A snippet of the river was visible through the bushes and trees and the trail itself was clear, though somewhat overgrown and wild. At first there was nothing to see except the path itself, until a black and white dog appeared on the path, its teeth set in a snarl. Emma knew this dog and knew what would come next. She decided not to stick around to see the terrible man who owned the mongrel. Every instinct forced her to turn and run.

Horrible panting and growling sounds seemed to fill the forest around her, but she did not turn around to see her pursuers again. She was almost clear of the forest when her foot caught on a root growing across the path, sending her crashing to the ground so suddenly that she had no time to react to help soften her landing. As she hit the damp, cool ground, her head bounced off of an unseen rock in the undergrowth. For a moment she seemed to be looking at the world through a darkening tunnel. Then everything went black.

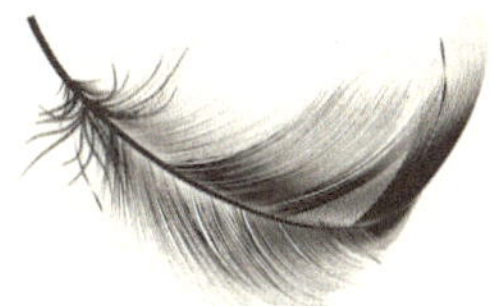

CHAPTER TWENTY NINE

Lille, Northwest Territory, Canada, 1902

As the grieving widow, Olivia did not think she could have been much more miserable, but she had been terribly wrong. Although she no longer had to worry about her financial security, there was no other benefit to life with Callum, unless she were to count the fact that he genuinely loved Violet and did anything he could to make her happy. She did not count this fact however, as she saw his love for her daughter as a liability to the girl's well-being.

Being the fool, she had believed him when he had said that he would be patient while she mourned the loss of her first husband. He accepted the fact that she did not love him, though he was arrogant enough to believe that it was only a matter of time and proximity. He really believed that in time she would come to love him because of everything that he had done for her.

Any time he felt that her attitude was ungracious, he had reminded her of this fact. It felt more like a business partnership than a marriage, which in a sense, Olivia realised it was. She had never loved Callum and was sure she never would. In fact, having blamed him for the death of her husband, she had loathed the sight of him. After avoiding him as much as possible she suddenly found herself married to him. Worst of all, she knew that her decision was more out of spite toward her family than out of a need for security.

The regret for her decision hit her the moment they had been pronounced husband and wife. It grew worse with each passing hour that night. Because of what he had said to her in his proposal of marriage, she had assumed that the arrangement of their marriage was to be platonic until she felt ready to consummate the marriage. She had been wrong. Callum had made it clear from the first night that although he could accept that it would take time for her to get over Fisher and for her feelings for her new husband to evolve, he would not tolerate some farce of a marriage. According to Callum it was her *duty* as his wife to share his bed in every way and he expected her to fulfil his needs. It was immediately clear to her that he did not care what *she* wanted or what *she* needed. He only cared about himself. Every time he touched her she cringed and crawled in her own private hell. What made matters worse was the fact that she had brought it upon herself. She was trapped like a fly twitching helplessly in a spider's web.

Every morning Olivia awoke enveloped in a feeling of disgust. She was disgusted with Callum and the thought of him touching her, and the awful feeling of him being inside her. There was no comparison to what she had shared with Fisher. That had been a joy she had looked forward to every time they could be together. With Callum it was a form of torment; all she could do was close her eyes and wait for him to finish and roll over to his own side of the bed. It made her feel ill.

Her new husband disgusted her in every way, but the disgust she felt for herself was much worse. It warped the way she saw herself as a woman and the way she saw her life. Even though she had married this man, she could not escape the feeling that she was no better than a common whore, because his money was the only thing she could ever be interested in. There was no way she would ever love him or *truly* want to be with him. The worst of it all was that she really had no interest in the money either, so she could not shake the feeling that she had married him for nothing. Not only had money never meant much to her in the first place, but things were so bleak and grey to her now that she could not bring herself to care about anything except the care of her daughter.

As if things could be any worse, Olivia also found herself to be completely isolated in her new sham of a marriage. Margaret and Harold had not attended her wedding; to be fair, she had not invited them or anyone else for that matter. They had not spoken since she had declared her intention to marry Callum. Estranged from her family and her best friend, she had never felt more alone in her life. If it weren't for Violet, she did not think she could carry on.

Every day she filled her time with her daughter, the only light left in her life. It worried her how much time they spent on their own. She did not want to isolate Violet in the same way that she had isolated herself when she shut her sister out of her life. It already tortured her enough that she had taken Violet's family away from her, despite how much she loved them, despite how much the poor girl had already lost.

Given the chance, she would have spent more time with the other mothers in the tiny town, but she could sense a wall between them any time she came around. Perhaps it was because she was now the mine manager's wife, which put her in a different social strata, not that *she* would ever care about such things, but the other women might. It was more likely, she surmised, that they judged her for marrying so soon after the loss of her loving husband. She could not help but wonder if any one of them would have chosen differently if they had been put in her position. This was a pathetic defence, she knew, but it was not fair that her own choices should impact her innocent daughter too.

Before long she had decided that it was easier to avoid these women and their awkward silences, but with the loss of her sister as a confidante, and the tense expanse in her marriage, she felt incredibly alone in the world. It was not fair that Violet had to bear the weight of her mother's need for human contact, though she never seemed to mind. Olivia was assuaged by the fact that her little girl loved her mother dearly and loved the time they spent together. Besides, when Violet was old enough to attend school with the other children, her magnetic personality would allow her to make her own friends and have her own life apart from her mother. What Olivia had not considered was that this self-imposed isolation from the other women in her world, and from her family, would put her in a terrible position of danger.

When things went from bad to worse, she felt she had nobody to turn to and nowhere to go.

They had been married for less than four months when Olivia found out how much of a tyrant she had bound herself to. He had let her know in the morning that he would not be home for dinner; the owners of the mine would be visiting for the day and he would be having dinner and drinks with them. It was late when he got home that night; Violet had been asleep for hours and the house had been quiet. Olivia sat at the kitchen table embroidering the hem of a dress she was working on for Violet with little flowers in light and dark hues. Because she was not adept with embroidery, having taken it up when she was already a grown woman, and because she wanted it to be perfect, it was taking forever to create each little petal. Though it could be an exhausting task, she also found it to have a tranquilising effect and she could pass the time away without constantly thinking of the misery that she had made of her life.

When he came stumbling through the door that night he seemed to be in a good mood. He was talking and singing to himself and laughing at something only he was privy to. Olivia had never seen him quite so inebriated. Although he often enjoyed a nightcap after dinner, she had noted that he rarely got even tipsy, leading her to assume that he needed to be in control more than he wanted to cut loose. But this night was obviously different.

Not interested in entertaining her stinkingly drunk husband, she started to put her embroidery away so that she could head to bed. He stood in her way, swaying and grabbing at her. “Where do you think you’re going? I thought we might do a little dancing or something.” He grabbed her and started to clumsily dance her around the room, then he buried himself in her neck and tried to kiss her but she pulled away.

“You’re drunk,” she said as she tried to get free of his grip, but despite his weakened state, he was still too strong to resist.

"So what? Can't a man enjoy a good time once in a while? Hmm?" He was subtly slurring his words.

"You can have all the good times you want. I won't stop you. But I'm tired and I'm going to bed."

"Well nobody said we couldn't have our good times in bed." He grinned his wolfish grin and pulled her closer again. He was breathing his venomous breath into her face and she tried to turn away from him, but he just held her tighter. She knew that her strength was no match for his.

"I'd rather not when you're in this state. Why don't you just…"

Before she could say another word he slapped her so hard across the face that the mark of his hand would be showing for days, leaving a bluish black bruise to turn a putrid greenish yellow, so that she was ashamed to leave the house for fear of someone seeing. She covered her cheek with the hand he had let go to strike her, but he still gripped her other wrist so tightly that it hurt.

"You are *my* wife now and you will do as you're told. If you want to continue to enjoy the generosity of my nature, you'll start to behave like the good wife I know you can be. If not, you're going to see a side of me you'll wish you would had never known." Callum twisted her arm and put his face so close to hers that she could feel his breath on her skin. "Do you understand what I'm saying to you?"

She had no words; she had nothing left. She nodded but she did not speak.

"Good," he barked at her and slapped her again on the side of her head, though not as hard as he had hit her the first time. "Then get in the room and get your clothes off. Maybe tonight will be the night we start a family of our own. It's time we give Violet a little sister or brother don't you think?"

Olivia closed her eyes and used all of her will to force herself to nod in agreement again, but still she said nothing. Her chest was hitching with the urge to sob, but she wouldn't let herself; she felt that she needed control of something at this moment. Callum released his grip on her wrist and she stepped back before carefully making her way around him to make her way to the room, to do as she was told.

That was the first time he hit her, but it was not the last. At first she was enraged with him and would make plans for how to get her revenge on him for how he dared to treat her. Still, she did what he demanded and did her best not to anger him. As things progressed it seemed to take less and less to provoke him. In time Olivia became convinced that he did what he did not because he was angry with her or frustrated with his marriage, but because he *enjoyed* it. Not only did the violence grow in frequency, it grew in intensity. She had come to see Callum Hollis, her husband, for the monster he really was. She had come to see herself as a ghost of the woman she once was.

CHAPTER THIRTY

When Emma awoke to the sound of John calling her name nearby, she was extremely disoriented. Still laying on the cold, hard ground, she was damp and chilled to the bone. Shivering uncontrollably, she came to understand where she was as the memory of her fall came back to her. Her head throbbed as she pushed herself up and she had to pause for a moment to fight the urge to vomit. She realised that she had likely suffered a concussion after being knocked out for what seemed a long time, judging by the gathering darkness and the feeling of her heartbeat pounding in her head like a hammer. John called again, closer now and she forced herself up onto her hands and knees, then slowly stood, feeling a little shaky on her legs. She was still swaying a little when he appeared in front of her on the trail.

"Emma!" he cried when he saw her standing in the forest. "What have you been doing? Are you alright?"

Her voice came out in a teeth-chattering croak. "I fell. I was knocked out. I think it was a while ago because I'm freezing."

"Oh shit!" John exclaimed and took off his jacket to put over her shoulders. "There, now let's get you home and into a warm bath right away. Are you okay to walk? Are you hurt?"

"Just my head I think. I can walk, but I think I'll hold onto you if that's okay."

"How about I'll hold onto you? Want a piggyback ride home?"

Emma could not help but laugh but the laughing hurt her head so she stopped and waved away his offer. "I'll pass. That would probably just hurt my head more. I really am okay. I just feel a little wobbly. Let's just hold hands."

"Alright, let's get moving then. I don't want you to catch hypothermia if you haven't already."

"Wait!" Emma stopped him before they started heading home. "I was out here looking for Mom and Charlie. Her car was here when I got home but I couldn't find them anywhere. Max was still in the house, but I thought they must have gone for a walk or something. Then I couldn't find them and there was a horrible dog and then I fell."

John stopped her in her panic. "They're okay. They're at home now. Charlie's already in bed; she's so wiped out from their day. Your mother decided they should make a day of it to get some time out of the house so they hiked up the trail to Bellevue. It's not that big of a hike, but Charlie was pretty impressed with herself and figured she should get some extra treats for energy. That's why they were late for lunch."

"Thank goodness!" Emma sighed heavily in relief. "I could not make sense of where they might have gone. With everything that's been going on I think I just panicked when they weren't home where I thought they would be."

"Everything's okay Emma, now that I've found *you*. We were just as confused about why *your* car was here but you weren't. When you still hadn't returned by the time I got back from work, your mother sent me out to look for you. She's pretty worried. She'll be relieved to see you're okay, aside from the goose egg on your head."

With Emma reassured, they made their way back along the river. Even though she was bitterly cold, Emma still found herself watching the woods as they neared the house, wondering if the woman Felix spoke of was lingering there. She knew this was likely the figure she had seen the night she herself had been lured into the forest, just like what had happened to Helen in her time here. With each passing moment she was coming to understand that much of her experience could be compared with Helen's, though she knew she was more fortunate because of the support she had from her family. John had taken time to come around, but he trusted her, despite everything she had put him through in the past, and eventually knew that he had to let his own notions fall away if he were to be able to truly take care of his family. She could not ask for a better husband.

Feeling overcome with emotion, she squeezed his hand and turned away from the forest to watch him in the early evening glow. He was already looking at her, but she saw with vivid clarity that it was not John holding her hand after all. It was *him,* and he was grinning at her. Although she could see being so close to him that his jaw was chiselled and his deep-set eyes could entrance any woman with a pulse, she was horrified by the sight of him and pulled her hand away so quickly that she fell back and hit the ground. Her head felt like it might actually explode when she struck the gravel road, although she caught herself in time so that she broke her fall painfully with her hands and was lucky that she did not break her wrists.

"Jesus Christ Emma! What are you doing? You're lucky you didn't hit your head again!" It was John's voice. Through the darkness she could see that it was John's face too. She began to cry quietly and John got down on his knees beside her and took her in his arms, rocking her gently. "Shh, it's okay Em. I'm sorry. Are you okay? What happened?"

It took a moment before she could stop crying long enough to speak clearly. "It was him! *You* were him. I don't know how. I don't even know if it was real any more. I feel like I'm losing my mind."

John did not ask any more questions. He simply pulled her up off of the ground and wrapped an arm around her shoulders as he led her the rest of the way home. Charlotte had seen them from the window where she had been watching and she ran out onto the front porch to bring them inside.

"She fell and hit her head in the woods," John told her. "We should get her inside and get her a warm bath and something to drink. She might have a concussion."

"Maybe we should bring her to the hospital then," Charlotte suggested, a note of worry in her voice.

"No. No hospital," Emma interjected. "I have no interest in sitting there for hours for them to tell us what we already know. Just stay with me and keep an eye on me like they would have told you anyway."

Charlotte begrudgingly accepted but only if Emma agreed to go if she started feeling worse or if she happened to lose consciousness again. Emma agreed to her mother's terms and let them take care of her for the rest of the night. Still shook up from her encounters with the man and his awful dog, she had no interest in being alone for the night anyway.

John stayed with her while she warmed herself in the bath. When they came back downstairs, Charlotte had prepared some hot cocoa, which made Emma nostalgic for her childhood when her mother could fix most problems with a hug and warm cup of cocoa. They sat and sipped their cooling drinks as Emma once again retold the story Felix had shared with her at the hospital.

"I wanted to get out of here tonight and spend some time at your place," she added once she was finished with the story. "But obviously my plans were thwarted. I'm sure that was no accident either."

"Maybe you're just feeling a little paranoid after hearing what happened to John's aunt. It's pretty close to home when it's family, even if you didn't know her. I'm sure one more night won't make a difference, and then we can get packed up tomorrow and head to my place. It's not like we have much choice anyway, now that Charlie's already fast asleep. You probably shouldn't be going too far after your big adventure either. And *we're* not going anywhere, are we John?"

"That's right. We'll be right here. You can get some rest tonight and head out tomorrow once you're ready to go."

"Sounds good to me. It's not like I have much choice anyway."

They spent the rest of the evening distracting themselves with old movies on the television until Charlotte finally drifted off, snoring lightly with her arms crossed over her chest and a frown on her face. She looked like she was contemplating some unsolvable problem. Emma woke her and they headed up to bed after what had been a draining night.

Once they got into bed Emma was no longer tired, though her head was still hurting. Fortunately the ibuprofen she had taken was starting to take effect so it was not nearly as bad as it had been earlier. John kissed her goodnight and she told him that she was going to stay up a little longer to read because she was not ready to go to sleep yet. As he rolled over she opened her end table to rifle for something to read. The journal she had found when they had gone to Lille on the hike that day was sitting on top of the other books and magazines she kept stored there for light reading before bed. The sight of it was a bit of a shock, as it had completely slipped her mind with all of the drama that had been going on.

Its cover was a beaten, faded brown leather, but it was still intact. She gently turned to the first page, listening while John's breathing slowed as he drifted off to sleep. Her heart was thumping furiously as she turned the delicate yellowed page to the first entry in the hand-written journal and began to read.

CHAPTER THIRTY ONE

Lille, Northwest Territory, Canada, 1903

"Are you sad Mommy?"

After receiving no response, Violet prodded her mother again. "Mommy? Why don't you want to play with me?"

Olivia snapped out of her stupor, took her daughter's hand and reassured her. "I'm fine sweetie. I'm just tired today. I didn't sleep very well last night."

"Maybe you need a nap. You can take one with me today if you want. I don't mind as long as you don't steal the covers."

Olivia laughed despite herself. "That sounds really great actually. I might just do that. Now finish your lunch."

"I am Mommy. You need to finish yours too." She looked at Olivia with concern, though she was too young to understand what her mother was going through.

"I will," Olivia lied, "but I think I'll wait until later. My tummy feels a little upset right now." Her hand instinctively went to her abdomen. But she had lied once again. She seemed to be doing a lot of that lately. Not really sick, Olivia was sore. All morning long she had been reliving what had happened between her and Callum before he left for work. It was a daily chore to try to keep her pains from Violet, who was growing more and more curious as she got older. Nothing got past her, but she was still young enough to fall for her mother's lies about what was happening to her.

Olivia always had some excuse for why she was not feeling well, for why she seemed sad, for why she was in pain. Careful to frame each story in a light which would not upset her daughter, she became a master storyteller, but she had no pride in the creativity of her deception. Olivia had come to see herself as a liar and a coward, covering up for the sins of a man she hated with all her heart. Her behaviour puzzled her, but she continued on anyway. Through the fog of her thoughts she had considered the possibility that she had gone mad from loneliness and abuse and that she was no longer capable of doing anything to defend herself against the monster she shared her bed with. But she knew that was just an excuse.

Having remarried while she was still freshly grieving for her first husband, she had not allowed herself the time she needed to overcome her loss. Now she felt she never would. As a result of her choice to estrange herself from her closest confidante, her sister, she felt trapped and alone. Worst of all, it had been her own decision.

Because she and the other women in town avoided each other more and more each day, she grew paranoid and isolated. Sure that she was a common topic of conversation amongst them, she wondered what they had to say about her. She wondered if they had any idea what was happening to her, and if they did, whether they even cared. Olivia was a pariah. But she was sane, like it or not. Insanity could not be used as her excuse for staying with a man who was destroying everything that was left of her. Olivia knew that she was sane, but her choices were far from it.

Before Callum had left for work that morning, she thought she would break the news to him once again that she was not yet pregnant. Knowing how upset it would make him, she decided to tell him just before he left so that he could take the day to get over it before taking his frustrations out on her. But she had been wrong. It had not mattered that he had practically been halfway out the door when she had told him, he would not waste the opportunity to turn on her like a wild dog.

"Useless bitch," Callum growled as he slapped her across the face. Olivia put her hand to her cheek, feeling the warmth of his slap as it drew her blood closer beneath the surface of her skin. "I do everything for you and you can't manage to give me this one thing? What's wrong with you?"

In a rare moment of defiance, she shot back at him, though her voice was quiet as she tried not to wake Violet who was still sleeping. "Maybe I'm not the problem."

He turned on her like a viper, his eyes wide with rage. "What did you say?"

She knew what he expected of her, that she would say 'nothing' and grovel in fear, but for some reason this morning she could not bring herself to do that, though she knew she should. "I said, maybe I'm not the problem, maybe it's you. Fisher and I had no problem conceiving." She hesitated for a split second, considering the enormity of what was about to come out of her mouth. "But then again, he was a real man. I actually *wanted* to be with him. Maybe it makes a difference."

They stood face to face for a moment, his face contorted in a hideous painting of rage, hers, a picture of calm defiance. Having no idea what the consequence of her words might be, she stood strong, ready for anything. The thought crossed her mind at that moment that he might actually kill her. In that split second she thought, *What do I care?* Then she quickly answered her own question with, *Violet...*

The little girl's smiling face, which looked so much like her father's, was in her mind when she felt the blow of his heavy boot. Callum kicked her without warning in the stomach. She went flying back to the floor, unable to breathe, as he had knocked the wind out of her and all she could do was writhe on the floor as she fought to catch her breath. Again the thought of death crossed her mind as she panicked for air, but before long she was gasping and spluttering through hot tears.

Callum said nothing more as he grabbed his hat and headed out into the crisp spring morning, slamming the door behind him as he went. Olivia stayed there on the floor until she regained enough strength to stand. It shocked her that Violet had slept through it all, but she was glad the girl was still asleep, so that she could have some time to herself to think.

Gingerly, she poured herself a cup of tea and sat at the kitchen table, looking out at the day as it was waking up. It was going to be a beautiful day it seemed, but she knew that there was nothing in it besides her daughter to bring her even a sliver of happiness. Things could not continue on this way. Repeatedly this morning the thought of her own death at the hands of her so-called husband had crossed her mind. The frightening part was how little it had bothered her, as though some part of her was secretly wishing for the release that it would bring from her self-imposed prison.

In that moment when he had attacked her, she had thought of her daughter. *What would happen to her if I was gone?* The right thing would be for her daughter to go to her family, to stay with Margaret and Harold, or heaven forbid, her own parents. Anything would be better than leaving her alone with Callum. But it would not be like Callum to do the right thing and he would likely try to keep the girl for himself. As her stepfather, he might just be able to get away with it.

When she considered the horrors that he might subject Violet to if left to his own devices, she began to despair. In the same moment it occurred to her that even if he did not kill her, she was not doing her daughter any favours by remaining in such misery. If he was willing to do the things he did to her, out of some sense of ownership and control, how could she assume that he would not eventually turn on her daughter in the same way. He was not really her father after all, and though the closeness of their relationship made Olivia feel ill with guilt, she knew that the fury of not having a child of his own grew more and more with each monthly disappointment. *What might he subject Violet to someday if given half the chance? How would he treat my little girl if I actually* did *bear his child?*

"How would you feel about visiting your cousins tomorrow sweetie?"

Violet's eyes popped open wide in gleeful surprise. "Really? I haven't seen them in forever Mommy! I'd love to go!"

"Okay then, we will. But the only way we can is if you keep it a secret. You can't tell Callum okay?"

"Why not Mommy?"

Olivia had been ready for this question. "Because sweetie, he'll want to come with us."

"That's okay, Mommy, I don't mind. He can come with us too if he wants. Don't you want him to come with us?"

"Of course I do honey." Olivia choked on her words as she prepared to manipulate her little girl. "Just as much as you do. There is one problem though."

"What problem?"

"Well, you know how much Callum works. It's probably going to be a while before he can take some time off to go. He'll probably want us to wait for him. Who knows how long that might take. But if we keep it a secret, we can go ourselves tomorrow. We won't have to wait so long. What do you think? We can wait until he's ready if you think that's best."

The wheels were turning in Violet's head. Olivia could see her being pulled between what she wanted: to see her cousins as soon as possible, and what was good: to tell the truth and wait if Callum wanted to join them. Because she was so little, Olivia was hopeful that the desire to see her cousins would outweigh her desire to be a good girl. It did not take long for her to decide.

"Okay, I won't say *anything*. Then we can go tomorrow *for sure*?"

"For sure," Olivia promised. She had no intention of breaking that promise.

It had been a tense night for Olivia. She had been walking on eggshells, wondering if Violet might slip up and reveal their plans to Callum. There was also the threat that he might lash out at her again, but she did her best to be sugary sweet, though it infuriated her to do so. It was her mission to stay out of his way and avoid any possibility of conflict. This was not a foolproof plan of course, as he did not require provocation to come at her, and he was likely still smarting from her show of defiance that morning. But it had turned out to be a quiet and uneventful night and she even noticed that Violet did her best to keep to herself, likely anxious that she might say or do something to upset the plan she had with her mother.

Olivia had packed a light bag for Violet, doing her best to avoid attracting any attention to what she might be doing. She knew that she was being paranoid, and that nobody would even care why she was catching a ride to Frank. Anyone who cared to even consider it would likely assume she was visiting her sister for the first time in ages. Still, she could not help but shiver as she waited to get on their way.

The morning was much colder than it had been for weeks and she felt that it must be a part of the curse which surrounded her like a fog. More than the chill of the morning, she shivered out of fear. She could not help but imagine a scenario where Callum just happened to be strolling by, or maybe even watching her, ready to stop them from leaving. She did not know what she would do if that happened; she simply hoped everything would go as planned.

It took until they were halfway to Frank before she could calm her nerves and convince herself that Callum was not going to catch her and stop her. For the first time in years she breathed a deep sigh of relief and basked in the feeling of freedom, even if it was going to be short-lived for now.

When she arrived on Margaret's doorstep for the first time in too long she was not sure what she should expect. Having turned her back on her dearest friend and only sister for something which now seemed so trivial in light of all she had endured at the hands of her husband, it did not escape her that she had chosen a brute she had despised over someone whose love and support she had always been able to count on. If Margaret slammed the door in her face she could not blame her, but she hoped that instead she would find forgiveness.

Finally, after what seemed an eternity, Margaret opened the door with a look of consternation, clearly not expecting a visit from anyone. It seemed to take a moment for it to register that her sister was actually standing right in front of her, so that Olivia was concerned that her fear might be right after all, and Margaret was not happy to see her. She hoped that the sight of her niece might at least temper her reaction so as not to upset the child too much. But after a moment of shock, Margaret grabbed Olivia and hugged her tightly. Olivia's many bumps and bruises cried out in her sister's grasp, but she barely felt them. It felt so good to be in Margaret's arms once again. So good to be in the arms of someone who truly loved her, even after all that had happened.

Margaret cried tears of joy as she whisked the pair into the kitchen and poured up some tea to warm them after their cold trip down the mountainside. Olivia was not sure how to say what she needed to say, but she knew she would have to wait until after their tea when she could send Violet to play. She needed time alone with her sister to reveal what had been happening with Callum and to share her plan to escape the prison of their marriage. Until then, she kept the conversation focused on what had been happening with Margaret and her family during their estrangement. Though things had been good for them with the business, as always, she readily admitted that it had been tough for them all to adjust to life without the frequent visits from her and Violet.

When they were alone, Olivia broke down and told the story of what her life had been like with Callum. She felt ashamed at how long she had stayed and allowed him to treat her as he had, but she also felt elevated, as though she could float away like a feather on the wind. The heavy weight which had been lifted from her, just in finally being able to tell her truth, was freeing. It occurred to her that this was the second time that she had experienced this sense of freedom just since leaving Callum's house. She was almost giddy with the thought of being away from his clutches.

When her story was told and there was nothing left to say, Olivia wiped her tears and held her sister's hand across the table. Margaret pleaded forgiveness. "I'm so sorry I was not there for you. I should have never let it go on so long."

"How could you be there for me when I wouldn't even let you? How were you to know what I was going through? Everything that has happened since the last time I laid eyes on you has been of my own doing because of my own stubborn stupidity. You are not to blame for any of it."

"I should never have broken your trust in the first place. I knew you wouldn't be okay with me discussing your private life with our parents. It was a stupid, thoughtless mistake. I am so sorry. None of this would have ever happened if I had just minded my own business. You were in such a bad place. I should have fought harder to stop you from making such a life-changing decision during your time of mourning; I knew you weren't thinking straight. It looks like we might share that stupidly stubborn trait after all."

"My obsession with taking revenge on our parents by cutting them out of my life, out of *Violet's* life, was self-centred and immature. They are far from perfect and I do not agree at all with their priorities or their way of thinking, but I've proven that I'm not so perfect myself, so who am I to judge? Losing Fisher far too early and this time away from you has shown me that time is precious, especially when it comes to time spent with family. I can promise you that I will *never* take that for granted again."

"I can't believe what I'm hearing! I'm so happy, but I can't deny that I am definitely shocked at such an enormous turnaround."

"Losing almost everything, including yourself, can teach you a lot about what's really important in life. Today is the start of a new life for me. I need to make sure that I'm wise enough to accept the support I'm going to need from those who love me the most. That has to include our parents, for Violet's sake *and* mine."

"A new life. Does that mean you intend to leave that bastard?"

"That's exactly what I intend to do, starting today."

Margaret put her hand over her heart and sighed loudly. "Thank goodness! I don't think you should ever set foot in that house again. That man's an animal and he's not to be trusted for a single second."

"I wish it were that simple, but he would just come here and cause a commotion. I don't want that, for Violet's sake."

"What do you mean? You can't be considering bringing that precious child back there now that you've gotten her away from that man."

Olivia shook her head and waved away her sister's concern. "Of course not. Violet's going to stay right here with you. I've already packed her a bag."

"Okay; but what about you? You can't seriously be thinking about going up there and spending the night alone with him. Look at the things he's done while Violet was there with you. What do you think he might do if it were just the two of you? What if he's suspicious of the fact that you've left Violet here with me after all this time?"

"I've already thought of that. I plan to tell him that *you* came to see *me,* and that although I had been shocked to see you, things went swimmingly well. I'll tell him that Violet begged to return to Frank with you to spend the night after so much time apart and that I couldn't refuse. I'll tell him that you will be bringing her back tomorrow. I can't see why he wouldn't believe that."

"But *why*? I don't see why you have to go back, when you can just stay here safely with us!" Margaret pleaded, but Olivia's mind was made up.

"I really have taken the time to think this through to ensure the best chance at success. I don't trust Callum to just take this lying down. God knows what he'll do when his pride is hurt. I want you to go today to buy a pair of train tickets to Calgary for Violet and I. Send a telegraph to our parents to let them know that I will be bringing their granddaughter so that we can stay with them for an extended period of time. We'll leave on the first available train."

Margaret's eyes grew wide with surprise. "Really? You're going to go stay with our parents? Not that I'm complaining really, but why don't you just stay here with me?"

"Because our parents don't live *here*. I think it would be wise for me to get as far away from that man as I can until I can find some way to get a divorce. I'm sure Father will be able to help me with that detail. Even then, I'm not sure that there's anything left here for me." She quickly added, "Aside from you and your family of course. You can come to see us whenever you want to though. Our parents would be thrilled to have a house full of children I'm sure."

"You really have thought this through haven't you?"

"I've had nothing but time to think. It's been torture. Now is the time to act and this is the first step. Will you help me?"

"Do you really need to ask, you ninny? Of course I'll help you. If I had my way, you'd never go near that man again. I'm still not sure if going back there is a good idea."

"Going anywhere near Callum Hollis is never a good idea, but I've got to be patient and smart about this. I can't take any foolish chances. And don't worry so much about me; I've managed to survive for this long with that monster. One more night won't *kill* me."

Leaving Violet behind had been more difficult than Olivia had realised, as it had been ages since she had been away from her little girl. There was a sense of relief in the fact that she was safe with her aunt and happy to be with her family once again. Leaving Margaret to return to Callum had been equally difficult. After the time they had spent apart, making up for lost time could not be accomplished in such a short visit. It saddened her to think that she would be returning to Frank only to leave again, and there was no telling when she might see her sister. It didn't change what needed to be done though. She knew that if she stuck to her plan she would have the best chance of escaping her marriage with as little ordeal as possible, if that was even possible with a man like Callum.

Being sure to get home as early as possible, she had his dinner waiting when he returned from work that evening as she always did. He had noticed immediately that Violet was gone and she took her chance to relay the story she had concocted to put him off. He grumbled about Margaret being a busybody and that she had better keep their personal business private. Then he finished his dinner without saying much more about it, which surprised her, as she had expected more of an uproar over her nerve to talk to anyone but him.

Hoping to keep the evening quiet, she settled in with her embroidery by the stove as Callum had his nightly drink and read a book he had been working on for weeks. She made an offhand comment about warming some water for a bath and offered to leave the water for him when she was done. He waved her off as he was engrossed in his book and she left unsure of what he wanted her to do, which was typical. This was a tactic he used so that he could complain later about whatever choice she made in lieu of his response.

Taking a bath was a time-stealing task, as it took forever to pump the water, warm the many pots on the stove and climb the stairs to bring them to the bathing room to fill the tub. With Violet gone for the evening, she did not have her usual routine to concern about which gave her the extra time, and she thought it might be a good idea to be freshly bathed in case her resourceful sister indeed found a way to get her out of town as soon as tomorrow. Olivia was giddy with excitement at the possibility and couldn't help but smile. She had just finished washing and rinsing her hair when she heard the sound of Callum's footsteps coming up the stairs.

The door was closed, but was not locked, as she had learned early on in their relationship that to do so would enrage him. As far as he was concerned, she had no right to refuse her husband the opportunity to stare at her or to grope her while she was naked and vulnerable in the bath. Such moments had been bliss with Fisher and hell with this man. All she could do as the door drifted open was take solace in the fact that tonight would be the last night she would ever have to do as he expected her to do. It would be the last night he would ever put his filthy brutish hands all over her. But tonight, like most nights, she would have to endure. Her thoughts returned to Margaret and she wished that she was sitting by a warm fire right now with her sister, wishing she had never left the warm nest of her home.

Callum closed the door behind him out of habit to keep the warmth in the room. Apparently he was planning on staying for a while. He rolled up his sleeves as she stared straight ahead, trying to seem natural and unsure of what that was. For so long she had lived in misery but had to pretend out of a sense of survival to be happy, though she knew that he had never fooled himself into thinking that she actually *was* happy with him. There was no hiding that fact or he would feel no need to beat her the way that he did. Though she wondered if he would have beaten her, even if she had returned his feelings initially, if it was just something that was in his nature.

No; he did not believe her lies about being happy with him, but he expected her to carry on with the lie, or *else*. It was just another opportunity for control. Olivia often thought that he would not prefer for her to love him, because it was always the perfect excuse to hurt her without conscience. Now that a part of her knew she would soon be free, she did not know how to put on the act, but she did her best anyway.

Callum removed his cufflinks and rolled up his shirt sleeves. Olivia frowned, knowing this meant he intended to touch her and she would have to let him. Again she regretted leaving the safety of her sister's home, but she pushed the thought away and commanded herself to be fully in the moment, as much as it horrified her to not escape to somewhere else, somewhere he was not. It was important that she remain on her guard and fully aware at every moment. She knew how sly her husband could be. Sometimes he had ways of making her tell him what he wanted to know whether she wanted to or not, but there was too much at stake for that now.

He started to massage her shoulders first and she had to fight the urge to tense up, though again she wondered how she had responded in the past before she had an actual escape plan. Had she tensed up then? Had she fought the urge? She could not remember and so she took the safe route and fought the urge. When he moved his hands to her breasts, massaging them softly as they floated in the water, she closed her eyes and wished for it to be over as quickly as possible. To her surprise she got her wish and he went back to rubbing her shoulders and her neck.

"It must have been a real surprise to have your sister show up here today," he began. Olivia was immediately on guard. Why was he bringing this up *now*? She had hoped the conversation on the subject had been done earlier, but clearly he had more to say. The feeling of vulnerability increased as she worried that he might be more angry about her visit with Margaret than she thought. It had surprised her that he'd had so little to say about it during dinner, as he always had to have his say and she had to listen. He had no interest in her opinion so she kept it to herself.

Thinking quickly as she had learned to do with this man, though it often was not quick enough to avoid a slap or a punch, she decided to appeal to his ego to put him on the spot, acting as though she had presented him as the good husband. "You don't mind her stopping by do you? I told her you would be happy that I don't have to be so alone all the time anymore. She was happy to hear that you and Violet are so close. I told her, *a girl needs a father in her life*. But she pointed out that she needs her family too, especially when they live so close. I told her that you would agree wholeheartedly, since Violet means so much to you." She fought the urge to hold her breath as she waited in anticipation for his reply. After spewing her rambling stream of thought she wondered if he could feel the rabbit pulse of her heart through his hands on her neck and did her best to steady her breathing.

"Of course I want what's best for Violet," he said in a soft voice without hesitation. Olivia was put at ease. She would do whatever it took to get through this hellish night and then tomorrow she would be a free woman for the rest of her life. Though she was young, she knew she would never marry again, and she was fine with that. All she wanted was a life with her daughter, with her *family*. Then he leaned in to be closer to her ear. "I have to ask though, do you think that having a lying whore for a mother is really what's best for her?"

Fighting the urge to jump up and flee, knowing that he would just overpower her, and that the tub was not a safe place for that to happen, she knew she had to continue on with the ruse and do her best to defuse the situation. But what *was* the situation? Why was he calling her a liar? She was terrified to refute him, but she had no choice given his accusation, "I... I didn't lie to you Callum! You know I never lie to you. I know better." Olivia tried again to appeal to his enormous ego, with a different approach. At times she thought he behaved more like a father than a husband with all of his demands, so she knew to behave like he was the one in charge.

"Then why did you tell me that Margaret stopped by when one of my men told me that he saw you this morning, loading my daughter into a carriage? Are you calling him a liar?"

Olivia flinched as though he had slapped her and he tightened his grip on her shoulders "No… no of course not. But he was obviously mistaken. We were right here this whole time. I swear on my…"

Olivia was not able to finish what she had been saying because Callum had suddenly gripped her shoulders painfully hard and pushed her down under the water. She fought and struggled, seeing his face floating above her, her vision of him warped by the water as she thrashed wildly in the tub for release. He pulled her back up out of the water and she gasped for air, gulping it in case it might be taken away again.

"Callum! What are you doing?" She screamed through her tears. "Let me go!"

"Why? So you can lie to my face and treat me like shit? I know what you're up to. You had no intention of bringing Violet back here. But when I'm through with you, I'll be going to pick her up. She's not going anywhere, and neither are you." Again he forced her head under the water without warning.

Intent on gaining the freedom she had so desperately longed for, Olivia fought with everything she had to get her head above water, to take the breath she so desperately needed. As she fought she thought of Violet and the life they would have together, she thought of her sister and the love they had found again, having never really lost it in the first place. But these would not be her final thoughts.

Instead, in the moment before she had to give in and take the final dying breath which should have finally set her free forever from any pain or suffering and rejoined her with the only man she could ever love, she thought of the man whose face loomed menacingly above her. Strangely enough, as he took her final moments from her, she was no longer afraid. All she wanted in those final hellish moments was to seek her vengeance on this man. She swore he would never take her daughter for his own.

As the water filled her lungs and her life slipped away, she cursed Callum Hollis to a life of torment at the hands of her own angry and wounded spirit. In her mortal rage, she did not stop to consider that she was cursing herself as well. In the moment that she crossed from the world of the living to the realm of the dead, she knew that she had damned herself to be tied to this monster for the rest of eternity. Once again, she had bound herself to him. Once again, she had only herself to blame.

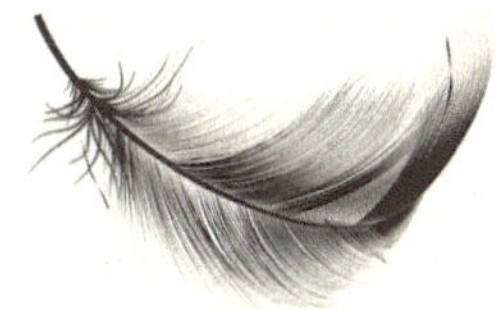

CHAPTER THIRTY TWO

Emma had started reading the journal in bed while John drifted off to sleep, and had been instantly entranced. She could not help but feel a sense of guilt in the act of reading someone's private thoughts, but she put it aside using the excuse that it did not matter because they were long gone, as the journal dated back to the turn of the century. It had been a heftier read than she had expected from a hand-written personal journal and she had finally decided to slip out of bed and continue her reading at the kitchen table with another cup of hot cocoa. Before long she was furiously rereading and marking passages to share with her mother and John, though she was careful not to actually write on or damage the book, as she was sure it must have some historical significance to someone. By the time she finished reading, she had no doubt.

The inscription in the front of the journal indicated that it had been penned by a man by the name of *Callum Hollis.* At first Emma had asked herself if she had heard the name before, as it had a ring of familiarity, but she chalked it up to her exhaustion and runaway imagination and carried on reading. It was clear that the man had started writing as an outlet for an obsession which had started when he fell in love with a married woman named Olivia, after helping to deliver her baby girl.

Early on in the journal she noted how he had posed as a friend, knowing the husband would have no choice but to oblige, as he was one of his employees. Callum Hollis had been the manager of the coal mine in Lille and Olivia's husband Fisher had worked for the mine as a carpenter. Through his writing Callum revealed how he felt about his deception of the unwitting couple who had welcomed him openly after what he had done for Olivia and their daughter Violet:

> *There are times when I look at Fisher and wonder what he would do if he knew of the indecent thoughts I have every time I'm near his wife. I know that I should feel guilty, that he's a good man who has welcomed me into his home and trusted me with his family. I also know that I would betray his trust in a moment, given half the chance.*
>
> *But I don't feel guilty. I feel nothing for Fisher except a deep envy and resentment for everything that he has that I do not. And why? Why would a woman like Olivia give herself to a man like him with nothing to show for all the hard work he's done because he doesn't have the brains God gave him? Why ?*
>
> *Olivia would be better off with me, but I fear she will never know, unless some stroke of good fortune (or bad - depending on how one looks at it), were to end their marriage. I know she would never betray her marriage, she is too good and loyal a woman. But if for some reason she were no longer married, I know that she would want me just as much as I want her.*
>
> *I could give Olivia and Violet a life that Fisher never could. It drives me mad to know that things will probably never change.*

Emma was intrigued. Who would have buried this book and why? Had Callum Hollis himself been the one to hide it? If so, for what reason? The only way to find out was to continue reading. Already she found that she had a serious dislike for this man, but was curious about why she had been drawn to this journal in the first place. It had all been so surreal. There had to be a reason.

As she read on she saw a gradual change in the man's thinking, as his obsession with an unattainable woman continued to rule his life. In time he shifted from *wishing* things could be different somehow to *planning* for how they could be different. He seemed to be growing impatient and his way of thinking always supported his entitlement to do as he pleased, regardless of who got hurt. In time he finally decided to take action in a small way, and though she knew that one man kissing another man's wife was never the right move, it would have been looked down upon so much more in this context, when even married couples avoided displaying their affections in public. It seemed his fixation was causing him to lose his inhibitions. He had decided that he would take what he wanted however he could:

> *Tonight was the night after all! Everything went off without a hitch. I managed to find an excuse to keep Fisher busy just before the stroke of midnight, while ensuring that I would be with Olivia when the time came. It made for the perfect excuse. She never knew what had hit her, but I could tell that she had wanted it just as much as I had. She would never admit it of course, she's too proper a woman for that, but a man can tell.*
>
> *Better yet, she was totally unaware that Fisher walked back into the hall at the perfect moment, just in time to witness our sweet embrace. The coward left without saying a word to me about it. Had the tables been turned, I would have pummelled the man, but he did nothing. More evidence that he does not even deserve her.*
>
> *I can only hope that Olivia will make the choice to keep our indiscretion to herself. If she does, it will give Fisher reason to question why she would be keeping secrets from him. His trust in her will be destroyed. If she does decide to tell him the truth*

things could get sticky, but I'll cross that bridge when I come to it.

I can feel it in my bones; the tide is beginning to turn. It's just a matter of time.

Emma sat back in her chair shaking her head. It was so strange to have this kind of insight into the mind of a man like Callum Hollis. If he was not a full-blown narcissist, he definitely was a self-centred, arrogant son-of-a-bitch. Without knowing them, her heart went out to this innocent couple whose lives were being toyed with by someone who claimed to be their friend.

In her heart she hoped that Olivia had told Fisher everything soon after, but her mind told her that was likely not the case. She wondered what she would do herself if put in the same position. On the one hand, it would be easy to convince herself that it meant nothing because it was a friend, or make the excuse that her husband would be better off not knowing, since she did not return whatever feelings the man had and it would really just hurt his feelings and destroy a friendship. That was assuming that Olivia did not have feelings for Callum, though she did not know how any good woman would not be able to see such a dog for what he really was.

On the other hand, it would be difficult to keep a secret like that from your husband without feeling guilty, as though you had done something wrong that needed to be kept hidden. Most wives would probably feel fine about destroying a friendship if she knew the man to be a snake like Callum. But of course, Emma knew she was making assumptions again. She was assuming that this woman Olivia *knew* how Callum felt about her and what he was up to and that probably was not a fair assumption to make.

Though she was sickened, she was also intrigued to see how things turned out, so she continued reading. Callum commented on running into the woman after what he had done, but it was clear that everything he said about their interactions was warped in his mind to be what he wanted it to be, regardless of how Olivia behaved or what she said.

Soon after, he made an entry which shocked Emma to tears. She had not expected to have such a visceral reaction to anything she might read in this distant narrative. A part of her had obviously connected with the couple this man was targeting, because when she read that Fisher had died on the job under Callum's direction, she felt partly sad and partly sick. It no longer mattered whether Olivia had told him anything, because he was gone. In his writing, Callum acknowledged that he was partly to blame for what had happened that night:

> *Fisher is dead. A part of me feels responsible for what happened. Though the trestle needed to be fixed before the line could open again, halting all progress for moving the coal, there was no reason it couldn't have waited for the morning when the storm might have calmed. But that was not how it worked out. I saw my chance to stick it to Fisher as my subordinate and I took it.*
>
> *I won't say I intended for his death to happen; I have no control over the fates after all. My intention was to take him away from his wife for a night of frigid misery in the Rocky Mountain winds. I also won't say however that a part of me isn't happy that things turned out the way they did. As I said, I'm not in control of the fates, but clearly, they have decided to favour me anyway.*
>
> *Fisher's death has opened a door that had been closed to me before. I will not deny my own fate and ignore the opportunity that has been laid at my feet. It will be a matter of patience. It will be a matter of time. But mark my words: Olivia will be my wife. It was always meant to be.*

"Monster," Emma whispered to herself then jumped at the unexpected sound of her own voice. She stopped to sip her drink which had grown cold. Taking a pee break would be a good idea anyway. By the time she was back the kettle would be warm again and she could get right back to reading, though she was concerned about where things were headed now that Fisher was gone. Her connection to the vulnerable Olivia grew stronger.

When she returned to reading she hesitated, asking herself if she really wanted to know what happened next. Even though she was concerned about how the outcome might affect her feelings, she could not deny that she was invested in knowing how things turned out for Olivia and her young daughter Violet. The entries had slowed for a while and the dates between them grew more expansive, until finally Callum indicated that it was time to move his plan forward. As time progressed he noticed that Olivia was still devastated and was growing more and more desperate, as she still had not left the house she and Fisher had shared, which was not the norm in a busy mining community like Lille. The mine needed the house she was living in for the man who had replaced her husband, but Callum had been in no rush to kick her out, biding his time when he would ask her to be his wife. He believed that the fact that she was staying there still showed that she was waiting for him to finally ask, but he knew that they had to wait at least long enough for things to have the air of decency. It had been a difficult wait.

Even if she did not want to marry him, he knew that her remaining in the house meant that she had no other viable options, which made her desperate, which made her vulnerable. Callum had no qualms with exploiting her vulnerability to get her under his roof and into his bed.

When he described his proposal, Emma was devastated that Olivia had not had the chance to tell him where to go right then and there, but she was completely destroyed when he wrote about his elation at her acceptance of his proposal. How could she not see what a monster he was? She had to at least realise the part he had played in Fisher's death. It was difficult not to judge her for her horrible choice so soon after losing her husband, but Emma reminded herself that the times were different and that a single mother with no work back then could count on ending up homeless, destitute and probably dead.

At first things seemed tense in the marriage from what Emma could gather from Callum's frustrated writings. Horrified that he had forced Olivia to sleep with him from the start, even though she had objected, Emma found herself hating him even more than she already had. So when she read that not only did he continue to force himself on her night after night, knowing that she did not even want him, but that he had dared to hit her, she had to take a break from reading. She was furious, yet was stuck with a feeling of helplessness, knowing that there was nothing she could do to affect the past, knowing that this trauma had happened to a real woman. Emma could only imagine how Olivia had felt day after day living with this man.

As the writings continued, so did Callum's excuses for abusing Olivia. Emma noticed that the beatings were growing in frequency and intensity. Her heart was pounding as she feared where this tragic story might be heading. Still, she was not prepared for the entry when he admitted that he had finally lost control. Emma had to step outside so that she could sob without waking the whole house when he revealed the truth. She had to take a few moments to regain her composure before she could read on about what he had done that night:

I am a doomed man. I have killed my wife.

It wasn't on purpose, I merely wanted to scare her, to punish her for her betrayal. In my attempt to teach her a lesson, I have taken her life. In a manner of speaking, I guess I am to blame. I took it too far this time. But the truth is that Olivia herself was really to blame. If she had not betrayed me, then lied about it to my face when given the chance to come clean with what she had done behind my back, then none of this would have happened. If she had been the dutiful wife she had promised to be when I took pity on her plight and married her, I would have never had a reason to strike her. But it is all a moot point now. Olivia is dead.

Now I may pay the consequence for losing control of myself in the moment. People are bound to wonder where she has gone, especially if Violet is still with me. Now that she has reconnected with that damn busybody of a sister, it will only be a matter of time before she comes looking for her and starts poking her nose around demanding answers.

It took all night to dispose of the body. I had to wait for cover of darkness before I could do anything, but the deed is now done. There is no reason to worry that anyone would find her now. All I can hope is that I was not seen by any of the neighbours. It was a filthy and grisly job, but it had to be done. The worst part of it all was using the bath water that I had just drowned her in to get cleaned up, but this was not the time to be squeamish about such things.

In the morning I will pack up a few essentials and give my notice to the mine. I'll gather Violet from Margaret's and tell her that Olivia is waiting at home to see her daughter and that she sent me to collect her. If I leave town immediately, no one will ever know that Olivia is even gone. And if anyone saw me tonight, I will have put some distance between myself and their queries.

Though it will be difficult, I must try to get some sleep now. Tomorrow will be a long day and I will have to be on my toes. If everything goes as planned, maybe I won't be a doomed man after all.

"Fucking animal!" Emma raged and slammed the journal down, then caught herself and covered her mouth with her hand. She listened intently, making sure she had not awakened anyone with her reaction to Callum's confession. It was stunning to know that he had done something with her body and had likely gotten away with it, considering the fact that she had found the journal buried in the dirt in a deserted town which had reverted nearly to its natural state since all the buildings had been moved. Still, she decided not to jump to any conclusions. The only way to find out how things had turned out would be to read on. Emma knew it would be a difficult task.

It infuriated her to see how little value he held in this poor woman's life. He had destroyed who she was then took all she had left. All Emma could hope was that even if Callum had gotten away with what he had done to Olivia, that he was not able to steal away with her young daughter as he had planned. The thought of this innocent child at the mercy and under the influence of the devil who had tormented then murdered her own mother in cold blood was more than she could stand.

Emma yawned and avoided looking at the clock, determined to find out everything she could before she returned to bed. She knew she would never be able to sleep unless she knew how things had turned out for Olivia's only child, who had now lost both of her parents. The thought of her growing up without them was devastating. She hoped that Callum would have had a change of heart and left the child with her real family to grow up with someone fit to raise a child. Perhaps Olivia's sister would have put her foot down and refused to return her niece to this monster unless her mother was with him. Surely, she knew not to trust him.

It would be even better if he had been caught and arrested before being able to get his hands on little Violet. The thought of someone putting a child through this, a little girl like her own, made her wish there was something she could have done to help, and this was what made her feel helpless. She reminded herself that whatever had happened, these people were long gone. There was nothing she could do to help Olivia or Violet at this point.

Still, Emma found herself to be more invested in this story than she had ever imagined she would be and she could not help but wonder why. All she knew was that she identified with Olivia, simply because she was a woman and she was a mother, and because of her own past. Emma knew what it meant to be vulnerable. Her situation had been very different of course. With everything she had gone through, John had been there for her through it all, never giving up on her, even after all she had put him through. She was reminded every day how fortunate she was to have found such a good husband and father and a story like this made her even more grateful to have such a loving and forgiving man in her life.

For so long she had struggled, insecure with the thought that he would resent her for the things she had done while she was ill, worried that he would be forever waiting for her to slip again. And he had been worried, when all this had started, worried enough to contact her mother and have her come to visit. Again, she had not been herself, though this time it had been something completely different. A pang of guilt struck her when she reminded herself that the only reason he had been so worried was because she had been keeping the truth from him, again failing to trust in his love. She assured herself that from now on, she would not allow herself to feel insecure about John's love for her. He was a good man who had stood by her through the worst; there was no reason to be afraid.

Preparing herself for what she might learn, Emma reopened the old journal and returned to where she had left off. Perhaps if someone more familiar with the tragic history of the Crowsnest Pass had been the one to read the account and had noticed the date Callum had recorded, they would have seen what was coming. But Emma had not grown up in the mountain town and she knew little about the colourful history of the place. And though she knew about the event which he would retell, she had not memorised the date, or even the year when it had occurred. In the end, she got her wish that Violet would not leave the town of Frank to go live with the man who had murdered her mother, forever lost to the only family she had left.

April 29, 1903

Today has been a nightmare. I could have never imagined that an act of God would take the only thing I had left: my precious little Violet. All I had planned, all I wanted for her, gone. Gone! How can it be that yesterday I awoke a man with a family, the family I had wanted, and now today…today I have lost it all.

It was still dark when I was nearly thrown from my bed by a violent shaking and shuddering of the earth. At first I was convinced that there must have been a massive explosion at the mine here in Lille, or that one of the shafts had collapsed, or even that we had experienced an earthquake, which would have been extremely rare in this region. But it was none of those things.

When I checked my watch, I could see that it was only 4:10 a.m., which explained why it was still so dark outside. I had not slept that long at all when I had been awakened by the violent event. When I was dressed and emerged from the house, I saw a massive greyish white plume of what appeared to be smoke, but turned out to in fact be dust. There has been a great disaster!

For reasons yet unknown, the northeast face of Turtle Mountain has come crashing down, destroying everything in its path. The mine has been wrecked, there is nothing left of the rail line, and the eastern edge of Frank is gone! Crushed under all that limestone, as though it were never there. I helped in the search, hopeful that we might find little Violet alive, but I knew all along that there was little hope.

Margaret and Harold's house and hotel were both destroyed in the slide. Those who survived by some miracle have already been found. There will be no miracle for me it seems. I guess it is what I deserve. Perhaps my dear little Violet's life is the cost of my penance for taking her mother's life. But the child was worth so much more than her mother ever was, she was so dear to me, and my only real true love in life. She has shown me that the love of a parent is far greater and more sincere than romantic love or even marital commitment could ever be. I have lost more than I can ever get back. I can't help but think that God is punishing me.

At the same time, he has given me solace. Because of the slide, I needn't worry about producing an explanation for Olivia's disappearance. I need simply say that she and dear Violet were both staying with her sister last night and that they were both lost in the disaster. As long as no one saw what I did last night with Olivia's body, I have no reason to fear. Part of me says I should go now, just in case that is precisely what happened. Why take the chance to still be here if someone comes around asking questions or pointing fingers?

On the other hand, it has been a long day and I have been visible both in Frank, or what's left of it, and here in Lille. In all that time, no one approached me but to thank me for helping in the search effort. If that is the case and I am scott-free, it would be a foolish choice to leave behind such a lucrative position. This is everything I have worked for, and it would be a shame to allow this tragedy to be any worse than it is. It may be worth the risk. No matter what, I will have to get some rest and hopefully the right decision will come to me in my sleep. I have to believe that I don't deserve to lose any more than I have already lost.

This certainly was not what Emma had expected. She sat stunned in silence, staring at the tattered and yellowing pages in front of her. The gall of the man was astounding. The fact that he felt sorry for himself was ridiculous considering all that he had done. She felt guilty for thinking that Violet had been better off in the end than had she ended up with Callum Hollis, but the alternative had been so unfair. Emma wept quietly for the tragic loss of the little girl and her family. It suddenly occurred to her that he mentioned the time of the slide to be 4:10 in the morning. She had disregarded the chill that detail had given her as she had read it, until it occurred to her that this was the time she had been waking again and again, since before she had even come to live in the house. But it had not started until after they had been informed that they had inherited the house; she was almost sure of that.

It was astounding that this journal she had discovered in Lille, through the strangest of circumstances, at the old site of their current house, was so directly connected to the famous rockslide of Frank. Pushing away from the table, she left the kitchen and went to the backyard to look up at the mountain. It seemed peaceful, with the moonlight glowing brightly on its jagged face, and yet Emma felt it seemed more menacing than it ever had. Though she had often thought of all the people who had died in the disaster so near her home, somewhere near a hundred souls lost, she had never felt so close to the event, had never felt so personally connected to it than she did at that moment.

The book was obviously a historical treasure, though so much of what it contained was a horrible narrative of a sick man's terrible thoughts and deeds. Still, she knew that when she was done reading it, she would have to hand it over to the right people to take care of it and share it as a unique piece of history with the people who made up the fabric of the community as well as those who came to the Pass to enjoy the beauty of the Rocky Mountains and experience the mythical past of the area.

A part of her felt guilty for not bringing it to them earlier. Perhaps she should not have been the first to read it, but she had honestly forgotten about it with all that had been happening, and had felt compelled to read it when she had finally discovered it again. There was no denying that the circumstances of her finding it had been truly strange and would be hard to explain to the staff at the historical society, but she could probably leave out the really weird details and just keep it simple.

Upon returning to the kitchen, she had decided to finish with the confessions of Callum Hollis. There was nothing more to learn about what had happened to Olivia and Violet after all. Their story had been a terrible tragedy in the end. But she could not help but wonder why she had been the one who had been almost hypnotised into finding it and felt that she needed to see it through to the end. She was still sure that there was nothing she could do about it, but to not know would drive her mad. Overcoming her guilt for wanting to know the outcome for such a horrible man, she turned back to where she had finished reading.

Last night I dreamed of Violet. I knew it was her because she looked right at me and smiled, as though everything were just as it was before. She had always been so happy to see me when I would return home from a long day of work. I never realised just how much that meant to me until it was gone.

In the dream I tried to reach her, to hold her, to tell her that everything would be okay now, that I would keep her safe. But when I reached for her, she ran from me. I felt that I should follow her and she led me to the river which flowed past her aunt's house in Frank.

When I called to her she turned and smiled again. When I asked her to stay with me she giggled and put her little hand over her mouth the way she always had, then finally she spoke, saying, "Find me." Then she turned and ran on the path that runs along the river. I tried to find her, but she had vanished.

I know this is a sign. I am meant to stay. Someday, somehow, I will be with my little girl again. Our love was always meant to be, from the day I brought her into this world with my own two hands. A love like that cannot and will not be torn apart. I know she wants me to stay, so that is what I will do, whatever the cost.

As she read on, it disgusted Emma to learn that Callum had indeed gotten away with what he had done. It seemed no one had ever seen whatever he had done with Olivia's body and he had taken the risk to stay on as the manager at the mine. There were huge gaps in the dates from there on, and it seemed that when Callum did feel the urge to write down his thoughts, it was because he was suffering the torments of a guilty conscience. Many of his accounts came out much the same:

I saw her again last night. I saw Olivia. I filled the tub so that I could bathe. I'll admit that I often think of her when I do, for reasons too obvious to discuss further. After I had finally filled the damned thing, I went to my room to find clean clothes to wear to bed. When I returned to take my bath, there she was, plain as day.

But like before, she was not herself. She is a ghost of the woman, a demon. She is bloated and grey and her wet stringy hair hangs in her face. Her eyes bulge from their sockets like they did in those final moments when she looked up at me from beneath the water, but they are black and monstrous now. I am always struck by the sight of the blackened bruises which stand out on her neck, symbols of the death I brought upon her. When she opens her mouth in a menacing grin, I am sure that she will speak, and that when she does, I will have lost my mind, if I haven't already. Instead of words or breath, water pours from her mouth. It is a putrid reminder of what I have done.

I am sure she has cursed me and I do not know what I can do. When I first dreamed of Violet, I had hoped to see her again, even if it was only in a dream, but that has never since happened. Instead it is Olivia, over and over again. But if this is the price I must pay, I will pay it. I am sure I've lost my mind, but she is always so real when she appears. Regardless, I won't give her the satisfaction of chasing me away or guilting me into giving myself up in some pointless pang of conscience.

No. Instead, I will carry on living with her, or the terror that pretends to be her, until the day comes that I find my little Violet again. Despite all that I have done and all that I have been through, I know in my heart, I will see her again. I just have to be strong.

Without much more to say, aside from providing a narrative of the curse he was sure he was suffering through, Callum's entries became more and more sporadic, often with gaps for months at a time. Finally there was a change in the routine that marked his life, a life which involved longer and longer hours at work in the hopes of avoiding the ghost he was convinced was haunting him in his home. After complaints from too many unsatisfied customers, tests had determined that the coal from the mine was too poor in quality to make mining it lucrative any longer. This had meant that the town of Lille in its current location no longer made any sense.

By now, according to Callum's dates, it was 1912, almost a decade since the violently devastating slide which had taken so many lives.

I have to admit, the idea of leaving this place has brought me a renewed sense of hope. Could it be too much to ask for that when I go, perhaps the demon who has consumed so much of my mind, my life, my soul, might stay here where she took her last breath? I won't count on it, but this is the first time I have felt any possibility of a new life that I can look forward to.

The house will come with me, which is part of why I worry that my time with that wretched witch may not be finished yet, but there would be no other option anyway. I will be moving to a new administrative position with the mine but they need me to maintain my residence in the Crowsnest Pass. Lille will be hauled away, building by building to be spread throughout the various towns in the region. The teams of horses have been coming from afar to prepare for the massive undertaking. It is probably best that I remain in this house, lest its secrets be revealed to anyone else.

I was given the opportunity to choose where the house would be located, and I have chosen a spot just east of where Violet was lost. I could not be any closer to her permanent resting place. With everything I have seen, if I am not completely out of my mind (I am not convinced one way or the other anymore when it comes to that particular detail), then there is still a chance that she will find me and I can be with her. Maybe now she will find her way home and we can both finally rest in peace.

From then on, Emma noticed a more upbeat tone to Callum's entries, and she found herself resenting any possibility of happiness for such a horrible person, regardless of what he had gone through for so many years. As far as she was concerned, he had brought misery on himself, and he deserved everything he got and more, as he had never had to answer for what he had done to Olivia. She noticed that he rarely used her name any longer, as though he was afraid that just saying it or writing it would give her more power over him than she already had. It also allowed him to deny the gravity of what he had done and why he was being tormented, whether that torment was real or not. The thought of him moving on infuriated her, knowing that he deserved a life sentence of suffering for the life he had taken.

Something about his story suddenly rang familiar to her. She reread the passage to see what it might be and realised that his house was just east of the slide, which was where her house was located too, though it was not the only house in the isolated neighbourhood of about a dozen houses. Still, something was nagging at her and it finally occurred to her to get the notebook she kept to keep track of the stories that Felix had shared with her since they had met.

When she opened the book it was right there in black and white on the first page of her notes. The house had been moved from Lille, a detail she had not forgotten of course, but it had belonged to a man who had worked in management with the mine! Felix had referred to the man as 'Mr. *Harris*', not Hollis, but she had noted that Felix had not been sure, as it had been so long ago. There was no doubt in Emma's mind that the house she was living in was the house where Callum Hollis had lived, the house where he had murdered his young wife Olivia in the bath. It was starting to make sense, but there was still so much she did not understand.

Her notes revealed that he had continued to be haunted in the house of course, which was why Felix had told her what he knew of the man's story. Felix had surmised that he had taken his life because he could no longer take the torment. Emma hoped that Callum might reveal something, anything, that could help her to deal with her own torment, much of which she was sure that he was responsible for, now that she saw the connection. Pressing on, she felt that she was nearing the end of the journal. As she reached what she realised was the final entry, Callum revealed more than she could have ever hoped for.

I cannot continue with this life. It is no life at all. Since moving to this place, a place which was meant to be a fresh start, my torment has only grown worse. But I think I have figured out a way to end it all and find the peace, and best of all, the love I have been seeking since that fateful night all those years ago when I lost my beautiful daughter and became chained to the horrific scourge which her mother has become.

It is bad enough that she followed me here, though she is different here, like a faded version of herself. But in my dreams she is the same as before and she laughs at me as she assures me that she will never leave my side. In my dreams it is sometimes as though the house is still sitting up there in that ghost town, intent on staying near to her bones.

Though the thought of being stuck with her for the rest of my life is a horror no man would want to live with, I have always held the belief that it would all be worthwhile if I were only able to see my Violet again. My mother used to warn me when I was a small boy to be careful of what I wished for. I know now that she was right in so many ways.

I wished for that woman to be mine from the moment she came into my life and I got her, but it was never a marriage of love and she turned me into a monster I never knew I could be. I wished for Fisher's death, but it made no difference, as it was the outset of the curse that became my existence and nobody ever looked at me the same after. I wished to move to this place, here by the river, hoping to see my little girl, and now I have, but not in the way that I had hoped, and it is more than I can stand any longer.

I was right, she knows this house, she is drawn here. I am sure that she is searching for me. But every time I see her, she is always running away from me and I have never been able to reach her. I nearly drowned trying to save her in the river, But even though I had been so close, it had all been for nothing and she had vanished once again. I had hoped, but I know now that in this life it is never to be. But perhaps in the next life it is! It is my only chance.

I have told my elderly neighbour here much of what has gone on since moving to this place. I'm not even sure why. Perhaps I just needed to tell another living soul what I have gone through these past years. Maybe I needed sympathy. It was a foolhardy thing to do, I know. I am sure he either thinks, or knows, I am mad, or he may even be suspicious that I have a reason to have a guilty conscience. If I am completely honest with myself, and in this moment I should be, as these will be the last words I ever write, I did not care about telling him, because I knew it would come to this in the end.

I'm not going to chance being stuck here in this house with that witch for eternity, so I've decided to take a walk along the river until I find the perfect spot. It will be have to be somewhere quite visible, so that I am found as quickly as possible. I haven't decided yet what I'll do with the dog. It probably wouldn't be fair to stick the old man with him, but I'll decide that when I return.

When I have finished with this writing, I am going to make one last trip to the place where I last knew happiness, where I last had my family and still believed we might have a chance. This will be my last confession, as I will never tell another living soul what I have done. I guess I deserve that one last ounce of dignity, or vanity, so that I can go to my grave secure in the knowledge that my secrets will die with me.

After much consideration, I have decided to bury this lifetime of thoughts, or I guess at least part of a lifetime. Sadly,

I can't seem to remember what things were like before I was bewitched by my cursed wife. Nobody has ever found her, and now that the town of Lille is nothing but a whisper of the past, nobody ever will. And that is where I will bury this journal, with her bones.

Never to be found.

"He buried it with Olivia!" Emma exclaimed with shock when she read the final line.

CHAPTER THIRTY THREE

Ignoring the clock, knowing it was far too late to still be awake, Emma crept up the stairs like a cat, careful not to make a sound and wake her family. The adrenaline coursing through her veins assured her she would never sleep, so she laid on her back, listening to the steady sound of John's breathing, as thoughts of another man's life raced through her mind.

Before long her thoughts turned to Olivia, and she wondered if it could be true. Could she be buried in the place where Emma had discovered the journal? If so, what should she do about it? How could she even explain the circumstances under which she had discovered it in the first place? Once she decided that she would discuss it with her mother and John so that they could decide what to do together, she curled up on her side, snuggled into her husband's warm back and finally drifted off into a deep sleep.

It seemed that she had not been asleep for long when she was awoken by the sound of running water. Though she jolted up in the bed at the sound, John did not move a muscle and continued on with his dreamy rhythmic breathing. Emma slid out of the bed, careful not to jostle him as he slept, hopeful that her mother had been unable to sleep and had decided to take a late night bath, though with all that they had been through recently, that seemed a ridiculous choice.

Emma tiptoed to the bathroom door and knocked quietly, careful not to wake anyone who was sleeping soundly. When there was no response, she realised that she no longer heard the sound of running water. Because the door was inexplicably closed, she assumed there was likely someone in there and she shivered involuntarily. Drawing in a deep breath, she turned the doorknob and slowly pushed open the door, which seemed far heavier than she seemed to remember, as though it had been waterlogged and was set to tear itself from its hinges. Heavy as it was, Emma noticed that it did not make a sound.

As she stepped into the room, the door closed silently behind her and she wondered if she might be having a dream. The room was unusually warm and steamy and was lit by a few flickering candles that cast dancing flames across the ceramic subway tiles which surrounded the tub. The shower curtain was closed, but as Emma watched, a hand emerged, wrapping the curtain in its feminine grip, the fingers long and elegant with natural and neatly trimmed nails.

Now she was sure she was dreaming, but she felt powerless to wake herself, though she felt perfectly lucid. She wondered if she should feel more afraid, but did not sense that she was under any threat as the pretty hand pulled the curtain across, revealing a beautiful young woman with long dark hair piled up on top of her head sinking back into the tub as she locked her deep, haunting eyes on Emma.

"I was hoping you'd come." The woman smiled knowingly.

"Who are you?" Emma asked with trepidation.

"You know who I am," the woman replied with another smile, as though she thought Emma were being purposely obtuse.

"*Olivia?*"

"Of course. I'm sure you must have known I would have to come to you, with everything you've seen, and now, with everything you've learned. I thought you deserved to know why I'm here. I know *you* know I *really* am here. Helen knew too, but no one believed her until it was too late, and look what happened."

"*Lorraine*?"

"Yes, *Lorraine*, and everything that came before and after her."

"Why would you do such a horrible thing? You know what it's like to be without the daughter you love."

Olivia frowned and furrowed her brow. "Of course I know."

"Then how could you do this to another woman? Another *mother*? It was so unfair what happened to you, what happened to Fisher, what happened to *Violet*, but it does not give you the right to take another woman's daughter away from her and leave her to waste the rest of her days without ever being able to move on."

"Helen didn't just lose her daughter Emma. She lost *everything*. That was the last thing I would have wanted for her, which was why I tried to warn her. But I was too late. And when Leo refused to see the truth, there was nothing more I could do. I was not the one who took Lorraine. I did everything I could to stop it, but I don't belong here, so everything isn't much."

"What do you mean? Why don't you belong here? And who took Lorraine?"

Olivia was visibly frustrated. "You know that too. We don't have time for this. You need to know. You need to go." The stained glass crows jostled in their tree and glared menacingly down at her. She glared back at them fearfully and whispered under her breath, "He's watching." She turned to face Emma, ignoring the crows who seemed to be listening and watching, though they remained mere images cut from glass. "You don't have long. You've known all along. You can't afford to pretend anymore that you have all the time in the world. None of us do. I lost my baby. Helen did too. I might not have been able to stop that, but maybe you don't have to lose your baby girl too, if you'll just listen to me and get out of here as quickly as you can. Take your little girl, take your family and just go. There's no time to lose."

"I believe you, and I will. I have no intention of staying here one day longer," Emma assured Olivia, who remained immersed in the tub, the steam rising and condensing on her dewy olive skin. "But I need to know why this has all been happening. Can't you tell me that? None of it makes any sense.

I have a lot of the story, but I know I don't have it all. What happened to Lorraine? Why did she have to die? You know don't you?"

Olivia stared deeply into Emma's eyes and seemed to be weighing what would be best in the situation. After a moment's silence she sighed deeply and sank down into the water looking down at herself beneath the surface. "If I tell you, will you leave then? Will you leave now? I don't think you should wait for morning. It may be too late."

"I promise. I'll wake everyone and tell them we have to go right away, *after* you tell me what's been going on in this house for all these years. Deal?"

"Fine," Olivia agreed with a frustrated tone. "This has never been about me. It's always been about him."

"Callum Hollis?"

"Yes; the monster I married after my *real* husband died. The demon who finally took my life and doomed my soul."

"How is this about him? It seems that both of you have had a hand in terrorising the different families who've tried to make this their home. How are you any better than him? You look like you once did here now I'm sure, but I'm also sure that it was *you* I saw in the woods. It was *you* who have stood by the bedside of more than one person in this house, set to terrify them out of their wits! And for what? You know I'm right."

Olivia nodded in agreement, "Yes; I did all those things, and I'll continue if I must. I'll do whatever it takes to stop him. I damned myself when I swore in my dying breath to spend the afterlife dedicated to his eternal torment. At that moment I did not consider the consequences of my choice. When he was driven to take his own life, so near to this place, he too became trapped here, but he is so much stronger than I am here."

"But why?"

"Because I don't belong here. I'm buried up there." Olivia tossed her head in the direction of what Emma assumed was Grassy Mountain Road, which led to the hike to Lille, once Olivia's home and still her final resting place. "At least that's what I think the reason is. I am stronger when there, near my remains. That's how I was able to possess you once John left you on your own, so that you would uncover the truth. John returned and stopped you before you found me too. But what do I know? Maybe he's just stronger than I am; maybe his death weakened me. Maybe it's because he's always been so obsessed with my daughter. She's here somewhere too now. Maybe it's because he's just evil and maybe evil is *stronger* than good, stronger than *love*. There's little I can do against him now but try to warn those who come to live in this wretched house. I don't really know what else to say."

"But you don't warn anyone. You just torment them."

"It's about all I *can* do. I can't lead anyone to safety, so I try to push them there. I don't even know how this is happening right now, if it even is. Maybe it's because you know so much. Maybe you're better able to see the real me, the echo of the woman I once was. Again, I don't really know, but it's not usually this way for me. The best I can do is use the state I'm in to try and frighten away the decent people who come to make a home here. That and try to stay present, because he prefers when I'm gone. It's not what I *want* to do. It's what I *have* to do. It's the only way I can protect you from *him*."

"Why? Why is Callum out to harm the people who live here? Why did he kill Lorraine?"

"Because of Violet."

Emma's face twisted into an expression of confusion. "I don't understand. It doesn't make any sense."

"None of this makes any sense, but he has never been sane or good, so why should it? It all comes back to his deepest obsession."

"You?"

"No, not *me*; *Violet*. Callum convinced himself somewhere along the line that he was in love with me, but believe me, that man never loved me for one moment. He was not capable. I think he knew that he would never have a family of his own; maybe deep down somewhere he knew that there was something fundamentally wrong with him. But when he was there for Violet's birth, she became his focus, his *fixation*. I was simply a means to get to her, though I'm not sure that he even knew it until he married me. He had what he wanted, the little girl he believed he had some sick kind of kindred connection with, but he was stuck with her difficult mother as well. And I could never love that murderous son of a bitch."

"I still don't understand. Even if Callum was obsessed with Violet, why would that cause him to threaten those who live in his old house?"

"The whole reason that he put this house where it is is because it was as close as he could get to the slide without risking the mountain actually falling on him. He believed that if he stayed near where Violet had perished, then she might find the house and recognize it and come home. After all, he had already seen that it was possible for a spirit to stay behind. *I* showed him that."

Olivia fell silent and Emma watched her struggle to finish what she had to say. Her lower lip quivered as she sneered at the subtle movements of the sinister crows. The obvious hatred she felt for them seemed to spur her on. "The amazing thing is that he was right. She did recognize the house and she comes from time to time. I've seen her for myself."

"What do you mean, you've *seen* her?" Emma asked surprised, "If you're both, you know, ghosts, then haven't you spoken with her? I would think that this would be your chance to move on! You've found your daughter after all this time."

A tear rolled down Olivia's cheek and she turned to face Emma for the first time since starting her explanation. "I guess that's part of my punishment for cursing that monster as I took my dying *breath;* I have seen her from time to time, but she can never see me. My only solace is that she can't see *him* either. So I guess this has been hell for him too."

"Yes, but *he* deserves it," Emma interrupted,."*you* don't."

"I guess I *do*. The cost of vengeance is steep in the afterlife."

They both fell silent for a moment then Olivia continued. "All I've been able to do is try my best to chase away those who come to live here, before he does whatever he might do instead. I know that it can be terrifying for those who encounter me, but that is the *point* after all. I've never done anything to actually harm anyone and I never would, but *he* would. His motives change depending on who lives here. If they don't suit his purposes, he'll target them until they can't stand the torment and they finally leave." She paused momentarily, fighting back tears so that she could finish, saying what she had to say. "And if they *do* suit his purposes, like you and Charlie, like Helen and Lorraine: a ready-made family like the one I brought to him all those years ago, then the danger is even worse. He wants those little girls, and he'll do whatever it takes to get them. That's why you need to go, so you don't have any regrets to live with."

"There's got to be something I can do to help you," Emma pleaded. "To help *Violet*."

"There's nothing that can be done for me now. If something could have been done for my little girl, I would have done it a long time ago. There is nothing. Such is life, and such is death. The best you can do is to do as you promised now. Take your family and leave, before it's too late."

Suddenly the room fell dark and Emma reached out to Olivia, but she had vanished. The tub was empty. It was as though she had never been there. The rhythmic dripping of the faucet mesmerised Emma and she stared at the water droplets as they welled up until they were too heavy to hold on any longer, finally falling, only to be swiftly followed by another. As she stared, the dripping grew louder and more sporadic until it sounded more like a ragged barking than a dripping. The room grew even darker and began to tilt sideways, giving Emma a sense of vertigo.

As she laid her head on the cold tile floor and closed her eyes, the barking grew louder and louder still until it sounded more like yowling than barking now. No longer able to stand it, determined to get away from the sickening noise, Emma opened her eyes and was shocked to see that she was no longer on the bathroom floor. Instead, she was lying in her bed. The effect was incredibly disorienting. It took a moment before she realised that though the dream had ended, the yowling had not. Shaking off her sense of disorientation, she jumped up in the bed and turned to the window. The horrible sound seemed to be coming from the backyard.

John jumped up out of bed and went to the window, but Emma flew immediately to the door and down the hall to Charlie's room. She could hear John yelling from their bedroom that Max was in the backyard, but she had already known that somehow, just as she had known that checking her daughter's room would be a hopeless cause. To her dread, she was right: the little girl's bed was empty.

Acting on instinct she turned and raced back down the hall and down the stairs. As she ran past the panicked little dog who was now whimpering, she burst into tears, knowing that he almost never made a sound, and that he almost never left Charlie's side. Especially in the night, the two were inseparable. The sight and sound of his helpless fear filled her with terror.

Though she had not even heard him behind her, John reached the gate before she did and ripped it open violently, racing down the back lane without turning back to see if she was following him.

"Charlie! Charlie!" He screamed desperately for his little girl, but she did not respond. Emma's heart felt as though it might burst as she ran behind him, sobbing as she watched him disappear behind the bushes at the end of the lane which hid the pool in the river.

At the same moment that she heard her mother desperately calling to her from the house, she heard John's terrified scream. She could hear him saying over and over, "No! No! No!" Then she heard a loud splash. As she reached the path that led to the river, she saw a sight that would be burned into her mind for the rest of her life. John was reaching for Charlie in the water, which was as black as the night.

Their little girl was in the middle of the deep, dark pool, her dark hair fanning out around her head like a halo. The way the white gown she wore glowed in the moonlight and the way her arms spread out like she was reaching for the shore in all directions completed the effect. Face down in the water, just before her father grabbed her and tore her from the frigid stream, she had resembled an angel. *Her* angel, floating lifeless in the Crowsnest River.

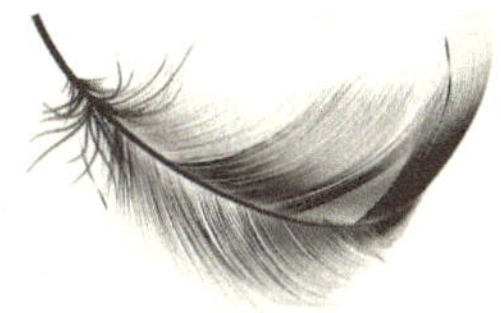

CHAPTER THIRTY FOUR

When a person loses someone, it changes them. Whether they loved them for a lifetime, or only had them in their life for what seemed a fleeting moment, it can never be enough. So there is a part that is always left longing, left wondering how things would be if only they had one more day, or even just a moment; if only they had one more *chance*. When it comes to loss, it is difficult to know what is worse: knowing what is coming or having no warning at all.

The most selfless of us hope only that the ones we care for need never have to suffer, whatever the cost to ourselves. But most of us selfishly long for the chance to say good-bye, whatever the cost to the ones we love. Whether selfless or selfish, it all comes from a place of sorrow, love and grief and matters only to those left behind. Except of course, when it also matters to those who have moved on, or rather, those who have *failed* to move on.

Emma felt numb to the words of the reverend as he finished the burial by tossing a few handfuls of dirt onto the coffin, which had already been lowered into the dark, damp earth. The rain had been coming down in sheets for the entirety of the burial service and she clung tightly to John as he shielded her from the onslaught with a wide black umbrella. She wished that he had forgotten it, so that her tears would be camouflaged by the pouring rain.

They escaped to the privacy of their car before they might have to speak to another person. Emma had been touched by how many people had come to pay their respects, but with everything they had been through, she could not answer one more question or even talk to one more person. Though she loved the mountains, and even the vehemence of the weather, be it rain, snow or wind, she knew she might never return. Even still, as they pulled away from the historic Hillcrest Cemetery, she never looked back.

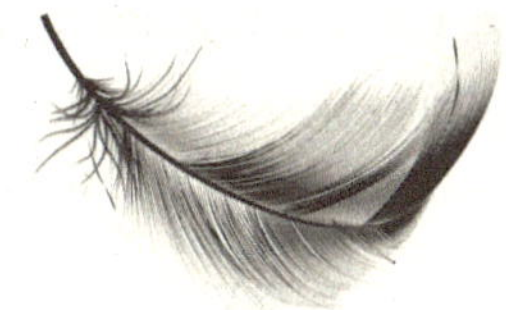

CHAPTER THIRTY FIVE

"They're not going to take *no* for an answer Emma. I know you're not so busy that you can't put aside one evening to let them thank you for everything you've done for the Pass."

"It's not that I'm too busy Marin, I just really hate these public functions."

"Well you might want to get over that if you plan on being some kind of bigshot writer someday."

"That's different and you know it," Emma pushed back. "Just thinking about everything that happened is traumatic for me, let alone talking to an audience about it."

Marin's tone grew serious and she softened her voice. "Maybe talking about it would do you some good. Maybe writing about it would be even more beneficial, in more ways than one. This could be a good starting point for you."

Emma was quiet for a moment before responding, "Maybe you're right." Marin gasped on the other end but Emma interrupted her before she could say anything, "I'm not committing to anything, *yet.* But I will consider it."

"That's great! For *now.*" Marin's tone changed again as she turned to other business. "In the meantime, you and John just need to sign the papers and the Crowsnest Historical Society will be depositing the funds for the purchase of the house in your account as agreed. I'm sorry it took so long to get this whole process dealt with. We really appreciate your patience. It took a lot of time and energy, not to mention my sanity, to get the town and the province on board so that we could minimise the costs to the historical society."

"No need to thank us. We didn't want any other families living there, so turning it into a tourist attraction, as twisted as I might think that is, is much better than the alternative."

"This is going to be great for the Pass. They're going to put the journal on display in the house, along with a digital presentation to discuss the history of the house. We're hoping you might write that for us. After all, I know you gathered the stories Uncle Felix shared with you during all your visits."

"I'll consider it."

"Really?" Marin asked, doubt clear in her voice.

"I really will," Emma assured her. "I promise."

"Alright; I can accept that."

"Great, now I should be go."

"Before you do," Marin interrupted her. "I thought you might like to know, they've exhumed Olivia's remains. They were exactly where you said they would be."

"Really?" Emma was clearly shocked. "What are they planning on doing with them?"

"They've already buried her."

"Seriously? Where is she now?"

"They've laid her to rest at the memorial to the victims of the slide. We hoped that might let her finally find some peace. To be near her daughter. It's the least we can do for her. I thought you might approve."

"I definitely approve," Emma assured her old neighbour and dear friend. "Thank you so much Marin. I never thought I would be happy to hear news of that house or its ghosts ever again. But I had asked once what I could do to make things better for her. Maybe, in some way, this was what I was meant to do."

"Maybe," Marin agreed. "You might be interested to know, since they moved her remains and buried her properly, no one has seen Olivia's ghost in the house still."

"And what about Callum?"

"People still claim to see him and his dog."

"*People*?"

"Sorry Emma. *I've* seen him and his dog. And I'm not the only one. Maybe he's finally getting what he deserves: an eternity to suffer alone."

As they said their good-byes and she hung up the phone, Emma felt a sense of relief for the first time in a long time.

CHAPTER THIRTY SIX

So this is it - the end. Although it's really the beginning.

As she sat in front of the muted glow of her computer screen, Emma struggled to find the right words, knowing she could never take them back. Hesitantly, she began to click the keys, the sound like slow summer rain on a metal roof, as she struggled to trust what she thought she should say, before finally allowing her heart to do the talking for her. Having finally reached the end of her first novel, all she had left to do was the dedication and acknowledgments.

For my dear friend Felix, who shared his stories, his community and himself, so that we might find the truth.

Feeling unsure of her climactic chapter, she turned back to read her own writing, to consider if she should change it somehow. It had been difficult to write such a traumatic moment in her life, but it had been cathartic too, as it was a subject that she and John typically avoided. Now she found herself afraid to read her own rendition of what had happened in those awful moments, on their final night in the house. Having already read and edited the remainder of the story, this was the one part she had avoided until now. But the time had come and the publisher wanted the book in their hands as soon as possible, so there were no excuses left.

Emma scrolled to the chapter she had not yet read and poured her attention into it, doing her best to be subjective. It was not as difficult a task as she had imagined it to be, until she reached the end and the images of her daughter in the pool, lit up like an angel in the darkness, came rushing back to her like a tidal wave. She swallowed hard and sniffed back a tear as she continued on to the end.

When I saw her floating there in the darkened pool, her hair and nightgown billowing around her, I thought my heart might burst and I would die there on the spot, at the edge of the Crowsnest River. While I stood frozen in place, John flew into the frigid water without hesitation, pushing his way through the weak current of the deep pool and quickly scooping her up, her tiny soaked body limp in his strong arms.

He placed her on the grass at the edge of the river and listened for her breathing, but heard nothing. All I could do was weep for the loss of my little girl as he fought with everything he had to save her life. I remembered Helen's story and the scene she had endured with her own family, a scene just like this on a night just like this. Though I wanted nothing more than to have my family back, to take them and run from this place, to somewhere they would be safe, I knew in my heart that all was lost and that our fate would be the same as theirs.

But when I heard Charlie coughing and spluttering on the ground, crying and asking her father what had happened and where she was, I had never been so grateful to be wrong in my entire life. She wrapped her little arms around her father's neck and I knelt down to embrace them both. In the distance I could hear the ambulance sirens wailing and my mother calling as she raced down the back lane to where we were.

Charlie was no worse for wear once they were able to check her over at the hospital. I knew that if John had been only a minute later, things might have turned out very differently. Again my thoughts returned to Helen and I felt a great empathy for the mother who had given up her life waiting for her daughter to return. I knew in that moment that I would have done the same and was glad that it did not have to come to that. We would never again return to that damned house.

Once they released Charlie from the hospital I asked John to take her and wait for me in the car while I checked in on Felix to let him know what I had learned and what had happened, but when I got there his bed was empty. Marin was still there. She looked at me and didn't say a word. Instead, she reached out her arms and held me in her embrace.

When she regained her composure she told me that Felix had passed peacefully in his sleep. She said that he had seen it coming, even though the doctors had said he was fine and could return home any day. I was reminded of his passing comments about how he was getting too old and how she had dismissed him. Maybe he had been trying to warn her too, to say goodbye.

"He just had to be right one more time." Marin shook her head and smiled at me, then she realised how late it was, "What brings you to the hospital this late? Is everything okay?"

"It will be," I assured her, "I just wish I could have let him know that."

"I'm sure he knows," Marin reassured me.

"I'm sure you're right," I agreed without hesitation.

Emma wiped a tear from her eye as she finished the final lines of the chapter she had been avoiding for months. She was reminded of the torrential swing of emotions that came with the revival of her little girl, followed swiftly by the loss of her dear friend. Felix had come to mean more to her than she could have ever imagined when she first met him. Together they had solved a great mystery. Hopefully, they had also given a restless spirit some deserved peace. She could never be sure of what became of Olivia and Violet, but she hoped in the deepest part of her heart that they had finally found one another, had finally found peace.

Before long she would take her own daughter to visit them at the end of the old Frank road, a pitted and pocked amusement park ride that crept its way through the slide. With a view of the river at the base of Turtle Mountain which could not be seen from the highway that ran through the most well-known path through the slide, Emma preferred the back road, as did most of the locals. It provided the best view of life, both plant and animal, which continued to survive all over the treacherous mountainside. More than once she had been privy to the lumberings of a carefree brown bear or the piercing cry of a bald eagle as it skimmed the surface of the water before snatching a bewildered River duck. It was the perfect resting place for a tired soul to find herself again.

"Mom, are you done yet?"

Lost in memory, Emma nearly jumped out of her skin at the sound of Charlie's voice, "What? Sorry, yeah, I'm all done for the day sweetie."

"Finally! Let's get going! We're going to miss the evening hatch if we don't get down to the river right now," Charlie complained.

"Okay, don't get your panties in a bunch!"

"Mom!"

"What?" Emma replied innocently.

"Don't be gross. Let's go! I've already packed our fly rods and fishing gear in the truck. Daddy said he'll have some sandwiches ready to go if we swing by the cafe before we go."

"Sounds good. How did I get so lucky, huh? I have such a great husband and daughter to take care of me."

"It's not luck, Mom." Charlie wrapped her arm in Emma's, and rested her head on her mother's shoulder. "You deserve it."

As they left the room, the computer screen which had been dark came to life, the cursor blinking dumbly a few lines below the end of the chapter Emma had finished reading. Without warning a message appeared on the screen, left to be found when Emma would return to the story she had bravely retold to share her ghostly encounters in the Crowsnest Pass, on the eastern slopes of the Rocky Mountains. The message left for Emma was brief and concise, and though it was simple and there was no name included, there would be no mistaking who it was from:

Together forever at last. Thank you Emma.

Printed in Canada